CHARLES NODIER

THE FOUR TALISMANS
AND OTHER STORIES

TRANSLATED AND WITH AN INTRODUCTION BY
BRIAN STABLEFORD

THIS IS A SNUGGLY BOOK

ISBN: 978-1-64525-169-9

THE FOUR TALISMANS
AND OTHER STORIES

CHARLES NODIER (1780-1844) was one of the pioneers of French Romantic prose; his salon at the Bibliothèque de l'Arsenal, begun in 1824 and known as *Le Cénacle*, brought together many of the key figures in the Movement and spun off other *cénacles* in which it was anchored, including Victor Hugo's. His best work consists of short stories and novellas.

BRIAN STABLEFORD (1948-2024) was a British science fiction writer, translator, and literary scholar who published over one hundred and twenty volumes of original fiction and over two hundred volumes of translations. He also wrote under the pseudonyms Brian Craig and Francis Amery. His original fiction includes the Hidden Swan series of novels, which began with *Halcyon Drift* (1972) and ended with *Swan Song* (1975), and the novels *The Werewolves of London* (1990) and *The Cassandra Complex* (2001). Among his important translations are *Monsieur de Phocas* by Jean Lorrain and *Mephistophela* by Catulle Mendès. He furthermore published numerous volumes of nonfiction, which include *The Mysteries of Modern Science* (1977) and, in four volumes, *New Atlantis: A Narrative History of Scientific Romance* (2016).

SNUGGLY BOOKS

Contents

Introduction

This is the final volume in a series of collections of the work of Charles Nodier, the great pioneer of the prose fiction of the French Romantic Movement. The volume entitled *Outlaws and Sorrows* assembles the fiction published during the first phase of his career, in 1802-1806; the volume entitled *Jean Sbogar and Other Stories* samples material from its second phase, works published in 1818-21; and the volume entitled *The Story of the King of Bohemia and His Seven Castles* includes the title novella, published in 1830, supplemented with some related works published in the following year. The present volume is one of three sampling material from the most prolific phase of Nodier's career, featuring material published between 1831 and his death in 1844. *Perfectibility and Resurrection* and *The Memoirs of Maxime Odin* are thematic collections, the former concentrating on stories and essays employing *contes fantastique* for the philosophical exploration of two topics that interested the author and the second collecting a series of stories focusing on a third subject of intense interest, amour.

This final volume is something of a miscellany, including a few more philosophical *contes fantastiques*, a few more stories of amour, and a handful of items that are difficult to categorize, concluding, by way of an appendix, with a translation of the 1831 essay "De l'amour, et de son influence, comme sentiment, sur la société actuelle" (tr. as "On Love and its

Influence as a Sentiment on Contemporary Society"), which might be seen as a foundation stone of the thinking that lay behind the composition of many of the items, summarizing the idiosyncratic attitude to "amour" exemplified in so many of the author's exemplary tales, and his idea of how that notion related to the contemporary condition of society—decadent, in Nodier's opinion—and thus to the current condition of literature within that society. In writing fiction Nodier was always very curious about exactly what he was doing, what he was able to do within the literary marketplace in which he was operating, and what he might have been able to do in a more hospitable environment. Seen as a disparate set or as a collage, the commentary element of the stories in the present collection composes an interesting evaluation of the nature and possibilities of fiction as a social phenomenon, and as a judgmental and consolatory force.

The stories assembled herein are unashamedly intellectual, especially when they protest about the intellectualism of fiction, championing a kind of simplicity and innocence of what the author knew himself to be incapable, having been irredeemably corrupted by his fervently eccentric self-education. In spite of that accepted paradoxicality, however, the author made every effort to practice what he preached, and to write stories that would do what he thought stories were supposed to do, even while incorporating commentaries that partly denied and defeated that object. That did not assist his popularity, then or subsequently, but it did help to make him a uniquely interesting and thought-provoking writer, whose preaching and practice had a powerful and positive influence on the Romantic Movement that he helped to found and shape. His was an eccentric genius, always likely only to attract the complete sympathy of a minority of readers, but it was nevertheless genius; his work was and remains a treasure trove still capable of provoking useful thought, even if the first impulse of modern thought (which would not have surprised him) is to reject the ideas dearest to his heart as so blatantly false as to be unworthy of serious philosophical attention.

The introductions to the earlier volumes in the series include a synoptic account of the author's early life, explaining—so far as is possible—the relevance of its circumstances to the pattern of his literary production and its thematic obsessions. That production was interrupted twice. In 1804, after Nodier identified himself as the author of an "ode" criticizing Napoléon Bonaparte, then the First Consul of France, and about to proclaim himself Emperor; he was imprisoned and then banished from Paris and placed under official police surveillance, making it difficult for him to place his work with publishers. Although he made a comeback in 1818-22, after the official surveillance was withdrawn and he was able to return to Paris, his first publications during that period were issued anonymously, and not long after he began signing his work again there was another hiatus, perhaps not unconnected with the increasingly hostile political climate of the Restoration, but more likely due to recurrent bouts of illness and his appointment in 1824 as the librarian of the Bibliothèque de l'Arsenal, when he became the host of the cénacle at which the leading members of the French Romantic Movement met regularly to discuss their work, their cause and their ambitions.

For one reason and another, it was not until 1830 that Nodier began publishing fiction again—but once he had resumed, he quickly became prolific, publishing a flood of works in the early 1830s, including a twelve-volume set of his *Oeuvres* collecting the work from his earlier periods of productivity and adding a good deal of new material. Some of that work had probably been written in the 1820s but had not been able to find publishers then, but most of it was undoubtedly new, representative of a new burst of enthusiasm and productivity. That revivification of his career was doubt-less assisted by a partial and temporary remission in his poor health, but 1830 was also a year in which the political and economic climate of Paris changed dramatically. The so-called July Revolution got rid of Charles X, and although it disap-pointed its republican instigators when the government of the day found a substitute king in Louis-Philippe, it instituted a constitutional monarchy to replace the oppressive absolutism of the former regime.

In truth, the change in the circumstances of everyday life brought about by the new monarchy was not so very great, and it did not take long for people to realize that; for a brief period, however, political censorship was considerably relaxed and publishers believed, at least for a while, that they had ac-quired a new and much greater freedom to publish what they liked—and to experiment in order to discover what the public could be persuaded to want. Nodier, along with all the other members of the Romantic Movement, took rapid advantage of that thaw to test the boundaries of public taste and toler-ance, as expressed in the willingness of publishers to deviate from their established ruts.

The presumed license granted to publishers was interpret-ed by the editors of several periodicals as an opportunity to publish more controversial work, and several of them began to promote the Romantic Movement enthusiastically as a regen-erative force in French literature. One of the periodicals that did so most pugnaciously was the *Revue de Paris*, to which Nodier had been contributing since its foundation in 1829, and which became his principal showcase throughout the 1830s, when it was owned by François Buloz, both for phil-osophical articles flamboyantly setting out his controversial theses regarding literature and its historical and psychological contexts, and for fiction in which he attempted to practice what he preached. Although the title reappeared in the 1850s, its original incarnation had been interrupted in 1845, not long after Nodier's death, and in its heyday he was its principal exemplary intelligence.

Inevitably, once he felt that he had a new freedom to explore and express his ideas, Nodier set about revisiting and refining the ideas that had fuelled his early fiction, in order to recapitulate and re-examine them from a more mature viewpoint, and most of the stories featured in the present collection represent aspects of that revisitation and sophistication. I have arranged the stories in the approximate chronological order of their publication, but that is probably not the order in which they were written; in particular, a group of three stories first published in one volume of the collected *Oeuvres,* "Lidivine," "Les Fiancés" and "Sibylle Mérian," were probably written much earlier than their publication, and almost certainly earlier than "Thérèse," which first appeared in a different volume of the *Oeuvres,* and "Baptiste Montauban, ou l'Idiot" (1833). "La Combe de l'homme morte," which also first appeared in 1833—similarly not in the *Revue de Paris*—might also have written during the fallow period of the 1820s, as might "La Mettrie, ou les Superstitions" (1831), which I have placed out of sequence in order to juxtapose it with "Sibylle Mérian," with which it shares a rather curious narrative methodology.

The last five stories in the collection were, however, definitely written in the order presented here, and although they are very disparate, they do represent a certain quirky evolution of ideas. It was entirely typical of the author to publish the purest of all his *contes fantastiques,* the Gallandesque fantasy "Les Quatre talismans" (1838; tr. herein as "The Four Talismans") soon after the novelette "Légende de Soeur Béatrix" (1837; tr. as "The Legend of Sister Béatrix"), which had illustrated the pious employment of fantastic devices within the Christian mythos. The latter story was itself published not long after a novella featuring a drastically contrasted methodology, interrogating the propriety and psychology of the *fantastique,* "Inès de Las Sierras" (1837), which had itself succeeded in the pages of the *Revue de Paris* the story subsequently retitled "Paul, ou la Ressemblance" (1836), which illustrated another of three aspects of *fantastique* fiction that Nodier had identified in an analytical 1931 essay translated in *Perfectibility and Resurrection*.[1]

"Les Quatre talismans" was followed in the pages of the *Revue de Paris* by two novelettes translated in other collections in the present series because they revisited the central themes of those assemblages, "La Neuvaine de la Chandeleur" (1838; tr. as "The Candlemas Novena") in *The Memoirs of Maxime Odin*, and "Lydie, ou La Resurrection" (1839) in *Perfectibility and Resurrection*, but the collection is concluded by the last of all Nodier's novelettes, "Franciscus Columna" (1843), penned while he was ill, and bringing together, in typically eccentric fashion, his fascination with bibliomania—first exhibited in "Le Bibliomane" (1831; tr. as "The Bibliomaniac" in *The Story of the King of Bohemia and His Seven Castles*) and a story of paradoxically-frustrated amour that repeats a pattern first laid down in his earliest publications (translated in *Outlaws and Sorrows*, and reiterated in *Jean Sbogar and Other Stories*), rounding out his extremely varied career in the most apt fashion possible. The present collection thus has links with all the other volumes in the series, and although it cannot be said to summarize or to complete them in a coherent fashion—an impossible task—it does help to illustrate the manner in which, in spite of their variegation, they do fit together as components of a life's work.

—Brian Stableford

---

1 That essay is, in part, a response to an essay by Walter Scott translated in an earlier issue of the *Revue de Paris*, "Du Merveilleux dans le roman" [originally "On the Supernatural in Fiction"]. The translation is credited to the antiquarian Auguste-Jean-Baptiste Defauconpret (1767-1843), who signed numerous other translations of English-language texts.

THE FOUR TALISMANS
AND OTHER STORIES

Thérèse

It is necessary to tell you that, since the failure of the assignats,[1] the Directoire had felt the necessity more than once to
put a great deal of metal into circulation. As it was reaching
its end and old people believed everything they were told,
the Directoire, which had let it be understood that France
was extremely rich in silver mines, dispatched squadrons of
well-paid explorers to all the old mines in the country, which,
whether they liked it or not, had never sent an obol to the
Treasury. I found myself appointed to an expedition to the
Vosges, where silver had been sought since time immemorial,
and whose *ballons*, cut by splendid roads, gave evidence of
immense and futile labor.

We were all young, all men of good humor and hope, all
devoted to our duty and impatient for discoveries. Our work

---

1 *Assignats* were paper money issued by the Constituent Assembly during
the Revolution, between 1789 and 1796, in order to ward off imminent
bankruptcy. They were originally bonds entitling their holders to purchase
property confiscated from the Church, with interest payments to be made
by the action of national assets, but were redefined as legal tender in
1790 in order to address a liquidity crisis; their exchange value declined,
threatening to increase the price of bread—an important shibboleth of
the Revolution—and the assignats ran into further trouble, blamed by the
government on forgeries manufactured abroad. The Convention replaced
them in 1796 with *mandats*, but the replacement also failed, as people
refused to exchange coin for them; the situation had become untenable
when Napoléon eventually abolished them.

was zealous and conscientious, and for a long time not devoid of hope. I remember that there was not one of us who, at the first strike of the hammer, had not discovered a seam; but the seam in question never led to anything, and the smallest expenditures of exploitation always exceeded by at least a third the most brilliant results. There was a succession of ecstasies and disappointments for which I had no terms of comparison then. I have perceived since that life is exactly similar.

We arrived, at the terminus of our false ambitions, at absolute discouragement. It was necessary then to spare the State a ridiculous expense, but that disinterested defection could only be supported by clearly-expressed calculation. I was not yet eighteen years of age, and all my science was reduced to a few dribs of Latin and a not-very-profound knowledge of a few specialties of natural history, among which mineralogy held a very small place. My comrades, who were able to distinguish at the fracture, by the odor exhaled by friction on contact with a fingernail or a lick of the tongue, all the inorganic substances then recognized by geology, had soon perceived my inaptitude, but they did not contest a rather jolly editorial merit that I brought fresh from a school of rhetoric directed by the good and judicious Droz;[1] and it is true that I translated their somewhat confused pages legibly when I succeeded in understanding something therein. It was therefore agreed that I would reside at a post fixed at a central point, where all the documents would brought to me, from which I would send all the dispatches.

1 Joseph Droz (1773-1850) was a teacher in Besançon before going to Paris in 1792, and returned there for a while later in the decade, when Nodier encountered him for the first time. He published an *Essai sur l'art oratoire* in 1799, having previously employed his expertise as an enthusiastic promoter and supporter of the Revolution. He went on to publish further essays on a variety of subjects and was eventually admitted to the Académie française. He was in Paris in 1803, when Nodier published several works of fiction, and published a romance of his own, *Lina* (1805), in which Charles Saint-Beuve identified Wertherian echoes.

The employees departed for the mines; the chief took refuge, as usual, in the urban delights of Épinal and my post was fixed at Giromagny near the *ballon* of that name, whose treasures, perhaps too rapidly abandoned, were the principal object of our investigations. By virtue of an particular surge of devotion, which was advantageously noted by me in my service notes, I reported a league toward the center, to a village known as the *Puy* because it was exactly at the base of the mountain, or the *Podium*, but it was neither that advantage of position, not that fortunate coincidence of etymology that had determined my choice of domicile—at least, I think so today, for then I scarcely knew what it was.

All of you who have traveled in all lands but have not seen the romantic gorge of the Puy have an essential voyage still to make, and have no fear that I shall anticipate the delightful sensations that it promises you by one of those artificial descriptions that depict nothing in the final analysis. In fact, I have never felt more profoundly the impossibility of depiction. When you arrive from Girmagny at the foot of the *ballon*, through the narrow route—and yet less opaque to the horizon than shadow and freshness, as the Latin poet puts it—that still ends at the cupola, so pure that one could believe that its elegant hemisphere had been carved which a chisel, or, according to the aspects of the sun, burned by a polisher; when you have traversed the maze of flowering bushes thrown obliquely through a lake of verdure, bright, silky and dappled, enlivened by a stream whose silver reflections bound all the way to the height of the lawn that searches it . . . alas, description, what do you want of me? All of you, as I said, who have visited every country but have not seen the romantic gorge of the Puy, will agree that more remains for you to see than you have seen.

But it would have been better to go there in 1799. What inspired in me such a profound predilection for the Puy was the very recent impression of an excursion that I had made

17

there a few months before, in the fervor of my entomological researches, in pursuit of two magnificent Vosgien insects, the *Lamia edilis* and the *Tamia Schoefferi*, and from which I had only brought back an amourette that had been well worth its price, for it was my first. That ineffable emotion of an adolescent heart had an influence on my literary vocation subsequently, and perhaps on the others. It furnished me with the principal details of two of my novelettes,[1] about which you scarcely care, and nor do I. When young, I savored the greatest pleasure in recounting the romance of my history everywhere; now old, I still amuse myself in rediscovering in my memories the history of my romance.

I had obtained lodgings in the Puy in the home of the honest Monsieur Christ, an ardent and supreme patriot, who had figured for ten years, in accordance with the intermittent favor of his opinions in the most eminent municipal functions of the locale, and who had returned, to the great displeasure of the aristocrats, after the eighteenth of Fructidor.[2] He was a man of righteous but absolute views who traced a political idea as an ox traces a furrow, and marched boldly in his principles with the intrepidity of the player of blind man's buff, to the right, the left or the center indiscriminately and in all conscience. I have seen ten thousand like him. He had three houses in the Puy and he established me in the most distant from the one in which he lived, because he had as many daughters as houses and they were all very pretty. I was well aware of that, but there was only one of them who produced in me the upsetting agitation that one senses more fully at eighteen than one can

---

1 Presumably *Stella, ou Les Proscrits* (1802), to which direct reference is made later in the story, and *Thérèse Aubert* (1819 but written much earlier). It is, of course, the earlier stories that provided the raw material for this one.

2 The coup of 18 Fructidor year V (4 September 1797) was a seizure of power within the Directoire, which suppressed a Royalist contingent that had gained a majority of seats in the recent elections.

express at forty-five. As that stubborn and delectable illusion disturbed my faculties in a manner rather prejudicial to my service, I would have had reason to applaud my placement as far as possible from the habitual subject of my distractions, if the thought of her had not followed me everywhere.

My small room on the ground floor, which I will gladly describe in compensation for not having described at my ease the valley of the Puy, was a straight parallelogram, horizontal to the courtyard and closed at the front by its glazed door and a large casement with little diamond-shaped panes, as is the custom in Alsace. Below that casement was an immense ash-wood table painted black by smoke, on which I laid out my documents and my copies. At the back of my lodging was an alcove with solid wooden doors, one of the extremities of which communicated internally with a kind of dressing-cabinet and the other with a prie-Dieu. If my room were ever transported to the stage in one of those fashionable compositions in which everyone can become the hero in turn, I beg the decorator not to forget that its interior was half-covered with pearl-gray paper, much blistered and very dusty, striped with two broad royal blue bands. One cannot be too punctilious in matters of that importance.

I usually got up at six o'clock in the morning—it was the end of May—in order to put in I don't now how many observations about which the Institute hardly cared and the Directoire no longer cared at all. At seven o'clock my bowl of *crème de ballon* was brought, sometimes by a domestic or one of Père Christ's elder daughters, and then I worked until midday; and sometimes by Thérèse, who was the youngest, and then I did no more work.

At midday I dined in Père Christ's house, and the women did not attend the meal. Fortunately, it was very short. I returned to my house; I picked up Saussure, Bergmann, Wallerius and my manuscripts, and I copied, analyzed and compiled for the rest of the day, not without seeing strokes as brilliant as a gaze sparkle under my pen, the dazzling play of which was more difficult to define than the capricious iridescence of my metals.

I tried in vain to expel them from thought and gesture, but they always came back, gliding over my paper in fiery furrows. That happened above all when Thérèse had come in the morning and she had placed her hand over my lips, or poured gold powder playfully into my inkwell. If my philosophical education had not been complete, I might have believed that the young woman was a magicienne, but I did not believe in magic, and that was all that my philosophy had taught me, or all that it had caused me to forget.

I was at least two years younger than Thérèse. She was lively, and yet reflective. Through her very nobility one saw something serious and powerful appear. There was within her the wherewithal to make a ravishing woman and a resolute man. Finally, the gaze that fascinated me often manifested additionally a thought imprinted with sadness and fatality, rapid, fugitive, inexplicable and promptly clarified by a radiance of gaiety, but which could not escape my gaze, for I was always looking at her.

I was amorous and timid; and the relative disproportion of our age, which the difference of sex rendered considerable, gave her a strange ascendancy over me. We loved one another a great deal, and we loved one another sincerely, but she had the advantage over me of knowing that, and I did not suspect it at all. So she addressed me as *tu* casually, a usage that the republican mores of her father's house, the simplicity of the local mores and, above all, having seen that I was younger— or, if you wish, more childish—rendered natural and easy for her, and when she did not address me as *tu*, I thought she was annoyed. I reciprocated, for my part, but more rarely and with less confidence, because she imposed on me so much when she was there that her presence, so desired—who would have believed it?—sometimes seemed importunate to me.

One morning, while playing behind my chair, and deliberately allowing the long tresses of her golden blonde hair to float before my eyes, she knotted several times between her fingers a black velvet ribbon passed around my neck.

"What's this, Monsieur?" she said to me, with the most severe tone of voice she had ever adopted. "Young as you are, so you already have souvenirs of amour? Is it a pledge? Is it a portrait?"

"No," I replied, taking out of my bosom a little steel cross suspended from it. "It's a cross blessed at the reliquary of Saint Claude, which my aunt Éléonore, a Benedictine nun, gave me on my departure, assuring me that it would protect me from all danger."

"All danger!" said Thérèse, raising her head and letting it fall back into her hands. "All danger! And what danger can you fear, poor and gentle young man whom no one would ever have the courage to hate? From all danger? Do you think so? Do you love me, Charles, do you love me? Give me that cross."

"It's yours!" I cried, at her knees, ". . . and as from today, what danger would I not brave? It's yours, my steel cross, like me, like my heart, like my life. Take your cross of betrothal!"

Thérèse understood then, doubtless for the first time, that I was mistaken in regard to the sentiments that it was possible for me to expect from her. That very impression must have suspended the course of her ideas for a time, for she made me wait for her response, tried it, interrupted it, and finally articulated it in an altered voice.

"Your fiancée, my friend? How could I be, since I'm married?"

I have no need to tell you that lightning could have fallen alongside me without astonishing me or consternating me more. It is a phrase cast in a mold, and so infallible in such a circumstance that there is no reader who could not substitute for it when the writer forgets it.

"Married! Since when?"

"Six months ago."

"Secretly?"

"It was necessary."

"Unknown to your father?" in pronouncing those last words, which contained not so much a question as a reproach, and which gave me an authority over her that the sad need to avenge my heart made me savor the advantage, I raised my gaze to Thérèse, who had remained standing; and she lowered hers.

"It was necessary," she repeated, with a more serious emotion, which had already changed object. "My father is a patriot and my husband is an émigré."

"An émigré! And married for six months! My God! Is the poor fellow well hidden, at least? Tell me that he has nothing to fear!"

"He has been under the protection of Heaven for six months, and for a moment under that of a steel cross that your aunt gave you, which has been blessed at the reliquary of Saint Claude."

"That steel cross, in fact, Thérèse . . . it's necessary that I believe in its power, since it's from the moment that it ceased to beat upon my breast that all my happiness has ended. May it protect him from his enemies, and may the misfortunes that awaited him only fall upon me!"

I scarcely knew myself . . . I scarcely felt Thérèse's hand pressing mine, or her tears, which sprinkled it abundantly. When I had recovered entirely, she had gone.

Oh, how I would have liked never to have come to the Puy. How I would have liked, above all, not to have come back!

Fortunately, my mission was reaching its end. Three days had not gone by when I received the order for my departure, and I was in such a hurry to leave that it would have cost me nothing to advance the moment.

I had for my labor the indefatigable hand, the diurnal hand and the nocturnal hand of the poet, and on the eve of the day, by then as impatiently awaited as it would have been dreaded a few days before, two hours after midnight surprised me at work, when a shrill cry became audible at my door, which resounded at the same instant under two or three blows, abruptly repeated. I opened it, and I saw Thérèse, distraught, launch herself into my room, her hair undone, her features upset, her feet bare, her body half-dressed in a disorderly cloak. All that I was able to remark was that it was a man's. My alcove was open; she hurled herself into it and slammed the door behind her, shouting: "Save me!"

A frisson seized me, chilling all my limbs. I did not understand either Thérèse's danger or my position with her in the middle of that night of terror, the anxieties of which were further augmented by a storm. Hailstones were bouncing off my windows, deafening on their leads; thunder was rumbling with a noise capable of waking the dead; lightning flashes, so multiplied that one could scarcely distinguish the intervals between them, were casting a kind of inflamed transparency on all the exterior objects.

My first thought was that the house of Père Christ had just been set ablaze by lightning. All that had been so brief that I had not had time to form another conjecture. My door opened again. This time I had not turned the key. There were six men armed with pitchforks and old sabers, who had entered almost before I had perceived them.

"Where's the fire!" I cried.

"Where's the émigré?" they replied.

I guessed.

The leader of the intrepid searchers, as luck would have it, was particularly well known to me. He was a former soldier

23

named Jean Leblanc, who had accumulated over several years the important functions of night-watchman, public crier and sergeant of the National Guard, and combined them with the function of Père Christ's jack-of-all-trades and the factotum of the Mairie. As honors summon honors, he had served me as a foreman or supervisor of the pioneers in the small number of local operations that I had reserved for myself, and I exercised upon him the species of ascendancy that the people willingly accord to a certain veneer of education that is not too spoiled by a stupid conceit.

"What the devil have you come to tell me about émigrés?" I said to him, "and where are you searching? In order to dare to make such a disturbance in my house at this hour of the night, and to be running the streets in this abominable weather, you must have had at least triple your enormous ration of Faucogney kirsch. Let me work, in God's name, for I have no time to waste with madmen."

"I'm neither mad nor drunk, my officer," Jean Leblanc replied, shaking his head. "An émigré was hidden in a neighboring house, that's publicly notorious. We flushed him out not ten minutes ago, and my comrades lost track of him a few steps from your door."

"Have you reflected," I said, placing my hand forcefully on his shoulder, "that the same road leads to yours, and that the bed of Suzanne Leblanc, the amiable and honorable wife of a man of your acquaintance, who only returns home at sunrise, is a surer refuge for an émigré than the cabinet of an extraordinary commissioner of the executive Directoire?"

At those words, the whole band uttered a noisy burst of laughter, with the exception of Jean Leblanc.

"In addition," he continued, in a rather sullen tone, but avoiding replying to me directly, as if he had not heard me, "these lights, which I have never remarked in your house at such an undue hour, prove that something is happening here, and that we haven't come without reason."

"They prove, friend Jean Leblanc, that you reason like an idiot. When one wants to hide someone in one's home one doesn't light the candles, one extinguishes them."

The bursts of laughter redoubled, and I thought I was saved. The inquisitorial squadron had already passed through the door when one of the worthy fellows took it into his head to say: "Why haven't we looked in the alcove?"

They came back in. "The alcove! The alcove!" cried Jean Leblanc.

"Although you're neglecting rather insolently the rules of subordination, Jean Leblanc, and especially the laws of the land, which forbid you to enter my domicile by night, for which I believe myself to be authorized to blow your brains out"—at that moment I seized my two pistols—"I want to give you satisfaction regarding my alcove. There's someone in my bed."

"Aha!" cried the troop. "We've got him!"

I set my back against the alcove, my pistols turned toward the assailants.

"There is someone in my bed; there is a woman there, the name and sight of whom are forbidden to any of you who is not in haste to die at this moment. However, in order to satisfy, with all my power, the patriotic ardor of Jean Leblanc, I will permit him to enter with me and to recognize by means of the hair and the hand the sex of the supposed émigré whom I am hiding from your pursuits. If anyone else dares to follow us, I shall kill him."

"It needs no more," said Jean Leblanc, intimidated, who desired no less than I did to put an end to his expedition. "Citizens, remain outside."

"Cover yourself with your headscarf and your hair," I said, opening the alcove, "and show your bare arm to this hero . . . Look, Jean Leblancc—is that an émigré?"

"Bounty of Heaven!" he said, laughing loudly in his turn. "Please God that all the damned aristocrats and *chouans* were like that! Peace would soon be made, at least on my side. But are you not, my officer, a proud hypocrite, at your age, to debauch thus the flower of our beauties, without having the appearance of touching them?" He continued, whispering in my ear: "There's no fooling me, damn it; that's poor Jeannette of the marsh road, whom you've indoctrinated with your fine words and sly tones. I'd give my head to be cut off that it's the blonde Jeannette, for there isn't another woman with an arm as delicate and such beautiful hair within ten leagues of the Puy—except Mademoiselle Christ!"

At that reticence, the temerity of which even frightened him, he bit his finger.

"Peace, Jean Leblanc! Keep your impertinent conjectures to yourself, and make sure, believe me, that Suzanne's alcove doesn't reserve a more important discovery for you!"

I thought that it was finally permissible for me to breathe. They had definitely gone; I drew the bolts. Painful, however, as the cruel embarrassment appeared to be that I had just escaped, I don't know whether the first moment that followed didn't appear even more intolerable.

You will understand that in that combination of circumstances, which gave my bed as a sole refuge to Thérèse, at two o'clock in the morning of a night so charged with emotions and terrors of every sort, every minute of which seemed to isolate us further from the rest of the world, there was more than enough to upset the head of an amorous young man of eighteen. My breast was beating with such violence that I doubt that it would be possible, even today, when the impressions of that age are disappearing, increasingly effaced by time, to express the agitations with a less lyrical emphasis and a less extravagant hyperbole than I did a year later in the little romance *Les Proscrits*: "There was a tempest in my heart as in nature."

I finally succumbed to that struggle of violent but confused thoughts, through which I could not discover the possibility of any fixed resolution, and I put my elbows on my table with a sort of bleak and mute stupor, in which I tried to lose even the faculty of reflection. I do not know how long that lasted.

Suddenly, my alcove opened; I heard footsteps heading toward me; I felt Thérèse's fingers sliding between my hand and my forehead. I turned slightly and I saw her, dressed in some of my clothes, coiffed in my Polish toque, which seemed too large for her head because she had gathered her long, thick hair therein, even more piquant than usual in that improvised accoutrement.

"Don't you think," she said to me in the tone of ease and abandon that only women are able to adopt at decisive moments, "that I look like Théophile?"

The Théophile to whom she was referring was a young man from Orléans whose excellent studies in mineralogy had given to me for a colleague in our scientific expedition, and whom I had just sent to Béfort, where he was to take the coach.

"It's striking," I replied, smiling, because I had grasped her intention immediately, "and you can return without danger, in that disguise, to your father's house. But is the unfortunate man for whose fate I would so gladly exchange my own also out of danger?"

"I believe so," she said. "I only escaped after having made sure of his departure; he has good weapons, a horse ready at the cottage where I saw you for the first time last year, and your steel cross around his neck."

"God be praised!" I exclaimed. "It's necessary to hope that this fortunate storm will protect him; but it's still a long way from here to the Huningue bridge, and I confess that I have more confidence, for the salvation of your husband, in his horse and his weapons than in the reliquary of Saint Claude and my steel cross . . ."

After having made sure of the exterior, I took her home. I went back more tranquil. I went to sleep.

Jean Leblanc came to wake me up at seven o'clock, in order to ask me, in a manner half humble and half cunning, to be kind enough to attest to the fine feat of arms that he had accomplished so gloriously the previous night, and of which no one, in fact, could render more pertinent testimony than me. I understood very well that he intended to make me buy his discretion at that price, and although the blonde Jeannette's reputation had already been subject to enough checks in the village not to merit very scrupulous protection, I was delighted to save it so cheaply. I even recall that I took pleasure in making of my certificate one of those magnificent historic amplifications of which the secret began to be lost after the *carmagnoles* of Barère[1] and has only been found since then in bulletins. If Jean Leblanc subsequently obtained some honorific decoration for his prowess—and I would not be overly surprised, given the manner in which they are usually awarded—that persiflage doubtless figured admirably in his dossier.

While I was writing, my friends had gathered their little caravan around me and were cheerfully making ready to get under way, with their mineralogical implements, my tin-plate boxes for herborizing and my butterfly nets. My room was full of people when Thérèse came in.

"There," she said, throwing on to my table a small package, neatly wrapped in a white sheet, "are a few effects that Monsieur Théophile forgot in my father's house." She added, with a significant glance: "We never forget anything."

---

1 Bertrand Barère (1755-1841) was a bloodthirsty leader of the Revolution, proscribed under the Directoire, given amnesty under Napoléon, exiled after the Restoration and—remarkably—allowed to return to France by Louis-Philippe, to resume his political career. He usurped the name of the carmagnole, a kind of coat favored by the revolutionaries, in order to apply it by analogy to their patriotic songs and oratorical extravagances. To make someone "dance the carmagnole" became a euphemism for sending them to the guillotine.

"Théophile less than anyone," one of my comrades interjected. "I'll wager that the scatterbrain forgot more than that in the lovely Thérèse's house, and that he also left his heart there, for he only talked about her with the enthusiasm of a lover."

"A lover!" cried Thérèse, laughing. "A lover! Oh, my lover is far away, if he's still running."

Those words, so fortunately appropriate to the circumstance, and which disguised a communication so essential and so difficult, relieved my heart of an immense weight. I did not need to know any more.

A week later I had not lost sight of Thérèse, nor the humiliating and sweet thought of my first amour frustrated in its illusions; but events were of a nature to distract me from my chagrin for some time. The coup d'état of Germinal[1] changed the aspect of France once again. Popular societies were reorganized under the name of constitutional circles, under the presidency of a regulator assisted by a secretary. The redoubtable law of hostages, interpreted as redoubtable laws are ordinarily interpreted—which is to say, in a manner to consternated all the classes of society, although, in the mind of the legislator it only threatened one—was about to be put into vigor. The terror reawakened, not like the lion of Billaud-Varennes, which would do it too much honor, but like the tiger on which Vergniaud speaks; the partisans of order held firm, but the others were the masters.[2]

---

1 This must be an error, as the reference is presumably to Napoléon Bonaparte's overthrow of the Directoire on 18 Brumaire Year VIII (9 November 1899).

2 Jacques-Nicolas Billaud-Varenne (1756-1819) was one of the instigators of the Reign of Terror, who warned the Club des Jacobins: "The lion is not dead when it is asleep, and when it wakes, it exterminates its enemies." Piere-Victorin Vergniaud (1753-1793) was one of the more moderate Revolutionaries, eventually guillotined for treason. He referred in a speech to the contending factions of the Revolutionaries resembling "two tigers tearing one another apart."

At Besançon I fell into the middle of a riot and was captured there. I was unlucky in the passions of my youth. Liberty treated me like amour, and although I cannot say, even today, of what I was accused, I only owe my life, in the division of votes, to the humanity of a juror, whose rigor would have spared me many miseries. It was scarcely a time to remember the Puy, its enchanted valley, its streams and its nymphs.

It is necessary to agree that I gained something from that escapade, in which I had made such a bold gamble without knowing why. There is nothing that softens the soul and disposes it to tolerance like misfortune, but that disposition increases in an incredible proportion in the face of the cruel legality of political passions in which the punishments are so disproportionate to the misdeeds. In times of revolution, whichever party is dominant, if you seek men of intelligence and courage, sincere exaltation, sympathetic sensibility and good conversation, have the State prisons opened. In forty years all that is generous in France has passed that way, and I doubt that much would have been lost if a national patriciat had been constituted on the basis of imprisonments instead of being constituted by diplomas and parchments.

Let us say more: the excellent citizens who demand the abolition of the death penalty in matters of opinion (and please God, if that frightful vestige of the barbaric sacrifices of our ancestors disappeared from our legislation for all crimes, that would be one great crime fewer!) are not only true philanthropists worthy of the gratitude of the society, they are also very judicious philosophers and very profound politicians.

There is nothing that solicits devotion like the cry of blood. Every man is magnified when he has the guillotine and its basket in front of him. I have seen thus innumerable victims of our discords and our reactions who have never been turned from their line because the scaffold as at the end of it, who would have turned back at the third step if it had been a matter of the admonition of a commissaire de police or a one-franc fine. What flattered us, what drew us on irresistibly—and I know this well—was the possibility, the hope, of dying, the emotion of the people who would watch us go, the vague idea that we would leave behind in the heart of a woman the memory of an enthusiasm, or at least a tenderness, of which we would retain a part. The representation of death, for a cause that one is accustomed to believe to be good, enables the denouement to be forgotten; and then, when one has the vanity of one's time or that of a character jealous of celebrity, it does not matter which hand will cast you under the eyes of history, even if it is the hand of the executioner. So see how they die, and kill them again, if you dare, the royalists, the republicans, the imperialists, the carbonari, and the proscripts of all colors. They are the envy of their judges.

The reaction of Germinal[1] was only exercised upon the émigrés and a generation of children who did not want terror by tradition, reasoning or instinct. The imprisoned émigrés were therefore, in the beginning, our natural friends, and the act of absolution that rendered us to our parents did not lessen that contracted amity under the weight of a common misfortune. We continued to visit them and serve them with all our strength, sometimes successfully.

There was nothing easier in those days than to obtain certificates of domicile for anyone in the villages of our mountains, where everyone is essentially aristocratic, because the insensate agents of democracy had revolted against their principles the class of people most interested in adopting them, by violating religious conscience and persecuting thought. It would be difficult to find a good Christian under a thatched roof who would not have willingly violated the express text of the commandments by taking the Lord's name in vain in

---

1 This presumably refers back to year II (1794), when the reaction against the Reign of Terror that culminated four months later with Robespierre's fall in Thermidor began in Germinal.

order to ransom the head of a prescript, and if that is a crime before the Lord in the eyes of casuists I cannot think that it is one in the eyes of humanity.

The courts martial that judged without appeal in the matter of emigration, and who were composed of honorable soldiers prejudiced against those unjust and unnecessary cruelties, ordinarily liked nothing better than finding a pretext for absolution, and it was a pleasure to see them release from accusation every day a marquis clumsily disguised under the mask of a peasant.

I remember on that subject an anecdote that will give some idea of that immense laxity of indulgence, a fortunate consequence of the ferocity of laws. We had a companion in periculous adventures named Léon de B*** whose destiny had been very romantic. Captured in Lyon, weapons in hand, amid the debris of Précy's column,[1] and condemned to death by the military commission of Orange, an entirely providential fault of form or circumstance brought him from his cell to the foot of the guillotine, with the sole expectation of mounting in the next day, just as the decree of the National Convention arrived which revoked that formidable tribunal and annulled its sentences. As a well-escorted cart was dragging him and twenty others to Paris to face the revolutionary tribunal, whose expeditive practices did not promise him any better luck, he perceived when he woke up one morning that his comrade in chains was dead, and succeeded in filching the cadaver's passport, of which the latter had no need in order to render to his last domicile.

The individual who had just made that extreme departure in such an opportune manner was a mountain man from Doubs named Antoine Renaud detained without cause, who

---

1 Louis Francois Perrin de Précy (1742-1820) led the royalist forces during the siege of Lyon in 1793, when that city was the center of a rebellion against the Convention. Précy fled the city with twelve hundred men but lost most of them during the pursuit.

happened to be the bearer of a nose so enormous that no other detail had been imagined to describe him in his description; and by virtue of a fortuitous coincidence with which poor Léon would not have been disposed to flatter himself in any other circumstances, the truly extraordinary nose that he owed to the bounty of nature justified that bureaucratic joke amply enough to rob him even of the appearance of an exaggeration. He was, feature for feature, the man of the *Cap des nez* whose passage through Strasbourg caused so much anxiety to the abbess of Quedlinberg and her four great dignitaries.[1]

In consequence, no protest was raised against his identity and he was transferred to Besançon, rendered to what was regarded as his natural jurisdiction. Unfortunately our unfortunate Facardin—that was his *nom de guerre*—had been born in Quercy, at forty-four degrees of latitude, and he had never succeeded in modifying even slightly in his pronunciation the harmonious and richly accentuated speech of that beautiful region. That would have done for him if he had proffered a single word before the court. He contented himself with proffering his papers in support of the characteristic configuration that served as his safeguard, and awaited the decision of his judges in a state of dejected silence that it cost him nothing to feign in such a situation. His southern sensibility, however, could not rest the unexpected joy of his acquittal, and he exclaimed the expression of his gratitude in an untimely Franc-comtois idiom that had never developed so much suppleness of rhythm and modulation outside of the region between Cahors and Figeac. We shuddered with terror in the audience when we saw the judges ready to fall about on their benches, and the president rising to his feet and repeating as distinctly as an immoderate desire to laugh permitted him: "The absolution is pronounced."

---

1 The reference is to an anecdote in Laurence Sterne's *Tristram Shandy*, devoid of any historical basis.

That story reminds me of another that is analogous, and I shall tell it as I heard it. It concerns an engraver from Nantua named Chavan, young then and probably still alive today, an intelligent, industrious and imperturbable youth—an artist, in the special sense that Genevans attach to that word—endowed, unlike Léon, with an almost miraculous aptitude for appropriating the manners, the language and the accent of any land: Spanish, English, Italian, Norman, Provençal or Bas-Breton, as the circumstance required; an *académie des inscriptions et belles-lettres* incarnate, a polyglot if ever there was one.

In the two years since he had been captured with part of a German regiment no one had succeeded in getting a word of French out of him or making him forget for a moment his inadmissible role as a *Kayserlich*. Cold, heat, hunger and thirst—and he was very thirsty—were only manifest in him, in his most extreme needs, by means of the language of gesture or a few incomprehensible articulations, against the impotence he had to manifest his indignation: the most comical scenes of despair. He could be surprised in a reverie, awakened with a start, struck unexpectedly, but his first cry never betrayed the secret on which his life depended. It was only in the evening, when the bolts had been shot, and in the midst of the most private communications, that he discarded the heavy and brutal stupidity of a rough soldier in order to amuse us with charming follies and develop before us all the riches of his encyclopedic game-bag.

The day of judgment arrived. Chavan, his features leaden, his eyes bleak and nostalgic, with the brutal appearance of a half-cretinous trooper, sat beside his defender without addressing a word or a glance to him. In his own identity Chavan was an important accused; he had been condemned to death three times as a deserter to the enemy, as a rebel of the Midi and as an émigré. Twenty witnesses recognized him under his name and the authority of their depositions could have been confirmed to the extent of the most absolute evidence by the slightest indication of the slightest emotion that might have altered his unalterable sang-froid. His sole means of salvation was the possibility of the existence of a perfect double born in the village of Kircheberg in the grand duchy of the Bas-Rhin, whose name he had taken and whose individuality he had concocted with a superiority of mimic talent that would have been the envy of a great actor.

Suddenly, the reporting captain announced that a fortunate chance had just enabled the discovery, among the court's interpreters, of a bourgeois from Kircheberg. There was no gaze that did not turn toward Chavan; but Chavan had not heard anything; he took a pinch of tobacco from his tinplate snuff-box, transported it with a solemn slowness above his large moustache, and savored it methodically. The interpreter had scarcely opened his mouth to enter into conference with the accused than the physiognomy of the latter appeared to broaden; a hilarity animated those features, so long depressed, gradually increasing to the extent of excitement, and words poured so abundantly from his lips that the ear most experienced in his Teutonic jargon would have had difficulty following it. The flow of words was threatening not to stop when the interpreter turned to the tribunal in order to attest that the soldier was his compatriot, and that unless he had been born in Kircheberg there was not a man in Germany who could speak the dialect as correctly.

Chavan was set free with a permission to travel. As he went down the stairs he perceived his interpreter, seized him by the hand affectionately, and whispered in his ear, in clear and fluent French: "When you write to Kircheberg, my dear comrade, I beg to you not to forget to give your respectable family my good wishes."

All our prisoners did not have the same skill and the same good fortune. There is one whose memory has left in my heart a profound impression of regret. He was a captain of cavalry named Scheyck, who had emigrated at the beginning of the Revolution with his regiment, and whom the stupid disdains of Coblentz, the ennui of inactivity, doubtless the love of his fatherland, and perhaps also some change of principles determined by age and reflection, had persuaded him subsequently, but too late, two or three months after the delays of rigor, to return to his homeland, stupidly abandoned in the confusion of a military escapade.

As he had no resources he had become a soldier again, and as he was brave among the brave, he had become a captain again. From his first stripe to his last epaulette there was not one of his promotions that had not been earned at a price of blood and which did not recall in his service some brilliant act of valor. Ill-fortune brought him to Besançon and as chance would have it he was recognized at a play by one of his former subordinates, who had made more progress and who exercised a senior employment in the local general staff.

Scheyck's honesty was too sincere for him to try to exonerate himself from an explanation. The law was inexorable; he submitted to it. After the four or five days that his captivity had lasted, we met in his room, as we had the previous day, during the hour of communication that prisoners were permitted, in order to empty a few glass of champagne. We were cheerful, as was customary, with the exaggerated gaiety whose expansion the very walls of the cell seemed to protect. There were, as usual, toasts, songs and delirium. At four o'clock an officer came in and asked whether Captain Scheyck was ready.

"He is ready," Scheyck responded, holding out a glass to him.

The unfortunate officer had come in search of Scheyck in order for him to die, and no one among us doubted that Scheyck had been judged that morning. The captain embraced us, marched to the stake smoking his pipe, measured his place on the ground as if he wanted to mark it in a bivouac at the head of his company, gave the order to fire as he would have commanded an exercise with blanks, and fell, by the sole weight of his body, his hand on his heart and his face to the sun. I have no hesitation in affirming that the republic never lost a worthier defender on the battlefield.

I have not yet spoken about one of the émigrés whose attentions and testimonies of affection touched me all the more because there was the sympathy between us that results from the harmony of character and the relativity of ages. He was about thirty and we had heard it assured that he had figured in the *corps de garde* during the artificial attack on the château of Versailles that prepared the bloody days of October. That prison document, confirmed by a bearing and manners of the *ancien régime*, well-served by the svelte attire and the most distinguished physiognomy that I had ever seen in my life, had earned him the nickname in the jail of "the queen's dancing-partner." Hippolyte Dam, full of affection for me alone, was reserved to the point of austerity with the rest of the prisoners, or polished to a point of formality that excluded even the intimacy of misfortune. His white forehead, crowned with little curls of rude and bushy chestnut-colored hair, never showed a crease. He was never seen to smile.

None of our friends had been equipped more promptly than Hippolyte with the evidence indispensable to save him from death, and since the progressive diminution of legal rigors had rendered executions extremely rare, his fate had ceased entirely to worry me. I was free and I had almost stopped going to the prison. The most advantageous turn that the affairs of a prescript could take then was to drag on in length. Bonaparte had only taken one step from Fréjus to the Tuileries, and France, fatigued by vengeances and assassinations, embraced with confidence the hope of a universal amnesty. I was, therefore, quite astonished to learn that Hippolyte had suddenly insisted, in spite of the court, on the solution of his affair; but that impatience did not cause me to conceive any other idea than that of his security. I was not alarmed, because I could not imagine that he would have been in such haste if the step had presented any uncertainty, and I went to bed quite tranquil on his account on the day of his judgment. It was six o'clock in the morning on the next day when Sister Marthe woke me up.

You will all recall that Sister Marthe was the providence of the sick, the consolation of the afflicted, the protectress of prisoners and the guardian angel of proscripts, who combined in her virile stature the inflexible energy of a hero with the virtues of a saint. You have also seen her, if I'm not mistaken, bedecked by the sovereigns of Europe with ribbons, crosses and medals, like a symbolic image of charity personified, bowing down humbly under the weight of those pious magnificences, thinking about the advantage she could extract from them for the relief of her poor.[1] She was not as superbly decorated then. She was simply Sister Marthe in a white headband and a black bonnet, a black serge skirt with a matching top and a blue apron with white spots in Orange cloth, with a little percale kerchief around her neck, bearing for all wealth a large silver crucifix, which she had often pawned in order to procure some aid for an indigent or some consolation for a condemned man. I had no better friend than Sister Marthe Biget, as she had no better friend than me, and her protection, if I had wanted it, would no more have failed me in 1814, with regard to kings and emperors, than it had done fifteen years earlier with regard to gendarmes and jailers.

---

1 The Sister Marthe in question, who resided in Besançon after the suppression of the French convents by the Revolutionaries, had been known in civil life as Anne Biget (1749-1824); she became internationally famous because of her voluntary work caring for the sick, including prisoners of war, and was decorated by the emperors of Austria and Russia as well as Louis XVIII and the King of Prussia. It is not unlikely that Nodier encountered her, but he is surely exaggerating the intimacy of their acquaintance.

The strange vicissitude of things! Her visit was so customary to me, when she needed to improvise a gratuitous speech for the defense of an insolvent accused, that I was not surprised, on opening my shutters, to see her sitting motionless at the foot of my bed.

"Well, Sister Marthe," I said to her, "what have we to do today? If it's a matter of your émigrés, you know that my name is not a good recommendation for them. If it's a matter of your deserters, I've already told you that I've sworn never to speak before the court that condemned Alleyme and Stevenard[1] between my hands, against the formal text of the law."

"It's not that," said Sister Marthe, wiping away a tear with one of her stout fingers; it's a commission from Hippolyte.

"Hippolyte!" I exclaimed. "What does he want?"

"Hippolyte," said Sister Marthe, with an astonished expression. "You don't know, then, that he was shot yesterday evening?"

"Shot!"

"At quarter past four. He refused to make use of his passport and his certificates. He named himself. Monsieur de Maiche exhorted him in vain. Abbé Artaud came to see him. He died in a Christian fashion."

At the same time she handed me a little pine box, the lid of which I opened while grinding my teeth.

I took out of it a small wad of cotton that enveloped a steel cross, beneath which as this note:

> *I am addressing to you by a sure path, my poor Charles, a cross that you gave to Thérèse. Of all that Thérèse and I have loved, this cross can no longer protect anyone but you. Thérèse died ten days ago, and I shall die shortly. Remember us both.*
>
> *Hippolyte.*

---

1 These names are untraceable anywhere else.

Baptiste Montauban; or, The Idiot

"I shall certainly not leave these mountains," I said to the hostess as I arrived with her on the doorstep, "without having seen this good Monsieur Dubourg of whom you have spoken to me. He was one of my father's closest friends. It's only seven o'clock in the morning; three leagues are soon covered when the weather is as fine as one could wish, and I can dispose of a day without prejudice to my affairs. It would be bad form not to have dined with him, in passing, would it not?"

"He wouldn't forgive you," she replied, "since not a week goes by when he does not ask for news of your arrival."

"I would not pardon myself either for having missed an opportunity to verify the worth of my prophecies. I predicted five years ago that his daughter Rosalie, who was then only twelve, would become one of the piquant beauties of the province, and I'm curious to know whether the little brunette with the blue eyes has made a liar of me."

"Be assured of the contrary," cried Madame Gauthier "One could go to Besançon, and perhaps to Strasbourg" (for Madame Gauthier that was the equivalent of the antipodes) "without encountering one like her; and with that, brought up like a charm and as good as gold; but don't go letting yourself get caught, to come back here in despair, as you do from time to time. Nice as you are, you'd be wasting your trouble and sighs this time, for it's been rumored for months that she's to be married."

"Damn it, Madame Gauthier, you still take me for a young man, although I'm twenty-four, with an established fortune and a serious position. Do you think that a trainee advocate for the bar of Louis-le-Saulnier gets infatuated like a law student or an advocate's clerk? Be reassured, my dear lady, and merely show me the route I have to follow to reach Monsieur Dubourg's house, for I didn't even know that his country residence was near here."

"You won't have any difficulty in the first half of the route," she replied. "You won't lose a moment on the well-frayed path that runs through the fields over there, along the stream bordered with willows, but once you've reached the foot of the hill that forms the valley it will be a different matter. You'll be in the Châtillon woods, which it's necessary to traverse in order to reach the château, and as they're only made by woodcutters, who trace many intersecting paths in their comings and goings there, I'll allow myself to say that even the local people sometimes go astray there. But there's no lack of huts and cabins on the edge of the woods, and you only need a hunting horn to procure a guide."

Grateful for that useful information, I saluted my hostess with a wave of the hand and set forth. I went through the country improvising speeches for the first act of my tragedy, with the delightful and immense preoccupation of a man pleased with his verses. So I was far advanced after an hour along the well-frayed little path that ran along a stream bordered by willows, and I was very fortunate, in keeping my direction, that the hill had not had the whim—which would have been strange in fact—to change its location

After having skirted the wood for some time, as Madame Gauthier had said, following fruitlessly a thicket so dense, that I could scarcely comprehend how a passage could be opened for a hare pursued by greyhounds, I was struck by the sight of a small house, all white—which is to say, freshly whitewashed—which backed up against the wood like an oratory crowned with foliage, and around which was a square tightly-trellised fence, from which vine-branches spread in all directions, with floating garlands of convolvulus and hops, and eglantine branches charged with flowers.

I took a few steps and arrived at the entrance to the pretty redoubt, which scarcely seemed appropriate to lodge two or three people. On a section of bench juxtaposed with the door of the house, which was likewise raised by a step or two above a vegetable garden a few feet square, a young man was sitting. I took the time to look at him, because he was not looking at me. He was probably too preoccupied to perceive my presence.

I cannot easily say what it was about the young man that suddenly excited my curiosity, my interest and my affection. I am not romantic, as everyone knows; but the place, the circumstance and, above all, the person, gave birth in me to a host of poetic melancholy ideas, which I was almost annoyed to blame on my composition. I ended up, however, taking a keen pleasure in savoring them in silence.

The young man, so absorbed in his thoughts that the slight sound I had made as I approached had not distracted him for a moment, was as handsome as one of those faces of which one dreams when going to sleep after a good deed, in a healthy slumber—which is truly the only manner of being happy that I know. He seemed delicate, even weak, and yet his pale and gracious face, inundated by the waves of curly blonde hair, would perhaps not have refused the expression of a strong masculine nature. Through the suave languor of his languid features the character stood out of habitual meditation and profound resolution. That surprised me.

What! I thought, privately. *Might you be envying in your sickened heart the advantages of which the blind distribution of fortune has deprived you? Might you be regretting the right that it has stolen from you to take an active part in the agitations of the multitude and to draw it by means of love or subjugate it by means of genius? God preserve you, poor angel!* I continued, drawing closer to him, for I had already loved a great deal. *Remain mild and pure, as I see you, in your futile strength; enjoy your solitude, and leave to the ridiculous tyrants of the old world, disappointed conqueror or dethroned king that you are on earth, the absurd empire that they have exercised for so many centuries.*

The young man turned his gaze in my direction and stared at me while I greeted him. He made a movement to get up, and I hastened to retain him on his bench, because he seemed to me to be ill.

"I beg your pardon, my friend," I said to him, "for having interrupted the course of your thoughts; reverie is so beautiful at your age. Can you indicate to me, without disturbing yourself further, the path through the wood that leads to the house of Monsieur Dubourg? It can't be very far from here."

He looked at me again, but his physiognomy had suddenly changed from an expression of timid benevolence to one of anxiety and alarm. He appeared to reflect.

"Monsieur Dubourg's house," he finally replied, as if he were seeking to collect some very confused memories. "Dubourg? Monsieur Dubourg? Monsieur Dubourg's house . . . ? Ah!" he continued, laughing. "There was once a beautiful house of that name, in which I lived when I was young. It was there that I saw for the first time angels that had taken the forms of women, flowers of all seasons and birds of all songs . . . but that wasn't in this world."

Then he let his head fall into his hands and he forgot that I was there.

I understood then that he was idiotic, or innocent, in local parlance. A marvelous society, ours, in which those two beings of election, the one who is inoffensive to all and the one who lives in solitude, are rejected scornfully to the limits of civilization, like poor children who have died unbaptized.

At the same moment the door opened close by, and I saw a woman about fifty years of age appear, who was better dressed than peasants usually are.

"What!" she said. "Baptiste, you receive a traveler without pressing him to accept milk and fruits and granting our poor roof the honor of procuring him a little shade and rest?"

"Oh, Madame," I exclaimed, "don't scold him, please! I've been here for a less than a minute, and his welcome has touched me in a manner that I shall remember forever."

Baptiste had not even heard his mother. He had fallen back into his reflections. His arms were folded, his head hanging over his breast, and he was murmuring confused words that I could not understand.

I followed the good woman into a rather vast room, of remarkable cleanliness, which had to be the best in the house. She made me sit down in a kind of armchair of honor, the seat of which was prettily woven of yellow and blue straw, while she ushered into the next room an entire flock of little birds of the mountain and the fields, which had scarcely been alarmed by my approach, and which obeyed her with a promptitude that was charming to see, so well domesticated were they.

She renewed the offers that she had just made, and sat down, on my reiterated refusal, asking me how, at least, I could be obliged in the white wooden house.

"I was telling your son when you arrived," I replied, "but he has completely forgotten me. The poor child, Madame, is very afflicted. Have you seen him in that state for a long time?"

"No, Monsieur," she said wiping away a large tear, "and it isn't even continuous. He's always sad, as sad as he's good, poor Baptiste, but he only lacks coherency in his ideas and in his actions, when certain words—which I refrain from employing, as you can believe—are pronounced before him, provoking these fits. Why those words trouble him I don't know; I avoid them, that's all. He was born so happy, the dear child, that he made in advance the hope and honor of my old age, but the good Lord suddenly changed his intentions in his regard."

Here tears became more abundant as she spoke the last words, and she begged my pardon for renewing such dolors.

"It's necessary to tell you, since you have the goodness to be interested in Baptiste," she went on, more calmly, "that Joseph Montaubon, my husband, was the best construction-worker in the Grand-Vau. That didn't prevent us from being very poor, because it was a very bad time for the trade, and my family, superior in condition to Joseph's, had paid an even more painful tribute to events; but that has nothing to do with the story. We didn't know which saint to thank when a rich and respectable man of the region charged my husband with the construction of a superb house, which you'll see if you go through the wood, for I believed that you're coming from Aval. When the house was built, all the way to the eaves, my poor Joseph went up on to the summit himself, as the chief workman, in order to plant the customary streamers of honor there. He had almost reached it when a section of the roof that he had, to our great misfortune, forgotten to fix, gave way underfoot. It was thus that he died.

"Monsieur Dubourg, who was and is the owner of the building, showed himself very sensitive to such a cruel misfortune. He had this small house constructed for my son and me, on rather productive ground, and even added a pension to it in order to subsidize the insufficiency of the income and shield us from all need. Finally, not content with that, he wanted to take responsibility for the education of Baptiste, who was then five or six years old, and who disposed everyone in his favor by virtue of his precocious mind and pretty face. So Baptiste was brought up in Monsieur Dubourg's house with the same cares and the same masters as his benefactor's lovely daughter, who was three years younger.

"That lasted for ten years, and Baptiste profited from it so well that he hardly lacked anything, so said the most knowledgeable people, to make an honorable way in the world. Monsieur Dubourg took the trouble to come here to assure me of that, adding in a serious but mild tone: 'You understand, Madame Montauban, that it's also time for me to separate Baptiste from my Rosalie. He's sixteen years old; she's thirteen and more. The young people are approaching the age when amour arrives; although brought up like brother and sister, they know that they're not, and perhaps I've waited too long to deflect them from that trap for their innocence. It's therefore necessary, my good friend, to take your son back into your own home until I've procured him the favorable position of which he's rendered himself worthy by his studies and his success, in a family even more opulent than mine, or some boarding school.

"'More than that is necessary, if you'll believe me; it's necessary that our children accustom themselves not to see one another any longer, in order not to feel the privation as keenly when they're separated entirely. I have my reasons for that, although nothing indicates to me any other relationship between them that that of a pure and natural amity.

"'Baptiste is an angel of tenderness and submission. Tell him that I shall never cease to love him, and make him understand, with your maternal heart and intelligence, that I have my motives for keeping him away from me. You won't lack pretexts, and if you succeed in convincing him that my happiness is at stake, I have no doubt about his resolution. However, if there's no other means, remind him of my own words. Tell him that the reputation of a daughter is the most precious treasure of a father, and that the voice of the public would soon impose on me a sacrifice more rigorous for all of us, if I didn't take prudent precautions in advance. Ask him not to return to Château Dubourg; I believe he's recognizant and will not be ingrate.'

"He went on: 'One more thing. As the sight of my house might inspire regrets in him that would trouble his repose with you, obtain a promise from him that he won't go any further from the forest in that direction than the place they call the Bec, because the wood extends there to the right and the left two long wings of thickets that surround the carriageway at the place where it's closed in a semicircle by the course of the Ain. You know that the first enclosures of my park are only visible some distance beyond that turning. As for his obedience, I repeat to you, don't worry about it. He'd die rather than break his word.'

"I had listened to Monsieur Dubourg quite nonplussed, because my mind had never been occupied with the danger that alarmed him, and yet what he said appeared to be so reasonable, that I limited myself, for all response, to expressions of thanks and deference. 'I understand,' he continued, getting to his feet, 'that your responsibilities will be augmented as mine are diminished, but that won't last long, for Baptiste is known to my friends under the most advantageous reports, and I expect news any day that he will be conveniently placed. In the meantime, receive from my amity these hundred louis d'or, in order to procure you both, in your solitude, a few of the comforts to which he is accustomed, and always count on me.'

"Having spoken thus, Monsieur Dubourg left the purse and departed, without wanting, in spite of my pleading, to take him with him.

"That was the epoch in which Baptiste came every year to spend a few weeks with me; he brought his books, his herbals and his scientific instruments. I was very happy. He found nothing astonishing, therefore, in his habitual displacement; I like to believe that he even desired it, that time as before. He had never been more handsome, more animated, more satisfied with life, although he had been naturally inclined to sadness since his childhood.

"It was thus for a few days, although I was afflicted that he was working so hard, for fear that—as was only too true—his health might not stand up to such continuous occupation. 'You have plenty of time,' I said to him one evening, 'to leaf through your authors over and over. We'll no longer quit one another until you have a place, and it isn't easy to find a region when there are so many scholars, especially since the revolution.' With that, I told him what Monsieur Dubourg had said to me.

"When I had finished, Baptiste smiled, made no reply, said his prayer, kissed me, and went to bed quite tranquilly.

"The next day, and the following days, he seemed dejected. He didn't talk. I wasn't astonished by that; I had often seen him like that. After a week, however—this was four years ago,—I thought I perceived that his mind was troubled. Unfortunate mother! It was as I had foreseen when he was stubborn in his studies in spite of me. From that time on he renounced his books, but it was too late. He said things that made no sense, or which signified things that I didn't understand. He laughed and wept without any reason; he was only content on his own; he talked to the trees and the birds as if they could understand him; and what is extraordinary, which I wouldn't dare to tell you if you hadn't just seen the proof, is that one could believe that the birds do understand him, by virtue of the facility with which they let themselves be taken by him. Might it not be possible, Monsieur, that the good Lord, who has given an instinct to those little animals to enable them to avoid their enemies, has also permitted them to recognize an innocent who is incapable of wishing them any harm and who only loves them in order to love them?"

That story had moved me greatly, and I believe that it will have produced the same effect on you, if I have found enough force to render it to you as I heard it, in its eloquent simplicity. I passed my hand over my forehead as if to brush away the cares that had descended upon it, and then I covered my eyes in order to dispense me of a dolorous explanation and a futile conversation.

"I've abused your patience for too long," Baptiste's mother said. "Let's return, I beg you, to what you might desire of us. There's nothing here that isn't at your service."

"Nothing, nothing," I replied, emotionally. "I only have to ask you about the forest path that leads to Monsieur Dubourg's house and will bring me back, for it's absolutely necessary that I return this evening."

"You've fallen as well as possible to be instructed, Monsieur; we're very close to it, but it isn't easy. Baptiste will guide you. Not a day goes by without him going to the Bec, to a certain place that I've forbidden him to pass, and this is precisely the hour when he goes hunting. I only beg you not to talk to him about that house, because it seems to me that the memory of his former sojourn with his benefactor isn't good for my child's reason."

"What testimony of my gratitude may I offer you for your service?"

"Oh, as to that," she replied, with a start, "you can't talk about it without mortifying me. We have no need of anything; on the contrary, we're in a condition to do something for travelers little favored by fortune, who rarely present themselves in these remote pathways. Furthermore—but it's a necessary condition—the unique thanks that I expect of you is that of paying no attention to any solicitations of that sort that Baptiste might dare to ask of you, because the customary object worries me. Will you promise me that?"

I did not hesitate. At the same moment, she clapped her hands twice, and all the little birds that I had seen a moment before hastened to the door with a confused chirping.

"Eh! It's not your turn yet," she continued, "impatient as you are. Your grain is not sorted and your troughs are not cleaned."

Then she clapped for a third time.

At that last signal, Baptiste came in, bowed, approached his mother, sat down on her knees, and wrapped an arm affectionately round her shoulders.

"There you are, very good and very handsome," said Baptiste's mother, kissing his forehead. "See, Monsieur, what an amiable child I have! A sweet and docile child, who will be my child all his life, as if I had kept him in the cradle! Do you think I have anything to lament?"

She was weeping, though.

"That isn't all, Baptiste. It's necessary to take a walk, because you haven't had any exercise today, although the air is so warm and the Sun so bright, So many butterflies have never been seen. You know, too, that we have two greenfinches from the last brood that are not females, and you've been thinking for a long time of replacing your goldfinch, which died of old age!"

Baptiste made it understood by means of gestures and cries that his mother had anticipated his desires,

"Go and put on your red gaiters, then, and your Polish hat with a red tassel, to do honor to Monsieur and guide him to the Béc d'Ain, where you can wait for him while hunting, as usual. I have no need to tell you that you'd give me pain by accompanying him any further."

I looked at Baptiste with a curious interest, to see what effect that prohibition would produce, for I believed that I had penetrated part of his secret in his mother's discourse. I did not perceive that the name of the Béc d'Ain reminded him of anything. He went to put on the Polish cap and the red gaiters, came back, kissed the good woman and ran on ahead of me whistling, while all the birds of the wood hastened to sing and flutter around him. I imagined without difficulty that they would have alighted on Baptiste's hat and shoulders if his companion had not intimidated them.

After walking for half an hour we traversed some woodcutters' huts. Children gathered in our passage.

"Oh, look!" they cried. "The innocent with the red gaiters, Mère Montauban's son, is going hunting without nets."

"Good hunting, worthy Bati! Bring us back some bird, a fat blue jay with moustaches, a lovely black and yellow oriole, or one of those mischievous woodpeckers that make holes in our trees."

"Even if it's only a greenfinch."

"No, no," Baptiste replied to them, "You won't have any more of my birds, as in the past, and I repent of having sometimes given you one. You imprison them in cages instead of retaining them by means of caresses. You clip their wings and make them suffer. You shan't have any more of my birds. The spirit of God is in the fluttering little bird; it isn't in the cruel infant that strangles it, mutilates it, kills and eats it. You're a wicked race, and the little birds of the sky are my brothers."

And Baptiste resumed his course in the midst of the laughter of the wretched children, who were doubtless astonished to find him more stupid and more insensate every day.

I would willingly have struck them, for I could not help liking Baptiste even more.

When we had arrived at the Béc d'Ain, Baptiste stopped as if an iron barrier had opposed his passage. He even recoiled a few steps and returned to the forest, calling to his birds.

"Oh, oh!" he said. "Where are you, the pretty, the dainty, the beloved? Where are you, the young singers of the thickets? Where are you, Rosette? Where are you, Finette? Must I believe that you don't love me any more, ingrates that you are, more wicked than women, if the owl hasn't eaten you! Come, little ones, come, my beauties! I have husbands to give you, two greenfinches of a single brood!" He threw his Polish cap on to the ground, allowing his long blond hair to spread over his shoulders. "Here, sleep in that, my daughters, and have no fear of humans, bird-catchers and snakes, for I'll watch over you like a mother over her chicks."

While he was speaking thus I had moved a little further forward. I plunged my eyes into the lovely water, so clear and so limpid, which bathes my dear Jura, the foot of the noble mountains that are your glory, where there are not too many cities and inhabitants! The Ain is another sky in which suns swim, and the Timave is perhaps the only one on earth worthy of being compared to it.

Baptiste's language extracted me from my contemplation. I approached his hat with a timid and halting step, but smiling internally at my credulity. The little finches were there, however. They crouched within it, huddling together, bristling their feathers in order to cover themselves better, like a tortoise hiding inside its shell, scarcely letting gleam outside an anxious eye that they would have liked to render menacing. I have no need to tell you that I withdrew suddenly, in order not to frighten them more.

"Although your hunt seems to me to be fortunate and complete," I said to Baptiste, "it's probable that you won't return this morning to the little white wooden house. Your mother recommended that you exercise, and I hope to still find you here when I return. However, I've remarked my path well enough not to mistake it, and I'd be sorry to retain you here against your will. But if I didn't see you again, Baptiste, I'd regret having quit you without leaving you some souvenir of my amity. Keep this silver watch in memory of me, unless you'd prefer a double gold piece to buy something that would suit you more. And don't refuse me!"

"A watch!" said the innocent, taking me by the hand. "Do you think that the sun will go out today? Gold? My mother has enough of it for the poor. What would I do with it in the midst of my birds?"

"You have nothing to desire, then, Baptiste?"

"Nothing, for my mother does not refuse me anything . . . except for a wretched knife."

That idea chilled my blood. I remembered what his mother had said to me.

"God preserve me, Baptiste, from giving you a knife. My good nurse, who is still alive, repeated to me a hundred times that that sad gift cuts attachments. And besides, people like you and me, my friend, don't carry knives. I've never equipped myself with that weapon of the carnivorous man, the butcher and the assassin."

Baptiste sat down beside his Polish hat and started talking to his finches.

I was observing him for a moment before continuing on my way when I heard myself named by a group of horsemen who wee going in the same direction that I was about to take.

"Maxime here!" they said. "Maxime on the edge of the blue waters of the Ain! Heaven be praised! Come on, then! The friends of Dubourg mustn't miss the nuptial benediction of his beautiful Rosalie, and it's already past noon!"

Wretch! I thought, and did not reply. Baptiste occupied me too much. He had, in fact, turned staring eyes upon them, but devoid of determined expression. I waited. I thought I saw him smile and then return to his birds. I decided that he had not heard or had not understood, and I joined my new traveling companions, without losing sight of him entirely. He seemed tranquil.

The wedding was as merry as a wedding. Men never seem so happy as when they are abdicating their liberty. Rosalie was charming, more charming than I had imagined, but also more anxious than is usual for a young woman who is marrying. Her soul was doubtless entertaining a vague memory of the beautiful days of childhood when she had dreamed of other amours and another husband. I felt a secret pleasure at that.

As for the groom, he was the complete type of the appropriate son-in-law in whom families obtain glory—which is to say, a tall fellow with a strong constitution, which no emotion had ever altered, endowed with the imperturbable self-confidence that plenty of fortune and a little custom give to fools: talking loudly and talking at length, talking about everything and laughing at what he said; forcing the others to take part reluctantly in the satisfaction he had with himself; a stout businessman, with a superficial smattering of physics, chemistry, jurisprudence, politics, statistics and phrenology, eligible by patent right and deep capacity; furthermore, liberal, classical, philanthropic, materialistic, and the best son in the world—an insupportable man.

I left as soon as I could, cleverly dissimulating my escape through the confusion of pleasures and celebrations. I was in a hurry to see Baptiste again.

When I arrived at the edge of the woods near the place where the Béc d'Ain plunges profoundly into the land, I was surprised momentarily to see the river traveled by a few agile small boats that I had not noticed in the morning. I supposed that they belonged to local people who were bringing provisions to Château Dubourg for the feasts of the evening and the following day.

Suddenly, the boats drew nearer, the peasants descended, and a rather dense group formed around something.

I am not curious; I don't know why I ran.

"It's really him," murmured a young fisherman. "It's the poor innocent with the red gaiters, Mère Montauban's boy, who must have drowned pursuing a swallow in flight, without recalling that the river was there."

"If he didn't have the intention, may God have mercy on his soul."

"Bati, the honest Bati—look what's become of him!"

The unfortunate child would not ask me for a knife again.

"Wait, wait!" I said, resuming sentiment and thought, and precipitating myself upon the cadaver. "Perhaps he isn't dead!"

"But how do you expect, my worthy young man, that he isn't yet dead, since it's one of our little ones, who was where we are, who saw someone from a distance throw himself into the Ain as the cavalcade of Monsieur Dubourg's friends commenced to emerge from the spur of the wood? We came when the little one cried out, and spent seven hours searching for the man, and now we've found him. So he's dead! And he's only too dead forever . . ."

"What luck!" cried a pretty little boy about ten years old, running into the wood. "I know where he's left his Polish hat, which is full of young greenfinches, like a nest!"

I went back across country then. I couldn't obtain any information about Baptiste's mother; she must have been dead, or returned to her village.

The wooden house has changed form. It has become very large, very populous and very noisy; so the little birds no longer go there; they avoid it carefully. Monsieur Dubourg's son-in-law has established a school of mutual education there, in which the children learn to envy one anther and hate one another reciprocally, and then to read and write—which is to say, everything they lack to make them detestable creatures. It's an Inferno.

Dead Man's Dale

It would have taken a lot in 1561 for the road from Bergerac to Perigueux to be as good as it is today. The great forest of chestnut-trees which still surrounds it was even more extensive, and the roads were even narrower. At the place where it seems to be suspended over a deep gorge, which was then called Hermit's Dale, the mountain slope that bottomed out in that valley was so steep and perilous that brave men scarcely dared to tackle it even in broad daylight. At eight o'clock on the eve of the first of November of that year—All Saints Day—it would have been completely impractical to attempt the feat, because the premature rigor of winter had added further dangers to the natural difficulties.

The sky, obscured from daybreak till sunset by a harsh wind-driven drizzle, mingled with snowflakes and hailstones, allowed nothing to be distinguished but the gloomiest horizons. Just as the darkness of the Heavens was confounded with the shadows of the Earth, so the sounds of the air were also mingled with those of the earth, in a horrible manner which made travelers' hair stand on end. The storm-wind, increasing from moment to moment, moaned like the voice of a crying child or a mortally-wounded old man crying out for help. It was impossible to tell whether the most frightful of these lamentations came from the height of the clouds or the echoes of the precipice, for the plaints of the forest, the neighing of stabled horses, the shrill whirr of dry leaves whipped up by whirlwinds, and the clatter of dead branches broken by the tempest all ran together. It was terrifying to hear.

The black and hollow vale of which I spoke just now opposed to that, at one point, a striking contrast, a fixed brightness, large and flamboyant, which expanded from below like the plume of a volcano; and from the open door with two battens that gave access to it, gusts of laughter emerged capable of cheering up despair. That is because it was the forge of Toussaint Oudard, the blacksmith, who had attained the age of forty without making a single enemy. He was joyfully celebrating the feast-day after which he had been named by the light of his furnaces and in the midst of his workmen, intoxicated by pleasure and wine.

It was not that Toussaint had never violated the sanctity of a saint's day to shoe a horse or put an iron hoop on a wheel, at least when he had to deal with an unexpected emergency suffered by travelers from abroad, and then he accepted no payment for his labor. Even so, his forge never relented in its ardor during the most scrupulously-observed holidays, because it served as a beacon—especially during bad weather—for unfortunate passers-by gone astray, who always found a welcome there. Whenever the peasants of the dale were called upon to describe the house of Toussaint Oudard, son of Tiphaine, the phrase most commonly applied to it was "Charity's Inn."

Toussaint suddenly came into the large kitchen adjoining the forge, where a few pieces of meat supplied by huntsmen and the butcher were roasting over a fire so fervent that the forge might have envied it, within the ample spread of one of those fine old fireplaces that seems ideally designed to serve the purposes of hospitality.

"See how well it's going," he said, cheerfully, addressing himself to an old woman sitting on a stool beside the hearth, her soft and serious features shining in the bright light of a copper lamp with three burners, which was secured by a bracket to the ancient plaster, stained black by smoke and by time. "It's my opinion that all the little ones are in bed and that a jolly flock of young women from the dale will provide you with good company for the night ahead, as usual. God preserve me from allowing it to be troubled by the cries of my children, long-deafened by the noise of the anvil, who wouldn't hear one another unless they howled like wolves. I've just sent them to my bedroom, where their cries won't reach you. Will you be so kind, mother, as to send us one of your maidservants with the rest of these meaty delicacies—the ripest and sourest that there are, if possible. Keep back a good portion, though, for any poor devils that the bad weather might bring us. As for your friends, try to regale them as much as they like with chestnuts gilded under the embers, while washing them down liberally with sweet white wine fresh from the cask, which will soften them up nicely. When there are no more, there'll be something else . . ."

Toussaint wiped away a tear and hugged the old woman before continuing: "I wouldn't leave you all this work, beloved mother, if my dear Scholastique were still alive—but God has decided only to leave you to mother my children, and to be a visible providence for their father."

"Everything will be done as you desire, my worthy Toussaint," said the worthy Huberte, as moved as her son by the memory he had awakened with his final words. "Have a good time for the little that remains of your feast-day, for the hours are passing quickly. When the monastery bell announces the first prayers for the dead, we'll have the leisure to think about them. Enjoy yourself heartily, and don't worry about your guests. Here come two here already, Heaven be praised, whom we'll do our best to receive well, and who'll be indulgent in forgiving the paltriness of our means, if our welcome doesn't respond to our good will."

"May the Lord be with them," Toussaint said, greeting the strangers, whom he had not noticed until then, "and may they treat my home as if it were their own! Tell them some good stories to help blunt the tedium of the hours, and don't spare the provisions; in a workman's house, every day brings its bread."

Then he embraced his mother once again, and went away.

The two men of whom old Huberte had spoken had risen to their feet momentarily in response to Toussaint's politeness; then they sat down again, silently, on the far side of the fireplace.

The first of them had the appearance of a person of some distinction. He wore a black jacket with laces, over which was folded a large white ruff with generous folds, well-starched and well-fluted. His legs were encased, to a point immediately above the knee—the height to which his cloth cape also descended—by a good pair of leather gaiters, fastened on the outside. His hat, pulled down, was embellished with a floating plume, which fell down over his eyes. His pointed and graying beard only testified a robust old age, and his discreet and elegant attitude gave him the appearance of a doctor.

The other, to judge by his small stature, had to be a child of common extraction, but his extraordinary costume had immediately attracted the attention of Huberte and the young women of the dale, who regretted being unable to make out his features through the enormous clumps of red hair that covered almost the whole of his face. He was clad in a pair of breeches and an exceptionally tight crimson doublet. The top of his head was hidden by a woolen skull-cap of the same color, from which the bright blond head of hair that lent him such a strange physiognomy burst forth in crimped curls. That bonnet of sorts was fastened under the chin by a sturdy strap, like the muzzle of a vicious dog.

"You will be better able to excuse us for failing in our duty," Huberte said, resuming her conversation and addressing the older of the two strangers, "if you understand that our poor and underpopulated country does not often have the honor of being visited by travelers like you. It must have been chance that brought you here."

"Chance or the fiery furnace," replied the man in black, in a hoarse voice, the sharp tone of which startled the younger women.

"It's sometimes the same thing," the dwarf put in, leaning back and letting out an ear-splitting burst of laughter, although he contrived not to render any part of his face visible, save for an immense mouth liberally equipped with teeth that were pointed like needles and as white as ivory.

Immediately afterwards, he set his stool beside the fire-irons and extended towards the brazier two very long and emaciated hands. The flame shone right through them, as though they were made of horn.

The man in black paid no immediate attention to that brutal banter. "My damnable horse," he went on, "carried away by fear of the storm, led me astray for three hours, from one woodland to another and one ravine to another, until it finally made the decision to throw me into a precipice, where I was left for dead. I think I'd covered a good thirty leagues, and I was only guided through the unfamiliar territory by the light of your forge and the grace of God."

"His divine will be accomplished in all things," said Mother Huberte, making the sign of the cross.

"The grace of God could do nothing less," the mischievous little man put in, "to assist the most illustrious, most reverend and most noble Master Pancrace Chouquet, former instigator of the Monastery of the Daughters of Saint Columba, minister of the Holy Gospel, rector of the University of Heidelberg and doctor in four faculties."

That statement was followed by a burst of laughter even louder than the first.

"By what right," cried the doctor, grinding his teeth, "does an uncouth lout of your kind dare to involve himself in my conversation, and to attribute names and titles to me that might not be mine at all? Where have you met me before?"

"I beg your pardon, my gentle master—don't get carried away," the fellow replied, stroking the doctor's cape and sleeve with his huge hand. "I saw you in Cologne while making my tour of Europe, in order to complete my education, in accordance with the dearest wishes of my father. I attended one of the lectures in which you were translating Plutarch into excellent Latin, when you suddenly stopped, quite at a loss— as if Satan had taken you by the throat—at the treatise *De Sera Numinis Vindicta*. It's beautiful and scholarly material. It's true that you had other affairs to see to that day—a bed was being warmed up for you behind the tomb of the three kings that was even more ardent than Dame Huberte's hearth. The story is rather amusing, and I'd willingly tell it if that were the desire of this amiable and happy company."

"And I," said the doctor, in a low voice, "if you mention the matter again, will shove it back into your soul with my dagger! It's surprising," he added, growling, "that a rogue like you should be received into such an honest house."

"I took him to be your servant," Madame Huberte told him. "I don't know him otherwise."

"Nor me, nor me," said the young women, huddling together like baby birds taken from a nest.

"Me neither," said Cyprienne, hiding her head between Maguelonne's knees.

"Oh, the mischievous children!" cried the traveler in the red skull-cap, from the corner of the fireplace, where he crouched down to pull out the burning chestnuts with sharp claws. "See how naughty they are, pretending not to recognize me in my Sunday clothes! Look how much he's changed, Madame Huberte, the little neighborhood horse-trader, Colas Papelin, formerly a clerk, now a groom, at your service. Honest Master Toussaint has not applied his iron to a single one of your mares that I have not previously washed, brushed, combed, smoothed, waxed, polished, brighter than a mirror, and whose horsehair I haven't teased with my fingers at all hours—or by night, at least. That's why I'm always well received at the forge—because the ostler and the farrier, as the saying goes, have only one hand."

While delivering this speech, he moved the thick curls of his flamboyant hair to the left and the right, uncovering his face. Laughing loudly enough to shake the walls, he displayed a rather ugly countenance, as pale and jaundiced as the wax of an old candle, furrowed with bizarre wrinkles, in the front of which shone two little red eyes, brighter than coals incessantly excited by the draught of a pair of bellows. Everyone started with alarm.

Dame Huberte knew perfectly well that she had never seen him before, but a feeling deep inside warned her that it was not a good idea to say so.

"If I've ever seen this phantom before," Pancrace muttered, "he must be the great Devil of Hell."

"It could well have been there," Colas Papelin replied, still laughing, "and I would have been as astonished as you are by the hazard which has found us both here. Who would have ever expected to find Master Pancrace Chouquet in Hermit's Dale?"

"In Hermit's Dale!" said Pancrace, in a thunderous voice. "Ah! Ah!" he went on, biting his fist.

"Ah! Ah!" Colas Papelin repeated, infernal mockery in his tone. "But do you not think, as I do, Doctor, that it would be rather amusing for we men of letters, among whom the love of instruction is combined with the love of gold and pleasure, to find out why this miserable vale is so called? The story must be a singular one, and it's my opinion that Dame Huberte—who knows all the good stories in the world—will tell us that one between two jugs of sweet wine."

"I don't much care for stories, my good man," replied Pancrace, making as if to rise to his feet.

"If it isn't that one, it'll be mine," cried Colas Papelin, putting the other back in his seat, gripping him with wiry arms that squeezed him like a vice. "Oh, we'll obtain great pleasure, Dame Huberte, from hearing you tell that one."

"I promised to tell it to my daughters," the old woman replied, "and it isn't a long story. It's necessary, first, to tell you that this country was even wilder and sadder than you find it more than a hundred years ago, when a holy man came to found a little hermitage on one of the rocky ledges that border the precipice. It was said that he was a rich young lord, and that he'd removed himself from the court for fear of not being able to find salvation there, but he was never known by any other name than Odilon—under which the Holy Father has beatified him, while he awaits canonization."

"Damn!" said Colas Papelin.

"At any rate," Huberte continued, "no one had any doubt that he had brought plenty of money with him, for in less than no time the face of the dale was completely changed. He brought in laborers to till the land, constructed a water-mill on the stream, built a little hospice, a presbytery, a monastery . . . and his generosity attracted tradesmen to the dale, of every kind useful to travelers. Their families still live here, albeit in mediocre accommodation, never ceasing to glorify the name of the Blessed Saint Odilon, who appointed them his heirs. That's why this valley is called Hermit's Dale—because he never left his hermitage, and, in imitation of God, he was good to men without ever being seen. The Lord has his soul before his face, exactly as it says in the prayer-book."

"The story is very edifying," said Doctor Pancrace, "and I would like to believe it on this occasion, although I have heard its like everywhere that monks are to be found—but it seems to me that the weather is getting better again: the wind has stopped roaring and the rain is no longer battering the windows."

"It would be pleasant to resume our journey immediately," Papelin remarked, gaily, keeping the doctor in his seat, "but it would be far too impolite to abandon Dame Huberte at the beginning of such a good and instructive narrative."

"The narrative is quite complete," the doctor replied, impatiently, "and has made clear everything that we could expect from it—which is to say, the origin and the etymology of this valley's name; there is not a word lacking."

"It lacks," Colas replied, "a change of fortune, a denouement and a moral, of a kind for which we students on the benches would not have thanked you when you took the trouble to explain the arguments of Master Guillaume Fichet[1] to us. Look, if you need proof: the venerable Madame Huberte is ready to continue now that she has got her breath back."

She had indeed resumed her story. "The Blessed Odilon had lived thus, in retreat and devoted to prayer, for nearly three quarters of a century, when a young man volunteered to assist him in his holy offices, who had attracted attention for some months by the devotion of his practices and the assiduity of his sacraments. As the young man had the knowledge of a priest, the eloquence of a preacher and the apparent piety of a saint—for no one had ever seen a penitent whose mortifications were so carefully-researched—the hermitage was easily opened to him. His name escapes my memory for the moment, although it seems to me that I heard it spoken not long ago."

"The name of that person is completely irrelevant to your story," murmured the doctor, gnawing at his fingers again.

---

1 Guillaume Fichet, 1433-c. 1480, was a rector of the University of Paris, who helped to establish the first printing-press in the city.

"Master Pancrace Chouquet," Colas Papelin repeated, in a more strident tone, "thinks that the name of this person is irrelevant to your story, respectable hostess!" He went on to add, crying out even more strongly: "Hear this! Your story can do without the name of the good apostle, who seems to me to be an infernal hypocrite—such is the opinion of Messire Pancrace, Messire Chouquet, and Messire Pancrace Chouquet! So you don't recall the name, Madame Huberte?"

The wretch wants to see me dead! the doctor thought, for his part, as he turned his eyes towards the door.

"Not yet," little Colas Papelin replied to his thought, choking with laughter.

"We had feared for a long time that the lure of the Blessed One's treasure might tempt thieves," Tiphaine's widow continued, having taken scant notice of these interruptions, "but we knew by this time that after having distributed a great part in charitable works—as I have mentioned earlier—he had divided the remainder between the parish and the monastery for the education of children, the solace of travelers and the repair of storm-damage. No one in the valley saw anything in the arrival of the young cleric, therefore, but a gentle source of comfort sent by the grace of Providence to ease the last years of the hermit. At least, we said to our old people, the holy man will have someone beside him to close his eyes, and to summon the blessings of Heaven upon his head by giving him the last rites."

"Oh, that was a worthy thought, brave woman!" cried Colas Papelin, sobbing. "I swear that I would have blessed the head of that benevolent old man myself, if God had permitted it! What says my master, Messire Pancrace Chouquet?"

Pancrace twisted his beard, shifted on his stool, looked at the door again, and made no reply.

"That's good," the old woman went on. "One night, Tiphaine sat up in bed beside me. It was thirty years ago today, on the Eve of All Saints, just before the morning mass for the dead."

"What?" said Colas Papelin. "Do you mean, my good mother, that exactly thirty years has passed since that day: that it will be thirty years to the hour, not a minute more and not a minute less, when matins sounds?"

"It must be, honest Monsieur Papelin," Huberte replied, "for it was in 1531. I asked Tiphaine what had woken him up at such an hour, thinking that he must be ill. 'Lie down,' he replied, 'and don't be afraid, old girl. It was just a bad dream, but I have to set my mind at rest before I go back to sleep, for dreams are sometimes communications from the Lord. It seemed to me that someone murdered the old holy man Odilon, and since I woke up I don't know what sort of commotion's got into me. Don't worry—I'll be back in a minute.' So saying, he ran to the hermitage with some of the workmen possessed by the same anxiety—and they found that their dreams had instructed them only too well!"

"The poor hermit was dead," said Colas. "Do you hear, Master?"

"He was dead when Tiphaine got there—but even though he must have fallen without offering the slightest sign of life to the eyes of his murderer, he had found enough strength afterwards to drag himself outside his cell, while the wretch searched fruitlessly for the imagined treasures that he would pay for with his soul!"

"And his murderer was the deceptive and detestable monster who had concealed himself within the amity and prayers that constituted his mask of devotion! Do you hear, Master?"

Pancrace's only reply was a kind of dull moan resembling the cry of an animal.

"It was him all right!" said Dame Huberte. "The grille of the cell had closed behind the Blessed One, by means of an apparatus which Tiphaine had devised, whose secret was unknown to the assassin."

"Caught at last!" cried Colas Papelin, with his usual horrible laugh. "A few moments more, and the good will be avenged. Do you hear, Master?"

"It wasn't like that," Huberte went on, shaking her head. "Tiphaine and his men found no one in the cave, and because the odor of bitumen and sulfur suddenly poured out of it, it was assumed that the stranger had made a pact with the Devil to escape the danger in which he was placed—which turned out to be the case, for we found out later that he had studied at Metz or Strasbourg under the vile sorcerer Cornelius,[1] of whom you must have heard."

"Oh, his bargain was dearly bought," Colas Papelin put in, letting out a new gale of laughter. "Do you hear, Master?"

"I hear," Pancrace Chouquet replied, in a tone of affected calm. "I hear the language of superstitious folly, with which papism has nourished these ignorant folk. May the light of truth descend upon them!" And he made a sudden movement to pull away from his companion. Colas Papelin did not attempt to detain him, but merely turned upon him an expression of derision and contempt.

"What is certain," added the old woman, slightly piqued, "is that what remained in the cave was a fragment of parchment, stained with blood and bearing the marks of five great black fingernails, like a royal seal, which guaranteed thirty years of respite to the homicide—or so it appeared, in a translation made by Monseigneur the great penitentiary, for it was written in a diabolical script."

"Either there's a ringing in my ears," murmured Colas Papelin, "or that's matins sounding. Do you hear, Master?"

"The assassin has never been seen since," Huberte concluded, "although he left a token of his presence behind: the hand

---

1Cornelius Agrippa (1486-1535) was a famous German philosopher, whose studies of alchemy and magic won him a belated reputation as a sorcerer that was dramatically enhanced by the false attachment of his name to a treatise on black magic.

of the Blessed One contained a thick handful of hair attached to a bloody piece of skin, which could not be detached from his grip."

"Good for Saint Odilon!" said Colas Papelin, rising abruptly to his feet and sending the doctor's plumed hat flying from his head with a sudden sweep of his arm.

One side of Master Pancrace Chouquet's head was bald, as glossy as if it had been seared by fire.

The doctor measured Colas with a menacing stare, gathered up his hat, and went to the door. He looked behind to see if the groom was following him, but the little man was amusing himself by using an iron poker to make the fire glow red, drawing out sparks that sprang up as far as the arched top of the fireplace.

The door closed again.

The entire group of women remained silent and motionless, weighed down by an uncanny terror, as if they had been petrified. Colas Papelin looked at them, laughing even louder. He bowed to them, brushing back his disordered hair with the coquettish grace of a man of the world educated in good manners and polite habits.

"Adieu, respectable Huberte, and to you, gentle maidens," he said, as he departed. "Thanks are due to you for the hospitality we have received, but I have other duties to perform—I must follow that gentleman along the road, lest he escape me."

An instant later, the creak of hinges was heard, and the sturdy shutters rebounded against the door.

"Is the Devil gone, then?" cried the blonde Julienne, lifting her tiny trembling hands towards Heaven.

"The Devil!" said Anastasia, putting her hands together in an attitude of prayer. "Do you think that's who he was?"

"He certainly gave the impression," Madame Huberte observed, gravely, "of someone who stopped telling his rosary beads a long time ago."

"Didn't he name himself?" Julienne replied, slightly reassured. "Colas Papelin and the Devil—it's the same thing."

"The two names are exactly synonymous," added Demoiselle Ursule—who was the niece and goddaughter of the parish priest—knowingly.

"I know where I've seen him before," said Cyprienne. "I've seen him stoking the fire in exactly that fashion, when I've fallen asleep at my distaff!"

"Me too," said Maguelonne. "I've seen him mischievously tying the tails of our goats together, when I'm on watch in the cowshed!"

"It must be him," said little Annette, the daughter of Robert the miller, suddenly, "who frightens our donkeys by whistling in the wood!"

"He wanted to scare us too," replied her sister Catherine, in a low voice. "The Evil One in the red jerkin has done more than one of his tricks on the banks of the stream in the dale."

"Deliver us, Lord!" cried old Huberte, falling to her knees.

One can well imagine that the young ladies followed her example quickly enough, and that they did not go their separate ways in response to the matins bell without having purified Dame Huberte's kitchen with prayers, the burning of incense and aspersions of holy water.

The following morning, as the people of the hamlet took themselves off to mass at the monastery, which was separated from the forge by a patch of scrubland, Toussaint Oudard suddenly quit the arm of his mother and stepped in front of his little flock, warning them with a gesture and a cry to go no further, for he wished to spare them the hideous spectacle by which his own eyes had been struck.

It was a corpse, so horribly lacerated, so contorted by the convulsions of agony, so shriveled and desiccated by the action of some celestial or infernal fire, that it would have been difficult to recognize it as human, were it not for the shreds of a black cape and a plumed hat that were trailing beside it.

And ever since that day, Hermit's Dale has been known as Dead Man's Dale.

Lidivine

In 1800 I was in the prisons of a provincial city, and I was not there for the first time. The cause of those petty misfortunes of a young man dispense me from blushing.

I shall not talk about the jailer and his wife, honest and charitable people who have left me a tender memory, but I cannot dispense with remarking in passing that the sad ministry of the jailer is one of the most honorable that there is in the world, when it is exercised with mildness and humanity.

Madame Henriey was infirm and almost always ill. But she had to represent her in the interior an old housekeeper whose name was Lidivine—"a name little known, even among the saints"[1]—whom the poor prisoners named "la divine," because they believed that hyperbolic name to be her veritable name. There is nothing, in fact, that can give us a more distinct idea of the Divinity than Christian charity.

Lidivine was seventy-eight years old, which did not prevent her from being lively, active, busy and ready for anything, as if she were no more than fifty. She was even light and jovial, for the first condition of hygiene is a clear conscience. There is a deep-seated gaiety of the heart that only belongs to good

---

1 This supposed quotation appears to be invented, as is the name Lidivine, although it has been used occasionally since the story's first publication as a forename; it can, however, be regarded as an alternative rendering of the same of Saint Lydwine, the patron saint of sickness, of whom Joris-Karl Huysmans was later to write a "biography."

people. Minds occupied with evil thoughts, on the contrary, easily become sad. There is a reason for that.

When I think of Lidivine I always see her in her clean white wimple and black costume, so brisk and so tight, and her silver heart attached to a velvet cord, also black, which had reddened slightly. She dared not wear visibly the cross that had been suspended from it—that was not yet permitted[1]—but she doubtless conserved it between her flesh and the cilice of wool or hair that she wore out of penitence. I never understood why Lidivine would be doing penance for anything; perhaps it was for having been pretty, for her healthy pallor and robust thinness had enabled her not to lose all the advantages of a good figure and an agreeable face,

What I am saying about Lidivine here is what we all thought, good or wicked; so the influence of Lidivine on the hardened and the most rebellious minds had something more powerful than force, which acted without one knowing exactly how, by a sort of providential fervor; Lidivine had the secret of affirming dejected hearts and consoling desperate hearts. When rabies aroused in the depths of the dungeon one of those demonic mobs that struggle with their irons and die without yielding, biting bloody bayonets, soldiers were no longer sent down there. Lidivine was sent down, and a moment later everything was calm.

God would not have believed that he had done enough for the prison of which I speak if he had only placed Lidivine there. She was seconded by her grandson in that noble and pious ministry. Pierre was a young man of twenty-three, weak in body but indefatigable in patience and courage, whom no care retained from lessening our annoyances and assisting our miseries. I could only give you an imperfect idea of his

---

1 Many religious orders were disbanded by compulsion after the Revolution and the symbols of their vocation banned; in 1800 the relevant edicts had not yet been repealed by Napoléon Bonaparte.

resigned but not dejected physiognomy, his blue gaze, his smooth blond hair cut at right angles, if I did not say that you might have remarked similar characters in the type of our good mountain peasants or in the images of saints traced by a naïve painter.

Pierre was not an important person even in prison. Having arrived there, according to our conjectures, by means of the protection of Lidivine, he was only the aide and servant of the warders. I learned later that that was his title, and the title in question, strangely enough, was a favor acquired by his good conduct. I shall explain that in due course, if the wick of my lamp is still burning.

At any rate, I had been drawn toward Pierre by the sympathy of age that brings young men together so rapidly, especially when they are unhappy, and by the sympathy of beliefs, the only social bond that our political discords had not broken. When his shirt was opened slightly by some work of strength, such as refreshing our camp beds by introducing a new bale of straw, or transporting an invalid, I had often seen the cord of a scapular floating over his breast. Perhaps some secret instinct also informed me that the Lord had imposed a common life of misery and devotion upon us, and that our wellbeing, like his empire, was not of this world.

Our room, number 6, was usually opened by Pierre, whom we all cherished; that was one of those attentions by which we recognized the benevolence of the jail, for the religious salute that Pierre addressed to us every morning was for us akin to a benediction spread over the day. Once, the bolts drawn late and more rudely, without regard for our slumber, announced to us the visit of another warder. That one was named Nicolas.

Nicolas was a good man that another kind of vocation, of which I am not informed, had engaged in the prison service and who had not adapted without effort, I suppose, to the spirit of his estate, but he had succeeded in it in masking his natural sentiments from anyone who did not know them. By dint of exercising his deeper vocal cords, the poor devil had succeeded in giving himself a hoarse and menacing voice, which he was able to render more formidable by convulsively frowning his thick but mild eyebrows, which were never destined to express anger. As that artificial complication must have cost him a great deal, he never responded more brutally than when his back was turned. One day, when he was caught weeping over a man who was about to die, and who was embracing his wife for the last time, he complained that someone had thrown snuff in his eyes. I have encountered twenty warders like Nicolas; men are never as malevolent as they appear to be.

"Where's Pierre?" I asked him, sitting up on my bed.

"Pierre, Pierre!" he replied, bitterly. "It's always Pierre that people ask for. One would think that there was no one here but Pierre. What does he do for you that others don't? Does Pierre bring you anything other than a pitcher of water and bread? A pitcher, here it is; bread, here it is; if you have dealings with Pierre go to find him, Pierre's in the dungeon."

"Pierre's in the dungeon!" I exclaimed. "That's impossible. What has he done?"

"What has he done? How do I know what he's done? Does that concern me? Do I get mixed up in what others do? A door opened too soon, a door closed too late, a letter secretly passed on without having been read, a slack and idle complaisance for your comrades or for you—he's quite capable of it, the little bigot."

Needless to say, Nicolas had turned his back while pronouncing those unkind words.

"It's infamous!" I said, interrupting him. "It's horrible! If the magistrates knew about it, such an abuse of power would be severely repressed. The dungeon is a very serious punishment, and no penalty can be inflicted on a free man except by the authority of the law. That vexation is unworthy with regard to Pierre, as it would be unworthy in your regard. I tell you that it cries vengeance!"

"Good," said Nicolas, looking straight at me this time. "Have you, perchance, mistaken your friend Pierre for a free man, like me, who can quit the house in the evening, asking for my wages? He's a prisoner like you, except that you're going to court tomorrow and the messieurs on high are perfectly free to send you home to your relatives if you have good witnesses, whereas Pierre has thirteen years still to do, since he's only done seven, and thirteen years in the galleys, truly, if the idea comes to the commissioner of the executive power, who retains him by favor, as in a house of pleasure. I agree that it's harsh, but what do you expect? He wasn't old enough to be guillotined."

The guillotine, the galleys, that honest Pierre, that admirable Lidivine, all the appearances that had struck me, all the notions that I had just collected in a two-minute conversation, were tumultuously confounded in my mind when the door closed on me again. I could no longer interrogate Nicolas, who would probably not have been in any humor to reply to me; but I thought I could still hear him, murmuring his refusal through the thick wall, in a tone graver than that of the bolts: "How do I know? Does that concern me? Do I get mixed up in what others do . . . ?"

I went to court, in fact, the following day, as Nicolas had announced to me, and I was acquitted by the majority of nine votes out of twelve. You will not be astonished if I add naively that the advantageous result of a count had never been more agreeable to me.

The first thing that occupied me when I found myself free was the story of Lidivine and Pierre. An old priest, recklessly saintly, had taken refuge in their family in 1793 in order to carry exhortations and hopes from there to his Christian flock, devoid of a pastor and altars. He was surprised while officiating and held out his hands to the irons, like a martyr of the first ages of the Church. His petty people of the hamlet defended him in spite of him, with the ardor that religion always inspires when it is persecuted. There were fifteen of them. Thirteen died on the confessor's scaffold, after having received his final benediction. The grandmother was more than seventy, the grandson less than sixteen, and, in accordance with the accurate expression of the warder, one of them was older than required and the other was not yet of an age to be guillotined. That was why Lidivine and Pierre were in prison.

In the meantime, Bonaparte had come back: Bonaparte, that giant of civilization, who brought it back ready-made, and who could not reaffirm it on its eternal bases, because God no longer wanted that. The revision of those exceptional procedures of a legislation of anthropophages had become facile. A large number of honest people took an interest in the fate of Pierre and Lidivine. There is nothing so common as finding hearts disposed to the reparation of evil when there is no longer any peril to hinder them. I am not talking about the efforts of my friends in prison, whom I saw often, because I already knew, by virtue of precocious experience, that the slightest official revolution could render them futile.

At the moment when the documents annulling their judgment reached me, fully authenticated and legalized, I flew to them, ten times happier than I was in quitting them on the day of my absolution. I brought Lidivine and Pierre twenty-six years of liberty; so I remember that impression as if I had neither suffered nor seen suffering since. It was at four o'clock in the afternoon, on a beautiful spring day, as the Franche-Comté sometimes has in April, but the hour had not expired, and the prisoners were still enjoying the last minutes of recreation in the courtyard in bright sunlight, very warm and very cheerful. In prisons there is a time and a place assigned to recreation; I can certify that.

"You're free," I cried, flinging my arms around Pierre and Lidivine in turn. I had some difficulty in making myself understood, but everyone else understood, and the emotion of those poor folk, who bathed their cheeks and hair with tears, explained my words well enough.

After that there was a great silence—a grave and sad silence, for there are other bonds to break, in a prison where one has lived for seven years, than those of captivity. Lidivine looked at those women, those convalescents and those invalids whose mother she had been for such a long time, and whom she had flattered herself with bringing back gradually to religion and to virtue; finally, she stopped in front of an old man, completely broken, whom the fatigue of age or the excess of joy had nailed in place.

"Oh, Georges," she said to him, "who will bring you your broth?"

Then she returned to me and, clutching my hand in her two hands, she said: "I'm truly free?"

"Yes, Lidivine."

"I could leave with you now, if I wished?"

"Yes Lidivine."

"You can take me right away to the house of the advocate of my prisoners?"

"Yes, Lidivine."

"You can show me those of the physicians of my invalids?"

"Yes, Lidivine; and the church will open to you again, for we're living under a human, just, enlightened government, which will sense the necessity of supporting its power on faith. God is the best of auxiliaries."

"You're right, my friend. Oh, if I were sure of not being a burden in prison . . ."

The jailer's wife embraced her and made an involuntary movement to retain her.

"That's good," she said, smiling, while she wiped her eyes with the back of hr hand. "I'm not yet so old that I can't earn my bread honestly in the home of my masters. Go and lie down bravely, you others, for four o'clock is chiming. We'll see one another again tomorrow. I don't want to leave . . . Where would I go, anyway," she added, "to be more useful or happier? There's no longer a house, a family and a village for me; even the cemetery wouldn't tell me anything, for my husband, my brothers and my children are no longer there. You know that they died far from here, and they've been put I don't know where. As for Pierre, that's something else; he's young, handsome, industrious, patient and, above all, God-fearing. If the world has returned to good, as you say, perhaps my poor Pierre will prosper. Come here, my child, so that I can bless you and bid you adieu."

Pierre had not yet spoken. He seemed to be plunged in a serious meditation and embarrassed to break the silence. Finally he drew nearer to Lidivine, at the appeal she had just made to him.

"Never, Mother," he said, firmly. "I've sometimes thought about the action I ought to follow when my term ended; I would have liked to be a priest, but I don't have the leisure to become knowledgeable. In any case, if the ministry of a priest is great, that of warder has duties that I like and from which I don't want to abstract myself. Nicolas needs an aide, and he knows now that my compassion for the difficulties I've suffered since childhood have never turned me away from my obligations. I beg you to permit me, Mother, not to leave the prison. It's the life that the Lord has made for me, and I won't renounce it."

The prisoners had gone. Nicolas no longer had any reason to constrain the expression of his good nature.

"Stay! Stay!" he cried to Pierre, weeping hot tears.

"Isn't it true that in my place, you'd have done the same?" said Pierre, turning to me.

"Yes, my friend, if I had had the courage."

Lidivine and Pierre died in the service of prisoners.

The Fiancés

It was at least an hour before sunset on the first of January 1685, and all the offices had finished when the doors of San Marco opened again for a double solemnity that summoned a large number of people to the church. Two small processions, equal in magnificence, had emerged at the same time from the Palazzo Morosini and the Palazzo Trevisano, in order to accompany to the baptismal font two children born during the previous night, and to request in their favor the waters of redemption. They entered at the same time through the two lateral doors and reached the holy baptistery at the same time, where the women deposited two cradles.

One of the groups was led by Onofrio Morosini, the son of the illustrious doge Francesco Morosini,[1] well-known for his great services of war and state that he had rendered to the republic, the second by Senator Bernardo Trevisano, the judge of the Quarantia, who heightened the splendor of his family by the renown of his knowledge, and to whom Italy entire did not oppose, in that century of decadence, a greater philosopher or a more skillful antiquary.[2]

---

1 Francesco Morosini (1618-1694) became Doge of Venice in 1688 after a distinguished naval career. There does not seem to be any record of his having a son called Onofrio.

2 Bernardo Trevisano, the supposed author of several alchemical texts, was actually said to have lived in the fifteenth century, but the most famous work attributed to him, *Il sogno verde*, only materialized in 1695, thus

When the nurses had uncovered the children's cradles, a sentiment of admiration was manifest in all parts, the exuberance of which could not be entirely repressed by the imposing sanctity of the location. Never had the day of birth allowed so much beauty to appear in the imperfect creature who had just been born; never, until that moment, had an intelligent soul appeared to animate its gaze, and it was impossible to doubt that the infants enjoyed the faculty of seeing and feeling, for they smiled when they looked at one another. It was remarked, above all, how much they resembled one another, and the ingenious and poetic imagination of the people easily supposed that they had been made for one another when it was learned the Providence had given Morosini a son and Trevisano a daughter.

Morosini's son was named Giovanni, and Trevisano's daughter Elisabetta-Maria, the name of her venerable grandmother Elisabetta-Maria Tagliapietra, Bernardo's mother.

One circumstance of which no one in Venice was unaware gave a bizarre interest to that unexpected similarity. For several generations the two families of Morosini and Trevisano had been divided by a hatred that had often degenerated into bloody disputes. Those altercations had calmed down, in truth, under Onofrio and Bernardo, noble and generous lords, whose mores had been softened by the study of the sciences; but they were believed only to have been put to sleep, and it had been feared that they might be renewed at the first opportunity, with more violence than ever.

That day, the witnesses could not help thinking that Providence itself had the intention of putting an end to it, and that it had contrived that strange encounter deliberately, in order to bring together, by means of a touching and sacred bond, two of the great patrician families whose dissensions never burst forth without endangering republics. That sen-

---

presumably prompting Nodier's dating of the present story.

timent was so natural that Morosini and Trevisano shared it without having communicated it verbally, and fell into one another's arms like two brothers finding one another after a long separation. After having exchanged the most tender embraces they promised, to the acclamations of the multitude, to marry their children in sixteen years, if the sympathy that seemed to be manifest in them on the day of their birth continued to strengthen with age; and that reciprocal engagement was so sudden that it was impossible to determine which of them had proposed it first.

Every month of every year of the lives of Giovanni and Elisabetta confirmed the hopes of the two noble senators. Their amour increased at the same time as their beauty, and it was incomprehensible that it could have been different, for no other person in the world was worthy of disrupting the invincible attraction that summoned them to confound themselves in a single soul.

They were, in fact, two ideal creatures, two exceptional beings, whose complete perfections of body and mind would have condemned them to eternal solitude if nature had not taken care to have them born at the same moment at the same point on the earth, like two rare flowers on the same stem, two birds of paradise with gold and azure plumage, under the same shade and almost in the same nest. Thus, their mutual tenderness did not even inspire the jealousy whose principal motive is in human vanity.

It would have been necessary, in order to aspire to deflect the amour of either one, to be deluded as to one's own value, and it was sufficient to see them to sense that Elisabetta was only made for Giovanni and that Giovanni was only made for Elisabetta. Any rival pretension to the happiness of those two celestial children would have betrayed the dementia of pride; but the hearts of young men and virgins dared not beat for them; people were content to admire them, and poets to sing about them.

I have already said—and who could need to be told?—that Bernardo Trevisano had imprinted in his time a great movement in the philosophical sciences; much is still made today of his *Cours*, his *Méditations*, his *Praelections fondamentales*, and above all his treatise on *The Immortality of the Soul*.[1] After having profoundly examined the doctrine of Democritus and that of Aristotle, he had delivered himself most particularly, under the auspices of Jean Caramuel,[2] Bishop of Vigevano, the most imaginative mind of the century, to the divine theories of Plato.

It is unfortunately rare, as is well-known, that an active and passionate thought which plunges into the mysteries of spiritualism stops at the useful and consoling notions of that precious study, but Bernardo was too thirsty for knowledge not to sound all the sources on which intelligence had drawn before him. His admirers admitted that he sometimes went astray in the numerical combinations of Pythagoras, and that the reveries of Caramuel, his master, regarding the cabala of letters, which he had scorned in his youth, influenced in a manner injurious to his glory the compositions of his old age. It is not useless to recount what determined that new direction in his work.

Bernard Trevisano, so favored by Heaven in the fortunate development of his Elisabetta, was suddenly afflicted by the most rigorous blows in the rest of his family. A wife who was still young, and who made his delights, was taken from him in a matter of days by a malady unknown to medicine. A son for whom he had high hopes, the sole heir to his name and an illustriousness that went back to the most ancient times of the republic, died in his arms, smiling, like an angel recalled to

---

1 None of these works appear in the list of works conventionally attributed to Bernardo Trevisano.

2 The Spanish scholastic philosopher and mathematician Juan Caramuel (1606-1682), a correspondent of René Descates, Pierre Gassendi and Athanasius Kircher, among many others.

God. Elisabetta herself hardly participated in material life. He compared her sometimes to those brilliant and pure fires that are often seen wandering over the earth but do not hold to it, the sight of which is enjoyed with intoxication, but which no power can fix, and which vanish at the slightest gust of air without leaving any trace of their passage.

"Alas," he cried, one day, "what is the point of these profound speculations in science? To what do the discoveries of philosophy lead, if it is not given to humans either to foresee the evils that menace them or to ward them off? Is not life, in fact, a tenebrous gulf, the bottom of which no one can know without having touched it, as the Euripus[1] was for Aristotle and the volcano for Empedocles?

"No, no," he went on, "the infinitely powerful being who has given me the instinct of verity, and who has permitted me to reignite the sacred flame in the hearth of ancient enlightenment, will not refuse me the price of so much effort and so many late nights. If it is too late to save the two parts of my soul that I have already lost, I shall protect my Elisabetta against death for a long time, or I shall deliver to the flames all my futile books, cursing the employment I have made of my foolish years, for the ignorance of the brute is a thousand times preferable to a knowledge that produces no fruits."

With that, he had everyone forbidden entry to his palazzo, and enclosed himself in solitude in the midst of his cabalists and Pythagoreans, with his fateful figures and his mysterious alphabets.

Morosini respected Bernardo's sadness for a few years, for he could only attribute the resolution of the great man to the need to nourish himself secretly with memories of his mourn-

---

1 The *détroit de Euripe* [strait of Euripus] is the channel separating the island of Euboea from Boeotia on the Greek mainland. Popular tradition related that Aristotle drowned there, having despaired of understanding its complex tidal currents.

ing. However, when the first of January 1701 approached, Morosni, who had arranged everything for the marriage of his son with Elisabetta, did not hesitate to penetrate into his friend's retreat, and the servants, who knew the conventions of the two families, dared not forbid him access to it. He therefore went into Bernardo's chamber and sat down.

"It's you, Onofrio," said the philosopher, turning toward him. "What do you want of me?"

"Can you ask me that? I've come to summon you to keep the promise you made me sixteen years ago at San Marco, the accomplishment of which interests the happiness of our children today. Are you capable of having forgotten it, and have people not been mistaken in assuring me that, far from occupying yourself with preparations for the wedding, you have had the disloyalty to send Elisabetta away a few days ago? Tell me that that is false, I implore you."

"It is true," replied Bernardo. "Elisabetta is not in Venice, but I am not disloyal."

"What!" cried Morosini. "Miserable family hatreds, as without excuses as without motives, have prevailed over the holiest oaths!"

"You are not judging me harshly enough to insult my thought," replied Bernado, holding out his hand.

"What, then, is the fatal key to this enigma, in which my reason is lost? Perhaps the derangement that your assiduity in labor and your systematic distancing from affairs had brought to your fortune has made you fear not being able to endow Elisabetta worthily? Disabuse yourself, my brother; Elisabetta is already too richly endowed by her beauty and her virtue. Giovanni has no need of your wealth to enable her to take the rank of a queen; he is my only child, and in the seven years since my father has gone to join his ancestors, the days and nights elapsed would not have sufficed for me to count the treasures that the old doge conquered in the Peloponnese and from the Turkish fleets of the Archipelago. But you're no longer saying anything."

"I'm astonished by your facility is supposing me to have such cowardly weaknesses. Elisabetta is still one of the most opulent heiresses in all the Venetian states, and I esteem Govanni sufficiently to give him my daughter if she were as poor as she is rich. A truce on your conjectures, therefore; you will not divine me. Listen—have you sometimes reflected on the unknown cause of human fatalities? Do you know on what our destiny depends?"

"I know it; our destiny depends, in the first place, on divine Providence, in the second place, on the good or bad employment we make of our faculties, and above all on our reason."

"That's true in principle, but Providence has general laws from which it never departs, because they are self-imposed; and wisdom consists of not contradicting the inevitable action of those universal laws by an imprudent ardor of enjoyment. The most infallible of all has been recognized by Pythagoras, who was perhaps more than human. The cabalists had groped their way along his path, and my master, Caramuel, has taken a few steps after them. What they were searching for, I have found. The fate of the whole of life is hidden from the eyes of the vulgar in the syllables of our name. It is their arrangement that determines the fortunate or unfortunate outcome of our enterprises, and it is from their combined harmonies that result, in accordance with certain cycles of years that are co-ordinated with them, in the apparently fortuitous eventuality of our affections."

"Alas," said Morosini, consternated, "have I heard correctly? Have you only combated so splendidly, since your youth the superstitions of magic and the reveries of judiciary astrology, in order to revert at fifty to the delirious hypotheses of Caramuel? You're smiling, Bernardo, and I comprehend that disdain. Forgive my sincerity. The extent and certainty of the knowledge that has placed you so high above the most savant and the most sage forbid me to contest it, but what consequences do you claim to draw from your system?"

"This: the century that will commence in a week will be bad for the human race. It is from it that an era of desolation will date that will doubtless end with the annihilation of the species. I find it, however, sufficiently benevolent and pacific for our children, if they have the courage to want to be happy at the price of a small sacrifice. The only year of the disastrous century that menaces them before the end of a long and brilliant career is the one that is about to open. They are only sixteen years old, Onofrio, and the rapid time that the sun will take to visit its twelve houses will not render them too mature for marriage.

"It would be easy for me to disarm your credulity, but I shall not attempt it. What I would obtain easily from your conviction, I have a right to expect from your affection, and if you wish, from your pity. Science or instinct, error or vision, my belief is formed irrevocably; and if your intelligence, more enlightened than mine, is repelled by a bizarre doctrine that inspired the same distance in me for a long time, you will at least spare, by granting mercy to my illusion, what there is of the most irritable in the heart of a father.

"It is not you who will accuse of exaggeration the precautions that paternal love inspires. You are not unaware, any more than I am, that if the dangers one fears for one's children are imaginary, the dolor that they cause is not. You can do better; you can demand of Giovanni that he avoid like death the opportunity to see Elisabetta, if only for a moment, if our misfortune permits him to discover her retreat. Obedient, I will lead his wife to the altar for him on the first of January 1702; rebellious to our pleas, you can announce to him on my behalf that he will only rediscover her in the tomb.

Morosini made no further reply. He embraced Trevisano tightly, and reported his words to Giovanni.

Giovanni was, as we have seen a little while ago, a perfect soul in a perfect body. Bernardo's doctrine appeared to him to be an error on the part of the genius, but he submitted, weeping, to the will of a father who would soon share the rights of his own. He even resigned himself without effort to Morosini's project, who had immediately resolved to have him spend the year traveling, either to add a necessary complement to his education, or to distract his heart from a dangerous preoccupation by means of the attraction and variety of new sensations. He departed, visited in succession Italy, France and Germany, and bore his regrets and his impatience everywhere.

The year had scarcely finished three quarters of its course when, in haste to savor the air that he had breathed with Elisabetta, he arrived in Padua, returning toward Venice.

It was the twenty-sixth of September, a solemn day in the annals of the Christian city that flourished over the ruins of the ancient city of Antenor. The anniversary of the festival of Saint Justine, a predestined young woman to whose memory the cult of the faithful has consecrated a monument within those pious walls that will doubtless never equal in magnificence the temple of Venus at Gnide, nor that of the Graces at Orchmene, nor the marvel of Delphi.

Giovanni, filled with a religious admiration, went through the rich hangings and the baskets of flowers, all the way to the sacred enclosure; he penetrated it in the midst of a cloud of perfumes and incense, which was floating, colored by all the hues of the rainbow by the reflections of the stained-glass windows, and knelt on the mosaic pavement in a chapel clad in sumptuous marble of rare and various colors, in which a golden reliquary resplendent with precious stones reposed on the altar, surrounded by a choir of virgins in white robes who were saluting it with their canticles.

O illusion more enchanting than all those that had struck Giovanni's senses thus far! One of those voices, which resonated in the depths of his heart, reminded him of Elisabetta's. He got up, bewildered, and attached himself without reflection to the steps of the group, whose song had concluded, and which had reached the parvis.

"See you soon, dear Giovanni," one of the young women said to him in a low voice, lifting her veil slightly, in order to allow herself to be seen, and letting it fall back. "Don't forget your Elisabetta, in order that Elisabetta does not forget you!"

After which she disappeared, and was lost in an instant in the midst of her companions.

He had seen her. It was Elisabetta.

The last three months of the year were long for his amour. It seemed that they would never end.

They did end, however.

Onofrio Morosini did not wait for the last day to go and remind Bernardo that the delay he had fixed was about to expire, and was glad to have been anticipated, for the philosopher, distracted from his austere studies by the milder cares of his life, had already surrounded himself with all the preparations for a brilliant wedding.

"May Heaven heap you with benedictions, dear Bernardo," he said. "We have no time to lose to crown the desires of our children. My Giovanni, ready to cede to the ardor that is consuming him, is visibly inclining toward the tomb. Pale, withered and languishing like a flower whose root has been touched by the plowshare, he has been fading for three months on my heart and under my tears; I've trembled a hundred times that his soul, scarcely suspended from his lips might be exhaled in a sigh."

"That's strange," said Trevisano. "I've received equally sad news of the health of my Elisabetta. My calculations cannot be mistaken though; and if my intentions have been followed, as I have reason to believe, no danger threatens them. Let us not be alarmed by these lax languors of two passionate hearts that are missing one another. It is a cloud that will dissipate at the first ray of amour. Return to Giovanni, therefore, and tell him that everything is disposed in my palazzo to receive the two spouses there. Another hundred hours, Onofrio, no more than a hundred hours, and your Giovanni's fiancée will be united with him forever."

The sage Bernardo did, in fact, leave the next day for Padua while the preparations for the nuptial feast were completed.

It was at least an hour before sunset on the first of January 1702, and all the offices had finished when the doors of San Marco opened again for a double solemnity that summoned a large number of people to the church. Two small processions, similar in their lugubrious appearance, had emerged at the same time from the Palazzo Morosini and the Palazzo Trevisano, and came to recommend to the prayers of the church two young people who had died during the previous night. They entered at the same time through the two lateral doors and reached the area under the keystone of the vault, the funereal rendezvous of the dead, at the same time, where the porters deposited two coffins.

Those unfortunates were Giovanni Morosini, son of Onofrio, and Elisabetta Travisano, daughter of Bernardo.

That is what I read in a very rare collection of Italian poetry to their praise, the date of which is not distinct present to me, which makes me dread that I might be mistaken by one year as to that of the event, something of scant importance in a historical vignette, even when the foundation is veridical.

Sibylle Mérian

When the Swedish General Rosander had consumed in foolish dissipation the immense fortune left to him by his father-in-law Mathieu Mérian,[1] counselor to the elector of Mayence, he could see no other course to adopt than to go and hide his merited poverty in a country where human eyes could not follow him; but he commenced by ensuring the life of a son almost in the cradle, who had cost his mother the light of day, by placing him in the protective hands of the famous Marie-Sibylle Mérian,[2] the child's great aunt, whose rich, exact and careful talent would be the eternal despair of painters of natural history.

The good Marie-Sibylle welcomed little Gustave de Rosander like a God-given son, for she had only had two daughters of her unhappy marriage to André Graff. Gustave, loved, caressed and nourished in good studies, came along

---

1 Matthäus Merian was the name of two Swiss engravers, of whom the elder (1593-1650) was the more celebrated, although the one featured in the story is the younger (1621-1687).

2 The naturalist and scientific illustrator Maria Sibylla Merian (1647-1717) was the daughter of the elder Mathäus Merian and the half-sister of the younger. She became the leading entomologist of her time, one of the first naturalists to make a detailed investigation of insect life. She published a seminal two-volume study of caterpillars in 1679-83. She traveled to Surinam in 1699 to observe tropical insects and published *Metamorphosis insectorum Surinamensium* in 1705. The pupil featured in the present story is fictitious.

so perfectly that nothing would have been lacking to fulfill all the wishes of his aged adoptive mother if he had given evidence of any penchant for observing her cherished insects and butterflies with her; but the surly child did not want to hear mention of it, and at twelve he could scarcely distinguish a pale and wan silkworm from the pompous caterpillar of a spurge hawkmoth.

"It's very easy for you, Great-Aunt," he said one day, with a sharpness that he showed very bitterly thereafter with regard to the Chevalier Linnaeus, his contemporary, compatriot and friend, "it's truly very easy for you to talk about the marvelous beauties of nature, you who have been able to admire them under the sky of Surinam, but if you have it at heart to make me share your enthusiasm, it's necessary to send me there with my aunt Dorothée and not to retain me in these hideous lagoons, in the midst of your larvae, your caterpillars and cocoons, which I have, thank God, avoided looking at all my life, so hard to swallow is the disgust that the spectacle inspires in me. I would like to believe that there are favored countries and races of election on earth over which God has deployed his power; but if the entire world resembles what I have seen of it, it appears to me to be scarcely worthy of the trouble that the Lord took in making it. I beg your pardon, my respectable Mother, for contradicting your ideas thus; I'm only seeking to educate myself, and it isn't entirely my fault that nature doesn't appear to me clad in the marvelous colors that your brushes lend it."

Sibylle did not judge it appropriate to confront Gustave's opinions head-on, because that is a poor means of enlightening the presumptuous ignorance of young people, whom it is easier to guide to the truth by progressive instruction. She smiled and kissed him.

"If it were only a matter of that," she said, "and you had a little confidence in my stories, I wouldn't have any difficulty dissipating all the doubts that have arisen in your little head regarding the wisdom and the power of the Creator. I won't even use for that the common privilege of voyagers, who have a passion for lying when they come back from far away. You know that I never impose in that regard. The people of election that you have divined by means of a fortunate instinct really exist, and I have seen them myself in traveling the world, so that you can rely on my narration with even more assurance than if you read it in the superb cosmographies of your famous great-great grandfather Théodore de Bry;[1] for that which he only had painted, I have been able to observe at close range, very carefully."

"Oh, I would have pleasure, dear maman," cried Gustave, "in hearing you recount those beautiful things."

"I'd like that," said Sibylle, "and I'll answer to you that they surpass by far the idea that you might have formed of them. Can you imagine, to begin with, that among those people everyone is born adult and perfect, without suffering any of the inconveniences of an age of apprenticeship and weakness?"

"It must be thus," said Gustave, "in a species veritably favored by Heaven."

"That's nothing yet; everyone there is born clothed, but not in foolish plumage like the birds or a coarse fleece like ewes. Those people come into the world clad in pompous accoutrements draped and floating like the togas of senators, or shiny and polished like the armor of knights. Some are embroidered so delicately and so artfully nuanced in their colors that the needles and looms of the fays have never produced their like. It's not rare to find some who display in their adornments all that coral, jet, lapis and gold have of the most dazzling, and others in which all those reflections are confounded, with an inexpressible harmony, in sparkling mosaics that have no

---

1 Théodorus de Bry (1528-1598) was the elder Matthäus Merian's employer and father-in-law. One of the friends of Nodier's father, who was instrumental in having him released from jail in 1804, was the prefect of Doubs, Jean de Bry, who might have been a descendant.

name among humans. Finally, one sees some who take the refinements of that magnificent luxury further, whose robes are enameled with more rubies, sapphires, amethysts, emeralds and diamonds than Monsieur Tavernier counted in the treasure of the great Mogul. I hardly dare speak to you after that about the undulating plumes that shade their crowns, because it's a matter of little consequence by comparison with others, but the whole composes an ensemble splendid to behold."

"I confess that I would have great difficulty believing in these miracles," Gustave replied, "if it were not you who are attesting to them; but it's also necessary to remark, my good friend, that thus far you have only talked about kings."

"That's because I've expressed myself poorly," Sibylle continued. "I don't disagree that there are simpler castes among them, whose attire, although elegant, offer a little less ostentation; but as they're all equal and it's to nature that they owe their rich exteriors, it's not astonishing to find that involuntary sumptuousness in the most common estates. I've seen simple carpenters with crimson robes heightened by black velvet ruffs, and masons enveloped in silk balandrans like burgomasters. That, however, is only a small fraction of their advantages. As they have numerous enemies, which is unfortunately common to all creatures, would you believe that the Lord has deigned to furnish them in advance with the weapons necessary to defend themselves, and that there is not one who does not carry his arsenal with him?"

"And what weapons has the Lord given them?" cried the young Swedish gentleman, who felt the bellicose blood of his ancestors seething in his veins.

"All those, Gustave, that are customary to men, and many others that men do not know, of which I cannot communicate the ideas to you without enabling you to see them: helmets, morions, armor, shields, sabers, cutlasses, rapiers, stilettos and daggers bristling with points that are barbed and are detached as they are withdrawn from the wound they have opened. Some bear burning acids that devour everything they touch and subtle poisons that kill their aggressors, although, in general, they prefer perfumes, and those the most elegant exhale at a distance would make amber and roses jealous. To return to their means of defense, there is no one in that population who is not provided with vigorous and sharp pincers, with which they pierce, cut and crush their adversaries' limbs.

"I could show you some whose suits of armor are sown with rigid and penetrating spikes; others that march protected by three sturdy, long, tightly-grouped and inseparable lances, like the Macedonian phalanx. They also know the usage of firearms and it is even more ancient among that people than among us; but those who make use of them only employ them in retreat, in the fashion of the Parthians. I have often witnessed exercises of those musketeers, and have even had occasion to see them in battle. I remember having remarked one who made more than thirty discharges in half a minute, which the most skillful sharpshooters hold to be almost impossible. In the end he stopped, probably for want of ammunition, and when captured, in order to escape his assailants, he trusted his wings."

"Wait, Aunt, in the name of Heaven," Gustave interrupted, abruptly. "The people you're talking about have wings?"

"I've forgotten to tell you that until now," replied the good Sibylle. "God would not have left such an advantage to the birds. Furthermore, there are powerful tribes who are even better endowed. Combated on the ground by an enemy superior in numbers, they precipitate themselves into the air, as I told you. If the rival army has the privilege of following them and threatens to overtake them in that infinite battlefield, the fugitive squadrons are content to fold their futile wings under the armor on their back and plunge underwater. There they organize a living flotilla, for they have with them, in their portable baggage, light skiffs, fast racing boats as rapid as a glance, with keels like those of tall ships, which triumph over currents by the force of oars, and in which intrepid navigators advance in serried ranks, brandishing the inflexible blades that nature has fixed to their breasts."

"That's prodigious," said Gustave, "but are those advantages not paid for at the cost of some grave inconveniences? Are their organs as good as ours?"

"Refrain from making the comparison," replied Sibylle. "It would be too humiliating for us. I will only tell you about their eyes, which have a solid, thick, damage-resistant, and yet diaphanous, cornea, shielded from all exterior accidents. They are almost always predominant and disposed laterally, in a manner to embrace, or very nearly, the entire circumference of the horizon; and their globe, ordinarily sculpted in facets, perceives objects by means of an incredible multitude of divergent gazes, each of which can awaken a sensation.

"You will also ask me, I have no doubt, whether they practice industry and take advantage of the materials that creation furnishes to us. There are further miracles there! What could I tell you about the expert economy of their architecture, the skillful organization of their fortifications, the inexhaustible resources of their strategy, the variety of their artifices of hunting and fishing, the perfection of their instruments, the lightness of their fabrics, the exquisite delicacy of their sculptures and the finish of their slightest works, that would not be far below the truth? It is necessary to live among them, as I have done, to be able to admire them."

"I shall certainly see them," said Gustave, adopting the resolute attitude of a man undertaking a distant voyage with its risks and perils. "But where does this extraordinary people live?" he continued. "Is it necessary to go in search of them far beyond Surinam?"

"We can see them tomorrow, if you wish to take the trouble," Sibylle replied. "They live everywhere, on the ground on which we walk, in the stream that bathes our meadows, in the air that you breathe. They live in the calices of flowers that have just opened, and even in the drops of dew that tremble in suspense from their petals; they quiver in the sand, murmur under the lawn, and dance and twirl in a ray of sunlight. My naval army has dropped anchor in a nearby pond; my musketeers are entrenched under a stone in the garden. I'm talking about insects."

Gustave, slightly piqued, bit his lips, but he did not want to contradict her. At dawn the next day he set forth with his great-aunt toward the unknown people of whose existence she had informed him, equipped for their only weapon and their only equipment with a small gauze net.

He acquired a taste for those discoveries, which became more instructive, more amusing and more gracious every day, and when death took him away from his worthy relative on 13 January 1717, he felt that he would never have been able to console himself if she had not introduced him previously to the milieu of the unknown people, the arduous study of whom furnished him with so much agreeable leisure and mild consolation.

Gustave de Rosander lived for a long time. He was knowledgeable, which is little; he was celebrated, which is nothing; he was tranquil, because simple tastes give peace to the heart; he was good, because the love of nature is a road to virtue; he was happy, because the calm of the mind and the benevolence of the soul compose the only true human happiness. That is all.[1]

---

1 This story bears a strong resemblance in theme and method to many essay-cum-stories written by S. Henry Berthoud, who became a prolific popularizer of science during the Second Empire. Nodier and Berthoud knew one another; although the latter was living in Cambrai during the late 1820s, he was already closely associated with Honoré de Balzac and Jules Janin, who must have taken him to Nodier's salon when he relocated to Paris; when Berthoud was appointed as the editor of the *Musée des Familles* in 1833 Nodier was one of the first writers from whom he solicited and obtained contributions.

La Mettrie; or, Superstitions

"Although the sun is reaching the end of its course, it is not yet day in the house of Nyctale;[1] be careful not to wake him. His sleep has probably been retarded by the croaking of a bird of ill-omen or the howling of a lost dog. The dreams that have arrived since have all emerged from the ivory gate, and he is awaiting those of the morning, which never fail to bring useful information for the conduct of life. Do not hope, however, to obtain some diversion therefrom, for today is Friday, an unfortunate day, a contrary and baleful day, *nigro notanda lapillo.*[2]

"But here comes Nyctale, who is following you pensively, although he has put his first slipper on his left foot and he had just stumbled into the threshold of his door while emerging from it. You have in order to master him some constellated stone or sympathetic talisman, since you convinced him to take part in your banquet in this house, which is the only one in the quarter where the swallows have not built their nests in the bays of the windows and between the joists of the ceiling.[3]

1 Nyctale [Night-bird] was the French name of a genre of owls, which retained a metaphorical significance after its literal meaning became obsolete.
2 Literally, "a day marked by a black pebble"—used by the Romans to refer to one that would go down in history as a bad one.
3 The French *hirondelle*, usually translated as "swallow," conflates that species, strictly defined, with the closely related species known in English

"Suddenly, however, his face darkens. Has he not sat down by mistake facing the evil Bohemian mirror, which a clumsy valet broke the other day; or might he have found his cutlery in a cross beside an overturned salt-cellar? I'm mistaken; he's occupied by a truly serious care; he's counting the guests one by one, and now you see him go pale and tremble; he has just assured himself for the third time that there are thirteen.

"From now on there will be no more repose for Nyctale. The most delicate dishes will change into poison under his hand, as at the harpies' feast, and he is only seeking a pretext to leave when the crown of burning candles whose neglected wicks are tilting reminds him, fortunately, that he is due to receive a visit or a message today at his lodgings. He slips away subtly, without anyone being able to divine the cause of his sadness and his impatience.

"Nyctale is a good and knowledgeable man, of sound advice, whom honest men esteem, who has shown himself adept in business affairs and conducts himself with prudence and firmness when required, but Nyctale is superstitious."

I said the other day, emphasizing an expression of Montaigne's, that one can never hammer the ears of men with the name of superstition enough to force them to understand that they are absurd in the meanings that they attach to words, insensate in the judgment that they bring to ideas and even more presumptuous than they are ignorant. It is that fantasy that determined me to charge with a long commentary the classic étopée[1] with which I have just acquainted you, and which you would be well founded in regarding as the worst of our great painter of characters, if I gave it to you as anything other than a detestable pastiche.

as the house martin.
1 This is a Frenchification of a word esoteric even in its native Italian, referring to a kind of illustratve report.

But, all things considered, I prefer to tell you what was said to me on that subject by my old and respectable friend Jacques Mauduyt one evening in Vendemiaire in year seven,[1] when we were dining together at Legacque's in a private booth—for he had the kindness of liking to hear himself talk in front of me, although I was then only a young student and a callow novice in philosophy; and as I was avid for knowledge, I took a singular pleasure in it for my part.

Now, if you have forgotten Jacques Mauduyt, who might well have gone the way of all reputations,[2] I congratulate myself on being able to inform you that he was a studious, savant, modest man perfect in mentality and morality, who had collaborated at a young age, without emerging from a sage and meritorious obscurity, with the endeavors of the Academy of Berlin, where he was the colleague and pupil of Voltaire, Maupertuis, Formey, the Marquis d'Argens, the King of Prussia and a host of more or less celebrated men of letters, of which the principal ones are classified here in order of talent; and that he exercised, in the epoch presently in question, the honorable functions of the president of a school, in which I formed myself, without knowing it for filling good or bad pages for the *Revue de Paris*, when I was no longer at an age to commence an apprenticeship in a more useful and more reliable métier.

One day, when he was giving me dinner at the Lointier of the Directoire on the terrace of the Tuileries he said to me, when the third or fourth chapter of the menu arrived: "This will merit your attention." I was listening with all ears, because

---

1 Vendemiaire of *an VII* of the Republic was in the year c1798 of the Gregorian calendar. Napoleon's Egyptian campaign was in full swing and the Directoire was in power

2 He has, but Nodier would have been familiar with a man with that surname, at least by reputation, who is cited as an authority on avian taxidermy in several reverence books of the early 1800s.

that was the moment when he was accustomed to develop before me all the riches of his erudition and his memory.

"Do you eat roast pigeon?" he said, consulting my thought with a penetrating gaze.

I don't know what effect such a question would have produced on you; what is certain is that for me, it was the object of one of those mental operations that is operated in the intelligence spontaneously, but in a very logical manner, and which holds it as if suspended momentarily over a new abyss that has just been discovered in the mental world.

No, I didn't eat roast pigeon.

I didn't remember having eaten roast pigeon. Why would I not eat roast pigeon if it were served now? What harm was there in eating roast pigeon?

Of that chain of thoughts I only delivered to Monsieur Mauduyt the material solution of the problem. I remained indecisive as to the motives determining my response; or rather, I made no attempt to disentangle them.

"No, Monsieur," I replied to Monsieur Mauduyt, blushing slightly, "I don't eat roast pigeon."

"In that case," he continued, with a marked intention to embarrass me, "we can have served to us, if your prefer it, a swallow stew or a skewer of sparrows."

"Eh!" I cried. "Who has ever taken it into his head to eat sparrows on a skewer or swallows in a stew?"

"It's not customary," Monsieur Mauduyt continued, "although the flesh of those little animals is fine, delicate, exquisite and easy to digest. But you haven't told me whether that reluctance comes to you from lack of habitude or whether it's systematic."

Then he turned to the waiter who was serving us, and without interrogating me further, asked him for half a pullet with cress.

"That's because I don't really know," I replied, "because I've never thought about it. Perhaps it's only a caprice."

"That's where you're mistaken," he said. "Caprice is an explanation good for idle minds who don't take the trouble to search themselves for a more rational explanation of their choices and resolutions. The human arbiter never stops at a design without being borne there by some movement that is appropriate to him, and which results from his natural instinct, or from the auxiliary instinct that his education has given to him, or the empire of an occult reasoning that has developed in him without his being aware of it, but which he can recover, by studying principles and corollaries carefully!

"That's probable," I replied aloud—*but*, I added silently, *it's a lot of philosophy with regard to the propriety of eating pigeon.*

"It's so probable that it's certain. The pigeon, the swallow and the sparrow are voluntary guests in the houses of man. One might think that nature had produced them expressly to entertain in his thought the memory of his origins state, and in order not to let him lose sight of his ancient relationship with the rest of the created world. They are not his vassals by right of conquest, but they love to live in the buildings that he has edified, and flock there eagerly as if they were made for them. They enchant him with the varied graces of their flight, their songs and their colors, for the pigeon glides with elegance and nobility, coos tenderly, deploys in the sunlight the riches of a robe clouded with a thousand reflections, and reproduces before our eyes every day the miracles of amour and inconsolable constancy of which poets are obliged to borrow the model.

"The swallow, more severe in its garment, as befits an exile, races, goes astray and disappears in the air. It goes a long way in order to prepare us to lose it; it comes from afar in order to console us with the idea of return. It only known how to whimper and lament, and its anxious murmur resembles years, because it has the care of a family. You know the information with which it is charged for us; it announces rain, it announces good weather, it announces the morning of the year and it announces the return of the good season; it bears the laborer's calendar on its dark wings. It taught our forefathers the art of rustic architecture; it teaches our daughters the solicitudes and joys of maternity.

"The sparrow, as skillful as a simple peasant, poor but robust, good-humored and always ready for a celebration, is lively, indiscreet, curious, petulant and clownish; it flies, hops and jumps in the midst of our flocks and our children. It chatters, it chirps, it whistles, it bears gaiety everywhere. A free inhabitant of the domestic roof, where it pays its rent in pleasures, we owe to it everything that it steals and gives it all that it requests, and it knows that so well that it never fails, when snow covers the ground where the seeds we have confided to it lie dormant, to come to the dining-room to demand the crumbs of the feast.

"In truth, don't you imagine that the first man who had the pigeons of his loft, the swallow of his ledges and the sparrow of his walls served at his table would be violating the holy laws of hospitality outrageously?"

"Now I know," I replied, "why I don't eat pigeons, swallows or sparrows, and I hold that it's a crime that ranks immediately after that of cannibalism."

"That idea is similar to almost all those that the practice of honest men has inculcated in you since childhood, and the mysterious significance of which you have not yet developed in your little brain, for I suspect that there is no supposed lie accredited the people that is not founded on some essential moral verity. Have you, by chance, heard mention of Monsieur de La Mettrie?"[1]

---

1 The physician Julien Offray de La Mettrie (1709-1751) became notorious as the most extreme materialist of the Enlightenment, and the author of *L'Homme machine* [The Human Machine] (1747), in which he extended René Descartes' argument that animals are automata devoid of consciousness to argue that humans have no soul separate from the

"There's no one who hasn't heard mention of Monsieur de La Mettrie. He's the official atheist of the King of Prussia, just as Bébé is the dwarf of the King of Poland."

"Atheist in all things," said Monsieur Mauduyt. "A physician who doesn't believe in medicine; a moralist who doesn't believe in virtue; a psychologist who doesn't believe in the soul; a courtier who doesn't believe in royalty. I saw him once, on a hot summer day, enter Frederick's cabinet, let himself fall on to a sofa after a rather abrupt little bow, plant his dusty feet on to a footstool, throw his wig on to an armchair, take off his cravat, and casually pull out his pocket handkerchief while the despot philosopher laughed between his teeth at his stupid rudenesss. That's because the king's atheist was slightly mistaken about his veritable attributions at Potsdam. Times had changed, not things, since Brusquet and Langeli. La Mettrie thought himself the equal of his master, but he was only his fool.

"Fool as he was, in his extravagance, I believe he entered while young into some secret conspiracy. La Mettrie had some good in him; I didn't know him well, but I much preferred his conversation to the diffuse verbiage of the director general of the academy and the cynical expansion of old Formey, the dimwit most fecund in *spropositi* that I ever heard in my life.[1] The true or false originality of La Mettrie was less fecund in witty and new quips, in ingenious paradoxes that he was able to enunciate in a gripping manner, and which, after having made reason smile, always left something to think about.

---

substance of the body. He developed as a corollary a philosophy of hedonism that alienated even those Enlightenment thinkers sympathetic to his atheism, and was rumored to have died after an orgiastic feast.

1 The philosopher Johann Heinrich Samuel Formey (1711-1797) was the son of French immigrants to Germany; he wrote in French and when he reformed the Academy of Berlin in 1744, during the reign of Frederick the Great, he made French its official language, helping to pave the way for the popularization of German philosophy in France and thus for the French Romantic Movement. The dismissal of his work as *spropositi* [nonsense] is very harsh.

He had the good fortune of being convinced by his ideas while developing them, and as he wasn't devoid of a certain imaginative verve, he often raised himself as far as eloquence when he was contradicted. Eccentricity is an annoying mental hitch, but eccentric men, as you'll have plenty of opportunity to observe, have an immense advantage in conversation over merely sensate men; they're almost never boring.

"On some occasion or other when we were to join the king in Berlin for a few days, I proposed to La Mettrie to depart with me the next day, sharing the expenses. 'Tomorrow's Friday' he replied, 'and I don't set forth on a Friday. For Saturday, I'm yours.'

"I stared at him to make sure that he wasn't joking. He was quite serious.

"We left on Saturday. Hazard had united at bedtime two or three carriages following the court. I had arranged to sup at the host's table. 'That was also my intention,' La Mettrie told me, 'but I've just verified that these messieurs number eleven; we two would make thirteen, and we'll sup in our room if it wouldn't suit you better that I sup alone, for I'm determined never to sit down at a table with thirteen places if it's possible for me to do otherwise.'[1]

"I smiled and had myself served in my room. He scanned it with a glance by the light of the candles that had preceded us. 'A spider!' he cried, taking out his watch with an anxious expression. 'Good, good,' he added, immediately, 'the sun hasn't set entirely.' Then he took his place, after having carefully established the symmetrical parallelism of his fork and his knife, which had fallen into a cross under the hand of a domestic.

"We didn't speak for some time. I couldn't see anything in the circumstances that had struck me but the caprice of a

---

1 Alexandre Dumas and Marie Nodier both commented in their memoirs of him that Charles Nodier was extremely reluctant to sit down at a table of thirteen guests, and Marie commented further on his superstitious inclinations.

singular mind or the overly prolonged irony of superior mind that enjoyed the foolish errors of the vulgar by exaggerating them deliberately; but as I had a mind to be clarified of that doubt, I finally broke the silence. 'May I ask you without indiscretion, my dear colleague,' I said to La Mettrie, 'why you never set forth on a Friday, if what you told me the other day was anything but an airy pretext or malign persiflage?'

"'Nothing is truer,' said La Mettrie, 'and I'll gladly tell you the reason. I won't cite the authority of the old traditions of all lands on the fatality of days; it's universal, it's probable, it's supported to an extent that they almost give certainty to the story, but you know that I only admit, in matters of reasoning, what is based on tangible facts. I won't ask you whether there are days in your life whose anniversary you see returning dolorously, after the quarter of a century that you've already lived; but if it were otherwise you wouldn't be human, or you wouldn't be worthy of being. It's only necessary that you admit that that sentiment natural to the individual is any less natural to the species, and that there are calamitous anniversaries in the history of nations as in that of a man.

"'Well, have you ever reflected on what happened before the eyes of the world more than seventeen centuries ago in the little land of Judea, the impression of which has been transmitted as far as us, especially in the naïve classes of society, through sixty generations? If you've forgotten, I'll tell you what it was. There was a man then, a poor and worthy man, a Nazarene worker, who had read fruitfully in his childhood and who had traveled in order to educate himself and to hide his life, who had penetrated the moral secret of all the myths of outdated religions, and who returned after twenty years to the land of his fathers, at the head of a dozen sages as wretched as him, the first to proclaim the truth in the face of all the tyrannies and all the religions of the old world. It was not a trivial matter, because no one had ever revealed to slaves that they were the equals of their masters without giving them the desire to make slaves of them, but he enveloped his lessons in a morality so conciliating and mild that the most superb and the most irritated allowed themselves to be fashioned, involuntarily, by the indulgence of his thought. He only drew one sword in his history, and he cursed it. The rich people of the earth rose up against him; the blind populace charged him with ignominies; the priests had him whipped and he found, as one always finds, a traitor to sell him and judges to condemn him. He was hung on a Friday between two thieves, to whom he addressed while dying, words of love and charity, with the mouth that had just pardoned his executioners.

"'That was a great misfortune for the human race, which, in any case, did not merit such a law or such a victim, but whose affairs he would have advanced for more than two thousand years if he had lived a human lifespan, as his good constitution and good mores seemed to promise him. Many revolutions have referred to his principles, but I fear that no one any longer did so with his sentiments, and that will imprint on revolutions to come an indelible stain of scandal and frenzy. You recognize the man of whom I speak and you know that his divinity to be more legitimate that that of any of the innumerable gods of Alexandre Sévère,[1] but that's not my fault, and when we make a god of the majority, like an academician of Berlin, under the good pleasure of the King of Prussia, it will be necessary to refrain from taking any other than the carpenter of Bethlehem.

"'Friday!' continued La Mettrie, excitedly, 'Friday forever execrable, when the generous patron of suffering humanity rendered his last sigh in opprobrium and torture! Fatal Friday, when the sun ought really to have been veiled by darkness, as ecclesiastic historians relate, if it had been anything but a sun—which is to say, an inorganic mass insensible to the

---

1 The third-century Roman Emperor Severus Alexander.

dolors of our organic and sensible matter. Friday, which ought to be effaced from the number of days, following Job's expression, in favor of doubling another day of the week, if there were one pure of crimes. Oh, let Friday, when justice died, die eternally, taking with it in its shroud all the virtues and liberties of the species!

"'Don't you think, too, my friend, that the bitter and profound conviction of a hundred million families who groan every Friday over the death of Christ, from Berlin all the way to Japan, is enough to excite some sad sympathy in the human heart? You would not dare to smile in an afflicted family in which the little daughter is mourning the loss of her doll and the grandmama the death of her pet monkey, but you would be devoid of compassion for the regrets of the immense family that was mourning the death of a god yesterday! For myself, in order to take part in the anguish of so many heartsick souls, I don't examine whether it's founded on reason, but whether it's sharp and sincere; and that why I don't undertake anything on a Friday.'

"I listened, wonderstruck, to that speech by La Mettrie, from which I have not retrenched a single word, because I wanted, above all, to give you an idea of the habitual forms of his logic and his elocution, in order to spare you the trouble of reading the useless or dangerous books he has left, of which the least fault is to be written without taste, without criticism and without conviction. I shall try to be more laconic in the rest of my story.

"'It's doubtless the same idea,' I said to him, 'that makes it repugnant for you to see the image of the cross depicted by a fork and a knife? Those two superstitions—allow me the word—are at least closely connected in the imagination of the people.'

"'The same idea and others too,' retorted La Mettrie. 'The image of a parricidal torture to which the populace of

Jerusalem had the sagest and mildest of philosophers subjected; the more vivid and more common image of a modern torture, horrible in its cruelty when it is inflicted on the guilty and for which indignation does not have anathemas enough when it strikes the innocent, how do you expect that odious cross not to sadden for me a meal in which two friends come together to exchange their thoughts and savor the pleasure of being together. If I flee the cross in the bloody theater of our homicidal executions, why would I condemn myself to find it in the intimacy of supper? That isn't all. That hideous figure is shocking for an eye fond of order, which enjoys the repose of a regular figure and which is obfuscated and revolted by the confusion of superimposed lines. That instinct must be natural to us, since Pythagoras made it one of the bases of his philosophy; and that's why all theogonies are in accord in seeing the emblem of divinity in the perfect triangle, from the shepherd astronomers through the Greek delta to the trinity of Tertullian and Bossuet. Our universal liking for equilaterals and parallels is moreover, the fundamental principle of the fine arts, and the man who cannot understand that would inferior even to a bee, so invariable in the uniform construction of its hexagon.[1] Yes, I can imagine that a chagrined genius, whom that linear anarchy and violation of parallelism afflicts too bitterly, might be reputed superstitious; but I sustain that an organization that is not slightly stirred by that barbarism of lackeys has nothing above the brute.'

"'With that facility of emotions and memories, my dear philosopher, it will not be difficult for you to explain your antipathy to the number thirteen, which the people, with their picturesque and figurative expression, call the *Judas point*.'

"'It horrifies you, as it does me, and I render thanks to your reason. Is it not painful to recall, in a society of thirteen

---

1 The text of *Rêveries* has "pentagon," but that is an obvious error, which seems unlikely to have been deliberate.

humans composed by chance that, in a similar number of brothers chosen by the most intelligent judge of the human heart that ever existed, there was a bandit capable of delivering his benefactor, whom he regarded as his God, to the executioner? What sentiment ought to awaken in you then, at the sight of your fellow guests? The least one can ask oneself is which one would be, at need, a delator and assassin? That number is extracted, moreover, from all ideas of order, for it expresses the first of the extranumeral figures of duodecimal calculation, the type of which is imprinted, as you know, in the twelve units of the phalanges of our four fingers, which are represented in their concrete number by the fifth digit, or the thumb. Now, these heteroclitic figures are repugnant to our spirit of method and harmony, like lines that deviate from the perpendicular.

"'But that isn't all. The calculations of the probability of life have proved to us that, out of thirteen men of different ages who are amusing one another around a table, nature ought to deliver one of them to death every year, save for the good fortune of chance. In a greater number, that sentiment is attenuated, lost in the multitude; here there is all the rigor of an arithmetical proposition and all the exigency of a problem awaiting solution. The cadaver is sitting at the banquet, as in the feasts of the Egyptians. That a tyrant who drives a million men to the conquest might reflect dolorously on the destiny to which that brilliant generation of soldiers will be subject within a century, you understand; and you want me to rejoice at a round table where I am exchanging with my comrades in life and habitudes a toast of hope and pleasure, which in a year's time I shall either not be rendering to all of them, or it will not be being raised to me by anyone.'

"'In truth, Doctor,' I said, 'it isn't me who would be so demanding now. I refrain from condemnation of everything; but I'll wager a hundred to one that you won't convince me as cheaply with regard to the appearance of a spider after sunset. I agree that a spider is a very disagreeable animal to see, but I must be very stupid if the hour has anything to do with it.'

"'Wait.' replied La Mettrie, laughing. 'Let's not proclaim the honors of your intelligence so lightly, and above all don't bet, for you might lose. The people are the pupils of times past, and superstition is their philosophy; they are wiser than you and me in such matters. You're not unaware that the numerous nation of spiders is distributed in different corps of arts and métiers, devoted to various industries, but equally hostile, and among them one can distinguish the weavers, which seize their prey in webs like bird-catchers, and hunters, which pursue it everywhere that they find it, like running dogs. The latter carry out their maneuvers in the houses of the poor on the track of nocturnal insects, and their clandestine encounters in the absence of the sun have nothing alarming for the observer. It's different for the ones that extend their nets during the day to the flies in apartments and the myriads of little creatures that dance in a ray of midday sunlight. They are only seen to draw away from the hole they inhabit when they are harassed by the obsession of the chambermaid whose broom has broken their industrious web more than once, and that transmigration occurs soon afterwards, when there is still time to suspend the weave elsewhere into which their prey comes to be caught.

"'The spider that I remarked as we came in, and which you will now find in the same place, because artificial light fascinates almost all animals, belongs to the skillful tribe of stationary spiders, which wait patiently above their trap like a country bourgeois clinging to the stem of his pipe or a poacher in his hide; and I have no reason to be astonished, on due reflection, that it was running—contrary to its habit, in the manner of Bedouins—over these walls, where it has nothing to do, our installation in your room having been bound to be

112

preceded by some belated and idle measure of tidying, unusual in these hovels. When the sun has set, the vagabondage of that displaced traveler no longer has a natural significance. It indicates then some unknown perturbation in its narrow domicile. You would not willingly go to bed in an old house where the rats were fleeing in legions, because you know that that phenomenon has always announced the imminent collapse of the building. I shall not explain to you the entirely material circumstances that warn them of it, and will present themselves to your mind. Is it not the same for the spider?'"

"'For the spider, even more intelligent and irritable,' I interjected. 'The spider, so sensitive to the slightest disturbance that, at the vibration of an instrument or a voice that causes its web to tremble, it jumps—or, rather, lets itself fall—to the center where all the radii converge . . . which has earned it, rather ridiculously, in my opinion, the reputation of a musician. I can easily conceive that, in the narrow container, the walls of which press it from all sides, it is forewarned a long time before a human being of the accident that threatens its dwelling.'

"'Since you have adopted that popular superstition on your own account in developing it,' said La Mettrie, 'I have no more need to justify it. I shall be content to add that it is not proven that the prescience of a spider is limited to announcing the accident of which we speak. We have not counted all the senses and all the secret instincts that it might have acquired, in accordance with its nature, for the conservation of its species. Exposed, in the interstices of a partition or under the thatch of a building, to the dangers of every sort that incessantly besiege the precarious habitations of poor folk, how do we know that it is not informed by some unknown organ of the slow progress of a conflagration that is still hidden, like marine bids or like our friends the swallows, of the tempest dormant in a scarcely visible cloud in the middle of a pure horizon?'

"'It would be necessary to ignore the most common mysteries of the organization of animals,' I replied to La Mettrie, 'to deny that possibility, which has in my eyes all the characteristics of plausibility; but since we're back to swallows, the infallible foresight of which, already attested by Virgil, I don't contest, can you explain to me as easily the ridiculous popular prejudice that attributes to them a fortunate influence over the interior wellbeing of houses where they deign to build their nests?'

"'Much more easily,' the philosopher told me, 'and you'd spare me that explanation if you'd taken the trouble to search for it momentarily for yourself. Fortunate, and a thousand times fortunate, is the house with swallows' nests. It is placed, above all others, under the auspices of the mild security for which pious souls believe that they have an obligation to Providence. And in fact, without seeking in the swallow a marvelous instinct of prophecy that poets accord to it a little too liberally, is it not permitted at least to suppose that it is not deprived of an instinct common to so many other species, which enables them to divine the most assured abode for a family in expectation? Have no fear that it will lodge under the inflammable straw of a rustic roof or the fragile beams of a nomad shack.

"'It has such a great fear of the mutations that overturn our temporary domiciles that it is seen fixing its preference on abandoned buildings, the ruins of which we are fatigued by stirring, and which are no longer disquieted by the movement of a turbulent population. *Men are no longer there*, it says, and it constructs its dwelling in a place that has already seen more than one generation pass without being disturbed by their movements. If it returns to towns and rural areas, it only settles in peaceful houses where no noise will trouble its little colony, in the shelter of which the solid hut that it builds so carefully can subsist long enough to spare it new labors next year. If you have observed it, our swallow is voluntarily prejudiced in favor of benevolent faces; like a stranger from a distant country it trusts in the procedures of a good welcome; it likes not being disturbed and abandons itself to those who love it.

"'I'm not sure that its presence promises wellbeing for the future, but it demonstrates it to me intelligibly in the present. Thus, I have never seen a house with swallows' nests without being prejudiced in favor of its inhabitants. There, I am sure, there are neither the tumultuous orgies of debauchery nor the din of domestic quarrels. The servants there are not cruel, the children are not pitiless; you will find some sage old man there or some tender young woman, who protects the swallow's nest, and I would go there with a million in my hand to hide my outlaw head without fear of tomorrow. The people who do not chase away an importunate bird and its chirruping brood are essentially good, and the good are favored by all the happiness that can be savored on earth.

"'You appropriate in such good faith and with such good reasons all the beliefs of the vulgar, that I would be astonished to find that you have objections to the most universal super-stition of the human race. However, I only glimpsed a smile of pity and a slight shrug of the shoulders on your part when the waiter upset the salt-cellar on the table just now. That is at least one prejudice of which your philosophy does not deign to absolve the people.'

"'A prejudice!' cried La Mettrie. 'A prejudice!' he repeated, emphasizing the word energetically. Do you know, my friend, what a prejudice is? It is, as its name indicates, something that was judged before us, a principle consecrated by the unanimous admission of nations, and against which arguments only remain in the head of a foolish and conceited dreamer who believes himself to be called to break without further appeal the decrees of experience. You are not mistaken regarding the movement that the brutal clumsiness of that bumpkin caused me, but you have not grasped the correct interpretation. The poor devil, who is perhaps not wicked by nature, will necessarily come to a bad end. He is marked by a fatal predestination, the accomplishment of which cannot fail; he upset the salt-cellar.'

"'Really!' I cried in my turn, immobile with stupefaction.

"'You did not remark that, as he came into the room, he bumped his foot heavily against the traverse, an inch high, that garnishes the door, and that he was holding the salt-cellar in his left hand, although he is not left-handed. Whoever has not anticipated the obstacle that presents itself to his foot in a house where he has been in service for a long time must never foresee anything. He lacks the means to memorize accidents and the judgment to avoid them; he does not even enjoy the finesse of tact that compensates a blind nag for the loss of one of its senses. The Romans went back inside their houses when they had stumbled on leaving, and it was a precaution well taken against the events of the day. A man who stumbles has slept badly, or has a bad deportment, or is in a fortuitous state of preoccupation that makes him vulnerable to all dangers. If he employs his left hand, without being exercised therein, in cares that demand precision and delicacy, he completes revealing to me a radical defect of his unfortunate organization. He combines the gross imprudence of an automaton with the indolent confidence of a fool.

"All the favorable chances of life belong to foresight and dexterity, for skill is nothing but mental dexterity. As the hand is the essential utensil of fortune, misfortune is the infallible lot of the disgraced man who lacks skill and exactitude in the material operations of the hand. The Latins were so penetrated by that idea that they only had one word for representing the gauche and the sinister; and I posit, in fact, that we shall be able to reconstruct, solely by means of the etymology of words, the entire edifice of human wisdom, when our stupid logomachies have finished ruining it. At any rate, you will be able to cite to me, between today and tomorrow, if you consult your memories, deaf, one-eyed and lame individuals who have become great men, commendable artists, illustrious citizens and happy fathers of families, but I admit that I am still to find one who was born one-armed.

"'As for the baleful presage that one can take from the overturning of the salt-cellar.' La Mettrie continued, 'that is a question more commonplace and facile, and I doubt, to tell you the truth, that you proposed it to me seriously . . .'

"As I insisted, with a smile that probably testified that my conviction was not complete, he went on in these terms:

"'Salt has been at all times the emblem of wisdom, and I cannot tell you why today; but I know that an emblem has a reason and that one does not attack it without wounding a verity. That is true to the point that I willingly share the disobliging prejudice that people have against a young woman who omits the salt while setting the table, for it is rare that one remembers a duty of conduct when one has a mind negligent enough to forget its representation. The usage of salt is not circumscribed like that of bread; it is a primary necessity everywhere there is a family, and it is for that reason that it has become the symbol of hospitality among the ingenuous or ingenious tribes that we call savage. The action of spilling salt indicates among them the refusal of protection and amity to suspect strangers, in whom one fears thieves and murderers, and that thought would sadden me at a feast of Lucullus in the cabinet of Apollo.

"'You only see here the blunder of a clumsy valet, and I agree with you, for that indirect insult of a mercenary host is not the fault of his will. But are you devoid of commiseration for the disgraced being who does not know how to make use of his foot to avoid tripping over a threshold, or how to make use of his hand to find the just equilibrium of a salt-cellar, or how to make use of the range and exercise of his eyesight to put it in its place? The unfortunate fellow has nothing else to do than go and hang himself, if he still has sense enough to calculate the action of a body gravitating at the end of a rope, the weight of which is augmented in proportion to the square of its velocity . . . and if you survey in your thought the interminable series of accidents more difficult to avoid that might occasion his petulant stupidity, do you not experience some sympathy for a poor family that has such domestics?

"'For myself, I have no hesitation in assuring that the house in which the salt is upset most frequently is necessarily the most unfortunate in the world, because it is the one in which people have the least order, economy, skill and foresight, and the things I have just listed are the principal elements of the wellbeing of households.'

"'There is nothing more veritable, my good friend, and I admit in advance the same interpretation for the unfortunate prognosis that good women take from the rupture of a mirror.'

"'That presage is even more serious,' said La Mettrie, 'because a mirror, fixed in a solid frame, is much less subject to hazards, and the gleam of its polish alerts the most distracted at a distance. Its substance also opposes sufficient resistance to light percussions that it is hardly ever broken without using violence. Now, one can only expect frightful misfortunes everywhere that imprudence and gaucherie are complicated by force and power. That principle can be extended to the most important applications, and history would prove that it enters into the economy of states as well as that of the hearth; but I owe you another observation that will not take us as far from our subject, which is that it is quite natural that the lesions of a mirror awaken an idea of fatality in the imagination of the people who transmit the verities of experience and sentiment that ignorant philosophers call superstitions. The limpid and correct repetition of the image of a person has something fantastic in itself, singularly appropriate to strike the mind with a sort of vertigo; and the mutilation that multiplies the effect of the mirror by destroying its unity produces, as everyone admits, an effect that emerges from the order of common sensations. It is not only a superstition, to make use of their language, but an impression.'

"'I have experienced it without rendering account of it,' I replied to La Mettrie, 'but you have made me think twice about the habitude of precipitate judgments, and I would scarcely dare to propose to you now to return to the dining room of the eleven guests, since our supper is finished, if the wicks of our candles, which are buckling under a chaplet of ardent disks were not announcing to me that the circle of the host's table is due to increase by a numerous excess of company.'

"'You remind me,' replied La Mettrie, bursting into laughter, 'that the man of the salt-cellar has forgotten to give us candle-snuffers, and I recognize the pernicious imp that dominates him by that lack of precaution. It's very little for him to dishonor the house of his masters if he doesn't expose them to being burned by negligence. The induction of which you speak is in any case, in the language of the people, only one of those colorful periphrases that are familiar to them, and which are almost always enveloped in an exquisite sense, When a candle or a lamp alerts them of an impending visit, it makes them sense the necessity of retrenching the superfluity of the wick, which is both a concern of order and a concern of cleanliness. If the visit does not occur, the snuffer of the candles is still acquitted of an indispensable office that tradition had brought back to his memory very appropriately, and who might have saved his roof from the misfortune of a fire. Suppose that that had only happened once since the old information of popular wisdom had been repeated, and tell

119

me whether you know many other philosophical theories that had rendered similar services to a village. It's a question that we can submit, if you wish, to the Academy of Berlin.

"'At present,' he continued, throwing down his napkin, 'I'll accompany you all the more willingly to the drawing room because I have long been fatigued by the howling of a dog, whose funereal barking seems to threaten the quarter.'

"'Good, good, you're not a man to fear that omen, at least, for which science has no explanation.'

"'Science could find ten of them, if it searched hard,' said La Mettrie. 'You'll tell me, no doubt, that it's quite natural that a stray dog should lament at the door of a hospitable shelter to which it has followed its master more than once before being separated from him by some fatal accident, and demand in its manner some scraps of food, the leftovers of the host's table and the servants' parlor. I agree very willingly, provided that you agree in your turn that it's different for the stray dog whose original instinct summons it from afar to the walls of a hospital or the casement of a dying man. Why should it not be provided with an organ that promises it a prey, which is so well matched to its destination, in the almost providential combinations of nature, that it can be seen everywhere impatient and attentive to facilitating the decomposition of an individual from whom life has retired, as if to render more rapidly the elements that compose it to the eternal laboratory of its creations?

"'The vulture descends in good time from its mountains in the wake of armies; it marks the battlefield with a surer eye than the captains, and, a long time before the effusion of blood, it soars with a horrible joy around the population of the living who will be a mountain of the dead for its feast. The crow alights on the summit of a new gallows, and takes possession of it as soon as the executioner. The seagull flaps its wings in the footsteps of the fisherman and extracts in expectation the tithe of his nets. In the cities of the Orient, the public gravedigger is often preceded by the hyena, which prowls, with its frightful yawn, through the empty ditches. As soon as night falls it introduces itself in packs into walls where contagious scourges are exercising their ravages, and waits, mouth agape, to be thrown cadavers. In our homeland, the ox has scarcely fallen under the butcher's sledgehammer than the air is obscured by a cloud of devouring insects, black and tanned scarabs, and green and blue flies, which come to collect in the place of sacrifice their share of the flesh and blood.

"'If you have ever killed a mole in your little garden, you will not have been long delayed in seeing rush around it a buzzing swarm of burying-beetles in lugubrious robes, with yellow strips like those of panthers, which hasten to inter the quadruped, still palpitating, in order to confide the deposit of its still-warm entrails to their hideous posterity. And you are astonished that a dog, returned to its primitive state by a fortuitous circumstance that has disengaged it from the duties of domesticity, recovers the fatal foresight on which all its means of existence repose in future? I don't know whether I'm mistaken, but if I ever heard, under the window of a dwelling where I had been surprised by a sudden malady, the savage cry that is only familiar to its species, trailing in long moans, I would understand perfectly what it wants.'

"Having said that, La Mettrie headed for the drawing room, where I accompanied him, and it was there that our conversation and my story concluded. All that it seems to me to be appropriate to add is that the famous materialist died a short time later, and that he died a Christian."

"I'm not astonished by that," I replied to Monsieur Mauduyt. But those impressions are too distant from me today for me to be able to say very positively whether I attached to that response the sense of a corollary logic, or whether I was only making an epigram.

What I do remember more clearly is that we went to take coffee at Peyron's, which then occupied the corner of the northern gallery of the Palais-Égalité, inhabited since by Lemblin, who has, I believe, conserved the reputation of its perfumed mocha and its delicate liqueurs. The young and pretty person who was sitting at the mahogany counter would probably have caused La Mettrie himself to lose the thread of his lofty philosophical speculations. However, I came back to them momentarily.

"What you've told me, my dear master, has struck me strangely, but it's only thus far a skeptical dissertation in the manner of Bayle. You haven't deigned to make me party to your conclusions."

"I extract two therefrom, at least," Monsieur Mauduyt replied, "and since you ask, here they are:

"The first is that it is necessary not to judge too lightly things that are the most absurd in appearance, because there are a great many positive verities that are easy to demonstrate, which escape demi-savants.

"The second is that intelligent people are never embarrassed in proving anything that they wish."

"So much the better," I said, warmly. "Intelligent people only have an interest in promoting good and useful ideas, and the representative government that we have the honor of possessing has placed us under the direction of intelligent men."

Monsieur Mauduyt looked at me fixedly again, replaced his spectacles in their case and handed me the Chaigneau brothers' *Journal du soir*, which he had just scanned, indicating to me the session of the councils.[1]

"Look!" he said to me.

---

1 The *Journal du soir*, printed by the Chagneau brothers, was one of the most prominent Parisian newspapers of the revolutionary years, from 1789 towards, and continued publication during the Empire. As a reporter for the *Journal de l'Empire*, subsequently the *Journal des Débats*, Nodier routinely recorded sessions in the Chambres and various associated committees.

Paul; or, The Resemblance
A Veritable and Fantastic Story[1]

I shall begin by declaring loudly that if it were necessary to re-nounce one of the immortal masterpieces of Homer, the *Iliad* and the *Odyssey*, and a royal edict or a formal act of parliament were required for that, I would try to learn the *Iliad* by heart before losing it, but it is the *Odyssey* that I would keep. I would not hesitate for a moment.

I agree that that opening might seem too magnificent for a short story. It puts me in manifest rebellion against the eternal rule of classical exordium: *Non fumum ex fulgore, sed ex fumo dare lucem.*[2] It is necessary, however, to take it as it is, for I shall not change a word. Critics can say what they like.

What charms me in the *Odyssey*, what penetrates me in reading it with a mixed sentiment of admiration and ten-derness, is the sublime good faith of the poet, who recites children's stories ingenuously as he has heard them recited, and ornaments them at pleasure with the richest colors of the

---

1 In the version of this story reprinted in *Contes de la Veillée* the editor dutifully adds a note to say that it was originally published in the *Revue de Paris* in 1836 under the title "Un domestique de M. le Marquis de Louvis, histoire veritable et fantastique." Subsequent editors reprinting the story have preferred the substitute title, as have I.

2 "Not to bring smoke from light, but to bring light from smoke"—a compliment addressed by Horace in his *Ars poetica* to Homer, adopted as a dictum in the teaching of rhetoric.

imagination and genius, because he has leaned nothing better in the conversation of old men, heroes and sages. His stories are marvelous, in truth, but the man who has confidence in his stories is even more marvelous than them. When Alcinous, king of the Phaeacians, allows a few doubts to escape regarding the probability of so many strange events observed in a few years of navigation, Ulysses refrains from responding with reasoned arguments; he limits himself to continuing, and Alcinous does not insist. That is because two things are essential to poetry: the poet who believes what he is saying and the listener who believes the poet. That combination has become rare, and so has poetry.

Our era participates to a great extent in the double state of those enfeebled bodies of which death has taken almost entire possession. In the one, a suave and tender melody like a song anticipatory of Heaven, is sufficient to soothe the agony, and the inspired poet arrives in his time. In the other, the material sensibility of which can only be awakened by caustic and corrosive irritants, another poet arrives who tears and burns in order to extract a scream of life. They are the two ultimate missions of art, and when they are accomplished, all is finished.

There is genius in those ultimate efforts of poetry; there is perhaps as much in the naïve and credulous abundance of Homeric compositions; it is necessary to struggle against the prosaicism of a worn-out speech, against the monotony of a creation too fully described, in which scholars no longer see anything but capricious aggregations of elementary molecules, and against the dryness of the ashen heart that present society bears, and which no longer palpitates. That is difficult and admirable. But where now, on earth, is the poetry of things? Where are the angels of Isaac and Tobit, the tents of Boaz and the laundresses of Nausicaa? I cannot give you news of them.

The great epic voyager of antiquity, whose stories I love so much, would be very surprised if he had to recommence his immortal fable today. He would be told that his Circe is, at the most, the Narina of Levaillant, or the Obérea of Bougainville.[1] His sirens are seals or sea-cows, Charybdis and Scylla are rocks, Polyphemus a one-eyes anthropophagous Patagonian—the fortunate influence of discoveries and progress! Do not ask that sublime story-teller about the centuries for which they were made, and which did not know him; you would be even more ingrate and unjust than them; you would not be giving him alms.

One of my friends recently wrote on this matter, in cheerful jest:[2]

> *But there treasures of taste, amour and poetry.*
> *What will replace them? Idiosyncrasy.*

Alas, yes; under the baroque influence that has made a rose a *phanerogam* and a butterfly a *lepidopteron*, it is necessary not to expect anything better of our anthropomorphic civilization. I am as sorry about that as you are.

It is for that reason that I have sworn no longer to read works marked with the seal of knowledge and intelligence, and you would not believe how difficult it is to find any that do not have that fatal cachet since mutual education by the

---

1 The naturalist and voyager François Levaillant (1753-1824) shared Jean-Jacques Rousseau's idea of noble savagery, and described an ideal type of that myth in "Narina," a name that he attributed to a young African woman with whom he had a relationship during an exploratory voyage undertaken in the 1780s. His portrayal is similar to the image of the inhabitants of Tahiti constructed by Louis-Antoine de Bougainville (1729-1811) in reports of his voyage of 1768, which attributed the name Obérea to the island's "queen."

2 The lines originate from a letter written by the one-time doyen of the Faculté de Médicine in Paris, Guy Patin (1601-1672), but they might have been quoted by someone of Nodier's acquaintance.

Jacotot method has put transcendent literature within the range of all intelligences.

Oh, if I had been Monsieur de Montyon,[1] with all the agreeable conditions that permitted him to endow his heirs so richly, I would have founded fine prizes in favor of the ignorant and the simple, and I would have taken pleasure in seeing them distributed, at the judgment of mothers and little children. What fine premiums I would have attached to the publication of an ingenuous book in which faith takes the place of science, experience that of study, and sentiment that of cleverness, in which the natural would make one forget if necessary, the absence of talent—if it is proven that talent is anything other than natural! With what munificence, nevertheless more economical and more facile than his, I would have liked to reproduce in abundance every year, for the instruction and wellbeing of the multitude, those delightful compositions that seize the soul by means of sympathies so vivid, and which penetrate it with such useful and pleasant information: the *Odyssey*, the *Voyages of Pinto*, Perrault's *Contes*, the Fables of Pilpay, Aesop and La Fontaine, *Télémaque*, *Robinson*, *Don Quixote*, *Les Hommes volants!* [2] One knows full well that it

---

1 Jean-Baptiste de Montyon (1733-1820) founded three prizes in the 1780s, the first one awarded for virtuous action, the second for a literary work seemed useful to the improvement of mores—both judged by the Académie française—and the third for scientific work, judged by the Académie des sciences. The first and second, in particular, received frequent scathing mention in works by authors associated with the Romantic Movement.

2 Most of the works on this list are easily recognizable, even when the titles are given in abbreviated form. The voyages to India and the Far East recorded in *Pilgrimage* (1614) by the Portuguese adventurer Fernão Pinto, were thought at the time to be wildly exaggerated. *Les hommes volants* is the title of the French translation of a novel published in English as *The Life and Adventures of Peter Wilkins* (1763; by Robert Paltock), although it is possible that the work that Nodier has in mind is the similarly-disguised *La Découverte australe par un hommme-volant* (1781; by Nicolas Restif de La Bretonne).

is only a question of books by men, but what men and what books those I have just mentioned are, great God! That would be money well employed! That would be a library of veritable "humanitarian progress," and the people who adopted them would be a people worthy of envy, a people worthy of living on the air they breathe and being warmed by their sun. Perhaps Monsieur Herschel will find them on the moon.[1]

In the meantime, I have not renounced recounting stories which I am often the only one to believe, and I would like to know why, my stories combining all the reasons for belief that one can seek in histories, the plausibility of the events and the honesty of the disinterested witness who narrates them. I ask you, in fact, what interest I would have in imagining that the wolf had eaten Little Red Riding Hood if it had not eaten her?—and may it please God that the wolf had not eaten Little Red Riding Hood and that someone could prove it to me soon, for that grief still counts among my troubles, even though they are so numerous.

These things are not invented, and one only says them with regret when one cannot dispense with saying them in order to obtain healthy moral inductions and excellent rules of conduct. Like those that emerge from the catastrophe of Little Red Riding Hood—to wit, firstly that it is necessary never to confide one's secret to the malevolent, and secondly that it is necessary not to let little girls go out on their own. I would like to be informed of a work of elevated philosophy or politics, solemnly crowned, which has brought more useful items of information into families, and accredited them in a more universal manner by means of a more naïve and more popular symbolism. I know full well that a book that I cannot

1 This *conte* was first published a year after the publication of the New York *Sun* "Moon hoax" describing discoveries allegedly made by the astronomer John Herschel with a new lunar telescope; the series of articles was rapidly translated in French newspapers, where it achieved a similar *succès de scandale*, giving rise to various items of spinoff.

understand is far above Little Red Riding Hood in the insur-
mountable height of its unintelligibility, but is not the book
I do not understand, which is only understood by a fifth or a
tenth of the nation—and that is not very many people—beyond the providential range of the necessary instruction that
belongs to everyone? In a good civilization, the people who
are not "progressing," have not "progressed" and probably
never will "progress," merit consideration nonetheless.

Everyone is free, in any case, to occupy his imagination
in his own manner and "to appropriate," as one philosopher
puts it admirably, "in the myths of a rational intellectuality,
that which harmonizes most identically with the spontaneous
sympathies of his individual and intimate estheticism." That
is clear enough!

Have you more faith, perchance, in Saint-Simonism than
in fairy tales? Ask a priest! In neo-Christianity? Ask the pontiff
who was resurrected on the third day. In the phalanstery? It
will be opened. In Monsieur Reinganum's lottery?[1] It will be
closed. In the French Church of Monsieur Châtel?[2] The bells
are ringing for mass. There is one of them for every taste. Only
come to me, I say, indolent and credulous but tender and
gracious minds who take more pleasure an interesting fables
than in all those vain theories of pride, even if those superb
lies are destined to become, unfortunately, verities and laws.
Permit the children to come, for there is no danger for them
in listening to my stories, and you know me well enough to
believe me. This one, in any case, will be clad in an authority

---

1 Henri Reinganum was a member of a notable family of bankers based
in Frankfurt, who organized lotteries in France in the 1820s and 1830s.
2 Ferdinand Châtel (1795-1857) was a priest who founded a schismatic
sect in Paris in 1830, which he called the Église catholique française,
occasioning considerable scandal by virtue of his liberal views. Nodier
could not know in 1836 that Châtel would be forced into exile
in 1842, and that his community would be dispersed after an attempt
made to renovate it in the wake of the 1848 Revolution.

that is worth more than mine. It was communicated to me by a man whose rare and perfect qualities I would perhaps have tried to describe if it had been permitted to me to attach his name to these fugitive pages. Now that he is named, his eulogy is made.

On the fourth of August 1834 the Marquis de Louvois arrived in the Pyrenees in a caleche.[1] On the seat of his carriage was a young domestic whose anterior history will not take up much space. Paul was the son of a livestock merchant favored by fortune, the brother of nine other children, who decimated the risky fruits of the petty paternal commerce. Paul was, in consequence, only too happy to enter the service of Monsieur de Louvois, and that will be easily understood if one knows his master.

For some time the carriage had been following the uneven road that overlooks the pleasant valley of Argelez, over which the eye wanders with pleasure, going upstream through bushy clumps of trees, amid which the ruins of an old feudal tower sometimes loomed up, as famous for its traditions as it was picturesque by its aspect. In the distance, a few patches of smooth and resplendent white stood out against the obscure and mobile backcloth of the most magnificent vegetation; a pointed steeple pierced the rounded crowns and a village could be divined, almost entirely veiled by the richness of the shade, like a curtain of verdure.

Traveling thus, under the postillion's resounding whip, the Marquis de Louvois' caleche, overtook for the last time an old man on horseback, who seemed to be attempting to keep it company, and whose inappropriate competition doubtless disquieted the sensibility of the noble voyager. Finally, it was done; neither the man nor the mount had reappeared there-

1 This title, famously associated with Louis XIV's minster of war in the early eighteenth century, still existed in 1834, but its holder was relatively undistinguished.

after, all the way to the relay of Pierrefitte, and Monsieur de Louvois, freed from the care of that unequal contest, hastened to ask for horses.

Horses were rarely lacking at the relay of Pierrefitte, but the road was often lacking when the waters of the torrent of Canterets, swollen by a violent storm, overflowed furiously into the plain, and the fourth of August 1834 was one of those days. It was necessary to stay overnight at the station of Pierrefitte, which is one of the sorriest extremities to which the Pyrenean tourist can be reduced between the banks of the Tot and those of the Nivette. Monsieur de Louvois resigned himself to it, and took the courage of his position as far as possible. In spite of the poor appearance of the food, he decided to have supper.

At the extremity of the long table where he was placed, another place had been set, and an old man did not take long to sit down there after a modest salute; he was the presumptuous cavalier who had attempted, an hour before, to match his fatigued charger with a sprightly team in harness, a circumstance by which Monsieur de Louvois had been struck, as you will recall. He cast his eyes over him, moved by a simple impulse of curiosity, and brought them back several times, which was the effect of interest and sympathy.

The man had a noble and mild appearance; thick white hair shaded his respectable head; his gaze, which Monsieur de Louvois often encountered, appeared to be animated by an uncommon expression; and the involuntary tears that he sometimes shed betrayed in interior disturbance that was attempting to expand. A conversation did not take long to be established and to lead to an opportunity.

I shall not change anything in this story, not even the proper names, which I can alter, like anyone else, in accordance with the conventions of fiction when I need to invent them. I promised in the beginning an authentic story in which the imagination of the storyteller plays no part, a narrative without adornment and without disguise, such as nature and society give from time to time to those who seek them, and that is the story I am writing. Perhaps there is some indiscretion in designating so overtly persons from whom I have neither received nor asked for permission, but what is the point of enveloping with mysteries of fiction a narration that has nothing offensive for anyone and which, in certain respects, is honorable for everyone? At any rate, even if I am condemned formally, I will be absolved in regard to intention. I ask no more, for this is not the work of a writer but a fireside chat destined not to emerge from a small circle of good people, in which I have enclosed my audience, my literary pretentious and my reputation.

"You must have been astonished," said the old man, "to see me just now so obstinate in following you; and that ambition, so inappropriate to my age, might have given you a poor opinion of my judgment?"

"No, in truth," replied Monsieur de Louvois; "I only supposed that encountering me, foreseen or not, was not entirely indifferent to you, and that you had some communication to make to me."

"It is necessary to explain, if you will authorize me to do so," said the aged traveler, "but how can I do it? My sole design was to attract the attention of a young domestic sitting in front of your carriage, who did not appear to recognize me. It is only too probable moreover," he added, stifling a sob and putting his hand over his eyes to contain a tear, "that we were both seeing one another today for the first time. Dare I ask you whether he has been in your service for a long time?"

"For two years," said Monsieur de Louvois, "and I have known him since childhood; I obtained him from his family."

"From his family," repeated the old man. With those words he raised his eyes to the heavens, and tears escaped him in abundance.

"Speak, speak!" cried Monsieur de Louvois. "I cannot comprehend anything of this mystery as yet, but I feel a profound need to understand you and to console you; perhaps I shall succeed."

A sigh that expressed doubt, and an inclination of the head that expressed gratitude, were his only immediate response. Finally, he continued: "You will permit it, then; and it only remains for me to ask your forgiveness for anything in my words at which your mind and your reason might revolt. The disturbance into which today's impressions have thrown me does not leave me the strength to decide myself between what it is necessary to believe and what it is necessary to deny.

"My name is Despin; I am the maire of the small town of Gaujac, where the Comte de Marcellus has a château. Four months ago, at the most, I was as happy as one can be on earth. My wife and I have a fortune of three hundred thousand francs—which is to say, much more than is necessary to live in pleasant ease and to do a little good around oneself, when one had simple tastes and one lives without ambition. All of ours was to leave, with an honest name, the agreeable dependence that we has enjoyed to an only son aged twenty-two years, who recompensed our cares by the best qualities and the most tender affections. Death took him away from us; our happiness ended there. We have lived too long!"

At this point, further tears interrupted Monsieur Despin. After a moment of silence, he continued:

"A stone surmounted by a cross, that is all that remains of him. By my inconsolable grief, Monsieur, you can judge that of a mother. Often, during the brief moments of sleep that Heaven accords to my fatigued eyes, my old wife steals away from my bed in order to go and weep in the cemetery over the tomb of her son. Recently, on a cold and damp night, I perceived her absence and I got up to search for her, or rather to find her, for I knew very well where she was. However, she did not respond to my voice, and I arrived at the place where the grave had been dug before perceiving her. She was lying there, motionless, unconscious. I thought for a moment, alas, that she had died thus.

"The movement of my departure had woken up a few domestics, who had followed me at a distance. Some of them carried her back to the house, another sustained me while I returned there. I had not yet lost everything; she had returned to life; they left us.

"My wife's physiognomy was extremely animated. Her eyes were shining with a strange light, which I had not noticed until then.

"'Perhaps our son isn't dead,' she said, squeezing my hand. 'Perhaps his grave is empty.'

"That language filled me with a new anxiety, because I feared that despair had damaged her reason.

"'Listen,' she continued, in the assured tone of voice of a person who wants to be believed. 'You know my devotion to the Holy Virgin and how I have always dreaded offending her. Well, I have dared to count on her protection in the misfortune that is overwhelming us, and everything announced to me that her divine bounty has responded to my hope. I have already seen her twice.'

"'Great God!' I cried. 'Who do you think you have seen?'

"'Her, in person,' she replied, calmly, 'and it was the splendor by which she is surrounded that had deprived me of my senses when you found me just now in the cemetery; but her words were as present in my ear as if I were hearing them at the moment. *You have prayed to me*, she said. *I come to those who pray to me in the sincerity of their heart. Send your husband toward the mountain; he will see again the child that you have lost.*'

"What would you have done in my place, Monsieur? I hesitated, however, for the frequentation of enlightened people and the habitude of reading had cured me of popular prejudices. Is that a great benefit? It must be, since the philosophers are so impatient to make everyone savor it. But the apparition was renewed several times in the same place, in the same circumstances. I know in my wife a simplicity of heart and an austerity of conscience that renders her incapable of any lie; no other illusion obscured her consciousness, for, to my great satisfaction, her despair, calmed by a promise from Heaven, allowed her to recover from day to day the serenity of mind that she had lost for three months. Her natural good sense was fortified because she had faith in that strange revelation, in which you doubtless only see evidence of madness.

"What can I tell you? Illusion or truth, her dream was at least a subject of consolation that the vain wisdom of men could not furnish her, and I hastened to subscribe to her hopes, with more confidence in the power of time, which cures all dolors, than in the accomplishment of the miracle. I had need of the miracle too, and what man could not have had need of a miracle to be reconciled with life? But I was not counting on it; I sometimes departed when the term announced in the holy apparition had come, and I quit my poor wife assuring her of a security that had not gained my soul.

"From that moment on I did not cease to wander in vain on the mountain, as I was awaited there, and I was due to depart the next day, perhaps to carry death to the most unfortunate of mothers, when this morning . . ."

"Well, Monsieur Despin, this morning . . . ?"

"When this morning, I saw my son sitting on the seat of your carriage; but he did not recognize me."

"Paul, your son, you say?"

"That is indeed the name of my son, and he is also my son, but he did not recognize me. He is my son, although he did not recognize me, and I don't know the reason. I saw him all along the road. I have just seen him again and talked to him for some time in the courtyard of the inn. He is my son. I asked about his age; he is exactly the same age as my son. He has his features. He has the sound of his voice. He has his accent. My son had a birthmark on his cheek; he has a birthmark on his cheek. If he arrived in Gaujac everyone would recognize him. I recognize him so well, myself, that I cannot be mistaken—and I am his father. But he doesn't recognize me."

Monsieur Despin's tears recommenced flowing and he remained plunged in a bleak silence, his elbows on the table and his head in his hands.

Monsieur de Louvois was profoundly moved. "Believe, Monsieur," he said to the old man, "that I would like to be able to prolong the error that has suspended your afflictions momentarily, if it depended on me to maintain it by lacking the truth. An incredible hazard has produced it, and I do not know whether it might not be more likely to augment your regrets than to soothe them."

"You are more capable than you imagine, Monsieur, of giving that appearance a species of reality," said Monsieur Despin, raising a suppliant gaze upon Monsieur de Louvois. "You are astonished by my words, and I understand that, but this last hope will explain. Paul's family is not well off, since it has been obliged to sell his services to a master. He is not my son; I believe that; but his resemblance to my son has deceived my despair, and it will deceive that of his mother. Is he not the son that a celestial protection has rendered to her? I am offering him a mother and a father devoted to his happiness; I am offering him all my wealth, of which I am ready to sign the donation, and Monsieur le Comte de Marcellus will not refuse to attest to what I have told you; he will no longer belong to anyone but himself; he will have no duties other than those imposed by an affection easy to content, and which only asks for affection. He was poor, he will be rich; he has served, he will be served; your generosity doubtless provides for his happiness; we shall substitute it without tenderness; we shall be loved, I'm sure of it, for we have loved in advance; we have loved him in another, and one is always loved when one loves. That is, everything tells me, the veritable meaning of a prediction whose verity became manifest yesterday in my eyes. Heaven does not work such miracles in vain; it wanted to repair toward your Paul a wrong due to chance, toward us a wrong of nature that took ours away. The indigent will have a fortune, and the mourning parents will have a son. Does it not seem to you, Monsieur, that it ought to be thus? Don't refuse me, I implore you, your intervention and your support. The aristocrats of the earth can sympathize without lowering themselves with a dolor that has interested the queen of Heaven. I have nothing more to do than die if you refuse me."

As he pronounced the last words Monsieur Despin squeezed Monsieur de Louvois' hands and moistened them with his tears.

The night had partly elapsed during that conversation and Monsieur de Louvois could not doubt that the old man's resolution was invariable. He went at an early hour into the room where Paul was sleeping fully dressed on one of the inn's camp beds, and he found Monsieur Despin on his knees, his eyes avidly fixed on the living image of his dead son.

Monsieur Despin got up, handed Monsieur Louvois the act of donation he had mentioned, accompanied by a payment of the sum of ten thousand francs, payable in case that strange proof did not succeed to the satisfaction of all parties, and withdrew, recommending to him for the last time the negotiation on which his life appeared to depend, by an respectful inclination and a suppliant gaze.

The movement that he made within the room had awakened Paul; he tried to leap up at the sight of his master and to excuse himself for not having been more diligent.

"Stay," Monsieur de Louvois said to him, "and sit down, in order to listen to me with all the concentration of which you are capable. Perhaps you have not heard recounted," he continued, smiling, "the story of the man whom fortune came to surprise in his bed, and perhaps you didn't imagine that it was yours. There is, however, nothing more true. One word, Paul, and you will exchange my livery for the coat of a prosperous bourgeois. One word, and you will be rich!"

"In truth, Monsieur," Paul replied, "I would not be surprised. That destiny has been predicted to me in childhood, and a few days ago it was announced to me in Auvergne. Monsieur will doubtless recall that he stopped to eat in a wretched mountain inn, where gendarmes arrived almost at the same time, with a kind of gypsy woman, whom they were taking to prison in the chief place, whose physiognomy struck him. That is because she was not a common witch, and one could see very well by her airs of dignity that she believed in her art. I was momentarily so tempted to believe it also that I dared not withdraw my hand when she seized it in her dry and sinewy hand and forced me, by means of a hard stare of her dark eyes, to deploy it before her. For myself, I turned mine away, so much did she make me afraid to see.

"'Oho!' she said, in a hoarse voice, muttering between her teeth. 'This is new. Would it suit you, my son, to have good fields in full yield, good meadows verdant in the sunlight, good flocks of sheep ready for shearing, two or three dozen good milch-cows, and as many calves bounding around, a country house that laughs at the south, from which the eye plunges with difficulty into the thickness of a beautiful orchard buckling under the weight of ripe fruit? Would it please you to relax from time to time in the city from the care of your lush farms in a good armchair of Utrecht velvet with long stripes, on the first floor of a spacious house in good condition, which belongs to you, as close as you please to a balcony laden with flowers, overlooking the main square, and to wait their indolently for the hour of an excellent meal while reading your newspaper, if the newspaper amuses you?'

"I could not help smiling, for the kind of life she was proposing to me was much to my taste. 'You will no sooner have entered the Pyrenees,' she added, 'pushing my hand away with a scornful anger, 'than that fortune will be offered to you, and you will have refused it.'

"I didn't understand very well how that could be the case, but I attached so little importance to the prediction of the adventuress that I haven't thought about it since."

The coincidence of those two mysterious events struck Monsieur de Louvois, for there is no mind so inured against the seduction of appearances that it is not astonished to be obliged to accord something to the intelligence of chance. After a moment of reflection, he made Paul party to what had passed the previous evening between himself and Monsieur Desprin, and opened before his eyes the formal document that was only awaiting his signature. He quit him then to give free course to his reflections. The affair was worth the trouble.

While all that was happening in the wretched tavern of Pierrefitte the sky had cleared; the turbulent waters of the torrent had reentered their bed and the relay horses, relaxed by a long leisure, were whinnying at the door, stamping their hooves on the granite paving stones like battle-chargers; the local farrier was trying surreptitiously to loosen a few screws in order to have a pretext for tightening them again, and Monsieur de Louvois was preparing to depart.

Scarcely a quarter of an hour had gone by when Paul entered his master's room with a modest but resolute air.

Monsieur de Louvois looked at him intently. "Well?" he said, laughing. "Is it to Monsieur Despin's son that I have the advantage of speaking?"

"No, Monsieur le Marquis," Paul replied, "it's to Paul, your domestic yesterday, who is likewise today and has no other ambition than to be so always, if you are content with his services."

"Have you reflected well?" said Monsieur de Louvois, astonished.

"I could reflect for ten years without changing determination."

Monsieur de Louvois seemed disposed to lend him a serious attention, and he continued: "I'm extremely touched by the misfortune of that family, and I would like to be able to procure them some relief. It's a duty that I would like to accomplish, if it accorded with mine, and I would have no need to be borne to it by my interest; but what that worthy old man asks, Monsieur, I am incapable of giving. He is seeking a son, and I already have a father. It is to my father that I owe the affection and the cares of a son, and the heart of a son cannot be bought at auction. The honest man who wanted to enrich me has a right to my gratitude, but I cannot offer him anything more. The sentiments that he requests belong to that other old man who has nourished me, who has brought me up on the produce of his labor, who has warmed me in his bosom when I was cold, who has wept by my cradle when I was ill, and who has founded on my good conduct and my gratitude the last hope of his old age. Do you believe that he would survive the idea that I had sold his name for money, that I had renounced the memory of his embraces and his counsels, that I had denied my nine brothers like a traitor and an accursed, in order to deliver myself casually to the pleasure of idleness?

"You will doubtless say to me, Monsieur, that my new estate would permit me to do him some good, that Monsieur Despin would not criticize that employment of my superfluity, and that there would be a means of redeeming at that price, in the eyes of men, my ingratitude and my cowardice, but what would justify me before my own conscience? It would be necessary, besides, for my father to want to accept that shameful indemnity, and I know him well enough to be sure that he would reject it with indignation. 'For what reason,' he would cry, 'would Monsieur Despin *fils*, of Gauhjac, who is unknown to me, gratify me with his alms? Who has asked him for them? Do I need to have recourse to him to furnish the maintenance of my nine children'—he would no longer be counting me—'in order to raise them in the fear of God and in the love of their family and their fatherland? If Monsieur Despin *fils* is too rich, if he is tormented by some remorse that obliged him to distribute his superfluity in works of charity let him look around him. Does he not know of difficulties to ease in his village, perhaps among his nearest neighbors?'

"I would also have become a stranger to my memories, to my amities of childhood, and to my fatherland as well as to my father. I would be recommencing a new life, the life of another who has loved nothing of what I have loved; and if it were abridged by shame, by chagrin, and by the very pleasures to which I would deliver myself in order to stun myself, would I leave the regrets that Monsieur Despin's son has left? Do you think, Monsieur, that my veritable father, insensible to the abandonment I would have made of his old age, would go to search the mountains for my resemblance? Oh, he would rather avoid it, have no doubt about that, for it would only remind him of my avarice, my baseness and my unworthiness. No, Monsieur, I shall not change estate; I shall not change fortune, because I do not want to change my name, because I do not want to change my family. I shall remain poor, but I shall remain my father's son, and I shall conserve the right to embrace him without blushing; that is worth more than money."

"Go settle the bill, my child," Monsieur de Louvois said to him, turning away to hide his emotion.

A quarter of an hour later, the postillion's whip struck the air with redoubled cracks. A post chaise rolled noisily under the coaching entrance of the inn. It emerged. Paul was perched on the seat, as on the day before.

A man attentive to what was happening in that house and who was wandering sadly in his chamber, invoking the aid of God, launched himself toward the window in order to convince his eyes of a new misfortune that he had not foreseen. Everything had just been lost by him, including hope. He had seen his son die for a second time; Paul had gone.

Monsieur Despin fell as if thunderstruck on the bed where he had not slept, and when an inn servant handed him Monsieur de Louvois' sad letter of adieu, he only cast a somber and dejected glance at it, because he already knew his sentence. Oh, with what strength did he have to arm himself in order to go back go his house! How did he present himself to his wife, so impatient for his return, and yet so sure of the result of his journey? What account did he give of his momentary hopes changed into eternal mourning? Religion alone can explain the resignation of the heart in such cruel proofs. There is an anguish within them that can scarcely be conceived, and cannot be described.

The story that I have just recounted, without adding the slightest circumstance to it, and without heightening it by artful ornaments that would have spoiled it for myself, can give rise to grave reflections. The positive philosophers who deny the intervention of a God in earthly things would give the honor of those marvelous coincidences to the power of hazard, because that is the name that one gives to God when one has made the desperate decision not to believe in him. Christians would see in it a more consoling and more elevating symbolism.

What, in fact, can the intercession of the most powerful do to console the widowhood of a heart that death has, so to speak, doubled—forgive me that expression, which is that of a sentiment and not that of a manner? Alas, it can only render appearances and forms; for the soul that animates them already has another abode, and it is to that one that it has instructed us to aspire, in order to replace what we have lost. The rest is only an illusion, which can deceive the eyes of a father momentarily, but cannot deceive his tenderness for long.

In order to recommence the life of a cherished individual who has been taken from us, it is necessary to recommence living ourselves; that idea might suffice to embellish death if death had any need to be embellished in the regard of anyone who has lived for a long time, but will life itself recommence? Yes, have no doubt about it, it will recommence! There is nothing in this creation that does not have its harmonies and its complement, if it is not the human heart; and the role of a day that it plays on the earth would only be one episode more in an ill-made drama if that drama of derision and cruelty were concluded by death. That is not to be feared, because it is impossible.

It is true to say that it would be necessary to have been dead to form exact notions regarding that mysterious future, and that is not common. There is, however, the case of the famous Icelander of Bessestedt,[1] who was taken alive out of his bier a week after his established death and lived for another ten years in the practice of good works, but without immediate communication with humans. That sage, named, or rather nicknamed Lazare Néobius—for criticism has not yet clarified that curious point of literary history—had spent all the time during which he was retrenched from the century in the intermediary world in which the good will receive the commencement of their recompense, and be disposed, by proofs milder than ours, worthily to receive an eternal recompense. He had rediscovered his family and friends there, after a rapture that would be thought inexpressible if he had

1 This "fact" was quoted in at least one other work, credit being given to Nodier, although the passage dutifully makes it clear that it is an invention. The Icelandic region of Bessestadt is mentioned in passing in Victor Hugo's *Han d'Islande* (1823), admiration for which was instrumental in forging the friendship between Nodier and Hugo.

not succeeded in expressing it very eloquently; and when he saw that he had fallen back into the dolorous toils of our life of preparation, he formed in his new exile the idea of a holy mission, which was imposed on him in order to stimulate the lukewarm fervor of the faithful and arm the weak against the invasion of false doctrines.

Such is the object of the admirable book of Lazare Néobius, on which I have extended myself a little more than my subject requires, because it is almost unknown, and so rare that no copy other than mine probably exists. It incurred, in fact, quite naturally, a double censure as soon as it appeared in the light of publicity: that of the Church, which did not believe itself authorized to receive, on the isolated testimony of a saintly man, a document supplementary to the revelation of the Gospel; and that of the temporal power, which judged, perhaps with reason, that the prospect of a future so facile and so pleasant, by diminishing the attraction that attaches us to our present existence, might loosen the bonds of social life to the benefit of the contemplative life.

That danger no longer exists today, or, rather, the contrary excess has become so alarming that one cannot hasten too much to bring a remedy to it. If society threatens to die soon, it is not the expansion of a pensive sensibility that is undermining it and will destroy it, not the intention to push intellectual and moral longevity beyond all limits; it is the deplorable instinct of a narrow egotism, which imprisons it in matter and forces it to discount its eternity at the price of a few sterile years that the present devours as quickly as it gives them. There is, therefore, no serious inconvenience now in delivering to tender and suffering souls those treasures of consolation and hope, which compensate them for the misfortune of living in a bad time and in an imperfect world.

I have even thought that sometimes, and if I have delayed so long in doing it, it is because I imagine that the age might one day lend my authority to my words. The idea of finally opening that unknown but certain world to the attention of my readers was still occupying me at the moment when I began to write these last pages, but sudden considerations have retained me . . .

And it seems to me, all things considered, that I would do better to go there in order to see for myself.

Inès de Las Sierras

"And you," said Anastase, "aren't you going to tell us a ghost story too?"

"If it depends on me," I replied, "for I have been a witness to the strangest apparition of which there has ever been mention since Samuel; but it isn't a tale; it's a true story."

"Good," murmured the deputy magistrate, pinching his lips; "is there anyone today who believes in apparitions?"

"Perhaps you would have believed it as firmly as me," I said, "if you had been in my place."

Eudoxie drew her chair closer to mine, and I began.

It was in the last days of 1812. I was then a captain of dragoons garrisoned at Gironne in the département of the Ter. My colonel thought it a good idea to send me to Barcelona, where a horse-market renowned throughout Catalonia was held on the day after Christmas, and he attached to me for that expedition two lieutenants of the regiment named Sergy and Boutraix, who were my particular friends. Permit me, please, to talk about both of them, because the details of their character into which I shall enter are not irrelevant to the rest of my story.

Sergy was one of those young officers that the schools give us, who have to overcome a few prejudices, and even antipathies, in order to be well regarded by their comrades. He had triumphed over them in a short time. His face was charming, his manners distinguished, his mind lively and brilliant, his bravery proof against anything. There was no exercise in which he did not excel, no art for which he did not have an inclination and a sentiment, although his delicate and nervous organization rendered him most sensible to the charms of music. An instrument that sang under skillful fingers, and especially a beautiful voice, filled him with enthusiasm that was sometimes manifested by exclamations and tears. When it was a woman's voice, and that woman was pretty, his transports went as far as delirium. He had often made me anxious for his reason.

You will easily appreciate that Sergy's heart was very accessible to amour, and he was almost never free, in fact, from one of those violent passions on which a man's life might depend; but the fortunate exaltation of his sensibility defended it against its own excesses. What that ardent soul needed was a soul as ardent as itself, with which it could associate itself and confound itself, and although he believed that he saw it everywhere, he had not thus far encountered it anywhere. The result of that was that the idol of the day before, stripped of the illusion that had divinized it, was no more than a woman the day after, and the most passionate of lovers was also the most fickle. During his days of disillusionment, when he fell back from the full height of his illusions into the humiliating conviction of reality, he had the custom of saying that the unknown object of his desires and his hopes did not inhabit the earth; but he still searched for it, leaping to deceive himself again as he had done a thousand times before.

Sergy's latest error had been produced by a rather mediocre little singer attached to Bascara's troupe, which had just quit

Gironne. For two entire days the virtuosa had occupied the highest regions of Olympus. Two days had sufficed to make her descend to the rank of the simplest mortals. Sergy no longer remembered her.

With that irritability of sentiment it was impossible that Sergy would not have a great liking for the marvelous. There was no region into which his ideas did not stray willingly. Spiritualist by reason or by education, he was much more so by imagination or by instinct. His faith in the imaginary mistress that the world of spirits had reserved for him was not, therefore, a simple play of fantasy; it was the favorite subject of his reveries, the secret romance of his thought, a kind of gracious and consoling enigma that compensated him for the sorry return of his futile trials.

Far from revolting against that chimera, when hazard brought it into the conversation, I made use of it more than once to combat his amorous despair, which was renewed every month. In general, taking refuge in an ideal life, when one knows exactly what it is worth, can make a considerable contribution to happiness.

Boutraix made the most perfect contrast with Sergy. He was a tall and stout fellow, as full as him of loyalty, honor, bravery and devotion to his comrades, but his face was very common and his mind resembled his face. He only knew moral amour—the amour of the head and the heart that disturbs and embellishes life—by hearsay, and he regarded it as an invention of poets and novelists, which had only ever existed in books. As for the amour that he understood, he made some use of it occasionally, but without devoting more care and time to it than it merited. His most pleasant leisure was devoted to the table, where he was the first to sit down and was always the last to quit it, unless the wine ran out. After a fine feat of war, wine was the only thing in the world that inspired any enthusiasm in him. He spoke about it with a kind of eloquence, and he drank a great deal of it without getting drunk. By virtue of a particular favor of his temperament, he had never fallen into the gross state that approaches men to brutes, but it is necessary to agree that he fell asleep just in time.

Intellectual life was reduced, for Boutraix, to a small number of ideas on which he had made invariable principles, or which he had reached the point of expressing by means of absolute formulae convenient for dispensing him of discussion. The difficulty of proving anything by means of a sequence of sound arguments had determined him to deny everything. To all inductions drawn from faith or sentiment he responded with two sacramental words accompanied by a shrug of the shoulders: *fanaticism* and *prejudice*. If anyone persisted, he leaned his head on the back of his chair and uttered a shrill whistle, which lasted as long as the objection and spared him the embarrassment of hearing it. Although he had never read two pages in succession, he believed that he had read Voltaire, and even Piron,[1] whom he regarded as a philosopher; those two fine minds were his supreme authorities, and the *ultima ratio* of all the controversies in which he deigned to take part was summarized in the triumphant remark: "See what Voltaire and Piron have to say about it!" The altercation usually finished there, and he carried off the honors, which had won him the reputation in his squadron as an excellent logician. With all that, Boutraix was a good comrade, and incontrovertibly the man who knew horses better than any other man in the army.

As we were proposing to drive, we agreed to make use for our journey to Barcelona of one of the *arrieros*, or carters, who abound in Gironne, and the facility of finding one had inspired a confidence in us that was mistaken. The solemnity

---

1 Alexis Piron (1689-1773) was a dramatist, like Voltaire, but was best remembered for his epigrams.

of Christmas Eve and the market two days later attracted an innumerable quantity of travelers from all over Catalonia, and we had waited for that day in order to procure the necessary vehicle. At eleven o'clock in the morning we were still searching for an arriero, and only one hope remained to us when we encountered him at his door.

"A curse on the carriage and the mules!" cried Boutraix, overcome by wrath and sitting down on a boundary-marker. "May all the devils in hell, if there are any, unleash themselves in your passage, and may Lucifer himself set a place for you! We aren't going, then!"

The arriero took a step back and made the sign of the cross.

"May God keep you in his holy protection, Master Estevan," I said to him, smiling. "Do you have passengers?"

"I can't say positively that I have passengers," the carter replied, "since I only have one, Señor Bascara, the stage-manager and *gracioso* of the comedy, who is going to join his troupe in Barcelona, and who stayed behind in order to accompany the baggage—which is to say, that trunk stuffed with clothes and rags, which a donkey couldn't carry."

"That's for the best, Master Estevan! Your carriage has four seats, and Señor Bascara will gladly permit us to pay three-quarters of the fee, which he will still be free to charge to the account of his director. We'll keep the secret for him. Take the trouble to ask him if he'd be so kind as to authorize us to accompany him."

Bascara only hesitated as much as was necessary to give his consent the appearance of a favor. We left Gironne at midday.

The morning was as fine as could be desired for the season, but we had scarcely passed the last houses of the town that the white vapors that had been floating since sunrise on the summits of the hills in soft and light curtains, developed with a surprising rapidity, embracing the entire horizon, and enclosed us in all directions like a wall. They soon condensed into an extremely fine rain mingled with snow, so intense and so dense that one might have thought that the atmosphere had turned to water or that our mules had drawn us into the depths of a river that was fortunately permeable to respiration. The equivocal element through which we were traveling had lost its transparency, to the point of hiding the edges and the nearest stretches of the road; even our driver could only assure himself that he was following it by sounding it continually with his gaze and his foot before taking his team forward, and those trials, often repeated, slowed our progress more and more. The easiest fords had, moreover, swelled in a matter of hours to become perilous, and Bascara did not traverse a single one without recommending himself to Saint Nicolas or Saint Ignatius, the patron saints of navigators.

"I'm really afraid," said Sergy, smiling, "that Heaven has taken literally the terrible imprecation with which Boutraix greeted the unfortunate arriero this morning. All the devils in hell seem to have been unleashed in our passage, as he wished, and we only need to sup with the devil to see his presage accomplished. It's annoying, you'll agree, to be subject to the consequences of that impiety."

"Good, good," replied Boutraix, half waking up "Prejudice! Superstition! Fanaticism!" And he fell asleep again immediately.

The route became a little more secure when we had reached the solid rocky shore of the sea, but the rain—or, rather, the deluge—through which we were swimming so painfully had not diminished. It only seemed to dry up three hours after sunset, and we were still a long way from Barcelona. We arrived in Mattaro, where we decided to sleep, in the impossibility of doing better, for our team was exhausted by fatigue. However, it had scarcely turned into the vast driveway of the inn when the arriero came to open our door and announce to us sadly that the courtyard was already cluttered with carriages that could not be accommodated.

"It's a fatality," he added, "that is pursuing us in this accursed voyage. There's no vacant lodging except Ghismondo's castle."

"Let's see," I said, jumping out of the carriage, "whether it's necessary to resolve ourselves to bivouac in one of the most hospitable regions in Spain; it would be a rude extremity after such a difficult journey."

"Señor officer," replied a muleteer who was smoking his *cigarro*, insolently leaning against the doorpost, "you won't lack companions in your disgrace, for it's more than two hours since everyone has been refused in the inns and the private house, where the first comers have found shelter. There's no lodgment vacant except Ghismondo's castle."

I had known that manner of speaking, familiar to people on such an occasion, for a long time, but the irksome response had never importuned my ear so disagreeably.

I made my way nevertheless to the landlady through a tumultuous crowd of travelers, arrieros, mules and grooms, and succeeded in attracting her attention by rudely striking a metallic utensil with the pommel of my sword.

"A stable, a room and a well-served table," I cried, in the imperious tone that usually succeeded for us, "and immediately! It's for the service of the Emperor!"

Well, Señor Captain," she replied, with assurance, "the Emperor himself couldn't find a place to sit down in my hostelry. As much food and wine as you want, if you're in a humor to sup in the open air, for thank God, it's not difficult to provide in a town like this one; but it's not within my power to enlarge the house in order to receive you. On my faith as a Christian, there's no lodgment vacant but Ghismondo's . . ."

"A curse on the proverbs of Sancho's country!" I interrupted, abruptly. "If that accursed castle really exits somewhere, I'd rather spend the night there than in the street."

"Is that so?" she said, staring at me. "In truth, you make me think so. Ghismondo's castle is no more than three-quarters of a league from here, and you will indeed find lodgings open there at all times. It's true that hardly anyone takes advantage of it, but you Frenchies aren't men to cede a good shelter to the demon. See whether it suits you, and your cart can be loaded with everything necessary to spend a joyous night, if you don't receive some annoying visit."

"We're too well armed to fear any," I replied, "and as for the demon himself, I've heard it said that he's a rather agreeable guest. Take care of the provisions, then, my good mother. Rations for five, each of whom eats like four, fodder for our mules, and a little too much wine, if you please, for Boutraix is with us."

"Lieutenant Boutraix!" she cried, bringing her extended hands together—which is, as everyone knows, an exclamation in gesture. "Mozo, two large panniers and true *rancio*."

Ten minutes later, the interior of the coach was transformed into the parlor of a good house, so luxuriantly garnished that one could not have introduced the thinnest of our voyagers; but, as I have said, the weather, which had not ceased to be menacing, appeared at least to be appeased momentarily. We did not hesitate to set forth on foot.

"Where are we going, Señor Captain?" said the arriero, surprised by those preparations.

"Where would we be going, my poor Estevan, if not to the place that you have indicated yourself? To Ghismondo's castle, of course."

"To Ghismondo's castle! May the beneficent Virgin have pity on us! Even my mules wouldn't dare make that journey!"

"They'll make it, however," I replied, slipping a handful of coins into his hand. "And they'll be compensated for that final fatigue by a copious meal. As for you, my dear comrade, there are three bottles of old Palamos wine in there, of which you can give me news. Only don't waste time, for we're all starving, and in any case, the sky is beginning to look sullen.

"Ghismondo's castle!" repeated Bascara, lamentably. "Do you know, señors, what Ghismondo's castle is? No one has ever penetrated it with impunity, without having made a preliminary pact with the spirit of evil, and I wouldn't set foot in it for a galleon's cargo. No, truly, I won't go."

"You'll go, on my honor, amiable Bascara," said Boutraix, putting a vigorous arm around him. "Would it befit a generous Castilian, who exercises a liberal profession gloriously, to recoil before the most inept of popular prejudices? Oh, if Voltaire and Piron had been translated into Spanish, as they ought to be into every language in the world, I wouldn't have any difficulty proving to you that the devil of whom you're afraid is a scarecrow of old women, invented for the profit of monks by some wicked water-drinker of a theologian; but I'll enable you to put your finger on that when we've supped, for my stomach is too empty and my mouth too dry to sustain a philosophical discussion at the present moment. March, then, brave Bascara, and be assured of always finding Lieutenant Boutraix between the devil and you, if he's reckless enough to offer you the slightest offense. Damn, that would be a fine thing to see!"

While speaking thus we had engaged in a rugged and winding path up the hill, to the sound of Bascara's sobbing "alases." He marked every step with effusions of psalms or invocations of litanies. I must agree that even the mules, slowed down by fatigue and hunger, only approached the goal of our nocturnal excursion in a surly and peevish manner, stopping from time to time, as if they expected a salutary counter-order, and turning their dejected heads piteously at each toise of the route they traveled.

"What, then," said Sergy, "is this castle of fatal renown that inspires such a sincere and profound terror in these good folk? A rendezvous of revenants perhaps?"

"Perhaps a thieves' lair," I replied, in a low voice, "for people never conceive a superstition of that sort unless it is founded on some legitimate motive for dread. But we three have three swords, three pairs of excellent pistols, and ammunition with which to reload; and in addition to our hunting knives, the arriero is certainly armed, as is the custom, with a good Valencian ganivet."

"Who doesn't know what Ghismondo's castle is?" murmured Estevan, in a voice that was already tremulous. "If these illustrious señors are curious to learn it, I'm in a state to satisfy them, for my late father went into it. He was a brave man, that one! God forgive him for having liked drinking too much."

"There's no harm in that," Boutraux put in. "What the devil did your father see in Ghismondo's castle?"

"Tell us the story," said Sergy, who would have thought the pleasure party more refined for a fantastic tale.

"After that, as well," the muleteer replied, "the señors will be free to go back, if they deem it appropriate." And he continued:

"The unfortunate Ghismondo," he said—and immediately paused, as if he feared being overheard by an invisible witness, but then went on: "Unfortunate indeed, for having attracted to himself the inexorable wrath of God, for I don't wish him any ill . . . Ghismondo was, at twenty-five, the chief of the illustrious family of Las Sierras so renowned in our chronicles. That was three hundred years ago, or very nearly, but the exact year is mentioned in the books. He was a handsome and brave cavalier, liberal, gracious and welcome everywhere for a long time, but too inclined to bad company, who did not knew how to maintain himself in fear and respect of the Lord, to such an extent that there were nasty rumor about his deportment, and he was almost entirely ruined by his prodigalities.

"It was then that he was obliged to seek a refuge in the castle that you have resolved very imprudently, retaining all reverence, to spend the night, which was the sole debris of his rich patrimony. Content to escape the pursuit of his creditors and his enemies—who were very numerous because his passions and debaucheries had stirred up trouble in many families—in that retreat, he finished fortifying it and confined himself therein for the remainder of his days, with a squire whose life was as bad as his and a young page in whom the corruption of the soul was in advance of his years; their household simply consisted of a handful of men-at-arms who had taken part in their excesses, and whose unique resource was to associate themselves with his fortune.

"One of Ghismondo's first expeditions had for its objective to procure a companion, and, like the infamous bird that soils its own nest, it was within his own family that he chose his sad victim. Some said, however, that Inès de Las Sierras—that was the name of his niece—secretly subscribed to her abduction. Who can ever explain the mysteries of women's hearts?

"I've told you that it was one of his first expeditions, because history attributes many others to hm. The revenues attached to this rock, which seems to have been struck by a celestial curse in all times, would not have sufficed for his expenditure if he had not supplemented it with taxes levied on passers-by, which are qualified as highway robberies when not executed by great lords. The names of Ghismondo and his castle soon became redoubtable.

"Is that all?" said Boutraix. "What you've just said happened everywhere. It's one of the necessary results of feudality, one of the consequences of barbarity in the centuries of ignorance and slavery."

"What remains for me to tell you is a little less common," the arriero went on. "The meek Inès, who had received a Christian education, was suddenly, on the day parallel to this one, enlightened by a bright radiance of grace. At the moment when midnight chimed to recall the faithful of the birth of the Savior, she penetrated, against her custom, the banqueting hall, where the brigands, sitting around the hearth, were distracting themselves from their crimes in the excesses of an orgy. They were half drunk. Animated by faith, she depicted for them in vivid terms the evil of their actions and the eternal punishment that would be their consequence. She wept, she prayed, she knelt down before Ghismondo, and with her white hand extended over his heart, which had once beaten with love of her, she tried to recall to it a few human sentiments. That, señors, was an enterprise beyond her strength, and Ghismondo, excited by his barbaric companions, responded with a dagger-thrust that pierced her breast."

"The monster!" cried Sergy, as emotional as if he were hearing the account of a veritable history.

"That horrible incident," Estevan continued, "did not hamper any of his license and his accustomed joy. The three guests continued to drink and sing impious songs in the presence of the dead young woman, and it was three o'clock in the morning when the men-at-arms, alerted by the silence of their masters, penetrated into the place of the feast in order to pick up four bodies lying in a flood of blood and wine. They carried the three drunkards to their beds without flinching, and the cadaver into its shroud.

"But celestial vengeance," Estevan continued, after a rather solemn pause, "the infallible justice of God, had not lost its rights. Scarcely had slumber commenced to dissipate the vapors that obscured Ghismondo's reason than he saw Inès enter his chamber at a measured pace, not beautiful, quivering with amour and sensuality, and clad as before in a light fabric ready to fall, but pale and bloody, trailing the long habit of the dead, and deploying toward him a flamboyant hand, which she came to impose heavily upon his heart, at the very place where she had pressed it in vain a few hours before. Bound by an irresistible power, Ghismondo tried in vain to draw away from the frightful apparition. His efforts and his dolor could only be manifest in a few dull and confused groans. The implacable hand remained nailed in place, and Ghismondo's heart was burning—and it burned thus until sunrise, when the phantom disappeared. His accomplices received a similar visit, and suffered the same torture.

"The next day, and all the days that followed for a year that was almost eternal, the accursed three found themselves interrogating one another with their gazes regarding the dream they had had, for they dared not speak about it. However the commonalty of peril and gain soon summoned them to new crimes, and the license of the night to further orgies, which they prolonged because sleep was redoubtable to them, and when the hour of slumber arrived, the avenging hand always burned them.

"The anniversary eventually returned of Christmas Eve— that's today, señors—and the evening meal had brought them together, as usual, when the hour of redemption sounded at Mattaro in order to summon the Christians to the solemn rites. Suddenly, a voice rose up in the gallery of the castle. 'Here I am!' cried Inès, for it was her. They saw her enter, throw off her funereal drape and sit down among them in her richest attire. Seized by astonishment and terror, they saw her eat the bread and drink the wine of the living; it is even said that she sang and danced, in accordance with the custom of the past, but suddenly her hand caught fire, as in the mystery of their dreams, and touched the hearts of the knight, the squire and the page. Then everything was finished for this temporary life, for their calcined hearts had been reduced to ash, and no longer sent blood into their veins. It was three o'clock in the morning when the men-at-arms, alerted by the silence of their masters, penetrated, as usual, into the place of the feast; and this time, they took away four cadavers. The next day, no one woke up."

Sergy had appeared profoundly preoccupied throughout the story, because the ideas to which it had given birth related to the ordinary substance of his reveries. From time to time, Boutraix uttered an expressive sigh, but which only expressed impatience and ennui. The actor Bascara murmured a few unintelligible words between his teeth, which seemed to add a muted, monotonous and melancholy bass note to the arriero's lugubrious ballad, and an oft-renewed movement made me suspect that he was telling the beads of a rosary. As for me, I admired those poetic shreds of tradition, naturally sewn together by the recitation of a simple man, which lent it colors that an imagination enlightened by taste does not always disdain.

"That's not all," Estevan went on, "and I beg you to listen to me for a moment longer before persisting in your dangerous project. Since the death of Ghismondo and his fellows, his detestable lair, having become odious to all men, has remained the property of the demon. Even the route by which one arrives at it has been abandoned, as you can see. It is only known, beyond any doubt, that every year, on the twenty-fourth of December, at midnight—that's today, señors, and it will soon be the time—the windows of the old edifice are suddenly illuminated. Those who have dared to penetrate these terrible secrets know that then, the knight, the squire and the page return from the bosom of the dead to take their places at the bloody orgy. That is the sentence to which they are subject until the consummation of the centuries. A little later, Inès enters, in her shroud, which she takes off in order to revel her customary accoutrement: Inès, who eats and drinks, who sings and dances, with them. When they have been cradled for some time in the delirium of their mad joy, imagining every time that it will never cease, the young woman shows them the still-open wound, touches their hearts with her blazing hand, and returns to the fires of Purgatory after having returned them to Hell."

The last words caused Boutraix to utter a convulsive burst of laughter that took his breath away momentarily.

"May the devil take you!" he cried, striking the arriero on the shoulder with an amicable blow of his fist. "I was nearly moved by that nonsense, which you recount rather well, and I felt disturbed, like a fool, when Hell and Purgatory returned me to myself. Prejudice, my Catalan! Childish prejudice, which is frightened by masks, old fables of superstition that no longer have credit anywhere but Spain. You'll soon see whether the fear of the devil will prevent me from finding the wine good—and by the way, that reminds me that I'm thirsty. Press your mules, if you please, for in order to see the supper served more promptly, I'd drink a toast to Satan himself."

"They were my father's own words, in a debauched party that he gave in Mattaro with soldiers like him," said the arriero. "When more wine was demanded of the master of the posada he replied: 'There isn't any more, except at Ghismondo's castle.'

"'I'll have some of that,' replied my father, who was as impious as a gavache,[1] 'and by the holy body of Christ, I'll have it even if Satan has to pour it. I'll go.'

"'You won't go! Oh, don't go!'

"'I'll go,' he replied, with a blasphemy even more execrable.

"And he was so obstinate that he went."

"With regard to your father," said Sergy, "you've forgotten Boutraix's question. What did he see that was so frightening at Ghismondo's castle?"

"That's what I've told you, señors. After going through a long gallery of very old paintings, he stopped on the threshold of the banqueting hall, and as the door was open, he looked inside rather confidently. The damned were at table and Inès was showing them her bloody wound. Then she danced, and

1 The word *gavache*, meaning ruffian or rustic, was adapted by Rabelais from Occitan.

each of her steps brought her closer to the place where he was standing. His courage suddenly gave way at the idea that she was coming to take him. He fell full length like a dead weight, and only came round the next morning on the threshold of the parish church."

"Where he had slept all night," said Boutraix, "because the wine he had drunk had prevented him from going any further. It was a drunkard's dream, my dear Estevan. May the earth be as light upon him as he found it mobile and shifting underfoot! But will we never arrive at this infernal castle?"

"We're there," the arriero replied, stopping his mules.

"It's high time," said Sergy. "The torment is commencing, and—a strange thing in this season—I've heard thunder rumbling two or three times."

"It's always heard at a similar epoch, near Ghismondo's castle," the arriero replied.

He had not finished speaking when a dazzling flash of lightning split the sky and showed us the white walls of the old manse, with its turrets grouped like a troop of ghosts over an immense platform of smooth and slippery rock.

The principal door appeared to have been locked a long time ago, but the upper hinges had ended up yielding to the action of the air and the years, along with the stones that sustained them, and the two battens, fallen back on one another, corroded by humidity and mutilated by the wind, were overhanging, ready to collapse. We had no difficulty in bringing them down. In the gap they had left in separating toward their base, where it would have been awkward to introduce the body of a man, some debris of the arch was amassed, which it was necessary to clear away before us. The robust foliages of aloes that had grown in their interstices fell under our swords then, and the carriage entered the broad passage, the paving stones of which had not groaned under the passage of a wheel since the reign of Ferdinand the Catholic.

160

We hastened to light some of the torches with which we had equipped ourselves in Mattaro, the flames of which, nourished by an impetuous current, fortunately resisted the wingbeats of nocturnal birds, which fled through all the cracks of the old building, uttering lamentable cries. The scene, which had, in fact, something extraordinary and sinister about it, reminded me involuntarily of the descent of Don Quixote into the cavern of Montesinos; and the observation I made thereof, laughing might perhaps have drawn smiles from the arriero and Bascara himself if they had still been able to smile—but their consternation was increasing with every step.

The main courtyard opened before us. To the left a large awning extended that served as a kind of hangar, once destined to protect the castellan's horses against seasonal bad weather, as was attested by iron rings placed in the wall at intervals. We rejoiced at the idea of being to garage our rig comfortably there, and that thought even appeared to relieve Estevan's anxiety, who was concerned above everything else with the welfare and repose of his mules. Two torches, firmly fixed to brackets that seemed to be prepared for them, threw a reassuring light over that shelter. The fodder with which we had charged the back of the cart, splendidly displayed before the team harassed by hunger, rendered him an expression of gaiety that was a joy to see.

"This is better, señors," Estevan said, somewhat reassured. "I understand that my mules can spend the night here, and there's a proverb that says that a muleteer is comfortable wherever his mules can lodge. If it pleases you to leave me some food in order to sup alongside them, I believe I can answer to you for them until tomorrow. There are enough good devils whom custom has rendered familiar to arrieros, and whose malignity is limited to tangling the manes of horses or brushing their coats the wrong way. As for us, poor creatures that we are, they're content to pinch us tightly enough to make a mark that lasts for a week, in the form of a yellow patch that all the water in the world won't wash away; to give us cramps that turn the calf over the leg-bone; or to weigh heavily upon our stomach, laughing like lunatics. I feel man enough to risk all that, in exchange for the grace of God and the three bottles of Palamos wine that the señor captain has promised me."

"Here they are," I said to him, helping him to unload the vehicle, "as well as two soft loaves and a quarter of roast mutton. Now the cavalry and its train are well lodged, let's go up to the infantry's barracks."

We lit four torches and set forth up the main staircase, through the debris by which it was obstructed everywhere. Bascara was placed between Sergy and Boutraix, who were encouraging him with their speech and their example, making fear yield to vanity, so powerful in a Spanish soul. I confess that that incursion, devoid of peril, had something adventurous and eccentric about it nevertheless, by which my imagination was secretly flattered, and I can add that it presented difficulties appropriate to excite our ardor. Parts of the walls had collapsed here and there, and raised before us in twenty places as many accidental barricades, which it was necessary to go around or to climb over. Planks, joists and entire beams fallen from the upper parts of the carpentry, overlapped and intermingled in all directions on the broken steps, the shards of which were angular and bristled under our feet.

The old casements that had provided light to the vestibule and the steps had fallen a long time ago, torn away by storms, and we recognized their vestiges by the sound of panes already broken, which the soles of our shoes caused to crackle. An impetuous wind, charged with snow, introduced itself with horrible whistles through the space that they had abandoned when falling in one piece two or three centuries before; and the wild vegetation, whose seeds had been strewn there by the tempest added further to the clutter of the passage and the horror of that aspect. I thought, without saying so, that the heart of a soldier would be borne more easily and more naturally to attack a redoubt or assault a fortress.

We finally arrived in the landing of the first floor, and paused momentarily for breath.

To our left, a long, narrow and obscure corridor opened, the darkness of which our torches, gathered in the entrance, could not illuminate. In front of us was the door to the apartments—or rather, it was no longer there. That new invasion only gave us the difficulty of entering, torches in hand, a square room that must once have received men-at-arms. At least, we judged that by two rows of dilapidated benches that garnished all its faces, and a few trophies of common arms, half-eaten away by rust, which still hung from its walls.

We traversed it, making three or four broken lances roll under our feet, and as many blunderbuss barrels. It ended in a right-angle turn to a gallery much more extensive in length but of mediocre width, the right side of which was still pierced by empty windows like those of the stairway, and the remains of a rotten door-frame were hanging there.

The floor of that part of the building had been so degraded by the influence of the atmosphere and by rainfall that it had abandoned all its mortar, which was only prolonged toward the exterior wall in a narrow and ragged fringe. In that direction one sensed it flexing and springing back with a suspect elasticity, and the foot engaged in it as if in a compact dust that only asked to give way. At intervals, the less solid parts were beginning to scale in bizarre gaping patches, that a curious tread more reckless than mine would not have sounded with impunity.

I drew my comrades abruptly toward the left-hand wall, where the passage seemed less hazardous. It was garnished with paintings.

"As true as there is no God, there are paintings," said Boutraix. "Did the drunkard who engendered that uncouth arriero come this far?"

"No," replied Sergy, with a slightly bitter smile. "He went to sleep on the parvis of the church in Mattaro, because the wine he had drunk prevented him from going any further."

"I didn't ask for your opinion," said Boutraix, aiming his lorgnon at the dislocated and dusty frames that covered the wall in unequal lines at a multitude of capricious angles, without their being a single one that was not more or less perpendicular. "They are indeed paintings and portraits if I'm not mistaken. The whole family of the Las Sierras has posed in this death-trap."

Such vestiges of the art of remote centuries would have fixed our attention in other circumstances, but we were in too much of a hurry to ensure our little caravan of a safe and comfortable shelter to employ much time in the examination of those defaced canvases, which had almost disappeared under the damp black coating of the years. However, when we reached the last portraits, Sergy approached his torch to one of them with emotion, and grabbed me violently by the arm.

"Look! Look!" he cried. "That knight with the somber gaze whose forehead is shaded by a red plume must by Ghismondo himself! See how the painter has expressed marvelously in those still-youthful features the lassitudes of sensuality and the worries of crime. It's a sad thing to see!"

"The next portrait will compensate you," I replied, smiling at his hypothesis. "It's that of a woman, and it was better conserved, or closer to our eyes; you'll be ecstatic at the sight of the charms of Inès de Las Sierras, for one can also suppose that it's her. What can be made out is already of a nature to produce a vivid impression. What elegance there is in that slim waist! What a piquant attraction in that attitude! How the arms and that hand, so perfectly modeled, promise beauties in the ensemble that escape us! It's thus that Inès must have been."

"And it's thus that she was," said Sergy, drawing me toward him; "from this angle, I've just encountered her eyes. Oh, never has a more passionate expression spoken to the soul! Never has life descended more vibrantly from the brush. And if you want to follow that indication under the scales of the canvas all the way to the mild contour where the cheek curves around that charming mouth, if you can grasp like me the movement of the slightly disdainful lip, where one senses all the intoxication of amour respiring . . ."

"I can form an imperfect idea," I continued coldly, "of what might have been a pretty woman of the court of Charles Quint."

"Of the court of Charles Quint," said Sergy, lowering his head. "That's true."

"Wait, wait," said Boutraix, whose tall stature permitted him to reach with his hand the Gothic cartouche with which the interior ridge of the frame was decorated, and who had just passed his handkerchief over it several times. "There's a name here written in German or Hebrew, if it isn't Syriac or Bas-Breton, but the devil take whoever can decipher it. I'd like as much to explain the Koran."

Sergy uttered a cry of enthusiasm

"*Inès de Las Sierras!* Inès de Las Sierras!" he repeated, pressing my hands with a sort of frenzy. Read it!"

"Inès de Las Sierra," I replied. "That's really it—and those three mountains in sinople on a golden field must be the speaking armories of her family. It appears that the unfortunate woman really existed, and that she lived in this castle. But it will soon be time to seek a refuge there for ourselves. Aren't you disposed to penetrate further?"

"To me, Messieurs, to me!" cried Boutraix, who had preceded us by a few paces. "Here's a drawing room that won't make you regret the damp streets of Mattaro, a lodgment worth of a prince or a military steward. Señor Ghismondo liked his ease, and there's nothing to say about the distribution of the apartment. Oh, a superb barrack-room!"

The immense room was, in fact, better conserved than the rest. Only the back received the light from two very narrow casements, which the favor of their disposition had preserved from the degradations common to the whole building. Its printed leather hangings and large antique armchairs had a certain air of magnificence, which their antiquity rendered even more imposing. The fireplace, of colossal proportions, which opened its vast flanks in the wall to the left, seemed to have been built for the evenings of giants, and the wood of demolition scattered on the staircase would have furnished us with a joyful fire for hundreds of nights similar to the one that was about to pass. A round table, which was only a few feet away from it, reminded us involuntarily of the impious feats of Ghismondo, and I admit willingly that I did not look at it without a slight frisson.

We required several trips to supply us with the necessary wood and to transport our provisions and our luggage, the economy of which the day's torrential downpour might have seriously compromised. Fortunately, everything was safe and sound, and even the costumes of Bascara's troupe, extended before the blazing fire on the backs of the armchairs, shone in our eyes with the artificial luster and belated freshness lent to them by the fake splendor of spangles.

It is true that Ghismondo's dining room, illuminated then by ten ardent torches skillfully fitted to ten old candlesticks was certainly better illuminated than the theater of a little town in Catalonia had ever been in living memory. Only the most distant part, the one that approached the gallery of paintings, by which we had entered, had not lost all of its darkness. One might have thought that it had gathered there deliberately in order to establish a mysterious barrier between us and profane vulgarity. It was the darkness visible of the poet.

"I have no doubt," I said, while occupying myself with my companions with the preparations for the meal, "that this will furnish the credulity of the inhabitants of the plain with a new pretext. It's the hour when Ghismondo returns every year to sit down at his infernal banquet, and the light that those casements must spread outside announces nothing less than a demonic feast. Perhaps it's on a similar circumstance that Estevan's legend is founded."

"Add to that" said Boutraix, "that the fantasy of representing that scene *au naturel* might have come to adventurers of good humor, and it's not impossible that the arriero's father really did witnesses a comedy of that kind. We're delightfully equipped to recommence it," he continued, lifting the costumes of the traveling troupe one by one. "Here's a knight's costume that seems tailored for the captain; I would recall feature for feature the intrepid squire of the damned soul, who was, apparently, good looking fellow; and this dainty costume, which will heighten the slightly languorous physiognomy of the handsome Sergy, will easily give him the more seductive air of a page. Agree that the invention is fortunate, and that it promises us a night of mad gaiety!"

While Boutraix was speaking he had disguised himself from top to toe, and we imitated him, laughing, for there is nothing more contagious than an extravagance between young brains. However, we had taken the precaution of conserving our swords and pistols, which, at a date close to their fabrication, did not contrast in too garish a manner without disguises. The heroes of Ghismondo's gallery, if they had suddenly descended from their Gothic canvases, would not have found themselves very out of place in their hereditary manse.

"And the beautiful Inès!" cried Boutraix. "You haven't thought of her! Would Señor Bascara, whom nature has dressed with external gifts of which the Graces would have been jealous, care to take on that role, for this one time only, at the general request of the public?"

"Messieurs," Bascara replied, "I lend myself willingly to pleasantries that do not interest the salvation of my soul, but this one is of a genre that does not permit me to take part in it. You will perhaps see, to your great distress, that one does not brave the powers of Hell with impunity. Rejoice as seems good to you, since grace has not touched you; but I attest to you that I renounce loudly these Satanic joys, and that I only request to escape them, in order to render myself a monk in some good house of the Lord. Only grant me, as your brother in Jesus Christ, whose name be praised forever, your permission to spend the night in this armchair, with some refection to sustain my body, and the liberty to pray."

"Well," said Boutraix, "that magnificent declamatory speech merits an entire goose and two flagons of the best. Keep your seat, my friend; eat, drink, pray and sleep. You'll never be only a fool! In any case," he added, sitting down and refilling his glass, "Inès only arrives at dessert—and I certainly hope that she'll come."

"God preserve us from that!" said Bascara.

I took my place opposite the fire, with the squire to my right and the page to my left. Facing me, Inès place remained vacant. I paraded a gaze around the table and, either by virtue of preoccupation or mental weakness, I also found that the amusement had something serious about it, which clutched my heart.

Sergy, who was more avid than me for romantic impressions, seemed even more emotional. Boutraix was drinking.

"How is it," said Sergy, that these solemn ideas of which philosophy makes a game never entirely lose their empire over the firmest and the most enlightened minds? Does human nature have a secret need to rise up as far as the marvelous in order to enter into possession of some privilege that once enraptured it, and which forms the most noble part of its essence?"

"On my honor," replied Boutraix, "I wouldn't believe in that supposition, even if you enunciated it in terms clear enough for me to be able to understand it. The effect of which you speak results quite simply from an old habit of the organs of the brain, which has retained, like a kind of soft wax hardened by time, the stupid impressions that our mothers and our nurses have inculcated in us in our infancy, and that is admirably explained by Voltaire in a superb books that I engage you to read when you have the leisure. To think otherwise is to reduce oneself to the level of that fellow who has been muttering the *Benedictus* for a quarter of an hour over his ration before daring to hazard putting his teeth into it."

Sergy persisted. Boutraix defended his terrain foot by foot, retrenching himself, as usual, behind his irresistible arguments: prejudice, superstition and fanaticism. I had never seen him so tenacious and so scornful in metaphysical combat; but the conversation did not remain for long at the height of those sublime regions of intelligence, for the wine was heady, and we were drinking it copiously, like people who have nothing better to do. It was midnight on our watches, and nearly one bottle more, when we all cried, in a transport of joy, as if that conviction had freed us from a hidden anxiety:

"Midnight, Messieurs, midnight! And Inès de Las Sierras has not come!"

The unanimity that we had encountered in such a puerile observation drew a long burst of laughter from us.

"Head and death!" said Boutraix, lifting himself up on two winy legs, the oscillation of which he tried to conceal beneath an air of nonchalance and abandon. "Although that beauty is in default at our joyous union, the chivalric gallantry of which we make profession forbid us to forget her. I raise this glass of red to the health of the demoiselle Inès de Las Sierras and her imminent deliverance!"

"To Inès de Las Sierras!" cried Sergy.

"To Inès de Las Sierras!" I repeated, approaching my half-empty glass to their already full glasses.

"Here I am!" cried a voice that came from the gallery of paintings.

"What!" said Boutraix, sitting down again. "The joke isn't bad, but who played it?"

I darted a glance behind me. Bascara, very pale, was clinging to the bars of my armchair.

"That rogue of a carter," I replied, "whom the Palamos wine has made merry."

"Here I am! Here I am!" repeated the voice. "Salut and good humor to the guests of Ghismondo's castle!"

"It's a woman's voice and a young woman," said Sergy, getting to his feet with a noble and gracious assurance.

At the same instant we discerned in the least illuminated part of the room, a white phantom that was running toward us with an incredible rapidity, and which, when it came within range of us, let its shroud fall. It passed between us, for we were standing up, our hands on the hilts of our swords, and sat down in Inès' place.

"Here I am!" said the phantom, uttering a long sigh and throwing to the right and the left the tresses of her long black hair, negligently retained by a few knots of poppy-red ribbon. No more accomplished beauty had ever struck my eyes.

"It's a woman, in fact," I said, in a low voice, "and since it's agreed between us that nothing can happen here that isn't perfectly natural, we have no advice to take except that of French politeness. What follows will explain the mystery, if it can be explained."

We took our places again, and we served the unknown woman, who seemed to be pressed by hunger. She ate and drank without speaking. A few minutes later, she had forgotten us completely, and each of the persons in that bizarre scene seemed isolated within himself, motionless and mute, as if struck by the petrifying wand of a fay.

Bascara had fallen at my side and I might have thought that he had died of terror if I had not been reassured by the movement of his palpitating hands, which came together convulsively in a sign of prayer.

Boutraix did not allow a breath to escape; a profound expression of annihilation had replaced his Bacchic audacity, and the brilliant vermilion of intoxication, which had burst forth a minute before on his assured forehead, had changed into a mortal pallor.

The sentiment that dominated Sergy had enchained his thought no less forcefully, but it was far less mild, to judge by his gaze. His eyes, fixed on the apparition with all the fire of amour, appeared to be striving to retain it, like those of a sleeping man who fears losing by awakening the irreparable charm of a beautiful dream—and it must be admitted that the illusion in question was worth the trouble of being conserved with care, for nature entire perhaps did not offer any living beauty that merited being put in its place. I beg you to believe that I am not exaggerating.

The stranger was no more than twenty years old, but passions, misfortune—or death—had imprinted on her features the strange and immutable perfection and eternal regularity that the chisel of the ancients has consecrated in the type of the gods. Nothing remained in that physiognomy that belonged to the earth, nothing that could dread there the offense of a comparison.

That was the cold judgment of my reason, pre-armed since that time against the mad surprises of amour, and it dispenses me from a depiction that each of you is free to provide at the whom of his imagination. If you contrive to imagine something that approaches the reality, you will be a thousand times further on than all the artifices of speech, the pen and the brush. Only—and it is necessary for the guarantee of my impartiality—allow to run over that vast and polished forehead an oblique streak, extremely light, which dies away an inch above the eyebrow, and in the divine gaze of which those large blue eyes spread the ineffable light, between lashes as black as jet, express if you can something vague and indecisive, like the disturbance of an anxious doubt seeking to explain itself. They are the imperfections of my model, and I can answer for the fact that Sergy had not perceived them.

What struck me most, however, when I was capable of occupying myself with such details, was the attire of our mysterious stranger. I had no doubt that I had seen it somewhere, not long ago, and I did not take long to remember that it was in the portrait of Inès. It seemed borrowed, like ours, from the store of a costumer skillful in scene-setting, but it was not as fresh. Her dress of green damask, still rich, but soft and desiccated, with a few withered ribbons attached here and there, must have belonged to the wardrobe of a woman dead for more than a century, and I thought, tremulously, that on touching it, the cold humidity of the tomb might be found there—but I rejected that idea immediately, unworthy of a rational mind, and I had returned fully to the free exercise of my faculties when, with an enchanting accent, the newcomer finally broke the silence.

"Well, noble knights," she said, allowing a reproachful smile to wander over her lips, "have I had the misfortune of troubling the pleasures of this agreeable soirée? You were only thinking when I arrived of delivering yourselves to the pleasure of being together, and when I came your joyous laughter was bursting forth to wake all the night-birds that have built their nests in the paneling of the castle. Since when has the presence of a young woman in whom the city and the court have found a few feeble charms alarmed gaiety? Has the world changed so much since I left it?"

"Pardon, Madame," replied Sergy. "So many attractions were made to surprise us, and admiration is mute, like fear."

"I'm grateful to my friend for that explanation," I said, immediately. "The sentiments that your sight inspires cannot be expressed in words. As for your visit, it was bound to excite a temporary astonishment in us, from which we have taken some time to recover. You know that nothing could announce it to us in these ruins, which lost their inhabitants a long time ago, and this wild place, the advanced hour of the night and the unaccustomed disorder of the elements, did not permit us to hope for it. You would doubtless be welcome, Madame, everywhere you deigned to appear, but we are waiting respectfully, in order to render you the honors that we owe you, for you to be kind enough to tell us to whom we have the honor of speaking."

"My name?" she replied, sharply. "Don't you know it? God is my witness that I only came in response to your appeal."

"To our appeal!" said Boutraix, stammering and covering his face with his hands.

"In truth," she continued, smiling, "and I am too conscious of propriety to act otherwise. I am Inès de Las Sierras."

"Inès de Las Sierras!" cried Boutraix, more consternated than if he had seen a thunderbolt fall beside him. "O eternal justice!"

I stared at him. I searched in vain in his face for anything that might betray pretence and deceit.

"Madame," I said, affecting a little more calm than I really possessed, "the disguises under which you have found us, which are perhaps rather unseemly for this holy day, hide nevertheless men inaccessible to fear. Whatever your name is, and whatever the motive is for which you have disguised yourself, you can expect from us a discreet and respectful hospitality;

we will lend ourselves willingly to recognizing in you Inès de Las Sierras, if that whim, authorized by the circumstances, amuses your imagination, and so much beauty gives you the right to represent yourself with more splendor than she could ever have had; that is the surest of all illusions, but we beg you to be persuaded that that confession, which does not cost our courtesy anything, could not have been extracted from our credulity."

"I am far from demanding such an effort," Inès replied, with dignity, "but who can contest me the title that I take in the house of my forefathers? Oh," she continued, becoming gradually more animated, "I have paid dearly enough for my first sin to believe the vengeance of God satisfied by that expiation, but may the belated indulgence that I await from him, and in which I place my only hope, abandon me forever to the torments that devour me if the name of Inès de Las Sierras is not my name! I am Inès de Las Sierras, the culpable and unfortunate Inès. What interest could I have in stealing a name that I have so much interest in hiding? And by what right do you reject the confession, already painful enough, of an unfortunate woman whose fate only demands pity?"

She allowed a few tears to escape, and Sergy drew closer to her with an ever-increasing emotion, while Boutraix, whose head had been supported for some by his arms, with their elbows on the table, let it fall heavily.

"Here, Señor," she said, taking a golden bracelet half-corroded by the years from her arm and throwing it down disdainfully before me, "is my mother's last present, the only jewel of her heritage that remains to me in the misery and the opprobrium of my life. See whether I am, in fact, Inès de Las Sierras, or a vile adventuress, consecrated by the baseness of her birth to the amusements of the populace."

The three mountains in sinople were encrusted there in fine emeralds, and the name Las Sierras, engraved in old letters, could be read there distinctly beneath the rust of time.

174

I picked up the bracelet respectfully and I presented it to her, bowing deeply. In the state of excitement that her mind had reached, she did not notice me.

"If you require other proofs," she went on, in a sort of delirium, "has the rumor of my misfortunes not reached as far as you? Look," she added, detaching the clasp of her dress and showing us a scar on her breast, "this is where the dagger struck me!"

"Woe! Woe!" cried Boutraix, raising his head and throwing it back, in an inexpressible disorder, on to the back of his armchair.

"Men! Men!" said Inès, in a tone of bitter scorn. "They know how to kill women, but the sight of their wounds frightens them!"

The movement, mingled with modesty and compassion, which she made to draw the flaps of her parted dress together and hide her breast from Boutraix's frightened eyes delivered the other to Sergy's, whose emotion was at its peak, and I understood his intoxication too well to condemn it.

A new silence was established then, longer, more absolute and sadder than the first. Abandoned, each in our own direction, to our particular preoccupations, Boutraix to an unreflective terror that had become incapable of reasoning, Sergy to the interior enjoyment of a nascent amour, the object of which realized the favorite dreams of his foolish imagination, and me to the meditation of the elevated mysteries on which I dreaded having formed reckless opinions in the past, we must have resembled the petrified figures of Oriental tales whom death has seized in the midst of life, and whose featured reflect forever the expression of the fleeting sentiment in which it has surprised them.

Inès' physiognomy seemed much more animated; but through the multitude of mobile aspects that an inexplicable enchainment of ideas made it adopt in turn, as if under the empire of a dream, it would have been impossible to determine the one that dominated her when she resumed speaking, while laughing.

"I don't remember," she said, "what I asked you to explain to me a little while ago, but you know that my thought cannot suffer the conversation of men since a hand that I loved, and which murdered me, threw me among the dead. Take pity, I beg you, on the weakness of an intelligence that is resuscitating, and forgive me for having forgotten for too long that I have not yet done honor to the greeting that you gave me when I came in. Messieurs," she added, standing up with an infinite grace and presenting her glass to us, "Inès de Las Sierras salutes you in her turn. To you, noble knight! May Heaven be favorable to your enterprises! To you, melancholy squire, whose natural gaiety is afflicted by some secret trouble! May days more propitious than this one render you an unalloyed serenity! To you, handsome page, whose tender languor announces a soul preoccupied by sweeter cares! May the fortunate woman who has fixed your amour respond to it with an amour worthy of you, and if you do not love as yet, may you soon love a beauty who loves you! To you, my lords!"

"Oh, I love, and I love forever!" cried Sergy. "Who could have seen you and not love you? To Inès de Las Sierras! To the beautiful Inès!"

"To Inès de Las Sierras!" I repeated, rising from my armchair.

"To Inès de Las Sierras!" murmured Boutraix, without changing place; and for the first time in his life he pronounced a solemn toast without drinking.

"To you all!" said Inès, approaching her glass to her mouth for a second time, but without draining it.

Sergy seized it and plunged an ardent lip into it. I don't know why, but I would have liked to stop him, as if I thought that he might be drinking death therefrom.

As for Boutraix, he had fallen back into a kind of reflective stupor that absorbed all of his soul.

"That's good," said Inès, throwing one of her arms around Sergy's neck, and with the other, placing over his heart for a time a hand as incendiary as the one of which Estevan's legend had spoken. "This soirée is nicer and more charming than any of those of which I have conserved the memory. We're all so cheerful and so happy! Don't you think, Señor Squire, that we only lack here the charm of music?"

"Oh!" said Boutraux, who was almost incapable of articulating anything else. "Will she sing?"

"Sing! Sing!" replied Sergy, passing his quivering fingers through Inès' hair. "It's your Sergy who is begging you."

"I'd like that," Inès replied, "but the damp in the cellars must have spoiled my voice, which was once beautiful and pure, and in any case, I only know sad songs, hardly worthy of a Bacchic tertulia, in which only joyful songs ought to resonate. Wait!" she continued, raising her celestial eyes toward the vault and uttering enchanting sounds by way of a prelude. "This is the ballad of *Nina Matada*, which will be new for you as for me, for I shall compose it while singing."

No one could imagine how much the animated movement of the improvisation lent to the seductions of an inspired voice. Woe betide the man who is writing his thoughts coldly, elaborated, discussed and tested by reflection and by time. He will never move a soul in its most secret sympathies. To witness the birth of a great conception, to see it launch forth from the genius of the artist, like Minerva from the head of Jupiter, to feel himself borne away in his flight through the unknown regions of the imagination on the wings of eloquence, poetry and music, is the most vivid of enjoyments that have been given to our imperfect nature; it is the only one that approaches on earth the divinity from which it takes its origin.

What I have just said to you is what I experienced at Inès' first notes. What I experienced a little later there are no terms in any language that can express. The two essences of my being were distinctly separated in my thought: one, inert and vulgar, whose material weight retained it fixed in one of Ghismondo's armchairs; the other already transformed, which rose into the heavens with Inès' words, and which received, at their behest, all the impressions of a new life, inexhaustible in sensualities. Be fully convinced that if some unfortunate genius has doubted the existence of that eternal principle, whose imperishable life is enchained for a time in the bonds of our fleeting life, and which is called the soul, it is because he had never heard Inès sing, or a woman who sang like her.

My organs, as you know, do not refuse that genre of emotion, but I am far from believing them to be delicate enough to submit to all of its power. It was different for Sergy, whose entire organization was that of a soul scarcely captive, only held to humanity by a fragile bond, ever ready to be released when he wanted to free himself therefrom. Sergy cried, Sergy wept. Sergy was no longer in himself, and when Inès, transported, was about to lose herself in inspirations even more sublime than anything that we had heard, she seemed to appeal to him with a smile.

Boutraix had woken up slightly from his bleak dejection and fixed two wide attentive eyes of Inès, in which the expression of an astonished pleasure had replaced momentarily that of fear.

Bascara had not changed position, but the sweet sensations of the virtuosa were beginning to triumph over his dread as a man of the people. He raised from time to time a face in which admiration was disputing with fear, and sighed with ecstasy or desire.

A cry of enthusiasm succeeded Inès' song. She poured a round of drinks and clinked glasses deliberately with Boutraix. He withdrew his with an ill-assured hand, watched me drink, and then drank.

I refilled the glasses, and I saluted Inès.

"Alas," she said, "I can't sing any longer, or this hall has betrayed my voice. Once, there was not an atom of air that did not respond to me and did not lend me a harmony. Nature no longer has for me the omnipotent harmonies that I interrogated, to which I listened, and which merged with my words when I was happy and beloved. Oh, Sergy," she continued, gazing at him tenderly, "it's necessary to be loved to sing!"

"Loved!" cried Sergy, covering her hand with kisses. "Adored, Inès, idolized like a goddess! If it only requires the unreserved sacrifice of a heart, of a soul, of an eternity, to inspire your genius, sing, Inès, sing again, sing forever!"

"I also danced," she said, leaning her head languidly on Sergy's shoulder, "but how can one dance without instruments? Marvel!" she added, suddenly. "Some favorable demon has slipped castanets into my belt." And she detached them, laughing

"Irrevocable day of damnation," said Boutraix, "now you have come! The mystery of mysteries is accomplished! The last judgment is nigh! She's going to dance!"

While Boutraix finished speaking, Inès had risen to her feet and begun with grave and slowly measured steps, in which the majesty of her figure and the nobility of her attitudes were deployed with an imposing grace. As she changed place and showed herself under new aspects, our imagination was astonished, as if another beautiful woman had appeared to our gaze, so much was she able to exceed herself in the inexhaustible variety of her poses and her movements.

Thus, by means of rapid transitions, we had seen her pass from a serious dignity to the modest transports of pleasure, which were then animated by the soft languors of sensuality, and then the delirium of joy, and then I know not what ecstasy even more delirious, which has no name; then she disappeared into the distant darkness of the immense hall, and the sound of castanets grew fainter in proportion to her distance, and diminished, always diminished, until it ceased to be audible in ceasing to be visible; then it came back from afar, augmenting gradually, and bursting forth when she suddenly reappeared under torrents of light in the place where she was least expected; and then she drew nearer to us, to the point of brushing us with her dress and clicking her reawakened castanets with a deafening volubility, which chattered like crickets, casting here and there through their monotonous racket a few piercing but tender cries, which penetrated the soul.

Afterwards, she drew away again, half-plunging into the shadow. Appearing and disappearing by turns, fleeing deliberately under our eyes and seeking to make herself visible. Then she was no longer visible and no longer audible, nothing could any longer be heard but a distant and plaintive note like the sigh of a dying young woman, and we remained bewildered, palpitating with admiration and dread, waiting for the moment when her veil, borne away by the movement of the dance, came to float and brighten in the light of the torches, when her voice would alert us to her return with a cry of joy, to which we would respond involuntarily because it would cause to vibrate within us a multitude of hidden harmonies.

Then she came back, and spun about her axis like a flower detached by the wind from its stem, launched herself from the floor as if it depended on her to quit it forever; descended upon it as if it depended on her not to touch it, not bounding on the ground; you would have thought that she had only to spring up therefrom, and that a mysterious decree of her destiny had forbidden her to touch it except to flee it. And her head, tilted with the expression of a caressant impatience, and her arms, gracefully curved in a sign of appeal and prayer, appeared to be imploring us to retain her. Sergy yielded, as I was about to yield, to that imperious attraction, and enveloped her in his.

"Stay," he said to her, "or I shall die."

"I'm leaving," she replied, "and I shall die if you don't come. Soul of Inès, will you not come?"

She fell, half-sitting, on to Sergy's armchair, her hands knotted around his neck, and this time, she had definitely ceased to see us.

"Listen, Sergy," Inès continued. "As you leave this apartment you'll see to your right a long, narrow, obscure corridor." (I had noticed it as we came in.) "Follow it for a long time, with precaution, over the broken paving-stones. March, keep marching! Don't be deterred by the infinite detours that will be presented to your sight; there's no means of going astray. Go down the steps by which it descends from floor to floor toward the cellars. Some are missing but amour easily overcomes the obstacles that have not held back, in order to come to find you, the footsteps of a weak woman. March, keep marching! You'll arrive thus at a winding stairway, even more dilapidated than the rest, but where I will guide you, for you'll find me up above. Don't worry about my owls, for they've been my only friends for a long time. The owls understand my voice, and through the vents of the sepulcher I inhabit, I'll send them back to the crenellations with all their chicks. March, keep marching! But come, and don't be long. Will you come?"

"Yes, I'll come!" cried Sergy. "Oh, rather eternal death than not to follow you everywhere!"

"Who loves me, follow me," replied Inès, uttering a burst of alarming laughter.

At the same moment, she picked up her shroud, and we no longer saw her. The obscurity of the distant parts of the room had already hidden her from us, forever.

I threw myself in front of Sergy and I seized him forcefully. Boutraix, returned to himself by his comrade's peril, had come to help me. Even Bascara rose to his feet.

"Monsieur," I said to Sergy. "As your elder, as your senior officer, as your friend, as your captain, I forbid you to take another step! Don't you see, wretch, that you're responsible here for all our lives? Don't you see that that woman—too seductive, alas—is only the magical instrument of which a troop of bandits hidden in this frightful lair is making use in order to separate us and doom us? Oh, if you were alone and free to dispose of yourself, I would understand your deadly aberration and could only feel sorry for you; Inès has everything necessary to justify such a sacrifice. But think that they hope to reduce us by isolating us and that if we must die here we ought to die otherwise than in a crude ambush, selling our lives dearly to the murderers! Sergy, you belong to us above all; you shall not quit us!"

Sergy, whose reason appeared to be combated by a host of contrary sentiments, stared at me, and fell devoid of strength on to his armchair.

"To us now, Messieurs," I continued, turning the door with difficulty on its rusted hinges. Let's pile up this old furniture in order to make a rampart. While it shakes under an almost infallible attack, we'll have time to put ourselves on guard, and hold out arms ready. We're in a condition to resist twenty brigands, and I doubt that there are as many here.

"I doubt it also," said Boutraix, when those precautions were taken and found ourselves around the table again, near to which Bascara had finally sat down, slightly reassured by our noble air of resolution. "The measures that the captain has just taken are advised by prudence, and the most intrepid warrior does nothing unworthy of his bravery in putting himself in shelter from surprises, but the idea that he has formed of this castle seems to me to be devoid of all plausibility; a band of scoundrels couldn't occupy with impunity, in the time we're living in, under the terror of our arms and in the midst of the indefatigable activity of our police, the ruins of an old building half a league from a big city. That's more impossible than all those whose possibility we denied a little while ago."

"Really!" I said to him. "Do you think, Boutraix, that Voltaire and Piron would share that opinion?"

"Captain," he replied, with a cold dignity of which I would not have thought him capable, doubtless inspired in him by the nature of the new ideas to which his mind was beginning to open, "the ignorance and presumption of my judgments merited that irony, and I'm not offended by it. I imagine that Voltaire and Piron could scarcely explain any better than me what happened just now before our eyes, but, whatever that event was and whatever might follow it, you'll permit me to think that the enemies with which we're dealing now have no need to find doors open."

"Add to that," said Bascara, "that a similar expedient is unworthy of the most maladroit thrives. Sending you that Inès, so well dressed, whom you regard as their accomplice, would excite your attention, not distract it. Do you suppose that they could have thought they would find a man mad enough—I beg Señor Sergy's pardon—to follow a phantom into a tomb? And if it was impossible to count on such a result, what would be the point of that prodigious apparition, which could only have served to warn you? Would it not have been more natural to let you pass the first part of the night in the blindness of a foolish confidence and wait for the moment when, surprised by sleep or wine, you would only give them the trouble of cutting your throats without peril, if your remains, rather light and more likely to betray them than to enrich them, had offered a bait tempting to their cupidity? Personally, I only see, in that explanation, the effort of an incredulous mind obstinate against the evidence, which would rather believe in the calculations of a false prudence than the miracles of God."

"Very well," I said. "One could not reason better, and I revert to your opinion. But if that explanation is no good, are you so sure that I don't have another in reserve? You seem rested enough now to hear it, and the perfect calm that has succeeded your terrors, so promptly dissipated, will furnish me, if necessary, with one proof more. You are an actor, Señor Bascara, and a very good actor, I can testify; you have proven it better tonight than you have ever done in Gironne. That marvelous singer, that incomparable dancer, who you have probably held in reserve for the opening of a theater in Barcelona, might you not know her? Might it not have been piquant to make a trial of her in an admirably directed scene, on the irritable sensibility of three passionate amateurs, whose enthusiasm might serve to guarantee your future success? Might your Spanish vanity not be amused at the same time, with too much complaisance, by the hope of inspiring some emotion of anxiety and dread in three French officers? What do you say to that, Monsieur?"

"Aha!" said Boutraix, smiling and finishing emptying his glass, for he was only seeking a pretext to become a great philosopher once again, as before. "What do you say to that, practical joker?"

Sergy, who had not emerged until then from his pensive dejection, raised a less sad and less distraught gaze toward us. The idea of rediscovering Inès alive on earth had brought some mollification to his dolor; he glimpsed the possibility of recalling her to our midst and seeing her again. He was listening.

Bascara shrugged his shoulders.

"Permit me," I continued, taking his hand. "That pleas-antry isn't in bad enough taste to irritate you, and we've had too much pleasure in it to deem you criminal. I will even add, without fear of being belied by my comrades, that each of us would gladly have paid for his place at the performance; but now the comedy has been played and you owe us the secret, as honest men whom one does not trick with impunity, and in whom a man like you is fortunate to find friends. Explain yourself frankly, let's destroy these ridiculous barricades, and have Inès come back. I warn you that any reticence prolonged beyond the limits that our politeness has set would become a bloody insult, for which you would pay dearly. Why are you not responding?"

"Because it's futile to respond," said Bascara. "A single moment of reflection would have spared you the trouble of interrogating me. I'm relying on you for that."

"Really, Monsieur? Again? It seems to me that I have been precise enough."

"Precision, so be it," replied Bascara. "But plausibility, where is that? Listen. Is it not true that you encountered me this morning in Estevan's vehicle? Is it not true that you took your places beside me? Is it not true that I could not have been expecting you? Is it not true that I have not quit you for a moment since?"

"That's true," said Sergy.

"That's true," said Boutraix.

"Let's continue," said Bascara. "The unexpected storm that surprised us as we emerged from Gironne—could I have foreseen that? Had I foreseen that we wouldn't arrive in Barcelona today? Had I foreseen that the inn in Mattaro would be full? Had I foreseen that you would form the temeritous project of sleeping in Ghismondo's castle, the mere sight of which makes the hair of travelers stand on end? Did I not combat that resolution with all my strength, and have I come here other than by virtually yielding to force?"

"That's true," said Boutraix.

"That's true," said Sergy.

"Wait," said Bascara. "With what design would I have organized this prodigious intrigue? With the design of trying out on three officers if the Gironne garrison the debut of a cantatrice and dancer—if it pleases you to call her that I won't oppose it—like the one you have just seen? Truly, Señors, you do too much honor to the munificence of a poor provincial

185

stage-manager in supposing that he gives such performances gratis. Oh, if I had an actress like Inès—may the Lord's mercy descend upon her—I would refrain carefully from exposing her to catch a mortal chill under the damp vaults of this accursed castle, or a sprained ankle in the ruins. I would even refrain from taking her to Barcelona, where there is no water to drink since the war, when she could make my fortune in a season in Milan or at the Paris Opéra. What am I saying, in a season? In a single evening, in a single aria, in a single step! Could La Pedrina of Seville herself, of whom there has been so much talk, although she only appeared once, and who woke up the next morning, it is said, with the treasures of a crown, even get close to her? A singer, you have heard her! A dancer who has not touched the parquet for an instant with her feet!"

"That's true," said Sergy and Boutraix, simultaneously.

"One more word," added Bascara. "My sudden calmness has surprised you, and why not, since it has astonished me? I understand it now. The impatience with which Inès withdrew announced that the moment of the apparition has finished, and that idea has soothed my mind. As for the reason why the three damned souls have not appeared, as usual, that is a more difficult question, but in which I take no other interest than that of Christian charity. It concerns more particularly, in all appearance, those who represented them."

"In that case," said Boutraix, "may God take pity on us!"

"A strange mystery," I cried, striking the table with my fist, "for I yield to that reasoning. What is it, then, I ask you, that we saw a little while ago?"

"What men very rarely see in this life," replied Bascara, his rosary in his hand, "and what a great many men will not see in the other—a soul in purgatory."

"Messieurs," I said, with sufficient firmness, "there is a secret here that no human intelligence can penetrate. It is doubtless hidden under some natural fact, the explanation of which would draw a smile from us, but which escapes the range of our reason. At any rate, it is important not to lend the authority of our testimony to superstitions as unworthy of Christianity as if philosophy. It is important above all not to compromise the honor of three French officers in the relation of a scene that is, I agree, very extraordinary, but the enigma of which, developed sooner or later, risks delivering us all to public derision. I swear on my honor, and I expect the same oath from you, never to speak in my entire life about what has happened tonight, so long as the causes of that bizarre event are not clearly known to me."

"We swear also," said Sergy and Boutraix.

"I take divine Jesus as my witness," said Bascara, "by the faith that I have in his holy Nativity, the glorious commemoration of which is being celebrated at the present moment, only to speak about it to my confessor, under the seal of the sacrament of penitence, and in order that the name of the Lord should be celebrated throughout the centuries."

"Amen," said Boutraix, embracing him with a sincere effusion. "I beg you, my dear brother, not to forget me in your prayers, for unfortunately, I no longer know mine."

The night was advancing. An unquiet slumber came to surprise us one by one. I have no need to tell you by what dreams it was agitated.

The sun finally rose in a sky purer than we could have hoped for the previous day, and without saying a single word we reached Barcelona, where we arrived early.

✳

"And afterwards?" said Anastase.

"Afterwards? What do you mean by that, pray? Is the tale not finished?

"I don't know why, but it seems to me that something is still lacking," said Eudoxie.

"What do you want me to say? Two days later we returned to Gironne, where we awaited an order to leave for the regiment. The reverses of the grand armée forced the emperor to gather the elite of his troops in the north. I found myself there with Boutraix, who had become devout since he had spoken in person to a soul in purgatory, and with Sergy, who had not changed amour since he had fallen in love with a phantom. At the first fire of the battle of Lutzen Sergy was beside me. He suddenly folded up and fell head first, struck by a mortal bullet, over the neck of my horse.

"'Inès,' he murmured. 'I'm going to join her . . .' And he rendered his last sigh.

"A few months later the army reentered France, where futile prodigies of valor delayed, without preventing it, the inevitable fall of the Empire. Peace was declared, and a large number of officers laid down their arms forever. Boutraix went into a cloister, and I believe that he's still there. I retired to the heritage of my forefathers, which I have no desire to quit. That's all."

"That's not," said Anastase sulkily, "the whole story of Inès. You must know more about it."

"The story is complete in its genre," I replied. "You asked me for a ghost story, and it's the story of a ghost that I've told you, or there never was one. Any other denouement would be vicious in my narrative, for it would change its nature."

"A bad defeat," said the substitute magistrate. "You're trying to avoid an explanation by means of a subtlety. Let's reason a little, if you please, for logic applies everywhere, even in ghost stories. You made a solemn engagement with your comrades to maintain an absolute silence regarding the Christmas night so long as the apparition was not clearly explained to you; you even submitted to that obligation by oath, and I remember it clearly, for I was only asleep at the commencement of the narration—which, by the way, dragged on somewhat in length. Now, you could only have been disengaged from that species of syntallagmatic contract—that is the legal term—by the conditional clarification on which it was founded, unless you suppose yourself to have been freed from it by the death of one of the contractants and the entry into profession of the other, which can be considered, in truth, as a kind of death; but I warn you that that declinatory plea cannot be admitted in the circumstances, which I can prove to you at your leisure if you persist in your conclusions. Thus, you are in a flagrant case of infraction of the contracted engagement if the condition resolved has not been accomplished."

"I beg you, Monsieur Substitute," I replied, "to spare me that litigation, never having had one in my life. I'm perfectly in regulation regarding the terms of my contract, which I could have refrained from reporting if I had not wanted to say everything. But the story that is being requested is another story; the clock is marking midnight and more; will you permit me to leave the key to the logogriph suspended for a month, like that of the old *Mercure de France*?"

"I adjudge," said the substitute, "that there might be reason to adjourn it, if it is agreeable to the ladies."

"Between now and then, your imagination can strive to search for the explanation that I promised. I have warned you, however, that this is a true story from beginning to end, and that there is nothing in what I am reporting to you of trickery, mystification, or thieves."

"Nor a ghost?" said Euidocie.

"Nor a ghost," I replied, getting up and taking my hat.

"Too bad, in truth!" said Anastase.

✳

"But if it wasn't a veritable apparition," said Anastase, as soon as I had sat down, "tell us what it was. I've been thinking about it for a month without finding a rational explanation for your story."

"Me neither," said Eudoxie.

"I haven't had the time to think about it," said the substitute, "but as far as I remember, it drew furiously upon the fantastic."

"There was, however, nothing more natural," I replied, "and everyone has head recounted, or seen with their own eyes, things much more extraordinary than those that it remains for me to tell you, if you're disposed to listen to me again."

The circle tightened slightly, for in the long evenings in a small town, people have nothing better to do than to lend an ear to fantastic tales while awaiting slumber. I entered into the matter.

I told you that the peace had been made, that Sergy was dead, that Boutraix was a monk, and that I was nothing more than a petty landowner at his ease. The accumulation of my income had almost rendered me opulent, and a heritage that arrived in addition enriched me with a ridiculous superfluity. I resolved to spend it on travel for education and pleasure, and I hesitated briefly over the countries I ought to visit, but it was only a feint of my reason, which was struggling against my heart. My heart was calling me back to Barcelona, and that romance would form, if this were the place for it, an accessory much longer than the principal one. What is certain is that a letter from Pablo de Clauza, the dearest of the friends that I had left in Catalonia, finished making up my mind. Pablo was marrying Léonore. Léonore was the sister of Estelle, and

Estelle, of whom I shall have little to say, was the heroine of the romance that I shall not relate to you.

I arrived too late for the wedding; it had taken place three days before, but the celebrations were continuing, as was customary, in fêtes that are sometimes prolonged beyond the honeymoon. It could not be otherwise in Pablo's family; he was worthy of being loved by a perfectly lovable woman, and is as happy today as he hoped to be then. That is seen from time to time, but it is unnecessary to be proud of it.

Estelle welcomed me as a regretted friend that one desired to see again, but my relationship with her had not given me reason to expect any more than that, especially after two years of absence, for this was happening in 1814, in the interval of the brief European peace that separated the first Restoration from the twentieth of March.

"We have dined at a better hour than usual," said Pablo as he came into the drawing room to which I had escorted his wife. "Supper will compensate us, but it's necessary to leave an hour at least for the cares of the toilette, and there is no one here who does not want to witness, in the boxes I've retained, the perhaps unique performance of La Pedrina. That virtuosa is so eccentric! God alone knows whether she won't escape us tomorrow."

"La Pedrina?" I said, reflectively. "That name has struck me once before, and in a circumstance memorable enough for me never to lose the memory. Is she not the extraordinary singer and even more extraordinary dancer who disappeared from Madrid after a day of triumphs, and of whom no trace was ever found? She doubtless justifies the curiosity of which she is the object by virtue of the talents that do not suffer any comparison in any theater, but I confess that a singular event of my life has made me blasé with regard to emotions of that genre, and that I am not curious to see La Pedrina herself. Permit me to wait in the Rambla for the time of our meeting."

"As you please," Pablo replied. "I believe, however, that Estelle was counting on you to accompany her."

Estelle came back, in fact, and approached me at the time of the departure. I forgot that I had promised never to see any dancer again, and never to hear a singer, after Inès de Las Sierras, but I believed that I was sure, that day, of neither seeing nor hearing anyone but Estelle. I talked to her for a long time, and I would be very embarrassed to say what was played to begin with.

Even the noise that announced the entrance of La Pedrina had not succeeded in moving me; I was still calm, my eyes partly veiled by my hand, when the profound silence that had replaced that temporary excitement was suddenly broken by a voice that it was impossible for me not to recognize. Inès' voice had never ceased to resonate in my ears; it pursued me in my meditations, it cradled me in my dreams—and the voice I heard was the voice of Inès!

I shivered, uttered a cry and threw myself to the front of the box, my gaze fixed on the stage.

It was Inès, Inès in person.

My first impulse was to search, to collect around me all the circumstances and all the facts that could confirm me in the idea that I was in Barcelona, that I was at the theater, that I was not, as I had been every day for two years, the dupe of my imagination; that one of my habitual dreams had surprised me. I strove to grasp something that could convince me of the reality of my sensation.

I found Estelle's hand, and I squeezed it forcefully. "Well!" she said smiling. "You were so sure of being pre-armed against the seductions of a woman's voice. La Pedrina has hardy begun, and you're beside yourself!"

"Are you certain, Estelle," I replied, "that this is La Pedrina? Do you know precisely whether it's a woman, an actress, or an apparition?"

"In truth," she said, "she's a woman, an extraordinary actress, a singer such as has perhaps never been heard, but I imagine that she's nothing more. Be careful," she added, coldly, "your enthusiasm has something disquieting for those who love you. You're not the first, it's said, that the sight of her has rendered mad, and that weakness of the heart will probably not flatter either your wife or your mistress."

As she finished she took away her hand entirely, and I allowed it to escape. La Pedrina was still singing.

Afterwards, she danced, and my thought, transported with her, surrendered defenselessly to all the impressions that she wanted to give it. The universal intoxication hid mine, but she augmented it further; all the time that had gone by between our two encounters had disappeared from our eyes, because no sensation of the same genre and the same power had ever reminded me of that one; it seemed to me that I was still in Ghismondo's castle, but in Ghismondo's castle magnified, decorated, populated by an immense crowd, and the acclamations that rose up from all parts rang in my ears like the joy of demons.

And La Pedrina, possessed by a sublime frenzy that only Hell could inspire and maintain, continued to devour the boards with her steps, to flee, to come back, to fly, chased or brought back by invincible impulsions, until, breathless, exhausted, annihilated, she fell into the arms of her accomplices, proffering with a heart-rending expression a name that I believed I heard, which resounded dolorously in my heart.

"Sergy is dead!" I shouted, weeping hot tears, my arms extended toward the stage.

"You're decidedly mad," said Estelle, retaining me in my place. "But calm down! She's no longer there!"

Mad! I said, to myself. *Can that be true? Have I thought that I have seen what I have not seen. What I believed I heard, have I really heard? Mad . . . great God! Separated from the human race*

and Estelle by an infirmity that will render me to public fable!
Fatal castle of Ghismondo, is this the punishment that you reserve
for the reckless who dare to violate your secrets? A thousand times
more fortunate is Sergy, in being dead in the fields of Lutzen!

I was sunk in those ideas when I felt Estelle's arm link with mine in order to leave the spectacle.

"Alas," I said to her, tremulously, for I was beginning to return to myself. "I must make you feel pity, but I would cause you even more pity if you knew a story that it is not permitted to me to tell you. What has just happened is, for me, only the prolongation of a terrible illusion from which my reason has never been completely liberated. Permit me to remain alone with my thoughts, and to put into them, so far as I am capable, a little order and coherency. The pleasures of a mild conversation are forbidden to me today; I shall be calmer tomorrow."

"You will be tomorrow as you please," said Pablo, who had just caught the last words in passing close to us, "but you certainly shan't quit us this evening. In any case," he added, "I'm counting, in order to decide that for you, on Estelle's insistence and on mine."

"Is that true," she said, "and will you consent to give us the time that you doubtless destine to occupy yourself with La Pedrina?"

"In God's name," I cried, "don't pronounce that name, dear Estelle, for the sentiment I experience doesn't resemble any sentiment that you could suspect, except perhaps terror. Why is it necessary for me to take my explanation further?"

It was necessary to give in. I sat down at the supper without taking part in it, and, as I expected, there was no talk of anything but La Pedrina.

"The interest that extraordinary woman inspires in you," Pablo said, suddenly, "has something so exalted that one can scarcely comprehend the possibility of augmenting it further.

194

It would be, however, if you knew her adventures, a part of which passed in Barcelona, but in a time in which most of us were not established here. You'd be obliged to agree that the misfortunes of La Pedrina are no less surprising than her talents."

No one replied, for everyone was listening, and Pablo, who perceived that, continued thus:

"La Pedrina does not belong to the class from which her peers ordinarily emerge, and in which these nomadic troupes are recruited whose destiny devotes them to the pleasures of the multitude. Her veritable name has been borne, in remote times, by one of the most illustrious families in Spain. Her name is Inès de Las Sierras."

"Inès de Las Sierras!" I cried, rising from my place in a state of excitement difficult to describe. "Inès de Las Sierras! It's true, then! But do you know, in that case, who Inès de Las Sierras is? Do you know where she comes from, and by virtue of what frightful privilege she enables herself to be heard in a theater?"

"I know," said Pablo, smiling, "that she is a rare and unfortunate creature whose life merits at least as much pity as admiration. As for the emotion that her name causes you, it cannot astonish me, for it's probable that it has struck you more than once in the lamentable ballads of our *Romanceros*.

"The story that it retraces in our friend's memory," he went on, addressing the rest of the audience, "is one of the popular traditions of the Middle Ages, which were probably founded on a few real facts, or a few specious appearances, and handed down from generation to generation in human memory to the extent of acquiring a kind of historic authority. This one, at any rate, already enjoyed a great credit in the sixteenth century, since it forced the powerful family of the Las Sierras to expatriate themselves with all their wealth, and to profit from new discoveries in navigation to transport their domicile to

Mexico. What is certain is that the tragic fatality by which they were pursued did not relax its rigor in other climes. I have often heard it said that in three hundred years, all the heads of the family died by the sword.

"At the beginning of the century whose fourteenth year we're in, the last of the noble lords of Las Sierras was still living in Mexico. Death had just taken his wife from him, and all that remained to him was a daughter aged six or seven years, named Inès. Never had faculties more brilliant been announced at such a tender age, and the Marquis de Las Sierras spared no effort for the cultivation of the precious gifts that promised so much glory and so much happiness for his old age. It would have been very fortunate, in fact, if the education of his only daughter had been able to absorb all his care and affection, but he soon felt the fatal need to fill with another sentiment the profound void in his heart.

"He fell in love; he believed that he was loved; he was proud of his choice; more than that, he congratulated himself on giving another mother to his beautiful Inès—but he gave her an implacable enemy. Inès' keen intelligence did not take long to grasp all the difficulties of her new position. She soon understood that the arts, which had only been until then an object of distraction and pleasure, might one day become her sole resource. She delivered herself to them thereafter with an ardor that was crowned by unprecedented successes, and after a few years she no longer had any masters. The most skillful and the most presumptuous of hers would have been honored to receive lessons from her; but she paid dearly for that glorious advantage, if it is true that in that epoch her reason, so pure and so brilliant, vanquished by obstinate fatigue, appeared to deteriorate gradually, and momentary aberrations had begun to betray the disorder of her intelligence at the moment when she seemed to have nothing more to acquire.

"One day, the inanimate body of the Marquis de Las

196

Sierras was transported back to his hotel. He had been found, pierced by stab-wounds, in a remote place, where no other circumstance presented itself that might cast any light on the motive and author of the cruel assassination. Public opinion, however, did not take long to designate a guilty party. Inès' father had no known enemy, but before his second marriage he had had a rival, signaled in Mexico for the ardor of his passions and the violence of his character. Everyone named him in the intimacy of his thought, but that universal suspicion could not be converted into accusation because it was not justified by any commencement of proof. Nevertheless, the conjectures of the multitude acquired a new force when the widow of the victim was seen to pass, after a few months, into the arms of the assassin, and if nothing had enlightened them since, at least nothing diminished the impression.

"Inès thus remained alone in the house of her ancestors with two persons who were equally foreign to her, and whom a secret instinct rendered equally odious, to whom the law had blindly confided the authority that it substituted for that of the family. The afflictions that had sometimes threatened her reason multiplied then in a frightful manner, and no one was surprised, although people were generally unaware of half her misfortunes.

"There was a young Sicilian in Mexico named Gaetano Filippi, whose anterior life seemed to hide some suspect mystery. A light smattering of the arts, a seductive but frivolous loquacity, elegant manners that gave evidence of study and education and intrigues in the commerce of society had opened access to the high society that the depravity of his mores ought to have forbidden to him. Inès, scarcely sixteen years old, was too ingenuous and simultaneously too exalted to penetrate the underside of that deceptive exterior. Her senses were disturbed by the revelation of a first amour.

"Gaetano was not embarrassed by the difficulty of making himself known under advantageous titles; he knew the art of procuring those he needed and giving them the appearance of the necessary authenticity to fascinate the most skillful and the most experienced eyes. It was in vain, however, that he asked for Inès' hand. The unfortunate girl's stepmother had formed the project of assuring her fortune for herself, and it is probable that she would not have been scrupulous about the choice of means. For his part, her husband seconded her with a zeal that doubtless concealed a secret motive. The wretch was in love with his ward; he had dared to declare it to her several weeks before, and he promised himself to seduce her. That was the profound chagrin that had been aggravating Inès' mortal distress so cruelly for some time.

"Inès' organization was similar to all those favored by genius to a superior degree. She combined with the elevation of a sublime talent a character that only asked to allow itself to be guided. In the life of intelligence and art she was an angel. In common and practical life she was a child. The simple appearance of a benevolent sentiment captivated her heart, and when her heart had submitted, it left no objections to her reason.

"That mental disposition is not deadly when it is placed in fortunate circumstances and under a sage direction, but the only being whose empire Inès could recognize in the sad isolation in which her father's death had left her only acted upon her to doom her; and that is one of the horrible secrets that innocence does not suspect. Geatano convinced her, almost without effort, to accept an abduction on which he made the salvation of his mistress depend. He had scarcely more difficulty convincing Inès that everything in the heritage of her ancestors belonged to her, by a legitimate and sacred right. They disappeared, and a few months later, abundantly furnished with gold, jewels and diamonds, they were both in Cadiz.

"There the veil was lifted, but Inès' eyes, still dazzled by the false glare of amour and pleasures, refused for a long time to see the whole truth. The society into the midst of which Gaetano had thrown himself, alarmed her sometimes by the license of its principles; she was astonished that the passage from one hemisphere to the other could produce such strange differences in language and mores; she searched tremulously for a thought that responded to her own in the crowd of tricksters, libertines and courtesans who composed his habitual society and did not find it. The temporary resources that she owed to an action for which her conscience was not yet completely reassured began to escape her, and Gaetano's hypocritical tenderness seemed to diminish with them. One day, when she woke up, she asked for him without response, and she waited for him in vain the following night; the next day she passed from anxiety to dread and from dread to despair; the frightful reality finally came to complete her misery. He had gone, after having despoiled her of everything, departed with another woman.

"He had abandoned her, poor, dishonored and, as a final woe, delivered to her own scorn. The spring of noble pride that reacts against misfortune in a soul without reproach ended up breaking in Inès. She had taken the name of Pedrina in order to hide from the research of her unworthy parents.' Pedrina, so be it!' she said, with a bitter resolution; 'shame and ignominy upon me, since my destiny has wished it thus!' And she was no longer anything but La Pedrina.

"You will easily understand that I must cease to follow her in all the details of her life; she has not given them. We only find her again at her memorable debut in Madrid, which placed her so promptly in the first rank of celebrated virtuosas. The enthusiasm was so vehement and so passionate that the entire city resonated with the applause of the theater, and the crowd that had accompanied her home with its acclamations and crowns only consented to dissipate after seeing her once more at one of the windows of her apartment.

"That was not the only sentiment that she had excited. Her beauty—which was in fact, no less remarkable than her talent—had produced a profound impression on an illustrious individual, who then held in his hands a part of the destiny of Spain, and whom you will permit me not to designate otherwise, because that anecdote of private life has not yet been sufficiently enlightened by my conscience as a historian, and because I am reluctant to add a very excusable weakness to the true or false wrongs of which fickle public pinion always accuse fallen kings.

"What is certain is that she did not appear on stage again, and that all the favors of fortune accumulated in a few days on that obscure adventuress, whose shame and poverty the neighboring provinces had seen for a year. There was no longer talk of anything but the vanity of her garments, the richness of her jewels and the luxury of her carriages; and, unusually, she was pardoned quite easily for that sudden opulence, because there were very few men among her judges who would not have been happy to give her a hundred times more.

"It is necessary to add, to the honor of La Pedrina, that the treasures she owed to amour were not exhausted in sterile fantasies. Naturally compassionate and generous, she sought out woe in order to repair it; she brought help and consolation to the sad redoubt of the pauper and the bedside of the invalid; she relieved all misfortunes with a grace that added to her benefits, and although a favorite, she made the people love her. That is so easy when one is rich!

"The name of La Pedrina made too much noise not to reach Gaetano's ears in the obscure place where he was hiding his shameful life. The produce of theft and treason that had sustained him thus far was now lacking to his needs. He regretted having mistaken the resources that he could have obtained from the debasement of his mistress. He dared to conceive the project of repairing his fault at all costs, even at the price of a new crime. That was what cost him the least. He counted on a skill too often exercised to inspire any suspicion in him. He knew Inès' heart, and the wretch did not hesitate to present himself before her.

"Gaetano's justification appeared impossible at first, but nothing is impossible for a cunning mind, especially when it is seconded by the blind credulity of amour, and Gaetano was not only the first man who had made Inès' heart beat faster, he was the only one who she had loved. All the aberrations to which her senses had yielded since had left her soul empty and indifferent; and by virtue of a privilege that is doubtless rare, but not without example, she had doomed herself without being corrupted.

"Gaetano's story, absurd as it was, had little difficulty in obtaining the credit of verity. Inès needed to believe it in order to recover some semblance of her vanished happiness, and that mental disposition is content with the slightest plausibility. It is probable that she dared not even hazard the objections that presented themselves in a host to her mind, in the fear of encountering one that was unanswerable. It is so pleasant to be deceived in the matter of amour, especially when one cannot cease to love.

"The perfidious individual had not, in any case, neglected any of his advantages. He had arrived from Sicily, where he had gone in order to dispose his family to permit his marriage. He had succeeded. His mother had even deigned to accompany him to Spain. In order to hasten the moment of seeing a cherished daughter of whom she had formed the most flattering idea. What horrible news awaited him in Barcelona! The rumor of La Pedrina's success had reached him, with that of her crime and her ignominy. Was that the price she had reserved for so much amour and so much sacrifice?

"The first idea, the first sentiment of which he found himself capable, was to die, but his tenderness had prevailed again over his despair. He had hidden his sad secret from his mother; he had flown to Madrid in order to talk to Inès, to make her hear, if there was still time, the cry of honor and virtue. He had come to forgive, and he forgave!

"What can I tell you? Inès, drowned in tears, distressed and palpitating, bewildered by remorse, gratitude and joy, fell at the feet of the impostor, and hypocrisy triumphed almost without effort over a heart too sensitive and too confident to divine it. That sudden change of role and position, which gave the culpable all the rights of innocence, is perhaps astonishing, but ask women! There is nothing more common.

"Inès' suspicion was reawakened, however, when she saw Gaetano in more haste to load the carriage prepared for their departure with treasures whose origin she could not recall without blushing than to remove her from her criminal amours. She insisted in vain on abandoning everything; he paid no heed.

"Four days later a journey by carriage ended in Barcelona, outside the Hôtel de l'Italie. An elegantly clad young man was seen to descend, and a lady who seemed to be hiding carefully from the gazes of travelers and passers-by. It was Gaetano and La Pedrina. A quarter of an hour later, the young man came out and headed for the port.

"The absence of Gaetano's mother confirmed the dread that Inès had begun to conceive. It appeared that she had obtained sufficient empire over her timidity to express them outwardly when he returned to his apartment. It is certain, at least, that a violent argument took place between them that evening, and was renewed several times during the night.

"At daybreak, Gaetano, pale, distressed and agitated, had several crates transported by the domestics aboard a ship that was due to set sail in the morning, and rendered there himself with a smaller casket that he had enveloped in the folds of his cloak. Having arrived at the vessel, he dismissed the men that had accompanied him under the pretext of some arrangements that still retained him, paid them generously for their trouble, and recommended them in the most express manner not to trouble Madame's slumber until he returned. However, most of the day went by without the stranger having reappeared. It was learned that the ship was en route and one of the men who had accompanied Gaetano, troubled by a somber presentiment, was tempted to make sure of that. He saw the sails disappearing over the horizon.

"The silence that continued to reign in Inès' room in the midst of the noises of the house became disquieting. It was ascertained that her door had not been locked from the inside but from the outside, and that the key had not been left in the lock. The hotelier did not hesitate to open it with a duplicate key, and a horrible spectacle was offered to his eyes. The unknown lady was lying in her bed in the attitude of a person asleep, and could have been mistaken for one had she not been bathed in blood. Her breast had been pierced by a dagger-thrust during her slumber, and the murderer's blade was still in the wound.

"You will easily forgive me for not having insisted on those frightful details; they were known at the time throughout the city. What is still unknown even to the people most touched by the fate of unfortunate woman—for it was several days before she was in a condition to collect and put in order the confused details of her story—is that the victim of that crime was the sublime Pedrina, of whom Madrid has never lost the memory, and that La Pedrina was Inès de Las Sierras.

"I shall return to my story," Pablo continued. "The witnesses summoned to that scene of horrior and the physicians who were summoned immediately, did not take long to ascertain that the foreign lady was not dead. Cares already belated, but urgent, were rendered with so much success that they succeeded in reawakening the sentiment of life in her. A few days passed, however, in the alternatives of dread and hope the excite public sympathy keenly. A month later, Inès' recovery seemed completely affirmed, but the delirium that had been manifested as soon as she recovered the power of speech, and which was then attributed to the action of a violent fever, did not yield either to remedies or to time.

"The poor creature had been resuscitated to physical life, but remained dead to intelligent life. She was mad.

"A community of holy women took her in and continued the attentive solicitude that her condition required. The object in all regards of an almost providential charity, it was thought that she justified them by a mildness proof against anything, for her alienation had nothing of the impetuosity and violence that ordinarily characterize that frightful malady. It was, in any case, frequently interrupted by lucid intervals that were more or less prolonged, and which offered hope, better founded from day to day, of a cure. They became frequent enough for most of the attention that had initially been paid to her slightest action to be relaxed; her carers gradually became accustomed to leaving her to herself during the long hours of the offices, and she took advantage of that negligence to escape.

"There was great anxiety, and the research was active; their result initially seemed fortunate enough to promise an imminent success. Inès had been noticed during the first days of her vagabondage because of the incomparable beauty of her features, the natural nobility of her manners, the intermittent disorder of her ideas and, above all, by the singular appearance of her accoutrement, composed at random of elegant but worn residues of her theatrical costumes, shreds of some glamour but little value, which the Sicilian had disdained to appropriate, and the bizarre assortment of which, with its borrowed appearance of luxury, made a singular contrast with the coarse sack that Inès had slung over her shoulder in order to receive the charity of the people.

"Her tracks were followed in that way to a short distance from Mattaro, but there the trail was completely effaced, and no matter where the investigation continued in the surrounding area, it was impossible to pick it up again. Inès had disappeared from all eyes two days before Christmas, and when people recalled the profound melancholy in which her mind seemed plunged every time she succeeded in disengaging herself from her habitual darkness, they did not hesitate to think that she had put an end to her days by throwing herself into the sea. That explanation came to mind so naturally that they were scarcely tempted to seek another. The unknown woman was dead, and the impression of that news made itself felt for two days. On the third day it weakened, like all impressions, and the following day, no one mentioned it any longer.

"Something extraordinary happened at that time, which contributed greatly to distracting minds from the disappearance of Inès and the tragic denouement of her adventures. There existed in the vicinity of the town where she had been lost the last vestiges of an old ruined manor known by the name of Ghismondo's castle, of which it was said that the demon had taken possession several centuries ago, and in which tradition made him hold a cenacle during the night of Christmas. The present generation had not seen anything capable of lending any authority to that ridiculous superstition, and no one was anxious about it any longer, but circumstances that have never been explained rendered its rights to it in 1812.

"There was no doubt this time that the accursed castle was inhabited by exceptional guests, who had delivered themselves there without mystery to the joy of a banquet. A splendid illumination burst forth at midnight in the long-deserted apartments and bore disquiet and alarm into the nearby hamlets. A few belated voyagers whom hazard conducted close to its walls heard the sounds of strange and confused voices, which were mingled momentarily by songs of an infinite sweetness. The phenomena of a stormy night whose like Catalonia could not recall in such a late season added further to the solemnity of that bizarre scene, the details of which fear and credulity did not fail to exaggerate.

"There was no talk the next day, and in the days that followed, of anything but the return of spirits to Ghismondo's house, and the concurrence of so many testimonies what were in agreement regarding the principal circumstances of the event ended up inspiring alarm in the police. In fact, the French troops had just been recalled from their garrisons to go and reinforce the remains of the army in Germany, and the moment appeared favorable for the renewal of the attempts of the old Spanish party, which then began to ferment in a very evident manner in the poorly submissive regions. The administration, little disposed to share the beliefs of the populace, only saw in that pretended gathering of demons faithful to their annual rendezvous an assembly of conspirators ready to deploy the flag of civil war again. A scrupulous visit to the mysterious manor was ordered, and that search confirmed, by virtue of evident proofs, the verity of the rumors that had rendered it necessary. All the vestiges were found of the illumination of the feast, and it was possible to conjecture, by the number of empty bottles that still garnished the table, that the guests had been quite numerous."

At that passage in Pablo's story, which reminded me of Boutraix's inextinguishable thirst and immoderate libations, I could not suppress a burst of convulsive laughter, which interrupted him for a time and contrasted in too bizarre a manner with the dispositions in which he had seen me at the commencement of his story not to occasion a sharp surprise. He stared at me, waiting for me to regain control of my indiscreet hilarity, and when I calmed down, he continued.

"The assembly held by a certain number of men, probably armed and certainly mounted—for forage also remained—was demonstrated to everyone's satisfaction, but none of the conspirators was found at the castle, and their trail could not be followed. The authorities were never enlightened in regard to that singular event, even in the epoch when it ceased to be reprehensible, and when there would have been some advantage in admitting what it had them been necessary to keep quiet.

"The troop charged with the little expedition was about to depart when a soldier discovered a strangely clad young woman in one of the cellars, who seemed deprived of her reason, and who, far from avoiding him, hastened to run to him, pronouncing a name that he could not remember. 'Is it you?' she cried to him. 'How long you've kept me waiting!' Taken into the daylight and recognizing her error, she dissolved in tears.

"That young woman, you have already guessed, was La Pedrina. Her description, sent a few days before to all the authorities of the coastal region, was present in their minds. They hastened to return her to Barcelona, after having subjected her, during her lucid moments, to a particular interrogation regarding the inexplicable night of Christmas; but it had only left extremely confused traces in her memory, and her testimony, the sincerity of which no one could suspect, only augmented the embarrassment, already very complicated, of the information.

"It only seemed demonstrated that a strange preoccupation of her sick imagination had made her seek a refuge in the manor of the lords of Las Sierras guaranteed by the rights of her birth; that she had introduced herself into it with some difficulty, taking advantage of a narrow gap left in the dilapidated doors; that she had lived there at first on her provisions, and, in the following days, of those that strangers had abandoned there. As for the latter, she appeared not to know them, and the description she made of their clothing, which was inappropriate to a living population, was so far removed from all probability that it was attributed without hesitation to remembrance of a dream whose features her mind had confounded with those of reality. What seemed most evident was that one of the adventurers or conspirators had made a deep impression on her heart, and that only the hope of finding him again inspired in her the courage to continue living. But she had understood that he was pursued, that he was menaced in his liberty, perhaps in his existence, and the most assiduous and obstinate efforts could not extract the secret of his name from her."

The last part of Pablo's narrative caused me to recall, under an entirely new aspect, the memory of a friend whose last sigh I had received. My breast swelled, my eyes filled with tears, and I raised my hand to them abruptly in order to hide my emotion from the people surrounding me. Pablo stopped, as he had the first time, and attached his gaze to me with an even more marked attention. I penetrated the sentiment that was occupying him easily, and I tried to reassure him with a smile.

"Tranquilize your amicable heart," I said to him, expansively, "regarding the alternatives of tenderness and gaiety that your singular story made me experience. There is nothing that is not natural in my position, and you will agree yourself when I have explained them to you. Continue, though, and forgive me for having interrupted it, for La Pedrina's adventures are not finished."

"Little more is required," Pablo said. "She was brought back to her convent and placed under a tighter surveillance. An old physician, well versed in the study of mental maladies, whom fortunate circumstances had brought to Barcelona a few years before, attempted her cure. He perceived immediately that it offered great difficulties, for the disorders of a wounded imagination are never more serious and, so to speak, more incurable than when they result from a profound disturbance of the soul. Nevertheless, he persisted, because he counted on an auxiliary that is always skillful in soothing dolor: time, which effaces everything and which is the only eternal constant in the midst of our temporary pleasures and chagrins. He wanted to combine it with distraction and study; he summoned the arts to the aid of her malady, the arts that she had forgotten, but the impression of which did not take long to reawaken, more powerful than ever, in that admirable organism.

"Learning, a philosopher has said, is perhaps only remembering. For her, it was invention. Her first lesson caused her audience to pass from astonishment to admiration, to enthusiasm and to fanaticism. Her success extended with rapidity, the intoxication to which she gave birth attained herself. There are privileged natures that glory recompenses for happiness, and that compensation has been marvelously adapted to them by Providence, for happiness and glory are rarely found together. Finally, she was cured, and was in a state to make herself known to her benefactor, from whom I obtained the story. But the return of her reason would only have been a further misfortune for her if she had not rediscovered at the same time the resources of her talent. You can imagine that offers were not lacking as soon as it was learned that she had decided to consecrate herself to the theater. Already ten different cities were threatening to steal her from us when Bascara came to see her yesterday and to engage her in his troupe."

"In Bascara's troupe!" I cried, laughing. "Be sure that she knows now who the redoubtable conspirators of Ghismondo's castle were."

"That's what you're going to enable us to understand," replied Pablo, "for you seem very well-informed regarding these mysteries. Speak, I beg you."

"He won't," said Estelle in a piqued tone. "It's a secret that he can't reveal to anyone."

"That was true a moment ago," I replied, "but that moment has operated a great change in my ideas and my resolutions. I have just been liberated from my oath."

I have no need to tell you that I recounted then what I had recounted to you a month ago, and you will dispense me without difficulty of recounting it to you today, even if you only have a vague memory of my first story. I'm not capable of lending it enough attraction to enable it to be heard twice.

"You are, at least, a good enough logician," said the substitute magistrate, "to extract some moral induction from it, and I declare to you that I wouldn't give a straw for the most piquant news, if no information for the mind resulted from it. The worthy Perrault, your master, knew how to extract grave and healthy morals from his most ridiculous tales."

"Alas," I replied, raising my arms to the heavens, "who are you talking to me about? One of the most transcendent geniuses who has enlightened humankind since Homer. Oh, the novelists of my time and even the makers of tales, do not have the pretention to resemble him. I will even tell you, between us, that they would be very humiliated by the comparison. What they need, my dear substitute, is the quotidian renown that one obtains with money, and the money that one always succeeds in gaining, well or badly, when one has renown. The moral that is requisite, according to you, is the least of their concerns. However, since you want one, I'll finish with an adage that I believe in my fashion, but which can perhaps be found elsewhere by searching hard, for there is nothing that has not been said.

"To believe everything is imbecilic.

"To deny everything is stupid.

"And if that doesn't suit you, it costs me little to borrow another from the Spaniards while I am on their terrain.

"*De las cosas mas seguras,*

"*La mas segura es dudar.*

"Which means, dear Eudoxie, that of all sure things, the surest is doubt."

"Doubt, doubt," said Anastase, sadly. "A fine pleasure, doubting! There are no apparitions, then?"

"You're going too far," I replied, "for my adage informs us that perhaps there are. I have not had the good fortune of seeing one, but why should it not be reserved to an organization more complete and more favored than mine?"

"An organization more complete and more favored?" cried the substitute. "An idiot, or a madman!"

"Why not, Monsieur Substitute? Who has given me the measure of human intelligence? Who is the clever Popilius who has said to it: *thou shalt not emerge from this circle.* If apparitions are a lie, it is necessary to agree that there is no truth more accredited than that error. All centuries, all nations and all stories bear witness to it. I have, moreover, a manner of thinking about the subject that is appropriate to me, and which you will probably find very strange, but from which I cannot depart. It is that humans are incapable of inventing anything—or, to put it differently, that invention is only an innate perception of real facts. What is science doing today? At each new discovery it justifies, it authenticates, if one can express it thus, one of the pretended lies of Herodotus or Pliny. The fabulous giraffe is wandering in the Jardin du Roi. I am one of those who incessantly expects the unicorn. Dragons, wyverns, endriagues and tarasques are no longer part of the living world, but Cuvier has discovered them in the fossil world. Everyone knows that the harpy was an enormous bat, and poets have described it with an exactitude that Linnaeus would envy.

"As for the phenomenon of apparitions, about which we were talking just now, and to which I would gladly return . . ."

I was, in fact, about to return to it, and with long developments, because it is a matter on which there is a great deal to say, when I perceived that the substitute was asleep.

The Legend of Sister Béatrix

Maria, gratia plena.[1]

It was widely agreed in France twenty years ago that all the treasures of poetry, without exception, are contained in Pomey's *Panthéon mythicum* and Monsieur Noël's *Dictionnaire de la Fable.*[2] A name unknown to Phurnutus, a fable ignored by Paléphate, a tender and touching story that does not go back to the *Métamorphoses*, any idea that had not been passed through the eternal template of the Greeks and Romans, was reputed to be barbaric.[3] When you had finished with the Aloïdes, the Phaëtonides, the Méléagrides, the Labdecides,

---

1 The line is from the *Ave Maria*, translated in the English version as "Mary, full of grace."

2 Jean-François Pomey's *Pantheum mythicum seu fabulosa deorum historia* (1619-1673 in Latin), rapidly translated into French and English (the latter as Tooke's *Pantheon of Heathen Gods and Illustrious Heroes*) became a standard handbook of mythology. The English translation by Andrew Tooke, headmaster of Charterhouse School, became a school textbook. François Noël's *Dictionnaire de la fable, ou Mythologique greque, latine, égytienne, celtique,* etc. (1801) was a supposedly comprehensive survey of all mythologies, edited by the inspector-general of public education appointed by Napoléon in the early days of the Empire.

3 Phurnutus was the signature used by Lucuis Annaeus Cornutus, author of *De natura deorum, sive poeticum fabularutm* (first century A.D.) Paléphate is the French rendering of Palaephatus, the pseudonymous author of a fervently skeptical text debunking myths as "incredible tales," only parts of which survived, probably written in the fourth century B.C.

the Danaïdes, the Pélopides, the Atrides and other unfortunate dynasties fatally avowed to the Eumenides by the learned
cabal of Aristotle, and above all by rhyme, only one course
remained for you to take, which is to recommence, and people recommenced. The patient admiration of colleges never
wearied of those beautiful myths, which did not say anything
to the mind and the heart, but which flattered the ear with
sounds purified by the sweet euphony of the Hellenes.

There was Bacchus, born prematurely to the sound of fire-
works, whom Jupiter sheltered in his thigh by virtue of the art
of Sabasius in order to accomplish there the requisite time of a
natural gestation. There was the son of Tantalus, served to the
gods in an *olla podrida* worthy of the Inferno, whose absent
shoulder-blade had to be replaced by an ivory substitute by
Minerva, hungrier than the rest of the immortals. There was
Deucalion repopulating the world with his grandmother's
bones—which is to say, by throwing stones behind him.
There were other absurd and solemn tales, of which it was
necessary to know the ridiculous, often obscene and impious,
details in order not to be considered ignorant and stupid in
the eyes of polite society. On the other hand, recompenses and
crowns were awarded to the fortunate child who succeeded
in assembling in his memory the greatest possible number of
those inept classics, and if I remember rightly, the principal
prelate of the diocese deigned to imprint to his triumph the
seal of his pontifical benediction. That method of intellectual
brutalization and degradation, which rarely failed in its effect,
was called education.

Our civilization, however, has not resembled for a great
many years the one that nourished it for so many centuries
with the puerile fables of paganism. The irony of Socrates dealt
the first blow to the phantoms of mythology; they vanished
under the whip of Lucian. A new belief was introduced, grave,
majestic and touching, full of sublime mysteries and sublime

hopes. With it descended into the human heart a multitude of sentiments that the ancients had not known, the holy fervor of faith, the noble enthusiasm of liberty, love, charity, and the forgiveness of insults. A poetry more appropriate to the needs of Christianity was born with it, and that poetry also had its myths and its stories. Why was that new source of marvelous inspirations and tender emotions neglected by the skillful artisans of speech who charmed with their narratives the ennuis and dolors of humankind? Why were pious and touching legends relegated to the firesides of old women and children, as unworthy of occupying the leisure of a delicate mind and a select audience? That can only be explained by the progressive deterioration of the precious naivety with which primitive ages obtained their purest enjoyments, and without which there is no more veritable poetry. The poetry of an epoch is composed, in fact, of two essential elements, the sincere faith of the person of imagination who believes what he is relating, and the sincere faith of the people of sentiment who believe what they hear recounted. Outside that state of confidence and reciprocal sympathy, in which different organizations are confounded, poetry is only a vain name, the sterile and insignificant art of measuring a few sonorous syllables in compassed rhythms. That is why we have no more poetry in the naïve and original sense of the word, and why we will not have any for a long time, if ever.

In order to recover its feeble vestiges, it is necessary to leaf through old books that were written by simple men, or sit down in some remote village, by the fireside of good people. It is there that touching and magnificent traditions can be found, the authority of which no one has ever bothered to contest, which pass from generation to generation like a pious heritage, on the infallible and respected word of old people. The sniggering objections of demi-education, so surly, peevish and stupid, which have no foundation, but which appeal to those who do not want to believe anything—because in searching for the truth that is forbidden to our nature, they find nothing but doubt—cannot prevail there.

The stories that are made there, you see, cannot provide material for any discussion; they defy the criticism of a demanding rationality that shrinks the soul and a disdainful philosophy that withers it; they are not confined within the limits of common probability, or even the limits of possibility, for what is not possible today was doubtless possible once, when the world, younger and more innocent, was still worthy of the miracles God made for it; when the angels and saints were able to involve themselves, without too much derogation of their celestial grandeur, with simple and pure people whose lives were spent between labor and the practice of good deeds. The facts that are reported to you have no need, in any case, of so much clarification; are they not the testimony of the aged ancestor, who knew them from his ancestor, and that one from another old man who was their eye-witness? And in the long succession of patriarchs nurtured in the horror of sin, was even one ever encountered who lied?

Oh, my friends, whom the divine fire that animated humans on the day of their creation have not yet abandoned entirely, you who still conserve a soul in order to believe, to feel and to love; you who have not despaired of yourselves and your future, in the midst of this chaos of nations in which one despairs of everything, come and participate with me in these enchantments of speech that enable to revive in thought the happy life of centuries of ignorance and virtue; but above all, do not waste time, I implore you. Tomorrow it might be too late! Progress has told you: *I move on*; and the monster does indeed move on.

Like the physical death of which the Latin poet speaks, primary education, that hideous death of intelligence and imagination, is knocking on the door of the meanest cottages.

All the scourges that writing drags after it, all the scourges of printing, its perverse and fecund sister, are threatening to invade the last refuges of ancient modesty, innocence and piety, under an escort of somber pedants.

A few more days, and the nascent world, which the science of evil goes to seize in its cradle, will know a ridiculous alphabet but will no longer know God; a few days more and all that remain, alas, of the children of nature, will be as stupid and wicked as their masters. Let us hasten to listen to the delightful stories of the people before they are forgotten, before they cause blushes, and their chaste poetry, ashamed by being naked, is covered by a veil, like Eve exiled from paradise.

I have sworn, personally, never to recount any others. The one that I am going to tell you is taken from an old hagiographer named Bzovius, an unknown continuator of Baronius, who is scarcely better known.[1] Bzovius regarded it as perfectly authentic, and I share his opinion, for such things are not invented. So I shall be careful not to change the slightest thing fundamentally, and as for the differences that might be found in the form, it is necessary not to impute them to my taste, but to that of the multitude, who would not care much for the painting of a naïve master if it were not heightened by a frame and refreshed with varnish. After that declaration, readers in whom the love of the beautiful and the true has not been adulterated by bad habits, will know what to do. They will leave my pastiche there and read, if they can disinter the old book in a library, good Bzovius, who recounts as hundred times better than me.

Not far from the highest summit of the Jura, descending slightly along its western slope, one could still remark less

---

1 Bzovius (Abraham Bzowaki, 1567-1637) was a Polish Dominican pseudo-historian who took over the *Annales Ecclesiastici* of Cardinal Baronius (Cesare Baronio, 1538-1607, most notable for his debates with Galileo) and is thus described by the Catholic Encyclopedia as a "continuator." Bzovius dates the legend of Saint Béatrix featured in this anecdote (there are several others) to the thirteenth century.

than half a century ago a mass of ruins that had belonged to the church and the monastery of Notre-Dame-des-Épines-Fleuries. It is at the extremity of a narrow and profound gorge, but much more sheltered on the northern side, which produces every year, thanks to the favor of that exposure, the rarest flowers of the region. Half a league away, the opposite extremity also allows the sight of the debris of an ancient seigneurial manor, which has disappeared, like the house of God. All that is known about it is that it was occupied by a family greatly renowned in arms, and that the last of the noble knights who bore its name died in the conquest of the tomb of Jesus Christ without leaving an heir to perpetuate his race. The inconsolable widow did not abandon a place so appropriate to entertain her melancholy, but the rumor of her piety spread far and wide with its benefits, and a glorious tradition consecrated her memory forever in the respect of Christian generations. The people, who had forgotten all her other titles, still call her "the Saint."

On one of those days when winter, ready to end, suddenly relaxes its rigor under the influences of a temperate sky, the Saint was walking, as was her habit, in the long avenue of her château, her mind occupied by pious meditations. She arrived thus beside the thorn-bushes that still terminate it, and she was a not a little surprised to see that one of the bushes was already charged with all its spring adornment. She hastened to approach it in order to make sure that the appearance was not produced by a residue of recalcitrant snow, and, delighted to see that it really was crowned with an innumerable multitude of beautiful little stars with an incarnadine radiance, she detached a branch carefully so that she might suspend it, in her oratory, from an image of the Holy Virgin that she had held in great veneration since her childhood. She returned home joyfully in order to bring her that innocent offering.

Either because that feeble tribute was really agreeable to the divine mother of Jesus or because a particular pleasure that cannot be defined is reserved for the slightest effusion of a tender heart toward the object it loves, the soul of the chatelaine had never opened to emotions more ineffable than on that pleasant evening. So she promised with an ingenuous joy to return every day to the flowery bush, and bring back a new garland.

One can believe that she was faithful to that engagement. One day, however, when the needs of the poor and the sick had retained her longer than usual, she had to hurry to reach her wild flower-bed; night arrived before her, and it is said that she was beginning to regret having progressed so far into that solitude when a calm and pure light, like that which descends from the nascent day suddenly showed her all her thorn-bushes in flower.

She paused momentarily, in the thought that the light might be coming from a brigands' camp, for it was impossible to imagine that it was produced by myriads of glow-worms emerged before their season. The year was still too distant then from the warm and placid nights of summer. Nevertheless, the obligation that she had imposed on herself came to present itself to her mind, and, reanimating her courage somewhat, she marched on lightly, holding her breath, toward the bush with the white flowers, seized a branch with her tremulous hand, which seemed to fall into her fingers of its own accord, so little resistance did it offer, and she resumed the route to the manor, without daring to look behind her.

Throughout the following night the saintly woman reflected on that phenomenon, without being able to explain it; and, as she was determined to penetrate the mystery, on the following day, at the same hour of the evening, she returned to the bushes in the company of a faithful servant and her aged chaplain. The soft light reigned there, as it had the previous day, and its radiance seemed to become more vivid as they approached. They stopped then, and knelt down, because it seemed to them that the light was coming from the sky; after which, the good priest rose to his feet alone, took a few respectful steps toward the flowery thorn-bushes, singing a church hymn, and went around them effortlessly, for they opened like a veil.

The spectacle that was offered to their gaze at that moment struck them with such admiration that they remained motionless for a long time, penetrated with gratitude and joy. It was an image of the Holy Virgin, carved with simplicity in coarse wood, animated with the colors of life as if by an unskillful brush and clad in garments that only revealed a naïve luxury—but it was from there that the miraculous splendor was emanated by which the place was illuminated.

"I salute you, Marie, full of grace," said the prostrate chaplain, finally; and by the harmonious murmur that rose up throughout the wood when he pronounced those words, one might have believed that they had been repeated by a choir of angels. Then he recited, solemnly, the admirable litanies in which faith has spoken without knowing it the language of the purest poetry; and, after further acts of adoration, he lifted the statue in his hands in order to transport it to the château, where it would find a sanctuary more worthy of it, while the lady and the valet, their hands joined at their foreheads inclined, followed him slowly, joining in with his prayers.

Needless to say, the marvelous image was placed in an elegant niche, where it was surrounded by odorant candles, bathed with perfumes, charged with a rich crown and saluted until the middle of the night with a canticle by the faithful. In the morning, however, it was no longer to be found, and the alarm was keen among all those Christians whom its conquest had filled with such a pure joy. What unknown sin could have attracted that disgrace to the Saint's manor? Why had the celestial Virgin quit it? What new abode had she chosen?

You will doubtless have divined that the blessed mother of Jesus had preferred the modest shade of her favorite bushes to the glare of a worldly dwelling. She had returned to the midst of the freshness of the woods, to savor the peace and solitude and the sweet exhalations of their flowers. All the inhabitants of the château returned there in the evening, and found her there, more resplendent than the day before. They fell to their knees in a respectful silence.

"Powerful queen of angels," said the chatelaine, "this is the dwelling you prefer. Your will shall be done."

And a short time afterwards, in fact, a temple embellished with all the ornaments lavished upon it by the architect, inspired in those centuries of imagination and sentiment, was erected around the revered image. The grandees of the earth wanted to enrich it with their gifts, kings endowed it with a tabernacle of pure gold. The renown of its miracles spread far throughout the Christian world and summoned to the valley a multitude of pious women, who settled there under the rule of a monastery. The saintly widow, more touched than ever by the light of grace, could not refuse the title of the superior of that house. She died there in old age, after a life of good works, examples and sacrifices, which were exhaled like a perfume at the foot of the Virgin's altars.

Such is, according to the manuscript chronicles of the province, the origin of the church and convent of Notre-Dame-des-Épines-Fleuries.

Two centuries had gone by since the death of the Saint, and a young virgin of her family was again, in accordance with custom, the custodian sister of the holy tabernacle— which means that she had the guard of it, and that it was her responsibility to open the tabernacle on solemn days when the miraculous image was offered to the piety to the people. She took care to maintain the ever-renewed elegance of her adornment, expelling the dust and harmful insects, collecting, in order to compose her crown or to ornament her altars, the garden flowers most gracious in their deportment and most chaste in color, and forming them into festoons, garlands and bouquets, which attracted in their turn, through the large window open to the rising sun, a multitude of crimson and azure butterflies, flying flowers of the solitude.

Among those innocent tributes, the flower of the hawthorn was always preferred in its season; and, counterfeited for all the others with an artistry whose secret the good nuns had stolen from nature, it reposed on the bosom of the beautiful madonna, in a thick bunch knotted with a silver ribbon. Even the butterflies were sometimes deceived by it, but they dared not alight on its celestial flowers, which were not made for them.

The custodian sister at that time was named Béatrix. Eighteen years of age at the most, she had scarcely heard it said that she was beautiful, for she had entered the house of the Holy Virgin at fifteen, as pure as her flowers.

There is a fortunate or deadly age at which the heart of a young woman understands that it is created in order to love, and Béatrix had reached it; but that need, vague and anxious at first, had only rendered her duties dearer to her. Incapable of explaining the secret movements by which she was agitated, she had mistaken them for the instinct of the pious fervor that accuses itself of not being ardent enough, and believes itself to be obliged toward the object of its love, as long as it does not love it to the extent of enthusiasm or delirium.

The unknown object of those transports escaped her inexperience; and among those that fell, if one might express it thus, under the senses of her ingenuous soul, only the Holy Virgin appeared to be worthy of that passionate adoration, for which her life could scarcely suffice. That perpetual cult had become the unique occupation of her thought, the unique charm of her solitude; it even filled her dreams with mysterious languors and ineffable transports.

She was often seen prostrate before the tabernacle, exhaling toward her divine protectress prayers punctuated by sobs, or moistening the parvis with her tears; and the celestial Virgin doubtless smiled from the height of her eternal throne, at that happy and tender mistake of innocence, for the Holy Virgin loved Béatrix and obtained pleasure in being loved by her. Perhaps she had also read in Béatrix's heart that she would always be loved therein.

An event occurred at that time which lifted the veil under which Béatrix's secret had been hidden from herself for so long. A young lord of the region, attacked by assassins, was left for dead in the forest; and although he conserved, at the most, a few faint appearances of a life about to be extinguished, the servants of the monastery carried him to their infirmary.

As the daughters of aristocrats possessed in that epoch, from childhood on, the formulae of remedies and the art of dressing wounds, Béatrix was sent by her sisters to aid the dying man. She put to work everything that she had learned of the useful science, but she counted more on the intercession of the miraculous Virgin; and her long and laborious vigils divided between the cares of a nurse and the prayers of a servant of Marie obtained all the success that she had hoped. Raymond opened his eyes to the light again and recognized his liberator; he had seen her a few times in the château where she had been born.

"What!" he cried. "Béatrix, is it you that I'm rediscovering, whom I loved so much in my childhood, and for whom the wishes of your father and mine, too quickly forgotten, permitted me to hope as a wife? By what fatal hazard do I see you again, enchained by the bonds of a life that is not made for you, separated without return from the brilliant society of which you were the ornament? Oh, if you have chosen this condition of solitude and abnegation yourself, Béatrix, I swear to you that it is because you did not know your heart yet.

"The engagement that you have contracted, in the ignorance of sentiments natural to everything that breathes, is void before God and before men. You have betrayed without knowing it your destiny as a lover, wife and mother! You have condemned yourself, poor and dear child, to days of ennui, bitterness and disgust, the long sadness of which cannot be soothed henceforth by any pleasure. It is, however, so sweet to love, so sweet to be loved and so sweet to revive by means of what one loves in the objects that one loves. The pure joys of an affection that doubles, that multiplies life; the tenderness of a friend who adores you, who embellishes all your moments with new fêtes, who only exists to cherish and to please you; the innocent caresses of pretty children, so fresh, so gracious, so glad to be alive, which a barbaric caprice would have abandoned to annihilation—that is what you will have lost, my Béatrix, if a blind obstinacy retains you in the abyss into which you have plunged!

"But no," he continued, with an even more ardent expansion, "you shall not misinterpret the intentions of your God and mine, who has only brought us together in order to reunite us forever. You will render to the desires of the amour that implores you and enlightens you. You will be the wife of your Raymond, as you were his sister and his beloved. Don't turn your eyes full of tears away from him. Don't snatch away your hand, which is trembling in his. Tell him that you are ready to follow him, and not to quit him again . . ."

Béatrix did not respond; she had not been able to find the expressions to render what she was experiencing. She escaped from Raymond's enfeebled arms and drew away, troubled, bewildered and palpitating, and went to fall at the feet of the Virgin, her consolation and her support. She wept there, as before, but it was no longer with an unknown emotion devoid of an object; it was with a sentiment more powerful than piety, more powerful than shame, more powerful—alas—than the Holy Virgin to whom she was appealing in vain for aid; and her tears, this time, were bitter and burning.

She was seen there several days in succession, prostrate and suppliant, and no one was astonished, because everyone in the convent knew her passionate devotion for Notre-Dame-des-Épines-Fleuries. She spent the rest of her hours in the wounded man's chamber, even though his cure had ceased to require assiduous cares.

One evening, at the hour when the church is closed, when all the sisters have retired to their cells and everything falls silent until the prayer, here is Béatrix, who goes to the choir at a slow pace, who deposits her lamp on the altar, who opens the door of the tabernacle with a tremulous hand, who turns away, shivering and lowering her eyes, as if she feared that the queen of the angels might slay her with a glance, and who drops to her knees. She tries to speak, but the words die on her lips or are lost in her sobs. She envelops her forehead in her veil and her hands; she tries to pull herself together and calm down; she makes one last effort; she succeeds in wrenching from her heart a few confused sounds, without knowing whether she is proffering a prayer or a blasphemy.

"O celestial benefactress of my youth," she said, "you whom I loved uniquely for such a long time, and who still remains the most dear sovereign of my soul, to what unworthy partition have I made you descend? O Marie, divine Marie, why have you abandoned me? Why have you permitted your Béatrix to fall prey to the horrible passions of Hell? You know, alas, whether I will cede without combat to the one that is devouring me. Today, it is determined, Marie, it is determined forever. I shall no longer serve you, for I shall no longer be worthy to serve you. I shall hide far away from you the eternal regret of my sin, the eternal mourning of my innocence, which even you do not have the power to render to me. Suffer however, O Marie, that I still dare to adore you; take in compassion the tears that I shed, which prove at least how much I remain a stranger to the cowardly treason of my senses; accept the last of my homages as you have accepted all the others—or rather, if my zeal for your altars was worthy of some recognition, send death to the unfortunate who implores you before she has quit you!"

As she finished speaking, Béatrix got to her feet, approached the image of the Holy Virgin tremulously, ornamented her with new flowers, seized those that she had just replaced, and, ashamed for the first time of the pious usage that she no longer had the right to make of them, she pressed them to her heart in the blessed sheath of the scapular, in order never to be separated from them again. After that, she darted one last glance at the tabernacle, uttered a cry of terror and fled.

The following night, a rapid carriage took the wounded knight far from the convent, and the young nun, infidel to her vows, who accompanied him.

The first year that went by after that was almost entirely spent in the intoxication of a satisfied passion. The world was a new spectacle for Béatrix, inexhaustible in enjoyments. Amour multiplied around her all the means of seduction capable of perpetuating her error and completing her doom; she only emerged from dreams of voluptuousness to awake in the midst of the joy of feasts, the performances of strolling players and the concerts of minstrels; her life was an insensate celebration, in which the serious voice of reflection, stifled by orgiastic clamors, tried in vain to make itself heard; and yet, Marie had not escaped entirely from her memory. More than once, in the preparations of her toilette, her scapular had opened mechanically under her fingers. More than once she had let a gaze and a tear fall upon the Virgin's withered bouquet. Prayer had risen to her lips more than once, like a hidden flame that could not be contained by ashes; but it had been extinguished there by the kisses of her abductor. In her delirium, however, something still told her that a prayer could have saved her.

She did not take long to prove that there is no durable love except that purified by religion; that only the love of the Lord and Marie escapes the vicissitudes of our sentiments; that, alone among our affections, it seems to increase and be fortified by time, while others burn so brightly and are consumed so quickly in our ashen hearts. Meanwhile, she loved Raymond as much as she could love; but a day arrived when she understood that Raymond no longer loved her. That day enabled her to foresee the day, even more horrible, when she would be abandoned entirely by the man for whom she had abandoned the altar; and that dreaded day also arrived.

Béatrix found herself without support on earth, alas, and without support in Heaven. She searched in vain for consolation in her memories, a refuge in her hopes. The flowers in the scapular had withered like those of happiness. The source of tears and prayer had run dry. The destiny that Béatrix had made had been accomplished. The unfortunate woman accepted her damnation. The higher from which one falls in the path of virtue, the more ignominious and the more irreparable is the fall, and it was from a height that Béatrix had fallen. She was frightened at first by her opprobrium, but she ended up acquiring the habitude of it, because the mainspring of her soul had broken.

Fifteen years went by thus, and for fifteen years, the guardian angel that baptism had given to her cradle, the angel with the fraternal heart who had loved her so much, veiled himself with his wings and wept.

Oh, how the fugitive years carried treasures away with them! Innocence, modesty, youth, beauty and amour—those roses of life, which only flower once—and even the sentiment of conscience, which compensates for all the other losses. The jewels that had once adorned her, impious tributes that debauchery pays to crime, furnished her for a time with a resource too promptly exhausted. She remained alone, neglected, an object of scorn for others as for herself, delivered to the insolent disdains of vice and odious to virtue, a repulsive example of shame and misery that mothers showed to their children in order to deter them from sin. She wearied of being a burden to pity and only receiving alms that a pious repugnance often nailed to the hands of charity, of only being helped covertly by people who had a blush on the forehead as they accorded her a little bread.

One day, she wrapped herself in her rags, which had been a rich costume when fresh; she resolved to go and request aliments for the day and shelter for the night from people who had not known her. She flattered herself that she could hide her infamy in her misfortune. She departed, a poor beggar, without any other wealth than the flowers she had once stolen from the Virgin's bouquet, and which fell to dust one by one under her desiccated lips.

Béatrix was still young, but shame and hunger had imprinted on her brow the hideous traces that reveal a hasty old age. When her pale and mute face timidly implored the succor of passers-by, when her white and delicate hand opened, shivering, to their gifts, there was no one who did not sense that she ought to have had another destiny on earth. The most indifferent stopped before her with a harsh gaze that seemed to say: "O my sister, how have you fallen?"

And her own gaze no longer made any reply, because she had been unable to weep for a long time.

She walked for a long time, a long time; it seemed that her journey could only end with death.

One day, in particular, she had traveled since sunrise along the side of a bare mountain on a harsh and rugged path without the sight of any house coming to console her lassitude; the only aliment she had was a few flavorless roots extracted from cracks in the rock; her shoes in tatters, had abandoned her bleeding feet; she felt that fatigue and need were about to cause her to lose consciousness when, as darkness fell, she was suddenly struck by the aspect of a long line of lights that announced a vast habitation, toward which she headed, with all the strength that remained to her. At the signal of a silvery bell, however, which awakened in her heart a strange and vague memory, all the lights were extinguished at the same time, and there was nothing around her but the night and silence.

She took a few more steps forward nevertheless. Her arms extended, and her trembling hands encountered a closed door. She sustained herself there for a moment, as if to recover her breath; she tried to attach herself to it in order not to fall, but her numb fingers betrayed her; they slipped under the weight of her body.

"O Holy Virgin," she cried, "why have I quit you?"

And the unfortunate Béatrix fell unconscious on the threshold.

How light the wrath of Heaven is to the guilty! Such nights expiate an entire life of disorder. The gripping freshness of the morning had barely commenced to reanimate a confused and dolorous sense of existence in her when she perceived that she was not alone. A woman kneeling beside her lifted her head with precaution and gazed at her intently in an attitude of anxious curiosity, waiting for her to recover her senses completely.

"The Lord be blessed forever," said the good tourière,[1] for sending us so early an act of piety to carry out and a woe to aid. It's an event of good augury for the glorious feast of the Holy Virgin, which we are celebrating today. But how is it, my dear child, that you did not think of ringing the bell or

---

1 A tourière is a nun in a closed convent who has the special duty of acting as an intermediary with the outside world, as a doorkeeper.

striking with the knocker? There is no hour when your sisters on Jesus Christ would not have been ready to receive you.

"Good, good . . . don't reply to me now, poor strayed ewe. Fortify yourself with this broth, which I warmed in haste as soon as I perceived you; taste this generous wine, which will render warmth to your stomach and flexibility to your painful limbs. Make me a sign that you are better . . .

"Drink, drink it all, and now, before getting up, if you still don't have the strength, wrap yourself in this mantle that I'm putting over your shoulders; put your little cold hands in mine, in order that I can recall the blood and the life to them, Can you feel your fingers becoming less numb under my breath? Oh, you'll be well in a little while!"

Béatrix, penetrated by gratitude, seized the hands of the worthy nun, and pressed them to her lips several times.

"I'm already well," she said, "and I feel that I'm in a state to go and thank God for the mercy he has shown me in directing me to this holy house. Only, in order that I might include it in my prayers, have the goodness to tell me where I am."

"Where would you be," replied the tourière, "if not at Notre-Dame-des-Épines-Fleuries, since there is no other monastery in this solitude for more than five leagues around?"

"Notre-Dame-des-Épines-Fleuries!" cried Béatrix—a cry of joy that was followed immediately by the most profound consternation. "Notre-Dame-des-Épines-Fleuries!" she repeated, letting her head fall upon her breast. "Lord have mercy on me!"

"What, my daughter?" said the charitable hospitaler. "Did you not know? It's true that you seem to have come from far away, for I've never seen a woman's garments that resemble yours, but Notre-Dame-des-Épines-Fleuries does not limit her protection to the habitants of the region. You cannot be unaware, if you have heard mention of her, that she is good to everyone."

"I know her, and I have served her," Béatrix replied, "but I have come from far away, as you say, Mother, and it is not astonishing that my eyes did not recognize immediately this abode of peace and benediction. Here, however, are the church, the convent and the thorn-bushes where I collected so many flowers. Alas, they are still flowering . . . I was so young when I quit them!" She raised her head toward the sky with the resolute expression that remorse that Christian self-abnegation gives, and continued: "It was in the time when Sister Béatrix was the custodian of the holy chapel. Do you remember, Mother?"

"How could I have forgotten, my child, since Sister Béatrix has never ceased to be the custodian of the holy chapel, since she has remained among us until today and will remain for a long time, I hope, a subject of edification for the whole community, since, after the protection of the Holy Virgin, we know no more assured point of support before Heaven?"

"I'm not talking about that one," Béatrix interrupted, sighing bitterly, "I'm talking about another Béatrix, who ended her life in sin, and who occupied the same position sixteen years ago."

"The good Lord will not punish you for those insensate words," said the tourière, clutching her to her bosom. "Distress and malady have affected your mind and troubled your memory with these sad visions. I have been living in the convent for more than sixteen years, and I have never known any other custodian of the holy chapel than Sister Béatrix. In any case, since you have decided to present to Our Lady an act of adoration, while I prepare a bed for you, go, my sister, to the foot of the tabernacle; you will find Béatrix there already, and you will recognize her easily for divine bounty had permitted that she had not lost in growing old the graces of her youth. I will come to find you again in a little while, in order not to quit you again until your complete recovery."

As she finished speaking the tourière returned to the cloister.

Béatrix staggered to the stairway of the church, knelt on the parvis and struck it with her head; then, slightly emboldened, she got up and advanced from column to column all the way to the grille, where she fell to her knees again. Through the cloud that obscured her vision, she had distinguished the custodial sister who was standing in front of the tabernacle.

Gradually, the sister drew nearer to her as she made her usual review of the holy place, rendering the flame to the extinct lamps or replacing the garlands of the previous day with new garlands. Béatrix could not believe her eyes. That sister was herself, not as age, despair and vice had made her, but as she had been in the innocent days of her youth. Was it an illusion produced by remorse? Was it a miraculous punishment, anticipatory of those that the celestial malediction reserved for her? In that doubt, she hid her head in her hands, and remained motionless against the bars of the grille, stammering at the end of her lips the most tender of her prayers of old.

Meanwhile, the custodial sister was still walking. Already, the folds of her garments had brushed the bars; Béatrix, overwhelmed, dared not breathe out.

"It's you, dear Béatrix," said the sister, in a voice of which no human voice could express the softness. "I had no need to see you to recognize you, for your prayers came to me such as I once heard them. I've been waiting for you for a long time, but as I was sure of your return, I took your place on the day that you quit me, in order that no one would perceive your absence. You know now what the pleasures and the happiness whose image seduced you are worth, and you will not go to them again. That is between us, for the century and for eternity. Reenter with confidence, then, the rank that you once held among my daughters. You will find in your cell, the route to which you have not forgotten, the habit that you left there, and you will don with it your original innocence, of which it is the emblem; it is an uncommon mercy that I owe to your love, which I have obtained for your repentance. Adieu, custodial sister of Marie. Love Marie as she has loved you."

It was, in fact, Marie; and when the bewildered Béatrix raised her eyes, inundated with tears, toward her, when she extended her palpitating arms toward her, uttering a prayer punctuated by sobs, she saw the Holy Virgin climb the steps of the altar, open the door of the tabernacle again, and sit down in her celestial glory beneath her golden aureole and her festoons of flowery thorns.

Béatrix did not descend to the choir without emotion. She was about to see again the companions whose faith she had betrayed, and who had grown old exempt from reproach, in the practice of their austere duty. She slipped into the midst of her sisters with her head bowed, ready to humiliate herself at the first cry that would announce her reprobation. Her head sharply agitated, she lent an attentive ear to their voices, but heard nothing. As none of them had noticed her departure, none of them paid any attention to her return. She threw herself at the feet of the Holy Virgin, who had never appeared to her so beautiful, and who seemed to be smiling. In the dreams of her life of illusions, she had experienced nothing that approached such happiness.

The divine festival of Marie—for I believe that it has been mentioned that it was the day of the Assumption—was accomplished in a mixture of gratitude and ecstasy, of which the most beautiful of past solemnities had scarcely given the idea to that community of virgins, as stainless as their queen. Some had seen miraculous lights falling from the tabernacle, others had heard the song of angels mingling with their pious songs and had paused respectfully in order not to trouble the celestial harmony. It was recounted mysteriously that there had been a festival in paradise that day as well as in the monastery of Épines-Fleuries; and, by virtue of a phenomenon foreign to the season, all the thorn-bushes in the country had flowered again, with the consequence that, outside as within, there a nothing but spring and perfumes. That was because a soul had reentered into the bosom of the Lord, stripped of all the infirmities and all the ignominies of our condition, and there is no festival that is more agreeable to the saints.

One sole anxiety obscured for a moment the innocent joy of the doves of the Virgin. A poor woman, suffering and very ill, had sat down in the morning on the doorstep of the monastery. The tourière had seen her and had soothed her imperfectly; she had made up a soft warm bed for her in which to rest her debilitated limbs, weakened by privation, and since then had searched for her fruitlessly. The unfortunate creature had disappeared without any trace of her being found, but it was thought that Sister Béatrix might have perceived her in the church, where she had taken refuge.

"Reassure yourselves, my sisters," Sister Béatrix said, moved to tears by those tender cares. "Reassure yourself," she continued, pressing the tourière to her bosom. "I have seen that poor woman and I know what has become of her. She is well, my sisters, she is happy, happier than she deserves to be and happier than you could have hoped for her."

That response appeased all dread, but it was remarked, because it was the first severe speech that had ever emerged from the mouth of Sister Béatrix.

After that, Sister Béatrix's entire existence flowed by like a single day, like the day of the future that is promised to the Lord's elect, devoid of ennui, devoid of regrets, devoid of dread, and without any other emotion, for sensible hearts can do without any, except for that of piety toward God and charity toward humans. She lived for a century without appearing to have grown old, because it is only the evil passions of the soul that age the body. The life of the good is a perpetual youth.

Béatrix died eventually; or, rather, she went to sleep calmly in the temporary slumber of the tomb, which separates time from eternity. The Church honored her memory with a glorious remembrance, by placing her in the ranks of the saints.

Bzovius, who has examined that story with the grave spirit of criticism of which canonical authors offer so many examples, is quite convinced that she had merited that honor by her tender fidelity to the Holy Virgin, for it is, he says, pure love that makes saints; and I declare—with scant authority, I agree, but in the sincerity of my mind and my heart—that as long as the school of Luther and Voltaire has not offered me a more touching story than his, I shall adhere to the opinion of Bzovius.

The Four Talismans

The First Day

> Work, take the trouble
> It is the foundation least lacking.

There was once in Damascus a very rich old man who was known as the Beneficent, because he only used his treasures to relieve the woes of the people, to comfort the sick and prisoners, or to shelter travelers; and he gathered a few of them at his table every day, for he was not proud, although he had succeeded in life. The oldest people in Damascus remembered that he had arrived there very poor, and that he had earned his living for a long time as a porter of burdens for merchants, after which, his petty savings having enabled him to go into business on his own account, he had been seen to raise himself to the highest degree of prosperity without giving rise to the slightest reproach, with the consequence that no one took umbrage at his good fortune, which he only seemed to enjoy in order to share it with everyone.

One day, three poorly-clad travelers bowed down by age, fatigue and misery arrived at the same time on his doorstep in order to request hospitality. The old man's slaves gave them water with which to wash, as usual, substituted clean and decent garments for their meager rags and dilapidated turbans, and distributed three purses filled with gold between them. Then they introduced them into the banqueting hall, where the master was waiting for them, as he did every day, surrounded by his twelve sons, who were handsome young men radiant with hope, strength and health, for God had blessed the Beneficent in his family.

When they had finished their meal, which was simple but copious and salutary, the Beneficent asked them to tell their stories, not in order to satisfy a vain curiosity, as most people would have done, but to inform himself of the means of assisting them in their enterprises and aiding them in their tribulations.

The oldest of the three, whom he had addressed, therefore began to speak, and expressed himself thus:

✳

The Story of Douban the Rich

Lord, I was born in Fardan, which is a small town in Fitzistan, in the realm of Persia, and my name is Douban. I am the eldest of four male children, the second of whom is named Mahoud, the third Pirouz and the fourth Ebid, and my father had all four of us from a single wife, who died young, which doubtless determined him to marry again, in order that another mother could care for us. The one that he gave us in that design was scarcely appropriate to serve his purpose, for she was avaricious and malevolent. As our fortune was reputed to be considerable she made a plan to appropriate it, and, my father having been obliged to absent himself for several months, she resolved to employ the time profitably to carry out her plan.

She pretended to soften somewhat in our favor, in order to inspire more confidence in us, and the first days were spent with more enjoyment than we were accustomed to find with her; the evil woman tempted us so much with the marvels of Fitzistan and the pleasure that we would have there in her company that we wept with joy. In fact, we departed a short time later in a closed litter, the curtains of which she never raised—out of respect, she said, for the law that forbids women to allow themselves to be seen. We traveled thus for sixty days without perceiving either the sky or the earth, so that we could not form any idea of the road that we had traveled and the direction in which we were taken.

We finally stopped in a dense and obscure forest, in which she thought it appropriate for us to rest under shade impenetrable to sunlight, and I have no doubt that it was the magical forest that encircles the mountain of Caf, which is, as you know, the girdle of the world.[1] We amused ourselves quite well in that place, drinking wines that she had brought, of which we did not know the usage. Those forbidden beverages plunged us into a slumber so profound that it would be difficult for me to determine its duration. Imagine the dolor of Mahoud, Pirouz and myself—for our younger brother Ebid was still asleep—to discover on awakening neither my father's wife nor the litter in which she had brought us.

"Our first movement was to run, to search and to call out loudly, all in vain. We understood easily the trap into which we had fallen, for I was already twenty years of age and my two older brothers only one year less, for they were twins. From that moment on we were abandoned to the most horrible despair and we filled the air with our cries, but without succeeding in waking our brother Ebid, who appeared to be occupied with a pleasant dream, for the unfortunate child was laughing in his sleep.

Our clamors became so loud that they attracted toward us the sole inhabitant of those frightful solitudes. That was a

1 Mount Qaf, an abode of wonders, was supposed by ancient Arabic folklore to rise from the ocean on the far side of the world.

djinni more than twenty cubits tall, whose unique eye scintillated like a fiery star and whose footsteps reverberated on the ground like rocks falling from the mountain. It must be admitted, however, that he also has a soft voice and gracious manners, which reassured us immediately.

"That's worthy shouting," he said as he approached us, "but it has had its effect, and I dispense you gladly from howling any more, inasmuch as I don't like noise. The gryphon flew away at top speed, without being asked, as soon as she heard you, and you're certainly not unaware, since you've put so much zeal into my interests, that my master King Solomon, deceived by that animal's false reports, had given her sovereign authority in my estates until the days when a human voice would come to trouble these solitudes. That was almost as if he had said eternity, for it was scarcely probable that you would have the whim one day to come and wail here instead of driving your parents mad in their domicile. Thank Heaven, all is for the best, and it only remains for me to reward you in accordance with your merits. You will see, little ones, that I know how to be grateful, for I shall gratify you three with everything that can fulfill the desires of a human on earth—to wit, fortune, pleasure and science.

"Firstly, for you." he continued, passing a ribbon around my neck and showing me a little casket suspended from it, "this amulet will have the property of enabling you to possess all the hidden treasures that we tread underfoot without knowing it, and enrich you with everything that is lost.

"You, whose looks are only mediocre," he said to Mahoud with the same ceremony, "will have the obligation to me of being loved at first sight by all the women you encounter on your route. It won't be my fault if you don't make a good establishment.

"You," he said to Pirouz, "will owe to this talisman the most universal empire that it is possible to exercise over the human race, since it will furnish you with an infallible means of calming all the pains of the body and curing all its maladies.

"Guard these precious jewels well," he added, "for it is in them alone that the marvelous talents you now have reside, and they will lose all their power the moment they are separated from you."

As he finished speaking the djinni turned his back on us and left us plunged in the most profound astonishment.

We only collected ourselves gradually, and without communicating our first reflections, which probably paused on the same idea. The djinni had only disposed three amulets in our favor, and it was probable that he did not possess any more; Ebid, who had not been summoned to the division, might take our sudden fortune ill, and might demand a new division, which would be equally fatal for us all, since the virtue of our amulets, exclusive to each of us who had just been endowed, could not be communicated to others. A sentiment of natural justice revolted our hearts against the caprice of that unequal destiny and made us an enemy ever ready to oppose our designs and trouble our enjoyments.

What can I tell you, Sire? We had the cruelty to abandon that innocent child, who only had us for a support, trying to persuade one another that the djinni would take care of him, but without any other real motive than the shameful dread of having him as a burden. That abominable action, which was to be the eternal torment of my heart, has not yet been expiated by all the misfortunes that I have suffered.

We walked for several days, making use of what remained of our provisions, and sustained by the brilliant hopes that we founded on our talismans. Mahoud, who was the ugliest of the three of us, and who saw in advance all beauties submissive to his conquering ascendancy, became more unbearable with every step in his impertinence and conceit. It was in vain that the stream from which we went to drink announced to him insolently twice a day that he had not changed his face. The insensate began to take pleasure in the reproduction of his image, and strutted in front of us in his ridiculous graces, in a manner to inspire more pity than jealousy in us.

Pirouz, who had never been able to learn anything, so limited was his intelligence, was no less proud of his science than Mahoud was of his beauty. He spoke with assurance about all the things that might be submissive to human intelligence, and boldly imposed baroque names on all the unknown objects that were presented to us in our journey.

As for me, who believed myself to be the best treated by far, since I had enough habitude of the world to know already that all the sensualities of amour and all the celebrity of knowledge could easily be bought for a price of gold, I trembled that my brothers might make the same reflection and I scarcely dared go to sleep without reminding them that our amulets would lose all their power in the hands of anyone who took possession of them. Even that precaution did not reassure me entirely, and I rarely yielded to the fatigues of the day without having buried mine secretly in the sands of the desert. During the night the slightest sound woke me up; I experienced anxieties that resembled anguish; I went to my talisman furtively and dug it up with my heart hammering horribly, and did not go back to sleep.

Those preoccupations, which were doubtless common to us, had given birth to suspicion and hatred between us, and we reached the point of no longer being able to live together. We decided to separate and to march in three different directions, promising one another, with our mouths rather than our hearts, to find one another again some day. With that, we embraced one another coldly, and bid one another an adieu that was to be eternal.

The next day I remained alone with my dreams, with no other nourishment than the wild fruits of the forest; they had been lacking since the morning, and hunger was pressing me cruelly when, at a bend in a profound ravine, I fell into the midst of a caravan of merchants or an ambush of nomadic thieves—I never knew which. However, I went to sit down with security in the densest part of the band, because my amulet had just revealed a mystery to me that I hoped to share with them.

"My friends," I said to them in a resolute tone, "you see among you a poor young man who possesses nothing in the world except these simple garments, but who can render you the most fortunate and most opulent of mortals. As I suppose that you have no other goal in your perilous voyage than to enrich yourselves with licit gains, I have come to offer you an immense and facile fortune, without any other condition than sharing it with you. If it is agreeable to you to give me half of a treasure that my ancestors hid in these solitudes, and which I need camels on order to transport to the nearest city. I take the divine prophet as my witness that I will cede the other half to you, and that it is considerable enough to fulfill the ambition of twenty kings."

On the hasty assent of the entire band, I said immediately: "Dig in the soil of this camp and divide the load in equal proportions between your camels and mine. I repeat to you that half is my share, and that I do not want any more, for Mahomet has inspired me to enrich the first believers that I found in the desert."

The event responded to my promise. The gold was almost at ground level, and all the camels were loaded before nightfall. Although the regions seemed completely uninhabited we mounted the most vigilant guard on the caravan, and as there was not one of us who believed that he could count blindly on the others I am inclined to believe that no one slept. We began to collect the first fruits of wealth.

The following days passed quite peacefully, enjoying the idea of our happiness and confiding our plans to one another.

243

As they developed in our minds, however, we conceived the possibility of extending their range in almost infinite proportions, and after a week the most moderate of the band was discontented with his lot, for the insatiable cupidity of wealth created for them, in the midst of their apparent prosperity, a relative poverty more difficult to support than the absolute poverty of the wretched of the earth.

I had remarked that disposition in my companions when we stopped to camp on the site of an ancient city, whose vast enclosure and superb ruins announced the old capital of a great people. My talisman revealed to me almost at every step treasures a thousand times more precious than ours, but our beasts of burden were already buckling under a burden that slowed their pace considerably, and in any case, the avarice by which I was possessed made me fear further divisions. Under the pretext of visiting the monuments whose munificence had only struck me, therefore, I drew away from the caravan in order to mark at my leisure, by means of easily recognizable signs, the places that concealed so many pledges of my future opulence, and I only returned to the camp exhausted by fatigue and hunger. I was strangely surprised by the agitation that reigned there at my approach, but I soon had the explanation of it.

"Young man," said one of the travelers, whom I had remarked as one of the most determined of the band, "we do not know who you are or where you come from, and in the ten days that we have been together you have not been able to tell us anything about the particular rights you claim to have over the treasure of which we have rendered ourselves masters. However, we are twenty, we have twenty camels, and the treaty that you have maliciously imposed on us has rendered you the possessor of half our camels and half our treasure, while half of the load of a single camel falls to each of us, as if some privilege imprinted on your forehead by the hand of Allah had delivered us to you as servants and slaves. The rules of natural equity require that these riches are divided equally between all of us, and we will still consent to that even though your pride and your perfidy merit a ruder treatment, if you accept the offer we are making you of a twentieth part of our charge. Otherwise, we shall examine the value of your entitlement in the severity of our justice, and we shall see whether it is not appropriate for us to take you to Bagdad as a prisoner in order to render an account of the origin of your deposit, the secret of which is probably hidden in the conscience of some assassin."

While he was talking I had reflected. My amulet, which gave me knowledge of buried treasures, did not reveal anything to me regarding their legitimate masters, and I had, in any case, advanced far enough in the study of politics not to hope that the most sacred entitlements could prevail against the state treasury. The immense fortune that I had just discovered and marked out consoled me easily for the loss of a few miserable millions, for I evaluated it as the equivalent of all the gold in circulation on the earth. I therefore contented myself with smiling with all the grace of which I was capable while meditating my response.

"What, my dear comrades!" I cried. "Has a difficulty so slight menaced to trouble our union momentarily? I have come to bring you myself the proposition that you have made me, and the sole regret I experience is that of not having made it before you. As much as each of you, and not more, that is the desire on which my mind has settled. Take nine of my camels, therefore, and charge the one that remains with the share that reverts to me. That's all I ask of you."

Having said that, I associated myself cheerfully with the communal meal, and afterwards went to sleep tranquilly, dreaming about the inexhaustible treasures of which I had just assured myself the conquest.

The next day, and for several days more, we continued to march without anything notable happening. From day to day, however, the caravan became sadder and more pensive, and it was easy to discern in each of our camel drivers alternate movements of jealousy and anxiety. There was even question of a few thefts, which led to bloody brawls among the adventurers, the least of whom had the wherewithal to buy a province.

On the other hand, the provisions were greatly diminished, and of all the rations, mine had become the most parsimonious. Ten times over I had regretted that the djinni had not accorded me, instead of the talisman that announced the deposit of treasures, one that would have allowed me to divine some unknown silo or even some nourishing root. We encouraged one another mutually to be patient, however, because out route was advancing. Indications known to all those who travel the desert enabled us to hope incessantly to arrive as a town or village and to establish ourselves there as sovereigns. Everywhere, sovereignty belongs to gold.

Finally, one day, delivered to my habitual alarms, I had scarcely succeeded in closing my eyes, at the moment when dawn was beginning to blanch the horizon of the desert, when I was suddenly woken up by the thrust of a yataghan that nearly plunged me into the eternal slumber. I only had the strength to open a dying eye by a crack in order to assure myself that my camel was no longer beside me, and to put a weak hand to my talisman, which was still there. A cry, which would have doomed me, was fortunately lacking my pain, and I suddenly fell into a deep unconsciousness, which my assassins mistook for death. Many hours went by thereafter, for the sun was in the middle of its course when I saw the light again.

I was lying on the edge of a stream, to which I had been transported in order to bathe my wound. A venerable old man whose white beard descended to his waist, and who was leaning over me, completing the dressing of the wound, appeared to be watching my gaze for some faint glimmer of life with a paternal solicitude.

"Divine prophet," I cried, "is it you who have descended from the heavens you inhabit in order to recall the unfortunate Douban to existence, or has the angel of death already transported me on his rapid wings to your celestial abode?"

"I am not Mahomet," he replied, smiling, "I am Sheikh Abou-Bedil, whom the ineffable foresight of the Almighty has led to this place in order to save you, and who has succeeded, with the assistance of your will, and the aid of a few simples with which nature is prodigal. Reassure yourself then, my son, for your wound no longer presents any danger. And you will recover easily in my house, where you will be treated with all the solicitude that your age and your misfortune merit. It is not far from here, and this litter of foliage, which I have had prepared for you, will make the road easier for you."

We arrived, in fact, in a few hours, and before sunset I was reposing on Abou-Bedil's mats

That sage old man had been the light of the Orient. A long-time counselor of kings, he had attached the memory of his name to that of an epoch of peace and prosperity that will live eternally in popular memory. Poets had composed songs to his glory, and cities had consecrated monuments him that testified splendidly to their gratitude. Unfortunately for him, the prudence of his administration had diminished disputes to such an extent that the indefatigable activity of men of law, who can never be idle, changed into implacable hatred for the settler of all arguments, gradually aroused against his beneficent authority the blind anger of the multitude. He relinquished power without waiting to be deposed, as he had anticipated it, and, stripped of all his wealth, he had obtained the mercy of taking refuge obscurely in the poorest of all his ancestors' manors.

He had lived there ever since, equally exempt from ambition and regrets, nourished on the milk of his flocks, clad in their fleeces, divided between the pleasures of meditation and the labors of agriculture, perhaps happier than he had ever been, because he had rapidly learned in his retreat that there is no estate, no matter how disgraced its fortune might be, in which a laborious life and a benevolent soul cannot be useful to people. Such was Abou-Bedil, who saved me from death, and whose good deed I have often cursed, because I have not been able to profit from it.

When I was completely recovered, I presented myself before him in order to kiss his venerable hands, but with a humility less timid than might have been expected of my fortune and my condition, my amulet having furnished me during my convalescence with a sure means of proving that I was not ingrate.

"Generous sheikh," I cried, rising to my feet in his arms, which were pressing me tenderly. "See in the fortunate circumstance that your good offices have been worth to me a signal mark of the protection of the perfectly just God that we worship, and who wants me to serve as the instrument of the reestablishment of your prosperity and your grandeur. A secret that I have inherited from my forefathers informs me that your ancestors have hidden in the foundations of this palace, over a long series of centuries, treasures that surpass in richness even the treasure of caliphs. You can make sure of them by turning over the stones of your subterrains and digging in the soil of your gardens, a few handspans below the depth that a spade can reach. Become opulent and renowned among men once again, then, Abou-Bedil; praise Allah, who can never be praised enough, and do not refuse the blessing of your faithful slave."

Abou Bedil appeared pensive, bit his lip, and made me sit down.

"My son," he replied, "God is great and his power is infinite. I am sufficiently certain of the effect of the remedies whose usage I have prescribed to you not to attribute the hallucination by which you have been struck to the vertigo that is sometimes the consequence of a poorly-healed wound. I have also heard talk, via my father, of the existence of those treasures, and you will perhaps be astonished that I have not sought to assure myself of their possession. That is because study and experience have taught me that there are only real treasures in moderation, which is wisdom.

"The innocent gifts of nature have been sufficient thus far for my happiness, and I shall not take the risk of adulterating the purity of a simple and docile life by pouring into the cup that God has given me the dangerous poison of riches; but your discovery, if it is true, removes from me the right to persist in a disdain that might be prejudicial to your own fortune. In all civilized lands a man who discovers a hidden treasure can legitimately claim half of it, and I would be failing in the duties of the most common equity if I deprived you of the advantages that so much gold acquired without toil and without peril seems to promise the inconsideration of your youth.

"You may therefore take possession of this wealth, if it really exists in the subterrains over which my manor is built. I only beg you, in the name of the gratitude that you testified to me a little while ago, which you ought to reserve more particularly to the sovereign author of all things, to leave me for my part the treasures buried under the soil of my garden, not because I imagine them to be more considerable than the former, but because they cannot be extracted without destroying the plantations from which I take my nourishment, and the flowers that I cultivate for the delight of my eyes. May God preserve me from ever sacrificing the perfume of a single rose to the foolish desire to accumulate in my coffers the corrupting metal that engenders all our woes."

Having pronounced those words, Abou Bedil retired to his baths, for it was the hour of ablutions.

For myself, I had workmen summoned, I took them into the subterrains, and I ordered them to take up the paving stones in their full extent, before my eyes. The purest gold ingots were heaped up there in such great quantity that after having loaded all the beasts of burden that it was possible to procure in the vicinity, I regretted having to leave behind almost as much as I was able to take away; but I did not fail to do honor to my moderation by exaggerating before the sheikh the value of the treasures that I was leaving him, as it had only depended on me to take them from him.

"You will know, then, where to find them," said the old man, smiling, "when you have exhausted those that belong to you, for I swear on the holy book, the Koran, not to touch them as long as I live. Now give the men who have worked under your orders all the metal that they have the strength to carry away, and order them to cover the rest with all the solidity they are capable of putting into their work. Let that gold be buried again in the entrails of the earth and remain there untouched by my hands. It will do less harm that way."

I was so impatient to enjoy my opulence that I was ready to depart at daybreak the next day. The sheikh was awake too, but it was in order to contemplate the sunrise and to visit his flowers. When he saw that I was about to set forth he said:

"My son, may Heaven be more favorable to you henceforth than it has been thus far. You are rich among all men, and wealth brings in its wake more misfortunes than you can foresee. Relieve those who are suffering and nourish those who are hungry; that is the sole privilege of fortune that is worthy of being envied. Avoid power, which is a trap set by the evil spirits for the most innocent souls. Similarly, avoid the favor of those who are powerful, for it is hardly ever obtained except at the price of liberty and happiness. Seek, however, to conciliate their benevolence and to assure yourself of their support, by the means that you would use to gain clients in the middle class—which is to say, by means of presents proportionate to their needs or to their cupidity. All the classes are equally submissive to the seduction of gold; it is only the tariff that changes. Do not disdain to buy at the same price the protection of courtiers, without which it would be insensate to count on the protection of the master. I have no more than a few words to add to my advice: be indulgent and merciful toward everyone; do not mingle in public affairs; and endeavor to learn a métier."

With that, Abou Bedil blessed me, and returned tranquilly to his roses.

While I traveled toward Bagdad, I meditated that sage advice, and I felt the necessity increasingly of signaling my entry into the city by making a magnificent present to the caliph; but I was unable to think about it without being alarmed by the sacrifice that I would be obliged to make by that prudent measure, and I paraded an anxious and jealous glance over my treasures, seeking a means not to be separated from them.

We finally arrived at the gates of the sovereign city, in a plain suitable for our encampment, which extended along one of the sides of the road. The opposite side was occupied by another caravan, which I had no difficulty in recognizing as that of the bandits who had robbed me in the desert, with their camels laden with my gold. Fortunately, the garments I had received from the liberality of Abou Bedil disguised me from their eyes, and I passed close to them in order to assure myself of their discovery without awakening their suspicion.

As I had accustomed myself to the loss of that wealth, which could only augment my embarrassment for the moment, that unexpected discovery suggested a plan to me that satisfied both my avarice and my vengeance, which I hastened to execute, after having put my escort on guard against such dangerous neighbors. I therefore went into Bagdad alone and immediately went to the caliph's palace, for it was the hour in which he held his audiences, which were open to everyone.

It is necessary to tell you, Sire, that the empire of the caliphs had just received one of those rude checks that finally caused its ruination, and the reigning sovereign had only found a means of remedying it by levying an exorbitant tax on his people, which threatened to become a source of sedition and revolt. It was in those circumstances that I presented myself before him, not without coloring my story with one of the lies that the mysterious origin of my fortune continually rendered necessary, for that is the inevitable inconvenience of any fortune that has not been acquired by a legitimate right or assiduous labor.

"Sovereign commander of believers," I said to him, after having prostrated myself three times and having struck my head three times against the pavement of his palace, "you see at your feet the unfortunate Douban, Prince of Fitzistan, expelled from his estates by the cruel ambition of a brother, who has come to seek a hospitable dwelling and a tranquil repose in yours. May the Almighty preserve me, however, from aggravating the changes of your empire with the expenses of an importunate hospitality. I have saved my treasures from the rapacity of my enemies, and the part that my frightful misfortunes have left me will suffice broadly for the needs of an existence worthy of the rank that I held in Persia. By a fatal hazard, I directed the smaller part of it by the ordinary roads, and that is what accompanies me today. The other, which I escorted personally through the roads of the desert, was stolen by my slaves, who left me for dead in a distant region.

"Miraculously saved from death, I caught up with the first part of my convoy this morning at the gates of Bagdad, and the Almighty permitted me to recognize the other in a nearby caravan as I was coming to dispose at your knees the assurance of my filial devotion. That one, which could dispense your people from the payment of a rigorous tax difficult to collect, and which would furnish you with all the gold necessary to satisfy the maintenance of your royal magnificence, will belong to you without reserve if you deign to receive the homage of it. It would be sufficient, in order to make it enter your treasury, for you to accord me a troop of soldiers disposed to take possession of it under my orders, and to authorize me to do justice to my assassins."

"We shall receive what you offer us, and grant you what you ask of us," replied the caliph, "but we shall not limit our favors to that. For three months, our grand vizier has sought to remedy the embarrassment of the empire without success, while the vivacity of your intelligence has just delivered us from it in an instant. Hasten to execute what you have proposed and take his place beside us, for such is our will."

That language struck me with confusion and terror, because I understood for the first time that a fortune cannot take the place of everything. I was scarcely initiated in the knowledge of vulgar letters, and, in consequence, incapable of exercising the functions of grand vizier, of which the distance in which I had always lived from affairs of state had caused me to conceive an extravagant idea. I only had the real aptitude of being rich, an estate for which I imagined one always has enough intelligence, and for which there is no lack of examples. In any case, it is necessary to admit, I esteemed my condition to be far above that of grand vizier, and even the caliph himself, and I had proposed to myself more than once, in my projects of future grandeur, to purchase one day the empire of the world.

I therefore declined, under the most specious pretexts that my imagination could suggest to me, the high favor with which the commander of believers honored me, and I was fortunate enough to color my pride with appearances of modesty and virtue. There is nothing easier than giving oneself the honors of moderation when one has nothing to desire.

That evening, the thieves of my gold were hanged, without them having been able to profit from it, and the treasure of which their crime had rendered them the masters passed into the coffers of the caliph, who did not obtain any more profit therefrom.

The next day, I bought palaces, country houses, sumptuous furniture and innumerable slaves, including women of all colors and all lands. In the days that followed I sent forth well-escorted caravans to collect from the city in the desert the immense riches that I pretended to have buried there, and I organized their voyages in such a manner that every sunrise ought to bring me, during a long sequence of years, as much wealth as I had amassed thus far. I had subterrains of a prodigious extent dug, in order to contain all the new treasures that the earth was to accord to my research, and I immediately abandoned myself to laxity and sensuality in the midst of my mistresses and flatterers, without any anxiety about the future, the service that I had rendered the caliph reassuring me completely regarding the efforts that my enemies might make to remove his protection.

A great deal of it was required, however, in order for me to be sheltered from all danger, and I had soon occasion to perceive that. By rendering the tax unnecessary I had irritated the tax-collectors, who always received the better part of all possible taxes. I had even aggravated the stupid pride of the populace, which suffers impatiently that anyone should meddle in its affairs, and did not want anyone to be able to flatter himself with having imposed independence on wellbeing upon it. I had humiliated the ambitious of the great, who blushed at seeing their honors repudiated by an adventurer, and the vanity of the rich, whose sumptuousness had been rendered impotent and ridiculous by my scandalous profusion. Far from being grateful to me for my refusal, the vizier regarded it as a surer means of taking possession of his power, by debasing it in his hands and making myself creatures among the people by means of largesse. The caliph, indignant at not being able to compete with me in magnificence, had exhausted his resources and his credit in vain by ruinous borrowing and he had remained enclosed in the poverty of his palace for some time, under the pretext of illness. Such was the state of things when I was told that the grand vizier was asking to speak to me.

I went to received him in great pomp and I introduced him, affecting an insolent humility, into the richest of my apartments. He was a man already old, whom I had always disdained to see, in spite of the sage advice of Abou Bedil, and whose physiognomy announced to me the most shameful avarice. His eyes were hollow, jaundiced and bloodshot, his face wan and weighed down by long eyebrows; his back was arched in a quarter-circle, like those of the unfortunate laborers who toil in the mines; his thin body, worn away by privations, tottered on its frail supports like an empty stalk that the harvester's scythe has neglected in passing. He was pressing over his chest a mantle of rich enough cloth, probably stolen from the remains of some predecessor, the worn weave of which no longer presented more than a thinly-wrought tissue to the daylight that threatened to break through in all parts. He lifted its flaps carefully before sitting down, in order not to expose it to the perils of friction, and he spoke to me thus:

"Traveler from Fitzistan, I would have the right to approach you with angry words, for you have forgotten the respect that is due to our august master in representing as a liberal homage what is only a very feeble part of the legal tribute that you owed to him; but his omnipotent forbearance imposes silence on our justice. I have therefore come to signify to you, in his name, and with regard to your quality as a foreigner, which might excuse your ignorance, that half of the treasures of which you have notoriously taken possession in many and various parts of his estates, which extend to the limits of the world, represent his sovereign property, and that you cannot retain them treacherously without incurring the just punishment inflicted for crimes of lèse-majesté—which is to say, death and confiscation."

At that last word, which had a particular emphasis in the grand vizier's mouth, his long and narrow lips lifted up at the corners; his little sunken eyes glittered with an ardent light, and his avid gaze assessed with a blink more rapid than lightning the value of my furniture and my jewels.

His intentions and his regrets were too manifest to escape, in me, the spirit of prudence, already proven, that is the wisdom and the torment of the rich, but my resolution was made with regard to the thieves of the court as to the thieves of the desert, and I had decided in advance to make all sacrifices, because there is no sacrifice that can compromise an inexhaustible fortune. I foresaw, in addition, that the caliph and the vizier would be obliged to bury a part of my riches, and as they were both much older than me, I knew that I would be able to recover one day the gold that they had stolen from me. It was, therefore, only a species of deposit that I hoped to recover before long, swollen by their own savings.

"Sire," I replied with a slightly forced smile, "although my treasures owe nothing to the succession of Abou-Giafar-Almanzor, the first caliph of Irak, and I make it a scruple not to collect any but those which come to me from my forefathers, I submit without reserve to the orders of our master, who can never be mistaken; I even beg him to accept all that I possess, instead of the half that he claims, glad of his sovereign bounty leaves me a mat on which to rest my head and a burnoose in which to envelop myself. I only ask to extract, if your grace will permit, these two cups, each carved from a single emerald by Ali-Taffis, which have contained the royal diamonds of my family since the reign of Taher the Great."

"Two cups, each of a single emerald and both filled with precious stones!" cried the grand vizier, bounding on my divan.

"I have long destined those two inestimable jewels," I continued, without emotion, "to enrich the particular treasure of the great minister who has imposed on this empire the mild wisdom of his laws. It is to you, Sire that they belong, and it is with the sole intention of offering them to you that I am conserving them. May they appear worthy to occupy a modest place among the magnificences of your palaces."

"Prince Douban," replied the grand vizier, raising his withered and crooked hands with an air of benevolence, "we are glad to recognize in this present, which is singularly agreeable to us, the sumptuous liberality of your illustrious ancestors, and we beg you to believe in our benign and infallible protection."

A moment later he had three hundred camels laden with my spoils, and he quit me, congratulating me with affable and laudatory words on my scorn for riches.

It had required a great deal for me to reach that high degree of human wisdom. I consoled myself effortlessly for one day of ill fortune, in the expectation of my convoys, not one of which failed. My houses were refilled, my subterrains crammed; gold invaded me from all directions, and as I could not abide spending it and distributing it, I sometimes feared that it would dispute with me the narrow space that I had reserved in which to live simply in the manner of other men. Two months went by thus in solicitudes and embarrassments, of which the poor at least have the good fortune of having no idea, and I believe that I might have died of the difficulty if the grand vizier had not judged it appropriate to put an eternal end to my worries by a new visit.

He presented himself this time in a different apparel—which is to say, accompanied by a hundred black eunuchs preceded by their chiefs, brandishing dazzling sabers around their heads, the aspect of which seized me with terror, for I had never been very brave, and nothing can render the heart more cowardly than wealth.

The abominable old man entered without being announced, sat down without being invited, and fixing upon me eyes red with wrath he said: "Infamous ghoul, so you have not feared to weary with your crimes the mercy of the caliph and that of Heaven. Not content with having robbed us of our right to half the treasures that you accumulate incessantly, you have contracted a sacrilegious pact with evil spirits to convert into gold the purest substance of our beloved people, including the nutritive elements that germinate in the crops and ripen in the fruits of the earth. Such crimes would have merited a punishment that would astonish the entire world, but the caliph whose bounty is infinite, softening the rigor of his justice in your favor, in consideration of the slight service that you once rendered to the land, and reducing your condemnation to the most favorable terms, wishes to content himself with having you strangled at the imminent festival of his glorious anniversary. The same sentence giving us the investiture of all your wealth past and present, originating from inheritance or acquisition, we deign to take possession of it here and now, before you, in order that you cannot pretext ignorance of any. With that, guards, let him be taken out of our presence, as soon as possible, for the sight of perverts is a torture for virtue."

There was nothing to respond to that speech, since my judgment had been pronounced. I therefore bowed my head humbly under the sabers of the eunuchs and got ready to go to the prison where I would await the imminent day of solemn executions. I had scarcely reached the door of my hall of ceremonies when the shrill and cracked voice of the grand vizier rang in our ears.

"Hola!" he said. "Bring back that wretch and have him stripped before my eyes of the magnificent vestments that he has the audacity to display in the midst of the public calamities that his spells have attracted to the land. The coarsest and vilest cloak is too good to cover him. Take care to place these sumptuous clothes in our vestry for some charitable usage for which we have reserved them, for we know a good man whose name is in benediction among the people, who is always dressed with an extreme simplicity because of his great modesty, who will heighten these rich garments further by his grace and fine bearing . . .

"Wait, wait," he cried, as if on reflection, "what is that casket hanging by that chain of brilliant metal over the breast of the infidel? Let me see it this instant! It is, in verity, as remarkable in its workmanship as its substance. To judge by its weight, it must be full of the purest gold; the stones with which it is incrusted are so fine that one might think them stolen from the crown of Solomon, and the sculpture is so delicate that it might have been wrought by peris. I proposed, at first glance, to make a present of it to Fatima, the youngest of my slaves, to whom I have never given anything, but I think that it would be better to conserve it in my treasury, in which it will veritably not be the least rare item."

As he finished that execrable speech, the old rogue passed the chain of my amulet around his neck.

"You are not mistaken at all regarding the value of that jewel, accursed thief whom God will punish with eternal torments," I cried, roaring with fury. "The casket that you have stolen from me is the marvelous talisman that gave me knowledge of all the treasures of the earth. If the impatience of your insatiable avarice could have been satisfied with the wealth I would have given you, in six months I would have changed all your palaces into gold and I would have enabled you to walk in your gardens on diamond sand. It would have been less costly to distribute kingdoms to your slaves that it has cost you today to take possession of a wretched imitation silver necklace. Die then of despair and rage stupid and detestable man, for the talisman of which you have unworthily taken possession has just lost all of its virtue in falling into profane hands. It will not even reveal to you, at present, the mysterious place where I have hidden my most precious riches."

In fact, the talisman had become mute, and the grand vizier already knew it. That idea had struck him a mortal blow; he was taken away unconscious, and I was dragged to prison.

A short time later the vizier died, in the midst of his sacks of gold, of the regret of not being able to increase their number. The caliph took possession of his heritage and my most hidden treasures, and he devoured in temporary sensualities the vain residues of my fortune, which only served to soften him and the corruption of his court. Even the people enervated their courage in delights and feasts. The enemy took advantage of those days of intoxication and delirium to plant its tents in the middle of the old kingdom of Abou-Giafar, and before the joyous anniversary of the coronation, when I was to be hanged, the entire empire had perished, because there had been one man within it who was too rich. Such were the real effects of the talisman that the djinni of the mountain of Caf had given me, for the ruination of a nation and perhaps for the misfortune of the world.

The government that succeeded that of the crowned thief took possession by turns of the direction of affairs in the name of justice and humanity, for it appears decidedly that that is one of the best possible means of deceiving people. Only the signal persecution of which I had been the victim was forgotten, because the splendor of my former estate had made as many rivals as there were rich men, and as many enemies as there were poor ones, and there was no one if Bagdad who had not, by means of violence or skill, taken a good part of my spoils. The dungeons were only opened to me after thirty years, by a popular insurrection, and I found myself fortunate to escape from the city where I had deployed so much sumptuousness, by courtesy of a conflagration.

My first thought was to return to the modest manor of Abou Bedil, not because I hoped to find him still alive, but because I flattered myself that he had not revealed to his heirs the treasure in his gardens. Alas, I did not succeed without long research in locating the place. The workers I had employed had remembered that mystery; a short time after my departure they had murdered the old sheikh and his family; the earth, dug up distantly all around, had yielded its fatal deposit to them. Not one of the nourishing plants that his hands had cultivated remained, which might have relieved my hunger. Thus, I had brought to his house, for the price of such kind hospitality, the most frightful misfortunes; and those horrible calamities, the depiction of which has followed me everywhere I direct my steps, were the produce of the talisman of gold.

It was therefore necessary to resign myself to my destiny, and extend my hand from city to city to the pious charity of passers-by, assisted more often by the poor than by the fortunate of the earth, whose prosperity dries up the heart as it had desiccated mine; for my blind opulence has not left from its short duration, I confess while blushing with shame and indignation, the trace of a benefit of little value of which recognition could now pay me the interest. Twenty years have gone by since then, and it is in that state of opprobrium that I arrived this morning in Bagdad, attracted, Sire, by the renown of your inexhaustible compassion for the wretched, in order to beg for a feeble assistance at your door, where I found these two old men.

✳

That is the story of Douban the rich, who had at his disposal all unknown treasures, and who had proposed, at the age of twenty years, to buy all the kingdoms and all the islands of the world, and who had lived for fifty years on the coarse aliments of prison and the uncertain resources of alms.

Although it does not appear to me to be very amusing, the beneficent old man of Damascus had listened with more attention than I would have been capable of lending to it myself if I were obliged to reread it. As the hour was advanced, however, he got up, blessing his guests, and adjourned them until the next day in order to hear the rest of their stories.

The Second Day

The next day, the three aged travelers returned to the house of the old man of Damascus at the time when they had been invited. They each received a purse of gold, as the day before, and sat down to a banquet with perfect contentment, for they had not been so generously welcomed or so fortunate for a long time. Douban the rich seemed particularly astonished to be at ease in his affairs, and to be living so largely.

When the meal had concluded, the good old man of Damascus turned toward the second of the three old men, who was to his right, and testified to him by a slight inclination of the head that he would have pleasure in hearing his story. That one did not have to be begged any further and he recounted what you are about to read.

✳

The Story of Mahoud the Seducer

Sire, I will not occupy you for a long time with the details of my childhood, for they have been reported to you with a great deal of exactitude by the one of my two companions who has had the honor of speaking before you. I am, in fact, his brother, Mahoud the handsome, nicknamed the Amour and Delight of Women, whose name resonated half a century ago in all the harems of the Orient. You know already how we were separated, and I confess that the disdain of my brothers for the scant charms with which I was endowed made me desire that moment with a keen impatience, although I was not long delayed in thinking that the djinni's talisman, which would make all beauties adore me, was bound to produce an exactly opposite effect on men. I therefore remained alone, as satisfied with my person as I was discontented with my situation.

The desert, sire, is a sad abode for a handsome man. I lived there very poorly and with great difficulty for several weeks, but I found compensation in the first habitations I reached. I have no need to tell you to what kind of personal advantages I owed the most gracious hospitality. I cannot, however, dispense with adding that it also brought with it annoying complications. Men are generally jealous, and the jealous are generally brutal, especially when they have received no education. All the countries I traversed were lands of conquest, but, unlike other conquerors, I almost never traversed them without being beaten.

One day, as I was escaping the pursuit of a hundred rival beauties, a pursuit that has its importunities, and I was hiding at the same time from the rough procedures of their lovers and husbands, I fell into the midst of a caravan of slave merchants, which was going to Imerette in order to purchase Georgians there. As I had heard it said that the most beautiful women in the world were to be found there, and I was no haste to exercise the proven empire of my merit or my talisman, I did not hesitate to engage myself among its servants for some vile office, in the certain hope of freeing myself at the first place where we found women. As you know, the hollow valleys in the flanks of the Caucasus are unfortunately quite deserted, and we were due to arrive in Imerette without encountering a single tribe.

The master of the caravan was a cunning man, jovial and facetious, who had divined the design of my voyage without difficulty and who took a malign pleasure in presenting my hopes and aspirations in a ridiculous aspect. "Comrades," he said one day, "we're approaching the end of our route, and we're going to put ourselves in possession again of the pleasant enjoyments of life, of which the desert has deprived us for such a long time. We shall be very fortunate, however, if the admirable Mahoud, the seductive prince of Fardan, deigns to leave us a few beauties to touch, for you know that he knows how to move them from the first day in the wake of his victorious chariot. O handsome Mahoud, whom nature has heaped with so many graces, will you refuse to be propitious to the good and faithful companions who have shared your hazards, and will they not have a single flirtation to glean behind your rich harvests? Enough pretty women flourish in the delightful countryside of Imerette to suffice for your plans of conquest without you reducing your friends to the misfortune of loving without being loved. There are few among them who merit being associated with a destiny like yours, and you ought not to dispute those with anyone. If only you had arrived in the land sooner, when the fall of the most powerful sovereign of the Caucasus put at my disposal the princess of Georgia, the adorable Zenaib, the unique pearl of the world, whom I sold last year to the king of China . . ."

"Zenaib, princess of Georgia!" I cried, with enthusiasm, for that name was for me a kind of marvelous revelation.

"In person," said the merchant, with a crushing sang-froid, "and it's thus that she spoke of you: 'Cruel man,' she often said to me, turning toward me eyes of a gazelle that would have melted a tiger's heart, 'if you sell my person to the king of China, as you propose, don't flatter yourself that you will sell him my heart. My heart is given to the handsomest of the princes of the earth, the charming Mahoud, the heir presumptive of Fitzistan. I don't know whether you have heard mention of him,' she continued, 'and I have never seen him, but he appears to me every night in my dreams. It is to him that the unfortunate Zenaib belongs forever, no matter what might happen.'"

At those words the entire troop burst out laughing convulsively, but I paid little attention to it. The image that I made of Zenaib absorbed all my thought, and I was already promising myself to have little regard for the vulgar tenderness of the daughters of Imerette. The following day we entered the city, without me having changed that resolution.

After having received from the slave merchant what was due to me for my services, I retired into an isolated kan in order to think freely about Zenaib and to seek the means of joining my princess across the immense distance that separated us. My imagination, naturally rather idle, not having furnished me with any, I had begun to abandon myself to the blackest melancholy when a public festival that was being celebrated in Imerette inspired me with the desire to emerge from my retreat in order to distract myself momentarily from the chagrins that were afflicting me.

There is no need to tell you about the effect that the sight of me produced; there was but one cry during my passage, and modesty forbids me to repeat it. The emotion of the youngest or the most reserved was only betrayed by a few sighs, half-stifled in seeking to make themselves heard. I returned home very late, because of the great competition of women pressing around me, which closed the roads to me. The entire evening was employed in receiving presents and refusing love letters.

"Alas!" I cried, with bitter disdain, rejecting those insensate testimonies of a passion that I could not share. "Alas that it isn't Zeinab, the unique object of my desires, Zeinab, whom you have stolen from me, my beautiful and tender Zeinab! At that price, I leave you without regret the empire of the world!" It's true that I did not have many pretentions!

I had appeared. The following days only augmented my embarrassment. You cannot imagine, Sire, how painful it is to be adored by all women. One could accommodate three or four, and a small surplus, but when it passes a dozen, there really is no means of standing it. And then, there are mild and facile passions with which one is always free to make arrangements, but those I had the misfortune of inspiring were so excessive and so violent that I cannot recall them without shuddering. There was soon no more question of anything but young beauties head over heels in love, who renounced the modesty of their sex in order to dispute the heart of an unknown adventurer. Some were suddenly deprived of the usage of reason; others delivered themselves to the ultimate extremities of despair. My arrival and my sojourn in the capital of Imerette were finally signaled by an insurrection unique in the annals of the world, which could not help attracting the attention of the government. I was taken before the king.

That prince, who was young and handsome, was waiting for me with an impatient curiosity in the midst of the great officers of his court.

"Is it you," he said to me, "arresting astonished eyes upon me, who call yourself Mahoud, Prince of Fardan?"

"That's me, Sire," I replied, in an assured tone, deploying all that I believed myself to possess of dignity and grace.

I must render that monarch the justice of declaring that he remained nonplussed for some time, as if stupefied, but, the secret power attached to my talisman resuming all of its empire, he abandoned himself so madly to the delirium of his hilarity that I thought for a moment that he was about to lose consciousness; and as the sentiments of kings are always contagious, the courtiers who surrounded him, forgetting the respectful constraint that his presence imposed on them, fell pell-mell on the steps of the throne, rolling in the most extravagant spasms of laughter that one can imagine. Even the guards surrounding me abandoned their weapons in order to hold their sides in both hands, in the almost frightening paroxysm of joy that commences to impinge on the confines of pain. That crisis was long, and perhaps appeared even longer to me than it really was.

"What!" cried the king, when he had recovered enough calmness to make himself heard, "It's you who have troubled the tranquility of my Estates with your baleful presence by casting the seductions of amour into the hearts of women? That prodigious triumph was reserved for those little round and stupid eyes, which let fall to the right and the left two squinting and surly gazes, or rather, to that broad flat nose, which surmounts from so high a twisted and poorly garnished mouth! Turn round a little, I beg you, in order that I can make sure that I'm not mistaken in divining a heavy protuberance behind your unequal shoulders. It's there, in truth—I take the whole world for my witness! And to complete the deformity, it only required," he continued, pointing with his extended hand "that the leg on which he is now standing with an affected nonchalance should equal the other in length. By the sun that illuminates us, nothing more surprising has ever been seen since the caprices of an imbecile sex have held the other in honor!"

After a moment of reflection he went on: "Odious reject of nature"—it was to me that he addressed those disagreeable expressions—"I order you to evacuate our realm of Imerette immediately, and, if it happens that you make the least of slaves fall in love with you before you leave, be warned that you will be hung tomorrow from the highest tree in the country, to serve as a scarecrow for scavenging birds."

That severe sentence was pronounced in such a manner as not to permit me the slightest reply. I exited modestly between my guards and I left the city in the midst of that insolent escort, veiling my face with my hands in the dread of exciting another of those sympathies for which I was menaced with paying so dear.

Having arrived outside the suburbs, where I had been greeted even more rudely, if that is possible, than I usually was, I started marching resolutely toward the frontier, without daring to look behind me. I traveled thus for two hours, prey to very serious meditations, for I had not had the leisure to recover from my kan the gifts and jewels with which the beauties of Imerette had just enriched me, when the hoof-beats of several horsemen that were following me closely caused me to fear a new misfortune.

"Stop, Prince Mahoud, if you please," shouted confused voices. "Handsome Prince Mahoud is that you?"

Almost sure, however, that those grave and robust cries had not been articulated by women, I faced up courageously the peril, and I saw four pages or icoglans, superbly dressed, mounted on magnificent white horses, caparisoned in silk and gold, accompanied by rich baggage carts.

"I am the Prince Mahoud that you seek," I replied, proudly, "and if there are no women among you, as I suppose, I can admit it to you without inconvenience for public tranquility. Now, what do you want with me?"

I shall not dissimulate from you, Sire, that the sight of me produced its customary effect on those idiots. After a moment of stupid jeers however they collected themselves, and the one who seemed to exercise a certain authority over the others, dismounting from his horse with a respectful embarrassment, came to bend his knee and humiliate himself at my feet.

"Sire," he said, striking the ground with his forehead, "may it please you to accept the timid homage of your slaves. The divine Aischa, our queen, who slipped this morning behind one of the curtains of the council chamber during your conversation with her august husband, and who knows its deadly results, was unable to forbid herself a movement of amour for your glorious and ravishing person. While awaiting more propitious days to recall you to her court, of which you are destined to be the ornament, she has ordered us to come to offer you these presents and these carriages, and to accompany you wherever it suits you to take us. 'Tell him, Chélébi,' she added, turning toward me eyes filled with the most touching languor, 'that the minutes of his absence are counted as centuries in the life of the unhappy Aischa, and that only the hope of seeing him again soon can submit my heart to the cruel torment of waiting for him!' As she finished speaking, she lost the color of her voice, and we left her almost fainted in the arms of her women."

"Get up, Chélébi," I replied, "And get ready to follow me. We have, alas, vast countries to traverse before I return to your sovereign's Estates, if I am ever to return to them. Let us submit to the will of the One who can do all things, and who will decide Aischa's destiny and mine."

After that I mounted a superb horse that had been brought by one of my slaves, and I hastened to the ultimate limits of the realm with all the urgency that the desire to escape my new conquest could inspire, for I had not yet made one so redoubtable. My soul was not entirely delivered from the dread that oppressed it until I had crossed the frontier of Imerette, where I left such profound memories.

Tender Aischa, I said to myself then, secretly, *may time, which triumphs over all things, render the dolor of our separation lighter for you. It will probably be eternal, for you do not know, sweet princess, that an invincible sentiment draws me toward the adorable Zenaib, the torments of which can only be appeased by my possession. Console yourself, if possible, and only attribute to prudence an abandonment that is imposed on me by amour. The fault is in the fate that condemns me to be loved.*

Thus plunged into melancholy thoughts regarding the regrets of which I was the object, I abandoned the bridle that was floating over my horse's neck nonchalantly, and delivered myself to the natural instinct of its species, which guided it to the first kan on the road.

I would abuse the attention that you have been kind enough to accord me, Sire, if I entered into the same details of all the adventures of my voyage, which was infinitely long; for, in spite of my impatience, I was obliged to advance in small stages, and I only stopped in the great capital of the kingdom of China, which, as everyone knows, is called Xuntien. Night had already fallen some hours before when I succeeded in establishing myself in an inn not far from the palace, where I attempted unsuccessfully to savor some repose. The thought that I was finally inhabiting the place where Zenaib respired, and the natural uncertainty that I experienced regarding the success of my enterprise did not permit me to close my eyes.

I got up with more diligence than I had done in my life; I dressed in haste in a few simple but gallant clothes and I headed toward the dwelling of the sovereign of all kings, my fact partly hidden by my mantle in order to hide it from the gaze of women. It is true that one only finds any in the streets that belong to the class of the people, all the others being retained in their houses by the extreme delicacy of their feet, which are the smallest, the most graceful and the most adorable in the world, but which cannot serve them to change place.

The sun had completed more than half of its course before I had reached the end of the magnificent avenue of trees that bordered the whole length of the principal façade of the palace. Reassured by the solitude that reigns in the vicinity of that beautiful abode, I had allowed my mantle to float, when a cry departing from a balcony informed me that I had been seen, and that it was too late to hide the features whose fatal ravages had already caused me so much embarrassment and inconvenience. I raised my eyes, perhaps imprudently, and a new cry was heard. A young princess, whose beauty I scarcely had time to remark through the trouble and pallor of her face, fell unconscious in the arms of her women, and the blinds, closed behind her, separated me from her forever.

"Unfortunate!" I cried, when I had returned to my lodgings, my forehead applied to the cushions of my divan. "Too seductive and too unhappy Mahoud, why is it that you are able to please all women, if the only woman whose heart can have any value for you, Zenaib, the divine Zenaib, must remain the prey of her victorious barbarian? But what part of that palace does my Zenaib inhabit? Where can I find her? How can I see her? How above all, can I been seen by her? Insensate hopes! Fatal amour! Deceptive illusions that too much success has nourished! Has nature given me so many advantages over other men only to make me feel more bitterly the rigor of my destiny?"

As I finished that lament, I hid my head entirely between my cushions, and inundated them with my tears. Chélébi came in at that moment to inform me of the presence of an old Moorish slave who was asking to speak to me.

"Let her speak," I replied, without deigning to turn my eyes, obscured by tears toward her. "What does she want with the sad Mahoud? What can she expect of the deplorable prince of Fardan?"

"It is really to you, Sire, that my message is addressed," said the old Mooress in a mysterious tone, "and I do not know these sorts of affairs very well if it does not fulfill all your desires. It is perhaps not without design that you stopped an hour ago under the favorite's balcony, but whether it was planned or by chance, amour recalls you there this evening, at midnight. This key will open the door in the grille that is locked at sunset, and a rope ladder, thrown from the window, will take you to the feet of the most amiable of princesses. Take the key, then, Sire, but respond, I implore you, and do not forget that Zenaib is waiting for you!"

At the name of Zenaib I took possession of the key that the old woman was striving to introduce into my languid hand and launched myself toward her in order to embrace her, in gratitude for such good news, but at the sight of her I recoiled in an irresistible horror, so execrable was the woman to behold, and I fell back in my place.

By virtue of a coincidence of circumstances only too easy to explain, the Moorish slave remained nailed to the spot, rolling terribly passionate eyes at me, to the expression of which nothing in all the terrors of nightmare can be compared.

"O most seductive of all men," she cried, softening as much as she could her shrill and cracked voice, "the aberrations of amour have no excess that is not explicable by the sight of you! Fortunately for you, however, nature does not oblige you to share the imprudent sentiments that you inspire. Deign to reflect for a moment, handsome prince, before accepting the perils of the rendezvous that is proposed to you. It is true that Zenaib does not lack beauty, but she counts among her slaves a woman who can dispute that advantage with her boldly, and who would lavish less dangerous pleasures upon your desires. The emperor is proud, jealous and cruel, and his vengeance might be mote terrible than you can foresee. So much perfection, alas, does not disarm it. The tender Boudroubougoul, whom you have before your eyes, would only aspire, on the contrary, to embellish your existence with the sweetest enjoyments, for her proven virtue guarantees, like the incomparable attractions with which you are provided, that you will never have rivals! Yield, yield, Sire, to the counsels of prudence, and do not reject the desires of Boudroubougoul, who implores you, the brown Boudroubougoul, your servant and your spouse!"

"Abominable monster!" I cried, getting up violently in order to avoid the odious embraces with which she was menacing me, "render thanks to the message with which you are charged if I do not strike you instantly with my canzar to punish your insolence and your treason. Return to your mistress and tell her that I will pay with my life if necessary, for the happiness with which she has flattered my hopes."

Boudroubougoul went out, launching a wrathful gaze at me, which left me in no doubt that her hatred was as terrible as her amour. I went to the baths, I perfumed myself with care, I covered myself with the most elegant garments I could find among the magnificent presents of the deplorable Aischa, and I was exact at Zenaib's rendezvous. The rope ladder was prepared; it only required, in order for me to climb it, the time to desire to do so.

I saw her, Sire, and the memory of that moment, impossible to describe, still makes the happiness and the despair of my life. Forgive, therefore, the involuntary emotion that embarrasses and suspends my speech.

Zenaib, lying on rich cushions strewn with flowers, raised herself up slowly, uttering a faint cry, for the excess of her passion had taken away almost all of her strength. I bent a knee before her and I took possession tremulously of her palpitating hand.

"Is that you, Prince Mahoud?" she said, opening upon me long black eyes that were resplendent with more fire than the morning star. "Is it you?" she continued, with an inexpressible languor, letting her head fall back on her swan-like neck, because her heart could no longer suffer the disturbance it was experiencing. As for me, I sought in vain a language to response to her, at the sight of the beauty that struck my gaze, of which the hours of Mahomet can only ever offer an imperfect image.

Meanwhile, our eyes met, and a reciprocal admiration took the place of any other sentiment; we remained as if swooning before one another, more reminiscent of insensible statues than lovers impatient to be happy.

At the same instant one of the door-curtains of the apartment was parted and the Emperor of China, followed by courtiers and soldiers, launched himself between us, brandishing his naked saber over our heads. Zenaib fell back on her cushions, unconscious, and I lay face down, dazed by terror, as if to hide from the assassins by which I was surrounded the deadly charms that had caused my misfortune. I did not know yet how much I ought to curse them.

"Deliver that unworthy slave to the vilest of my servants," the tyrant said then, "and let her never appear before me again. As for the impious individual who has dared to cross the threshold of this palace, take possession of the traitor, guards, and compete for the glory of making him die before my eyes in the most horrible torments. I will give a princedom of the Celestial Empire to whichever of you has a skilful cruelty in the closest conformity with the desires of my vengeance!"

He had not finished pronouncing that sentence before ten vigorous arms seized me and I found myself upright in the midst of my furious executioners. I leave it to you, Sire, to judge the anguish into which I was plunged when the curtain that had opened for the passage of the emperor was lifted again, and allowed the aged Boudroubougoul to appear. The infamous slave, whom I regarded as the secret artisan of my doom, advanced as far as the emperor's feet, prostrated herself and spoke thus:

"August sovereign of China and all the islands of the world, deign to moderate, in the name of your own gory, the just transports of a wrath only too well-founded, but on which you have just imposed yourself limits that it is not permissible for you to cross. When I revealed to you the treason of Zenaib and her perfidious accomplice, you will doubtless remember that I reserved for myself, for the price of a secret so important to the honor of your crown, the assurance of obtaining the first favor that I dared to implore of you."

"That is true," replied the emperor, "and I took as witness the gods of Heaven and earth."

"I therefore implore you with assurance," she continued. "Learn, powerful king of all kings, that jealousy alone excited me to betray the mystery that covered these criminal amours. The charming prince of Fardan had already rendered himself master of my heart, thus far inflexible, and I was ready to make him the sacrifice of my innocence when he dared to form the project of stealing your favorite from you. He had appeared to be touched himself by my feeble attractions, and the happiness of your slave would have surpassed all her wishes if the seductions of Zeinab had not broken such beautiful bonds. Render me the spouse who abandoned me, and I engage to fix the fickle fellow henceforth, in such a manner as not to lose him again. That is the favor that I ask of you."

"In fact," replied the emperor, turning his frightened eyes away from Boudroubougoul, "that genre of torture can leave nothing to desire of all those that the imagination of men could invent. Let the prince of Fardan be your husband, for such is our sovereign will. I will do more, faithful Boudroubougoul, in favor of such a worthy alliance. I grant you for your dowry the best fortress of Petcheli, and a guard of five hundred warriors, who will supervise the deportment of your seducer, for I do not intend that he should ever reappear to the gaze of the facile sex whose good graces he surprises so insolently. Let him be brought to my presence to hear his sentence."

The guards pushed me before the emperor, and I remained motionless there, as if felled by the thunderbolt that had just struck me.

There was a moment of silence then while I tried to explain myself, which was terminated by outbursts of such an extraordinary genre that I could not help raising my head in order to discover their cause. The sight of me had produced the same effect on the court of Xuntien as on the court of Imerette; but, as the Chinese are much more cheerful than the Georgians, their transports had something frightful that consternated me as much as my own misfortune. The emperor, above all, was prey to convulsions of laughter so delirious that his life seemed to be in danger, when he succeeded in sitting down, breathless, on one of the cushions, covering his eyes with a flap of his royal robe in order to avoid seeing me.

"Take him away," he said, "in the name of all the gods that protect China, and make sure attentively of the slightest circumstances of a marriage so well matched, in order that they might be inscribed in letters of gold in the annals of my reign."

The guards then arranged themselves in two lines, between which I was placed, beside my fatal bride. We descended thus into the streets of the city, which the first rays of daylight were beginning to illuminate, and in bright sunlight we traversed slowly a crowd that was incessantly augmented, to the unanimous jeers of the populace, for I understood the interests of my glory too well to leave my face exposed to the sight of women.

It was late when we arrived at Boudroubougoul's fortified castle. She was joyful and did not weary of heaping me with formidable caresses. Couriers, who had preceded us at a distance, had already disposed everything to receive us. The marriage was celebrated in the ordinary form, and the ferocious soldiers by whom we were accompanied had the cruelty of only quitting us at the nuptial bed.

You will permit me, Sire, to cast a veil over the horrors of the fate that the emperor's barbaric vengeance had reserved for me. They can, alas, be understood more easily than they can be described. Let it suffice for me to tell you that my captivity in that infernal dwelling lasted no less than thirty years, the minutes of which cannot be measured by any known species of time, for Boudroubougul's decrepitude seemed to defy the years. The more age weighed upon her, the more peevish and violent she became, and the more she feared, in her implacable jealousy, that I might escape the dire amour that I had had the terrible misfortune of inspiring in her. Even the precaution with which she had distanced all women only reassured her in part. She descended pitilessly into the mysteries of my heart in order to surprise a thought that might not have been of her, and the slightest discovery of that sort exposed me to the most odious treatments. I will leave you to imagine whether the opportunity presented itself frequently, and what it would be, great God, if you had seen Boudroubougoul.

I had nevertheless conserved my amulet preciously. I was reaching the end of my fiftieth years, and if that is no longer the age to please, it is at least that at which sensate people have acquired the maturity necessary to obtain a reasonable satisfaction from amour. I was still living, sad but resigned, in the presumptuous hope of that after-season, when I perceived one morning that the djinni's talisman had been stolen from me during my sleep. Only Boudroubougoul, who shared every night the accursed bed on which Heaven had amassed so much opprobrium and dolor for me, could have taken possession of it, in the false and ridiculous idea that the jewel was the pledge of some sentiment of youth of which my soul conserved a tender memory.

I leapt out of bed abruptly, ran to my wife's room, and saw the abominable old woman occupied in stimulating with the tip of a long iron skewer the ardent furnace that was finishing devouring the amulet. Nothing any longer existed but impalpable ashes that blackened the surface of the burning embers, but which still betrayed the appearance of its form. At that sight, a lamentable cry escaped my broken heart my eyes were veiled, and I felt my legs giving way beneath me.

"Perfidious individual!" cried Boudroubougoul, turning in my direction. "So it's thus that you betray the duties of such a well-matched bond, which has made your felicity for such a long time? This time, wretch, my vengeance is pitiless, and I shall not allow myself to be softened either by your tears or your oaths."

She was standing up, in fact, in order to strike me, in accordance with her constant habit, when an entirely new impression, of which she was not the mistress, constrained her to change her language.

"Oh! Oh!" she said, taking two steps backwards. "By what mystery has this boor been able to introduce himself within these impenetrable walls? Who are you, insolent stranger, who dares to present yourself without being announced in a woman's apartment?"

"Alas," I replied, with my eyes lowered, "do you not recognize in me your unfortunate husband Mahoud, the handsome prince of Fardan?"

"Can it be true?" said Boudroubougoul, after having considered me for some time with a mixture of astonishment and fear. "It's true!" she repeated, in a tone of bitter conviction. "So it's on you, ignoble and deformed creature, it's on you, accursed magician, that the lively and gracious Boudroubougoul has lavished, during thirty years of illusions, the treasures of her youth and her beauty! It's to you that I have sacrificed the flowers of the innocent charms that made the enchantment of the eyes and the delight of the world . . . !

"Get out," she continued, in a fit of anger impossible to express, pursuing me outrageously with the iron skewer that her hand had not dropped. "Disappear forever from my presence, and go to seek new conquests among the monsters that resemble you."

Boudroubougoul conducted me thus to the ramparts of the fortress, for all the doors opened before her. The last one closed upon me, and I arrived in the middle of the public square, regretting profoundly having advised myself sooner of such a facile means of reconquering my liberty. I had not lost with my talisman the slightly belated confidence that I founded on the good will of women. I sought their gaze, I watched out for their emotions, I expected their enthusiasm and their advances, but I obtained nothing but rejection. The day of my triumphs was gone forever. Trust after that the advantages of nature and the talismans of djinn!

The beginning of my story resembled the beginning of the story of my brother Douban the Rich, and the two stories also resemble one another in their conclusion. Obliged, like him, for twenty years, to subsist at the expense of public charity, I arrived in Damascus, where everyone indicated to me this hospitable house heaped with the benedictions of Heaven and those of the multitude. I was coming to request aliments for a day and shelter for a night, when I found those two old men at the door, one of whom is my brother. May the sovereign master of all things recognize the generous welcome that you have given me!

That is the story of Mahoud the Seducer, who had the gift of being loved by all women, who had disdained for twenty years the hearts of princesses and queens, who had moaned for thirty years under the yoke of the most abominable and wicked of creatures, and who had lived, since he had been liberated, on the petty alms of the people, like his brother Douban the Rich.

Although it appears to me to be scarcely more amusing than the first, the beneficent old man of Damascus had listened with more attention than you have probably brought to it yourself, and I beg you not to regard that observation as a reproach. But as the hour was late, he got up, blessing his guests, and adjourned until the following day hearing the remainder of their adventures.

The Third and Final Day

The next day, the three old men came together again in the house of the beneficent old man of Damascus, at the hour of the evening meal, to which they had been invited. They each received a purse of gold, as on the two previous days, and when the banquet had finished, their host, addressing the one who had not yet spoken, reminded him that he was also expecting the recitation of his story. The unknown traveler, who was a serious and circumspect man, passed his hand gravely over his bead, bowed in a dignified and polite manner to the father of the family and his children, and commenced in these terms:

The Story of Pirouz the Savant

Illustrious Sires, you will perhaps not learn without astonishment that I am the third brother of these two old men, and it is me of whom they have spoken under the name of Pirouz. I am better known today in the Orient by the title of the Savant, which was given to me in order to distinguish my excellence from the host of men who make a profession of science, at the risk and peril of humankind, without ever being signaled by a useful discovery.

280

It is me who received from the djinni of the mountain the talisman by means of which one knows the secret of maladies and the special electuaries that nature has produced in order to remedy them. He had probably not made that choice without reason, my inclination having always been borne to the research of the precious arcana that would be the foremost of human riches, if humans were able to know them. I received that favor with joy, because it opened to me the hope of a long future of fortune and glory, and I quit my brothers without regret and without envy. Smitten with their opulence and their personal advantages, they enjoyed a health that gave me no reason to believe that they would ever have need of me. I therefore took away my share of the provisions and advanced into the desert, collecting the various simples adapted to the principal infirmities of the species.

A few weeks went by; my sack was full of specifics and empty of provisions. I found myself rich in everything that could cure or soothe the suffering of humankind, with the exception of hunger, that positive evil, for which sages have not yet been able to provide any remedy except eating. What consoled me, Sire, in the torments that it caused me to experience, was that I was not unaware that there were many savants who had experienced it before me, and, if one can rely on the testimony of history, it is not absolutely necessary to go into the desert to find examples of it.

I was pressed by that importunate and humiliating necessity when my ear was struck by the sound of a few human voices. The noisy delirium by which those travelers seemed to be animated led me to hope right away that I was dealing with sick people, but I perceived with a certain satisfaction, I must admit, that it only announced the benevolent and communicative explosion of a banquet that was approaching its end. I slipped into it without dread; people who are hungry are so insinuating and persuasive! I was admitted without difficulty; people who are dining are so polite! I took part, with an entirely natural expansion in the good cheer and the joy of the guests, and I would have stayed there for a long time if a particular care had not summoned them elsewhere.

It was a funeral feast.

The king of Egypt had a favorite then, whom a passion for hunting wild beasts often drew in their pursuit into the most savage regions. He had stopped the previous evening, with his escort, in the place where we were assembled, and he had fallen victim to the vengeance of a mortally wounded tiger, which had left him lifeless alongside it on the desert sand. The grave had been dug, the cadaver was there, and that was why they were rejoicing while awaiting the funeral.

I had no sooner touched the dead man than I realized that he was alive. My sack furnished me with unknown balms and dictams of a heroic power, and when everything was ready for the burial my dead man mounted a horse.

The rarest good fortune that can arrive to a young physician is to make his debut in the practice by curing a great lord. The salvation of an entire people could not extract him from obscurity; that of a man of position makes his fortune—but mine was to be exposed to strange vicissitudes, and I shall only recount to you a part of them. I arrived in Cairo under the auspices of a courtier whom the favor that he enjoyed rendered at least the equal of the sovereign, and, in consequence, with an almost infallible perspective of profit and glory. Unfortunately for my patron and for me, the prince, who had need of a more assiduous friend, had just given my master a successor. When his favorite arrived, he had his head cut off, which is a kind of accident for which my amulet did not inform me of the slightest remedy. Science cannot provide everything.

By virtue of a compensation for which only physicians have good reason to congratulate themselves, the contagion that desolates Egypt every year was them inflicting horrible ravages.

The circumstance was propitious, and I took advantage of it in haste to cure all the sick, with the exception of those who preferred to die in accordance with the rules by adhering to the prescriptions that had killed their forefathers. Their number was considerable, and my reputation prevailed, but I did not obtain a great profit from it. There is no one as ingrate as a cured invalid. Men only appreciate health at its true value when they no longer enjoy it. It is different for the heirs of the dead, who never know its price better than when they are about to take possession of it. An heir is naturally grateful and liberal, and that is why the rich are almost never cured.

However, I did not have to justify myself in my practice for a single sinister, or even dubious, event, and medicine was envious of me. The college of doctors summoned me before the sovereign tribunal, in order to take account of the right that I had to cure, for it is not permitted, in that country, to save a man from death when one is not authorized to do so by a certificate that brings in a considerable revenue to the treasury. In order to be confirmed in the exercise of the profession of which I had recklessly usurped the privileges, it was necessary at least to prove that I had been prepared for it by preliminary studies of a very singular genre, among which the first requirement was the profound knowledge of the Coptic language. The sovereign tribunal before which the college of doctors had sent me, which did not know the Coptic language, sent me before the college of doctors, which did not know it either.

The first doctor who had to interrogate me asked me whether Sesostris had become blind in both eyes at once and, in the case that I shared the contrary opinion, which appeared the more probable to the savants, whether the eye that he had lost first was the right or the left.

I responded that the question seemed somewhat foreign to the art of curing, but that, if Sesostris had not gone blind in both eyes simultaneously, and if it was not the left one that he had lost first, then it appeared probable to me that it had been the right.

I can say here, without doing too much violence to my modesty, that that solution was welcomed by a rather flattering murmur.

The second doctor wanted to know my opinion on the color of the sacred scarab, which had always been reputed to be black until the arrival of a traveler from Nubia, where he had reported a green scarab. That difficulty did not present any very grave interest for human suffering, and I contented myself with declaring, in the sincerity of my heart, that God had apparently made scarabs of all colors, and that his slightest works were worthy of human admiration.

The third doctor touched more closely upon question with which my talisman furnished me with infallible means. He demanded that I explain to the learned assembly the secret virtues by which the abracadabra cured tertian fever, and I replied, this time without hesitation, that the abracadabra did not cure tertian fever. As the Egyptian physicians only cure tertian fever by means of the abracadabra, when they have the good fortune to cure it, that response excited general indignation. The college rejected me as a reckless and ignorant impostor who did not even know the Coptic language, and the sovereign tribunal sent me to prison in order to end my days there, with an express prohibition to cure anyone of anything, under pain of capital punishment. I spent thirty years wishing for death, but I had never been in better health, and I did not receive a single visit from a physician. That is the only mark of vengeance that they spared me.

After thirty years the young king of Egypt had grown old. Tormented by an unknown malady that defied all the prescriptions of science, and provided with a vitality that resisted all remedies, he recalled confusedly the miraculous cures of the Persian physician that had caused such a great rumor at the commencement of his reign. He ordered that I be brought, under the formal condition of paying with my head for the lack of success of a futile prescription. I accepted that terrible alternative with alacrity, although it did not seem to me to be conclusively demonstrated that my amulet had preserved its virtue for such a long time. There are so few faculties given to humans that do not lose a part of their properties and their energy over thirty years, and so few scientific reputations that survive for a quarter of a century.

I had no lack of opportunities on my route to reassure myself. Scarcely had I crossed the threshold of my cell than I found the street crowded with invalids, some wandering like specters escaped from the tomb, still half-veiled by their shrouds, others leaning on the arms of their friends and relatives; some lay on straw, extending suppliant arms toward me, others were carried in magnificent litters, having their slaves strew the road that I traveled with purses of gold and jewels. At a glance I recognized all the ailments; I cured them with a word and I arrived at the palace escorted by a population of resuscitated moribunds who were filling the air with their cries of joy and gratitude. I approached the royal bed, on which the prince was sitting, with the calm and proud security of a modest conqueror. Alas, how my confidence was mistaken!

The king of Egypt was not yet fifty years old, but his forehead bore the imprint of a centenarian decrepitude. His wan and leaden face, as if the livid hand of the angel of death extended were over him, had lost even the movement of life. His colorless lips scarcely conserved enough strength to part for the last breath that was about to escape them; only his eyes allowed a few residues of fugitive existence to be divined. Like two sparks ready to be extinguished on extinct embers. He tried to make a movement to summon me, but his hand betrayed him and remained icy on the rim that supported it.

A confused babble wandered over his paralyzed tongue, but I could not hear anything.

My condition was scarcely preferable to that of the dying man. I had no sooner perceived him than I divined my destiny from the horrible silence of my talisman. It did not suggest any thought to me, nor even a subterfuge that might take the place of a thought. An ordinary physician would have improvised the name of an unknown malady and that of an imaginary remedy difficult to find. He would have gained the time necessary to let his patient die, and so little was required! A physician by the instinct of nature and the benevolent aid of the djinni of the mountain of Caf, I did not know those skillful artifices. I darted around me a gaze of humiliation and despair, and I encountered the eyes of the king's physician, who was enjoying my confusion with an insolent smile.

My first thought was that the presence of one of those certified doctors was sufficient to neutralize the effects of the salutary amulet, although the djinni had not said so; but djinn cannot think of everything. Convinced that I would gain nothing by reflecting any longer I threw myself face down on the ground.

"Sire," I cried, finally, raising myself to my knees in a humble attitude of resignation, "either your majesty is not ill or the malady with which he is struck is hidden from my impotent knowledge. I am incapable of curing him."

At those words the king gathered the remains of his strength in order to bring his anger down upon me, but he could only make one gesture and utter one cry: "Put him to death," he said.

"Sire," said the physician, approaching the august invalid, "your indignation is legitimate and your vengeance too mild. Permit me, however, to indicate a means to render it useful to the conservation of these precious days, on which the propriety of Egypt and the wellbeing of the world repose.

Your majesty, who knows all that is known to kings, those visible gods of the earth, is not unaware that our law forbids us to afflict a cadaver and trouble by a sacrilegious study the holy repose of death. That impious science of Kaffirs and ghouls is wisely forbidden to us, but the divine Koran does not forbid us to extract the rare secrets from the entrails of a living criminal. If your paternal forbearance, which watches incessantly over the conservation of your subjects, deigns to accord this wretch covered with forfeits and ignominy to me, I believe myself to be sufficiently expert in my art to open him up and dissect him without touching the noble parts, and to discover in his palpitating viscera the mystery and the remedy of the dolors that are tormenting you, for only the love of your sacred person has inspired that prayer in me."

During that frightful speech, the marrow had frozen in my bones, and I awaited the tyrant's response with a horrible perplexity. A smile of hope ran over his pale mouth, and he inclined his head feebly as a sign of approval. I lost consciousness.

Then my hands and feet were bound, and I was transported thus in closed litter to the pleasure-house of the king's physician, a delightful villa whose elevated enclosure was bathed by the Nile.

Having arrived at the end of that fatal voyage, the slaves deposited me on a cedar-wood table, which appeared to have been disposed in advance for the frightful operation to which I was about to be subjected, while other servants prepared on a neighboring table the instruments of my torture: saws, knives, scalpels and sharpened lancets, the sight of which would have horrified one of those invulnerable heroes of whom the ancient poems of Araby sing.

I had turned my eyes away from them with a terror that broke my heart when a grave and slow tread imprinted solemnly on the steps announced to me the presence of my barbaric assassin. Oh, how I regretted then that the maladroit djinni who had endowed me, without my consent, with the sterile privilege of curing all human maladies, had not granted me in exchange the power to inflict them! With what devastating apoplexy I would have welcomed, without remorse, the king's physician! But I struggled uselessly under the convulsions of terror, and I fell back in my bonds.

"What do I see?" he cried, on perceiving me. "Is it thus that one receives the respectable guests who do me the honor of visiting me? Hasten to break those infamous cords and bring us cushions on which we can deliver ourselves at our leisure to the pleasures of sage conversation.

"And you," he continued, addressing a species of majordomo whom I had not yet seen, "try to surpass yourself in the preparations of a feast that will testify to this noble stranger, by its magnificence, how sensible I am to the glory with which his presence covers me today. When I have need of you for other services, I will take care to call you and acquaint you with my will."

He had not finished speaking when his orders were executed. A table strewn with flowers was covered with sorbets, jams, delicate dishes and exquisite wines, for the physicians of Egypt push to a incredible degree the refinement of taste for good cheer, and have no great scruple about infringing the precepts of the law; I don't know whether it is the same here. I was far from being reassured, however, or rather, I was commencing to imagine that the doctor was preparing to stupefy me with narcotic beverages to which I was not habituated, in order to proceed thereafter with his operation with less difficulty. At any rate, the scalpels and the lancets had not disappeared, and the sight of those menacing utensils shrank my appetite considerably.

The physician finally appeared to remark my consternation, of which he did not know the cause.

"What, my illustrious colleague!" he said to me. "Do you believe, by chance that it is the holy time of Ramadan, to disdain dishes that would awaken the sensuality of a santon? At least deign to reckon with this glass of old Shiraz, which I shall drink to the honor of your glorious success."

The revolution produced in me by that singular abuse suddenly rendered speech to me. "This is too much," I replied, weeping with anger. "I did not expect to see a man who exercises a humane and liberal profession adding such bitter irony to such black cruelty!"

"Get away!" he said. "You cannot seriously attribute to the most zealous of your admirers and your disciples the intention of that execrable pleasantry. I admit that the glory of opening up a great man like you is made to dazzle my pride, but not to the point of closing my eyes to the splendor of your knowledge and your talents. I followed close behind you this morning as you marched from your prison to the palace of the king of Egypt, and you rendered me witness to miracles so surprising that they seemed more like the work of a djinni than that of a man. Sire, you are a skillful physician, and the least of your formulae would be bought dearly by our academy."

Although my situation had changed little in appearance, I confess that those words penetrated me with a rather pleasant emotion, and that my self-respect triumphed momentarily over my fear. I drank a glass of Shiraz and recovered some courage.

"It is true," I said, with an expression of modest contentment, "that my practice has never been unfortunate, save for one sad occasion, and I defy the entire world to cite a single invalid that I have not cured at first sight, except for the king of Egypt, whom God will pardon the harm that he has done me, or wanted to do me."

"As for that one," replied the doctor, laughing, "you would have astonished me in an entirely different fashion if you had divined his malady, for I agree with your opinion that he is not ill. He has an iron constitution, used up before its time by all the excesses that precipitate the course of life, the satiation of lusts, the satiation of power, the satiation of crime. There is no longer anything new for his blasé organs, on this earth of which he is the terror, and that is why he is dying. Of all my clients he is the one who worries me the least, for I hold in reserve for him, for the first moment of ill-humor with which he has the misfortune of disquieting me, a sovereign potion that will procure him a radical cure for all his ills, and which will cure Egypt more infallibly still of the opprobrium and calamities of his reign. Don't be surprised not to have found the remedy for the dolors that are devouring him. Providence is too sage to have reserved such resources for the wickedest of all men."

"If I understand the value of that specific," I interjected, shivering, "it is regrettable for me that you did not make use of it sooner."

"That is what we shall see shortly," the king's physician went on, darting an oblique glance at his redoubtable implements. "Before then, we have to talk about something else, and at the point at which you and I are we can both talk without mystery. You penetrate with a glance the causes of all maladies, and you know in an instant the remedy appropriate to them. That is a point on which we are in accord, and which the observations I made a little while ago did not permit me to doubt; what I could not believe is that there was a school of medicine. in Egypt or elsewhere, that teaches that science, and you will permit me to imagine that you owe it to hazard rather than study."

An involuntary sentiment of confusion or modesty must have been manifest on my face then, and in my emotion, I lowered my eyes without responding.

"I have frequented, like you," he continued, "the courts of the most renowned sages, and I have learned that physicians know very little, or nothing at all. We reason with regard to maladies by approximation; we apply to then, out of habit, the remedies that have had some success in analogous situations, and we sometimes cure by chance. That is what our knowledge is reduced to, but it is sufficient for us to gain the confidence of the multitude, and to live in ease at the expense of credulous people. If you know another medicine than that one, you are even more knowledgeable than I thought, but I have reason to believe that you have not acquired the secret on the college benches. An honest and unreserved confidence can facilitate between us a good arrangement, of which I have no need to make you sense the urgency. You have had time to think about it."

At the same time he put a nonchalant hand on his lancets and displayed them on his knees with an affected distraction.

I had understood my physician, and I was only hesitating any longer over the terms of the capitulation.

"Such a secret," I said to him, "would be esteemed above all human treasures."

"But not above life," he said, negligently passing the most horrible of his lancets back and forth over a whetstone. "It seems to me that a pretty sailing boat, gallantly crewed, which would transport you far from the land of Egypt tonight, and a handful of Persian rupees that would give you the wherewithal to live while awaiting a clientele would be worth more to you than the honor of figuring one day in a cabinet of anatomy. That's paying high enough, in my opinion, in my opinion, in the position that you are in, for the communication of a few foolish words that you owe to the benevolence of a peri."

"Bring me the rupees," I retorted, "and let us go to see the boat, if it is ready, for I'm in haste to travel. You'll have the talisman.

I passed it around his neck, in fact, at the moment when the master gave the signal to depart. I praised with care the incomparable virtues of my amulet, but I carefully omitted, with good reason, to warn the doctor that it would lose its efficacy the moment that it fell into other hands, because that unfortunate circumstance would have annulled a bargain in which I had the greatest possible interest. It is, nevertheless, since that time that the physicians of Egypt have flattered themselves among those of all nations, of curing all maladies; but I can attest to you, Sire, that there is nothing in it, and that the physicians of that land kill their patients, like the others.

My resources did not take long to run out, but I believed that I had conserved some in my habitudes of a practitioner. I had seen and named a multitude of maladies; I had named and prescribed a multitude of remedies, and my memory had not abandoned me with the djinni's talisman. I therefore traveled the world, seeking out the sick everywhere, imposing most often at hazard the definitions of my pathology and the prescriptions of my pharmacopeia, and leaving the ordinary traces of the passing of a physician in the places through which I passed. I had some remorse for that in the beginning, because I have a naturally sensible soul, but I ended up making a rather facile habit of it, like other physicians, when I had determined in a hundred different consultations, that the most conceited members of that savant profession knew no more than I did. It always happens, in the final analysis, that the patient triumphs over the malady, or the malady triumphs over the patient, in accordance with the sentence of destiny or the caprice of nature.

I experienced a few failures, however, which compromised my reputation and put my safety in peril. I believed that it would not have been in question for a doctor in credit, whose consideration reposes on an old practical tradition and the confidence of a honorable clientele. Those can do anything they wish with the unfortunates who fall into their hands, and opinion dies not hold them to account for it, but it is something else for a poor physician without a diploma, who does not have, as they say, the *attachment* of the bleeding body and the legal privilege of exercising the art of curing without ever having cured anyone.

I was sacrificed without pity in all the cities where I established myself successively to the base jealousy of my colleagues, who divided up my patients joyfully the day after my departure, and never failed to bury them within three days, reserving the pleasure of attributing that bad outcome to the radical vice of the initial treatment. That fatality, which seemed to attach itself to my remedies everywhere, ended up by producing such a scandal that the law felt obliged to forbid me to practice medicine, under pain of losing my nose and ears. I was so weary of the science, and so jealous of conserving the principal ornaments of a human face in a good state, that I resigned myself to living on alms, following the funeral processions that I had so often seen set forth under my auspices.

I had reached that point of misery and debasement when hazard enabled me to encounter, the day before yesterday, at the gates of Damascus, these two old beggars, in whom I have recognized since my brother Douban the Rich and my brother Mahoud the seducer, whom the advantages of fortune and beauty have not rendered any more fortunate than me.

At those last words of Pirouz's story, the three brothers stood up and asked the beneficent old man for permission go embrace one another, like voyagers returned from distant journeys who encounter one another unexpectedly at the common terminus of all human beings, on the slope of decrepitude that leads to death. The old man authorized them with a nod of the head full of mildness and grace; and, getting up in his turn and wiping away a few tears, he embraced all three of them, after which he took his place again and had them sit down.

"It is for me," he said, "to tell you now, my dear friends, how I acquired the dazzling prosperity that crowns my happy old age, and which will become your share, for you see in me your brother Ebid, whom you left on the mountain of Caf. Console yourselves, beloved brothers, and be sure that on the day when the Almighty directed you to my dwelling he had forgotten everything, like me."

He continued:

✻

The Story of Ebid the Beneficent

My story will not take long to tell. There are few vicissitudes in the life of simple men, who obey their nature naively and submit to the inevitable laws of necessity with no resources and no secrets except for patience and labor. What I have done is what the universal instinct of conservation informs all our fellows. What I have become is what God has made me.

My cries troubled, as yours did, the almost inviolable silence in which the djinni of the mountain had reposed for centuries. He appeared to me as to you, but probably more impatient and more fatigued, for he had not expected a further importunity; so I will not hide from you that the sight of him filled me with terror, and I fell before him, trembling, without having the strength to oppose a word to his anger. Touched, however, by my youth and my weakness, he hastened to reassure me by benevolent discourse, which rendered me a little courage, because through the crude forms of his poor education, it revealed a great depth of good faith and natural honesty.

"Get up, poor child," he sad to me, "and leave me in peace without fear for yourself, for I don't wish to do you any harm. It isn't my fault, moreover, that you slept for so long, and I regret that you didn't wake up with your companions. As they had rendered me a service, and all trouble is worth a salary, I distributed between them a few baubles that I had inherited but of which I had no need for my own usage, the patrimony that my ancestors had left me permitting me to live here at my ease, insouciant and solitary, with no other ambition than to sleep late in the morning and eat away my hours. I endowed them with science, fortune and the gift of pleasing. They were all the jewels I had; a poor djinni can only give what he has. As for you, you find me with empty hands, and I'm almost as sorry about that as you are. See, however," he added, kicking an old leather sack that, to all appearances, had been left by some man who had, like us, gone astray in that sad desert, "whether you can obtain any advantage from this scrap metal; I don't have anything else."

After that, he disappeared.

My first concern was to examine my treasure, which consisted of bizarre implements that I believed I had seen before in the hands of workers, but whose usage I could not understand. The second was to have recourse to the provisions that you had spared for me and to assemble what remained in another sack, dividing the two burdens in an almost equal manner in order to diminish the fatigue of transporting them. I marched slowly, because I was weak, and I stopped frequently, because I was idle, as all children are; but I perceived with pleasure, after a few days, that habitude had rendered that toil easy and the burden light.

Soon, I reached places more favored by Heaven, where nature furnished me with enough roots and fruits to substitute for my exhausted provisions. I would gladly have stopped there if the cries of ferocious beasts had not made me anxious during the long nights, which were worrisome vigils for me. It was then that I learned the value of the objects in my leather sack. I imagined detaching strong tree-branches with one of my instruments, which is called a saw, driving them into the ground with a mallet, binding them together with robust stems that I obtained from reeds, and fortifying them with large stones, which I cemented with clay, with the aid of a trowel. I made myself an impenetrable enclosure, where I found repose every evening.

Nevertheless, I had not arrived at human habitations, and my ragged garments were beginning to fall apart. I contrived to make others with some flexible bark that came away easily under my hands, which I shaped with scissors and joined together with needles, by means of supple and solid filaments with which common plants furnished me in abundance.

I was initiated thus, by an apprenticeship of three years, in the labor of all métiers ; and when the adventurous fate of travelers led me to Damascus, I was neither rich, nor handsome, nor knowledgeable, my poor brothers. I was ignorant, indigent and disdained, but I was a worker. Sobriety had rendered me healthy and robust; exercise had rendered me supple and nimble; necessity, which is a good mistress, had rendered me inventive and adroit. I combined with that the contentment of the soul that renders one sociable and cheerful.

The sight of a city did not frighten me because I knew that people, united in society, had need everywhere to pay for a few aliments of intelligence, industry and strength. At the end of a day I had earned my day's sustenance; after a week I had economized the necessities of a day; after a few months, I was assured of life for a month, for it was necessary to take account of maladies, and even of idleness. A year later, I had a certain ease; ten years later, I was rich, in the reasonable acceptance of the word. Wealth consists of living honorably without being a burden on others, in a condition of modest and temperate ease that sometimes permits one to be useful to the poor. All the rest is nothing but luxury and vanity.

At thirty years of age, the care that I put into my work had attracted the attention of the manufacturers of Damascus. The most opulent of them gave me his only daughter of his own accord, for whom I would never have dared to ask. I recognized his generosity by means of my zeal, and God favored my enterprises. I had multiplied his fortune a hundredfold when he left it in my hands. Having arrived myself at the age of repose, for my benefactor had lived for a long time, I limited my ultimate ambition to sanctifying his memory by a good usage of the wealth that he had left me, and am thus advancing quietly toward the terminus of my quiet life, without having anything to regret but a cherished spouse and the friends I have lost.

You were included in that number, for I had never forgotten you. The fortunate event that has rendered you to my desire is one benefit more that I owe to divine Providence. After the rude ordeals of life that have been so painful for us, it remains for you at least to savor in the bosom of the family, the unalloyed leisure of a tranquil old age. That age is no longer that of vivid enjoyments, but it has its own, which also have their charm and their delights, and you will see that it is never too late to be happy. We shall recall together your hopes and your disillusionments, in order to enjoy the prosperous, albeit belated, circumstances that have enabled you to pass over the ocean of prideful illusions to a haven of salvation and wellbeing; and we shall easily fall into accord in agreeing that of all the talismans that promise happiness to vain human ambitions, there is none surer than work.

✳

The old man's discourse finished there, and you will not find it bad if I finish with him. I protest to you that I have felt the need to do so for a long time, and I regret having dragged you into the tedium of a languid narration from which I was unable to detach my imagination and my pen, but the amiable djinni who tells me stories in my sleep had lent this one graces that I have not rediscovered in writing it. You will judge whether the epoch has come in which I ought to renounce his promises, and I will learn from you whether I have also lost the modest talisman that has sometimes obtained a feeble right to your indulgence. That day will necessarily arrive, and perhaps it has.

Franciscus Columna

Perhaps you remember our friend Abbé Lowrich, whom we encountered in Ragusa, Spalato, Vienna, Munich, Pisa, Bologna and Lausanne. He is an excellent man, full of knowledge, but who knows a multitude of things that one would be glad to forget if one knew them as he did: the name of the printer of a bad book, the year of the birth of a fool, and a thousand other particularities of similar importance. Abbé Lowrich has the veritable glory of having discovered the real name of Knicknackius, who called himself Starkius, and not, if you please, Polycarpus Starkius, who wrote eight fine hendecasyllables on the thesis of Kornmannus de *ritibus* and *doctrina scarabaeorum*, but Martinus Starkius, who wrote thirty-two hendecasyllables on fleas. Except for that, Abbé Lowrich merits being known and being loved; he has wit, heart and an active and sincere generosity, and he adds to those precious qualities a lively and singular imagination that gives a great deal of attraction to his conversation, so that it does not fall into the infinitesimal details of biography and bibliography. I have played my part in that inconvenience, and when I encounter Abbé Lowrich in my perpetual voyages across the face of Europe I run to him as soon as I see him. That happened no more than three months ago.

I had arrived the previous day at the Two Towers hotel in Treviso but I had checked in very late and I had not set for in the town. In the morning, as I was going downstairs, I saw that I was preceded by one of those singular figures whose physiognomy depends on the side from which they are viewed: a hat such as one has never seen, fitted to the head as none is ever fitted; a red and green cravat, which surpassed by four full inches the collar of the coat on the left side and disappeared by as much on the right; trousers very unevenly brushed on one leg, the other leg of which was rounded out in a bulge with a sort of coquetry over the back of the boot; and finally, an immense portfolio, an irremovable portfolio containing so many book titles, so many notices, so many plans, so many sketches, so many inestimable treasures for the scholar, but which would not be collected by a rag-picker. There was no means of being mistaken; it as Lowrich.

"Lowrich!" I cried; and we were in one another's arms.

"I know where you're going," he said to me, after the exchange of a few amicable words; and when I had leaned that he too had arrived as recently as me: "You've asked for the address of a bookshop and someone has indicated Apostolo Capoduro, who lives in the Rue des Esclavons. I'm going there too, but without hope, for I've visited his shop twice in ten years and have never seen volumes there older than the romances of Abbé Chiari. The old bookshop is lost, completely dead, annihilated, and the barbaric times have arrived. But have you something particular to ask of him?"

"I confess to you," I replied, "that I quit the north of Italy with difficulty, without carrying away the *Dream of Poliphilus*,[1] of which I have heard mention as a very curious thing and which ought to be found in Treviso, it is said, if it is to be found anywhere."

---

1 Unlike the previous texts cited, the *Hypneromachia*, attributed to Francesco Colonna on the basis of the acrostic cited in the present story, printed by Aldus Manutius in 1499, is real, and is no longer rare, nowadays being available in several modern editions and translations. The "biography" of the author is, however, entirely Nodier's invention.

300

"If it is to be found anywhere," he exclaimed, "is a prudent reticence, for the *Dream of Poliphilus*—or, to express it more appropriately, the *Hypnerotomachia* of Brother Franciscus Columna—is a book that the old bibliographies designate by the characteristic phrase *Albo corvo rarior.* All that I can affirm to you if that if that white crow is to be found in some aviary, as it is impossible to doubt, it is certainly not Apostolo's. I even believe myself to be sufficiently sure of my fact to swear, by the manes of the Ancient Alde—may God surround him with an eternal glory—that if that clown Apostolo succeeds is furnishing you with a copy of the *Hypnerotomachia*, dated 1499, the second edition entering very nearly into the order of mediocre books, I intend and want to make you a present of it at the expense of my own purse, which that act of munificence would lighten considerably."

We went into Apostolo's shop at the same time. His pen suspended over a piece of paper, he appeared to be absorbed in profound meditations. He finally perceived our presence and appeared to recognize with joy the unforgettable face of the good Lowrich.

"Is it the Lord, dear Abbé," he said, embracing him, "who has sent you to me in order to extract me from the most mortal embarrassment in which I have found myself in my life? You can't be unaware that I have been publishing, for a few months, the *Literary Gazette of the Adriatic*, which is, as everyone knows, the most learned and the most intelligent of European gazettes. Well, that ingenious and savant gazette, which is destined to attract the admiration of the world and reestablish my fortune, is threatened with nor appearing tomorrow for want of six petty columns of feuilleton, which I am demanding in vain from my imagination fatigued by study and affairs. A malicious spirit must have conjured my ruin and brought disorder into my editorial office. The young muse who composes my articles of moral education is confined to bed; the composer who was to furnish me this morning with a cantata of a new genre has written to me that he cannot complete it for another week; and the profound calculator who treats questions of finance and political economy was put in prison yesterday for debt. Thus, in the name of Heaven, my dear abbé, sit down at this table where I have been sweating blood and water all night without being able to extract a line from my brain, and embroider me five or six pages of anything at all, even if it is only a short story that has not been used more than two or three times."

"Very well," retorted Abbé Lowrich. "We'll have time to occupy ourselves with your affairs when we've finished ours. We have not come to your establishment, my Parisian friend and I, from the depths of Norway, in order to substitute for the absent cantata of an idle composer and to pad out a feuilleton, but to see some books that are at least worth the trouble and expense of the voyage: a good well-certified first edition, a quinquecentiste of good date and good conservation, an Aldine volume of value, whose English and French binders have deigned to preserve the margins. Commence with that, if you can; we'll see thereafter. A feuilleton is soon made."

"As you please," Apostolo replied, "and I consent all the more willingly to it because that examination won't take up much time. I only have one volume that is worthy of being submitted to connoisseurs like you . . . but it's a volume," he added, taking a beautiful folio volume out of its triple envelope, ". . . a volume," he continued solemnly, when he had disengaged it completely from its vegetal prison, "a volume, in sum . . ."

And he handed the volume to Abbé Lowrich, looking at it with a gaze full of assurance and pride.

"Malediction!" murmured Lowrich, after having explored it with a glance, as was his custom. "The unknown treasure."

Then he turned to me, quite different from what he had been a moment before, his arms dangling, his eyes dejected, his forehead pale. "Malediction," he muttered, in French, in a voice scarcely articulated, so as only to be heard by me. "It's the damned book that I engaged myself to give you if it were found here, the original edition of the Poliphilus, traitor that it is, and as handsome, I swear to you, as if it had just emerged from the press. There are tricks of fate that are only reserved for me . . ."

"Don't worry," I retorted, laughing. "Perhaps we'll obtain it more cheaply than you think."

"And how much is Master Apostolo asking for this rarity?"

"Ah!" said Apostolo. "Times are hard and money is scarce. Once I would have asked fifty sequins from Prince Eugène, sixty from the Duc d'Abrantes and a hundred from an Englishman, but it's necessary today that I cede it for four hundred wretched Milanese livres, which are exactly four hundred French francs. I won't be beaten down by two *quarantani*."

"Four hundred famished rats that will devour your books from the first to the last!" Lowrich interjected, furiously. "Who the devil has ever seen four hundred livres demanded for a wretched old book?"

"A wretched old book!" said Apostolo, sharply, almost as animated as Lowrich. "A first edition of 1467, the first in Treviso and perhaps in Italy; a masterpiece of typography and engraving, whose figures can only be attributed to Raphael; an admirable work whose author has remained unknown until now in spite of all the research of scholars; in sum, a unique, or almost unique, item, of whose existence even you, Signor Abbé, were perhaps unaware, it pleases you to call a wretched old book!"

Lowrich's agitation had calmed down during that vehement tirade; he had sat down tranquilly, placing his hat on the counter of the bookshop, and he wiped the sweat from his brow like a man worn out be long and painful fatigues who had just found a place where he could rest and his ease.

"Have you finished, Apostolo?" he said, in a calm tone, pierced however by a hint of malign satisfaction. "It's just that I want the best for your glory and your interests, for, into the four words that you've just said to us you've squeezed four enormous stupidities, and if it pleased you to continue, I wouldn't have enough daylight to recapitulate them one by one—which wouldn't leave me the time to draft your indispensable feuilleton.

"First stupidity: it isn't true that this book is a Treviso edition printed in Venice in 1467, because it's a Venice edition printed in 1499, the last page of which has been removed in order to deceive you regarding the date, and I haven't paid any heed to that imperfection, which reduces the value of your copy by half. Your good fortune has put me in a state to remedy it, for I chanced to find the precious leaf the other day among some wrapping paper, and I carefully reserved it for an occasion that I didn't believe I'd encounter so soon. We'll see in a little while at what price I can cede it to you."

While speaking, Abbé Lowrich extracted the desirable page from his portfolio and fitted it carefully to the volume.

"That folio goes perfectly with my book," said Apostolo, "but I'm obliged to agree that it changes its nature slightly. Where the devil did I get the idea that it was the first Treviso edition?"

"Let's pass over that," said Lowrich. "We haven't finished. Second stupidity: it isn't true that the drawings in the book can be attributed to Raphael, whether the edition dates from 1467 or whether it was only executed in 1499, as you've just had the proof, Raphael having been born in Urbino in 1483, as no one can doubt—which is to say, sixteen years after the confection of the manuscript, which goes back to 1467, and even the greatest admirers of that sublime painter cannot suppose that he drew so accurately and so elegantly sixteen years before his birth. It was, therefore, someone other than

Raphael who executed these beautiful things, and I am not the only one, worthy Apostolo, who knows that.

"Wait a moment; I have only counted as yet two. Third stupidity: it is not true that the author of this book has remained unknown to all scholars to the present day, for all scholars know, on the contrary, and the majority of the ignorant are not unaware, that it is the work of Franciscus Colonne, or Columna, a Dominican in the convent of Treviso, where he died in 1467, whatever some stupid biographers say who have confused him with the savant doctor Francesco di Colonia, his near-namesake, who survived him by nearly sixty years.[1] They are both buried a few hundred paces from your shop, Apostolo.

"After what I have just told you, Apostolo, I can dispense with demonstrating to you that you have made a fourth blunder, worse than the other three, in supposing that the existence of your magnificent old book was unknown to me, and I don't know what retains me from proving to you that I know it by heart."

"As for that," replied Apostolo, hotly, "I defy you to do it, for it is written in an language so peculiar that there is not a living soul among my friends in Treviso, Venice and Padua who would dare to attempt to decipher a single page, and if you know it by heart, as you say, I consent to give it to you for nothing—a sacrifice that I shall make quite willingly, by reason of the excellent instruction that I would receive from you; for I was very close to advertising that volume in my *Literary Gazette of the Adriatic* from the false viewpoint that you know, and that would have caused me to lose forever the high and good reputation that I enjoy as a bookseller."

"What you have just said yourself," replied Abbé Lowrich, "about the veritably very bizarre style of our author, and the

---

1 Francesco Colonna's Wikipedia entry currently records his date of death as 1527, presumably relying on the source criticized by Lowrich.

vain efforts of so many doctors who have tried to interpret it, proves well enough that you are requesting a fastidious and insupportable verification that would take up our entire day. What would become of your feuilleton while I recite the *Hypnerotomachia* from alpha to omega? I accept your challenge, however, if you can content yourself with an experiment that is no less decisive but much more expeditious and facile. The chapters of your book are already too numerous to fatigue your patience, and I engage to deliver to you all the initials successively, commencing with the first, on which I see that you have just put your finger."

"Let it be done as it is said," retorted Apostlo. "And the first letter of the first chapter . . . ?"

"Is a P," said Lowrich. "Look for the second."

The litany was long, but the Abbé reeled it off all the way to the thirty-eighth and last chapter without hesitating for a moment and without making a single mistake.

"To divine an initial letter among twenty-four might happen by chance, without the devil being mixed up in it," observed Apostolo sadly, "but to repeat that trick thirty-eight times in succession it requires that the game be rigged. Take the volume, Signor Abbé, and never mention it to me again!"

"God preserve me," replied Lowrich, "from abusing your innocent candor to that point, O phoenix of bibliophiles! What you have just seen is only a conjuring trick scarcely worth of a schoolboy, which you will shortly be able to execute as well as me. Learn, then, that the author of the book judged it appropriate to hide his name, his profession and the secret of his amour in the initials of his thirty-eight chapters, which compose collectively a sentence of which I advise you not to demand the secret of the *Biographie universelle* of Paris, for it would make you lose the wager that I have just won against you. That simple and touching sentence is, however, easy to remember: *Poliam frater Franciscus Columna peramavit.*

Brother Franciscus Cololonne adores Polia. You now know as much about that as Bayle and Prosper Marchand."

"That's singular," said Apostolo, in a low voice. "The Dominican was in love. That's something new."

"Why not?" replied Lowrich. "Take up the pen again now, and let's search for a feuilleton, since you can't do without one."

Apostolo settled into his chair comfortably, dipped his pen in the ink, and wrote what follows, commencing with the title, of which I am far from making an overly long parenthesis:

FRANCISCUS COLUMNA
A Bibliographical Novelette

The Colonna family is certainly one of the most considerable in Rome and Italy, but all of its branches have not been favored by an equal prosperity. Sciarra Colonna, a passionate Ghibelline, who made Boniface VIII a prisoner of the Agnanis and was sufficiently carried away by his victory to give the sovereign pontiff a slap, expiated his violence cruelly under the reign of John XXII. He was exiled from Rome in perpetuity in 1328, his children degraded of nobility with him, and all his property confiscated to the profit of Étienne Colonna, his brother who had never abandoned the party of the Guelphs.

The descendants of the unfortunate Sciarra were extinguished, like him, in obscure poverty in Venice. In 1444 only one heir remained to so much misfortune, Francesco Colonna, born at the commencement of that year, doubly orphaned of his father, who had been assassinated the day before, and his mother, who died giving birth to him. Francesco, adopted by the piety of Jacques Bellini, the celebrated historical painter, and brought up affectionately among his children, showed himself worthy of the generous care that he received from his father and his illustrious adoptive brothers, Jean and Gentile

Bellini. From the age of eighteen he renewed in the history of painting the recent prodigy of the triumphs of the young Mantegna; Giotto had one rival more.

However, the fatality that had not ceased to be attached to Francesco's life did not permit his success to become glory; it is under the name of Mantegna or the Bellinis that the masterpieces of his brush are admired today.

Painting was far from being the exclusive object of his studies and his affections; he only accorded a secondary importance to it among the arts that embellish the abode of humankind. On the contrary, architecture, which raises monuments to the gods, solemn intermediaries between earth and Heaven, absorbed the greater part of his thought, but he did not seek its laws and marvels in the gigantic creations of contemporary arts, bizarre and often grotesque caprices of fantasy, which lacked, according to him, rationality and taste. Drawn away by the movement of the Renaissance, which was beginning to make itself felt in Italy, Francesco no longer belonged, except in relation to the faith, to the modern world that Christianity had renewed; antiquity had all of his admiration and all of his worship, and a strange alliance was operated in his mind between the beliefs of the religious man and the esthetics of the pagan. He took that preoccupation too far to see even in modern languages anything but rustic jargons more or less grossly corrupted by barbarities, which were only good for serving as interpreters in the material necessities of life, and could not rise as high as the eloquent or poetic translation of ideas and sentiments.

The result of that was that he had composed for his own usage a sort of intimate dialect into which Italian only entered for a few forms of syntax and a few mild inflections, but which related more immediately to the Homerics, or to Livy and Lucan, than to Boccaccio or Petrarch. That singular turn of mind, which was then the property of an original organization and a character destined, according to all appearance, to exercise a great influence over the century, had isolated Francesco from the rest of society. He generally passed there for a melancholy visionary prey to the illusions of his genius and insensible to the pleasures of communal life. He was sometimes perceived, however, in the palace of the illustrious Leonora Pisani, heiress, at twenty-eight, to the largest fortune that was known throughout the Venetian states, after that of her cousin Polia, the only daughter of the last of the Polis of Treviso; but it was Leonora's house that was in those days the sanctuary of poetry and the arts, and the influence of that muse summoned all the talents of her epoch around her irresistibly. It was soon remarked that Francesco appeared there very frequently, although more absorbed in reveries and madder than usual, but his visits suddenly relented and then he did not come any more.

Polia de Poli, whom I have just mentioned, was then in the Pisani palace, where Leonora had decided to spent the crazy weeks of the carnival. Eight years younger than her cousin, and more beautiful than Leonora herself, Polia, who was devoted, like many young women of high birth, to serious studies, took advantage of her sojourn in the capital of the scholarly world to perfect herself in areas of knowledge that are today entirely foreign to her sex, and the habitude of those solemn meditations had given her physiognomy something cold and austere, which passed for pride.

No one was astonished by that, for it was in Polia that the ancient Roman family ended that descended from Lelius Maurus, the founder of Treviso; she had been brought up under the eyes of an imperious and haughty father, so proud of the splendor of his race that he would have regarded as a misalliance the marriage of his daughter to the greatest prince in Italy, and it was also known that the treasures of which she would dispose one day could suffice for the dowry of a queen.

She had, however, granted Francesco a few testimonies of an almost affectionate benevolence in their first conversations; but she seemed to have gradually adopted a reserve that went as far as severity, not to say as far as disdain, and when he suddenly abstained from showing himself at the Pisani palace any longer, she no longer looked at him.

It was the month of February 1466. The spring, often precocious in that beautiful country, was commencing to heap it with all its favors. Polia was getting ready to return to Treviso and her cousin multiplied around her the various fêtes that could render a sojourn in Venice sweeter and more difficult to quit. One day had been taken for excursions by gondola on the Grand Canal and the wide and deep arm that separates the queen city from the solitudes of its Lido.

Francesco had not been forgotten in Leonora Pisani's invitations, and the letter that he had received had contained reproaches for his long absence so amiable and so touching that he could not conceive the possibility of a refusal. In addition, Polia was on the eve of her departure, as we have said, and it is permissible to believe that Francesco desired to see her again in spite of the ordinary coldness of his welcome; for, in reflecting further on the extreme change that had been so promptly manifest in their relations, he had ended up persuading himself that the capricious metamorphosis had a motive other than hatred. He found himself, therefore, on the steps of the Pisani palace, where the general rendezvous was, at the departure of the gondolas.

The masked ladies covered by similar dominos emerged in a crowd from the vestibule at the agreed signal, and each of them came to choose, in accordance with custom, with the decent familiarity that disguise authorizes, the companion whom it pleased her to give herself for the voyage. That method, more gracious and better understood than the one that has succeeded it in balls and assemblies, also offered inconveniences far less grave, the women never being more attentive to the care of their reputation than on the rare occasions when the protection thereof is entrusted to them alone.

Francesco was waiting, therefore, motionless and with his eyes lowered, for someone to deign to think of him, when a pretty gloved had came to lean on his arm. He welcomed the unknown woman with a modest and respectful urgency and conducted her to the gondola that was prepared to receive them. A moment later, the elegant flotilla was moving over the calm and polished surface of the canal to the rhythmic sound of oars.

The lady, who was sitting to Francesco's left, remained silent for some time, as if she needed to collect herself and to overcome, before speaking, some involuntary emotion. Then she untied the strings of her mask, threw it over her shoulder and attached her gaze to Francesco with the mild and serious assurance that self-consciousness gives to elevated souls. It was Polia.

Francesco trembled and felt a sudden frisson run through all his veins, for he had not expected anything similar. Then he tilted his head and covered his eyes with his hand in the dread that it would have been a profanation to look at Polia so closely.

"That mask is unnecessary," said Polia. "I have no reason to take advantage of the custom that authorizes me to keep it; amity has no need of it, and its sentiments are too pure for it to have to blush at their expression. Don't be astonished, Francesco," she continued, after a moment of silence, "to hear me speaking of my amity for you, after so many days of rigorous constraint in which I might have given you reason to doubt it. My sex is submissive to particular laws of propriety that do not permit it to abandon its most legitimate sympathies to the interpretations of the multitude, and there is nothing more difficult to feign in an accurate measure than an indifference of the heart that one does not experience.

"Today, I am about to quit Venice, and although I am destined to live very close to you, it is quite probable that we will never see one another again. There is no possibility henceforth of any communication between us except that of memory, and I do not want to quit you leaving you with a false idea of me and taking away an anxious and painful idea of you that would trouble the repose of my life. I have provided for the former by an explanation that I believe I owe you; I expect of your sincerity that you will reassure me as to the latter by means of a confidence that perhaps you also owe me. Don't be alarmed, Francesco; you will remain the sole judge of the propriety of my questions."

For a moment, Francesco had uncovered his lowered eyes; he dared to look at Polia; he collected her words with an avid attention. "Oh, Madame," he cried, "God is my witness that my soul has no secret that does not belong to you."

"Your soul has one secret," said Polia, "a secret that afflicts your friends, and which certain persons among them might have an interest in penetrating. Endowed with all the advantages that promise a fortunate future—youth, genius, knowledge and glory already—you are nevertheless abandoning yourself to the languors of a mysterious sadness, you are consuming yourself with an unknown worry, you are neglecting the work on which your reputation is founded and you are fleeing the society that searches for you, in order to hide in an almost impenetrable solitude for days that so much success ought to embellish. Finally, if it is necessary to believe the rumors that are circulating, you are on the point of breaking entirely with human society and imprisoning yourself in a monastery. Is what I have just said to you true?"

Francesco seemed agitated by a thousand various emotions. He needed a few moments to gather his strength.

"Yes, Madame," he said, "that is true; at least, it was all true this morning. An event that has occurred since then has changed the course of my ideas, without changing my resolution. I shall enter a monastery, and my engagements are irrevocable; but I shall enter it with a mind full of consolation and joy, for my existence is complete, and I cannot conceive being so fortunate on earth that there is anything further to desire. Born poor and obscure, but stronger than my fortune, I have only measured my misfortune by the immense void into which my heart had plunged. That void is filled by the most delectable of hopes: you might remember me."

Polia looked at him affectionately. "I would like," she said, "only to see in your words a simple play of the imagination or one of those condescending flatteries of politeness with which one pays adequately for amity. It seems to me that the affected language of cold people is not appropriate between us. I believe, therefore, that I am beginning to comprehend some of the things that you have said to me, except for your resolution. But," she added, smiling, "I do not comprehend them sufficiently."

"You are about to comprehend better," said Francesco, encouraged, "for I shall tell you everything. Pardon, however, the trouble and irresolution of my words, for of all the circumstances of my life, this one is the most unexpected.

"The strange situation in which I was born, without parents and without protection, almost without a friend, having fallen from a great name and an independent fortune, would doubtless suffice to explain my natural melancholy. It is a cruel confidence to make, that of a misfortune attached to the cradle that follows one for life. That idea, however, was the first one of which I was able to take account. I had to acquit the material debt before thinking for a moment about myself, and I have no need to tell you that I succeeded in that. After that, my courage became firmer; I scarcely regretted the grandeur and the opulence lost forever. I went further; I sometimes congratulated myself, in my childish pride, for only owing my illustriousness to myself, and being able one day to force the family that rejected me to envy the celebrity of my repudiated name. Such are the illusions of inexperience and vanity. A day had to come that would destroy everything and remind me of my misfortune and my negligibility.

"Alas," Francesco continued, "this is the mystery that your too-benevolent curiosity has testified the desire to know, and which reason made it a law for me to keep hidden in my bosom. But how shall I dare to reveal to you the sad and profound secrets of sick souls that philosophy and wisdom regard as a puerile infirmity of the mind, and above all while the elevation of your character holds you too highly placed for you to deign to accord them any other sentiment than pity? I am in love, Madame."

At that point Francesco stopped for some time, but, reassured by Polia's gaze, he continued in these terms:

"I loved without having thought about it, without appreciating the consequences of my extravagant passion, without fearing them for the future, for I was living entirely in the impressions of the present. I loved a woman who was designated to everyone by depicting the rare qualities in which she is clad, which combine with beauty all the perfections of intelligence and the soul, and whom Heaven seems only to have confided to earth in order to remind us of the inexpressible felicity of the condition that we have lost. I loved her, Madame, without remembering that she was noble among all the noble, that she was rich among all the rich; that I was poor Francesco Colonna, the unknown pupil of Bellini, and that all the efforts of fortunate labor would only ever bring me a sterile reputation. Such is the effect of the passion that dazzles, blinds and kills.

"When reflection had brought me back to myself, when I had sounded with a fearful eye and the bitter laughter of despair the abyss toward which I had made so much progress without being aware of it, there was no longer time to turn back; I was doomed.

"The first thought of the unfortunate is to die; that is as conveniental as it is natural, because it cuts through all questions and remedies all difficulties. But might not that desperate death, far from hastening the day when it would bring me closer to the day when I would approach her in a better world, separate me from her forever? That was a wholly new idea, which retained my arm as it was ready to strike; I measured the profound future of which the impossibility of suffering in resignation for few days was about to deprive me. I condemned myself dolorously to live, but without dread, in order to attain the moment when two souls, freed from all the bonds that have weighed upon them, can seek one another, recognize one another and be united forever. I made the person I love an object of worship for my entire life; I built an inviolable altar to her in my heart, and I devoted myself to it as an immortal sacrifice.

"You might say, Madame, that under my invincible sadness, that project, once settled might be mingled with some joy? I understood that that hymen, which commenced with the widowhood to end with the possession, was perhaps preferable to ordinary marriages, which end with bad days. I no longer saw in the years that remain for me to spend among men anything but a long engagement that death would crown with an eternal felicity; I sensed the necessity of isolating myself from society in order to meditate in an austere but delectable sentiment, which does not suffer division, and it is for that reason that I am embracing the duties of the monastic profession. God wants to pardon the weakness of his creatures; the oath that will devote me to him in three days is the oath that will unite me indissolubly with the woman I love, which will only give me rights over her in Heaven. Permit me to repeat in conclusion, Madame, that the accomplishment of

315

that design no longer costs anything to my resignation, since a generous compassion allows me to conceive the hope of not being forgotten."

"In three days . . . !" exclaimed Polia. "In truth," she continued, "I have had too little time to reflect on the secret that you have just confided to me to dare to settle on an opinion and above all on a judgment; but it seems to me that if the woman for whom you have conceived such resolutions is unaware of them, as I was unaware of them a little while ago, she was unworthy of inspiring them."

"She was unaware of them," said Francesco, "for she was unaware that I love her. Oh, doubtless my heart could have drawn ineffable consolations from the idea that she knew of my amour, that she was not absolutely insensible to it, and that she might have accorded it at least the memory of pity! Of all the torments of amour, perhaps the cruelest is to remain unknown to the person one loves; of all sentiments, the bleak indifference that one feels for a stranger is perhaps the most painful that amour can dread. But why cast into a peaceful and happy heart the dolors that one is scarcely capable of supporting for oneself? Either my passion would be rejected, as I suppose—and what would I gain then by verifying that sad doubt?—or it would be shared, and I would have to suffer for two. What am I saying, suffer for two? My despair is my life, since I have found enough strength to live with it. Hers would already have killed me."

"You take your suppositions too far, Francesco," Polia replied, sharply. "Who knows whether she might not experience the same anguish as you? Who knows whether she might not aspire at present to inform you of them? What would you say if that noble and rich young woman, whose splendor dazzles you but whose soul is probably no calmer than yours, what would you say, Francesco, if, freely, she came to offer you her hand, if, submissive to a respectable and inflexible force, she came to promise it to you?"

"What would I say, Polia?" Francesco replied, with a cold dignity. "I would refuse it. In order to dare to love the woman I love, it is necessary to a certain point to be worthy of her, and my most constant study has been to ennoble my soul in order to bring it closer to hers. By what right could I accept the privileges of a high position that society refuses me? With what effrontery could I sit down at the banquet of fortune—I, who have for my lot obscurity and poverty? Oh, a thousand times rather the horrible chagrin that is consuming me than the shameful renown of an adventurer rejected by the world and enriched by amour!"

"I haven't finished," Polia interrupted. "That scruple is exaggerated, but I understand it and I share it. Society, as it is made, demands strange sacrifices, and that one would perhaps be commanded of you by your character; but a character of the same temper as yours might respond to it with another genre of abnegation. Grandeur and fortune are capricious accidents of hazard, of which once can despoil oneself when one wishes. The artist and poet is the same everywhere; he has success and glory everywhere; but beyond an arm of the sea, the rich and titled woman who has been able to abdicate those vain privileges of birth is nothing but a woman. If that woman came to you and said: *I renounce my grandeur; I abandon my fortune; I am ready to become humbler and poorer than you, and to confide to you, as my sole support, the whole destiny of my life*, what would you respond, Francesco?"

"I would fall at her knees," said Francesco, "and I would respond thus: *Angel of Heaven, retain the rank and the advantages that Heaven has given you; you ought to be and to remain what you are, and the wretch who would be capable of letting himself be drawn to the tender and sublime impulse of your heart would never have merited occupying a place therein. He can no longer rise as high as you except by means of a constant resignation, facile for whoever hopes, especially for whoever is loved. It is not me who would make you descend from the rank at which God has not placed you without reason, to submit you to the vicissitudes of an anxious existence, poisoned by needs that would be renewed incessantly, and perhaps one day by incurable regrets.*

"My felicity is complete now; it has surpassed my hopes, since you have accorded me all that you could obtain from the obligations that your name imposes upon you. You love me, I will add, and you will always love me, since you have not recoiled before the resolution to give your life to mine. Your life, my beloved, I accept and I take as a sacred deposit of which I will soon render you an account before the Lord our judge; for life is short, even for those who suffer, whatever feeble hearts might say. This earth is only a place of passage to which souls come in order to be tested; and if your soul, as faithful as it is devoted, were to remain married to mine during the years that time still measures for us, all of eternity would be ours . . ."

Polia remained silent for some time.

"Yes, yes!" she cried, with exaltation, "God has not instituted a holier and more inviolable sacrament. It is thus that an amour such as yours ought to conciliate its hopes and its duties in a hymen of the heart, which other men do not know, and your spouse in Heaven would speak to you as I am speaking to you if she had heard you."

"She has heard me, Polia," Francesco replied, letting his head fall back into his hands with a torrent of tears.

"So," said Polia, as if she had not understood those last words, "in three days' time you will adopt the habit of one of the religious orders of Venice?"

"Of Treviso," retorted Francesco. "I am not forbidding myself even the happiness of perceiving her a few times more."

"Of Treviso, Francesco? Where you do not know anyone except me?"

"Except you," replied Francesco.

At that moment the hand of the young princess found itself linked with that of the young painter. "We have not re-

318

marked," she said, smiling, "that the gondola has stopped and that it has already returned to the Pisani palace; but we have nothing more to say to one another on earth. However, our last adieu is not without sweetness, if we have understood one another fully, and our first conversation will be sweeter still."

"Adieu forever," said Francesco.

"Adieu forever," said Polia. Then she refastened her mask and disembarked.

The next day, Polia was in Treviso. Three days later, the emblematic knell was sounded in the convent of the Dominicans which announces the profession of a new monk and his eternal death to society. Polia spent the day in her oratory.

Francesco submitted easily to his new destiny. Sometimes he regarded his conversation with Polia as a dream, but more often, he retraced it in its smallest details with a child-like enthusiasm, and went so far as to congratulate himself on having inspired, in his misfortune, an amour that did not fear in the slightest the vicissitudes of fortune and age. He accustomed himself in a matter of days to dividing his time between religious duties and the laborious leisure of an artist, sometimes painting the pure and naïve frescoes that are still admired in the convent of the Dominicans, although the proud insouciance of modern art has allowed them to deteriorate, sometimes reassembling in a book, a favorite object of his studies, all the impressions of his genius, and above all of his amour.

He had taken for the frame of that vast and bizarre work, in which he hoped to revive in its entirety the rather vague form of a dream, and nothing was more appropriate, according to him, than to represent, in its apparent confusion, the fortuitous enchainment of the ideas of as solitary abandoned to his thought. It is known that, by means of the rare moments when he was allowed to exchange with Polia a few tender words he had received the assurance, that she would accept the dedication of that strange poem, and he informs us himself that she aided him with her advice. It is thus that he renounced entirely the vulgar language in which he had conceived and commenced it (*lasciando il princiniato stilo*) in order to deliver himself there to the savant language in which he had neither models nor imitators, and which furnished him as his pen flowed with his learned preoccupations of an antiquary.

A year had gone by in those mild labors mingled with mild illusions, and Francesco had just set his hand to his work when the most devastating news that could desolate his heart filtered through the walls of the Dominicans. Young Antonio Grimani, later admiral and doge of the republic, but already the most brilliant of its nobles and the highest of its hopes, had just asked for Polia's hand, and it was added that Polia's hand had been accorded to him.

That was the day when Francesco was to present his book to Polia. He steeled himself under the blow that had just struck him, went to the palace and stopped on the threshold of the apartment.

"Come, my brother," said Polia, on receiving him, "come and communicate to us the marvelous secrets of your heart, a treasure that Christian humility refuses to the world, and of which we alone ought to obtain the confidence." At the same time, she sent away her women and servants with a gesture, and Francesco remained alone before her.

His legs were giving way beneath him, a cold sweat inundated his brow, his arteries were throbbing violently and his breast was swollen, as if it were about to burst.

Polia raised her eyes from the manuscript to the monk. Francesco's pallor, the bloody aureole that circled his eyes, exhausted of tears, and the convulsive tremor of his livid and limp hands, revealed to her what was happening in her lover's heart. She smiled proudly.

"You have heard mention," she said to him, "of my imminent marriage with Prince Antonio Grimani?"

"Yes, Madame," Francesco replied

"And what have you thought, Francesco, about that alliance?"

"That no man is worthy of contracting one such with you, but that Prince Antonio has more rights to it than anyone else, and that it appears to fulfill the wishes of Venice . . . and yours. May it be happy forever."

"I refused it this morning," said Polia.

Francesco looked at her as if to seek to discover in Polia's eyes whether her mouth might not be betraying her thought.

"You know better than anyone," Polia continued, "that my faith is engaged elsewhere, and irrevocably; but I must excuse your suspicions, for yours is assured to me by the oath that binds you to the altars, and I have never given you a similar guarantee. Listen, Francesco; tomorrow is the anniversary of the day that received your first vows, and it is in the last office of the morning that you will render them even more indissoluble and sacred by renewing them before the Lord. Have you, during the year, changed your manner of thinking about the nature and the necessity of that sacrifice?"

"No, no, Polia!" cried Francesco, falling to his knees.

"That's enough," Polia continued. "I have not varied any more than you. Tomorrow I shall attend the last office of the morning, and I shall associate myself with all the power of my soul with the vow that you are going to repeat, in order that you will know henceforth, Francesco, that between the heart of Polia and inconstancy there is also perjury and sacrilege."

Francesco tried to respond, but when the words reached his lips, Polia had disappeared.

The young monk had almost as much difficulty supporting his joy as his misfortune. He sensed that he did not have enough strength to be happy, for the mainspring of his life, worn out by so many contrary emotions, was ready to break.

The following day, at the last office of the morning, when the monks entered the choir, Polia was sitting in her usual place in the first rank of the benches of the nobility. She stood up, and went to kneel in the middle of the pavement of the great nave.

Francesco had perceived her. He renewed his vows in an assured voice, went back down the steps of the altar, and prostrated himself on the parvis. At the moment of the elevation he lay down entirely, throwing his crossed hands in front of his head.

When the office concluded, Polia left the church; the monks passed before the sanctuary one after another, with a profound genuflection; but Francesco did not quit his position. No one was astonished by that, for he had often been seen to prolong the duration of the prayer thus, in motionless ecstasy.

At the evening office, Francesco's attitude had not changed. A young monk came down from the stalls, approached, leaned over him, and took one of his hands in his own, tugging it in order to recall him to his customary duties. Then he got up, made the sign of the cross, looked up and turned to the assembled monks. "He's dead," he said.

That event, one of those that are effaced so rapidly in the memory of a new generation, had occurred more than thirty-one years ago when, one evening in the winter of 1498, a gondola stopped before the shop of Aldo Pio Manucci, whom we call "the elder." A moment later, the visit was announced in the study of the savant printer of Princess Hippolita Polia of Treviso. Aldo ran to meet her, introduced her, had her sit down, and remained struck by admiration and respect before that celebrated beauty, whom half a century of existence and dolors had rendered more solemn, without taking away any of her splendor.

"Sage Aldo," she said, after having deposited on the table a bag of two thousand sequins and a rich manuscript, "as you will be, in the eyes of the remotest posterity, the most learned and the most skilful printer of all the ages, the author of the book that I am confiding to you, will leave the renown of the greatest painter and the greatest poet of our dying century. The sole depository of this treasure, which I shall reclaim when your art has reproduced it, I have not wanted to deprive entirely of its possession the minds favored by Heaven who are able to savor the conceptions of genius; but I have waited, to multiply the copies, until the moment when I could demand them of immortal presses. You know now, sage Aldo, what I expect of you: a masterpiece worthy of your name and capable in itself of perpetuating the memory throughout the future. If that gold is exhausted, I will furnish more."

The Polia rose to her feet and leaned her two hands on the women who had accompanied her. Aldo followed her as far as her gondola, testifying his submission to her by respectful gesture, but without addressing a word to her, because he was not unaware that, having retired into an inviolable solitude for more than thirty years, she had renounced the commerce and conversation of men.

The book of which there is question here is *La Hypnerotomachia di Poliphilo, cioè pugna d'amore in sogno*, and not *Le Combat du Sommeil et de l'Amour* as rendered in translation by Monsieur Ginguené, author of the *Histoire littéraire d'Italie*. We do not claim—God forbid!—to conclude from that that Monsieur Ginguené did not know Italian. We have more indulgence for the distractions of talent.

"Sign that now as you wish," said Lowrich, as he stood up. "I don't have the habit of putting my name to these baubles, and Heaven is my witness that I have only ever accorded such historiettes to booksellers in exchange for books.

"May all the novelettes that you make in future," said Apostolo, "enrich your library with a volume like this one! It is yours, and I owe you twice as much."

"It's mine," said Lowrich, taking possession of it enthusiastically . . . "Or rather, it's yours," he continued cheerfully, passing it into my hands; I promised it to you this morning."

It is thus that the most magnificent of the copies of the *Poliphilo* became the giant of my Lilliputian collection, which figures there today *ne pluribus impar*. I submit it there willingly to the gaze of book-lovers, who cannot help recognizing in it a magnificent book . . . and not dear!

APPENDIX

On Love and its Influence as a Sentiment on Present Society

Creation would only have been a brilliant but ephemeral spectacle before the eyes of the great Spirit if he had not thought it good to perpetuate it in an immutable order by means of eternal reproductions. It is for that reason that he invented love, in a movement of affection or a fit of irony.

Then he deposited an organic phenomenon in the bosom of plants, an instinct in the bosom of brutes and a sentiment in the bosom of human beings. He told his work to grow and multiply, and the world and society that we know came about in consequence.

What you have just read is a summary of *Genesis*, of some other book that it pleases you to prefer to it.

Whether love was enclosed in a paradise decorated by God's own hands in order to serve as a nuptial palace for humankind is not the question. Nature entire, in the grace of its innocence and beauty, young nature, virginal and flowering, was a paradise for human beings. Why was it not for love?

A time came when that flower withered and fell, faded, to earth, where that paradise was closed, where winters accumulated upon springs and centuries upon years; the ruins of temples crumbled over huts and the ruins of kingdoms buried tribes.

Love alone lived above the social world, like the imaginary

fires that flutter above torches and candelabras when the ashes that produced them have already cooled.

Divine as it was, love was submissive to the vicissitudes of the accursed species in which he had incarnated it. It participated in its infirmities and miseries; it was debased by its opprobrium and lamented its anguishes. Like God and along with liberty, it is the only one of our thoughts that is assured of the same immortality as nature; it is reborn, young and creative, in all the revolutions of the worlds, and the worlds are reborn with it. But as it is the expression of the species, it is as mobile and as changing. The history of love is the history of the human species. It is a fine book to write.

The first of all loves, the love of the first two lovers, which inspired Milton with such beautiful pages, was bound to differ from all others. Eve was Adam's sister, since she proceeded from the same origin; she was his daughter, since God had formed her from the bone, flesh and blood of her husband. Once can imagine everything that such a sentiment comprised of the sympathetic, the touching, the grave and the solemn. All the affections of which humans contain the sublime seed were represented there. Plato, who was animated, unknowingly, with the spirit of a precursor, approached that myth of *Genesis* in his reveries, but he is as far from it as the thought of a great man is from the thought of a god. The hypothesis of the philosopher is the most ingenious of hypotheses; the revelation of the sacred writer is as great as creation itself.

It is necessary not to stop at those loves, which only live for us in a few lines of Moses and a few verses of *Paradise Lost*. I will say more. Their attraction has been effaced through the ages to such an extent that the intelligence to comprehend them cannot remain. A sensible soul lacks today the two most precious and most gripping seductions of love. They await another name.

Who would want love without mystery? And who would want love without rivalry?

The happiness of being loved consists less in the possession of a heart that is given than in the dubious, anxious and graduated surprise of a heart that is defended. The encounter that one contrives, the sad and soft gaze that one steals, and the quiver of a palpitating hand, which one often brushes before daring to seize it, are its supreme sensualities.

The impression of desire, respect and enthusiasm that the beloved object produces, the idolatrous attention that holds all minds suspended on her speech and all thoughts captive to her movements; the impatient disturbance that moves the crowd before her alone, when one is waiting for her; the murmur of joy that rises around her when one sees her; the confused and jealous anxiety that her preferences inspire, maintain, reanimate or console in turn—those are its supreme triumph.

The Latins made use of the same word to express the idea of loving and that of choosing.

There was nothing of all that in the terrestrial paradise; there was almost nothing of love there.

After that another came, which had to resemble the first in its moral character. The marriage of brothers and sisters, necessary for such a long time, conserved the principle of love in its chaste purity, but it no longer excluded its promises and its hopes, its bitter suspicions and its burning insomnias, its troubles, storms and tempests. A poet, who would have been nothing but a poet, might perhaps have put the first homicidal weapon in the hand of a deceived lover. The history or fiction of Scripture has a higher instruction. The consequence of that is that love of God was still the primary amour; otherwise, embittered pride, ambition betrayed in its projects, hypocrisy unmasked in its calculations, passions without tenderness and without grandeur, might have been the veritable vehicles of the disorders and misfortunes of humankind forever.

The system of alliance between members of the same family, which tightened natural bonds by multiplying them and brought no other changes into the domestic interior but the graces of a cradle and the caresses of a new-born, must have maintained the innocent felicity of the patriarchal age for a long time. That love, born under the same roof, in the games of two children, which ended, in the same tomb, with the slumber of two old people, could only be renewed in another form by imperfect images. Even genius, in delivering itself of its own accord to the instinct that permits it to create, has imagined nothing of the tender and enchanting that was not felt in that native effusion of the first sentiments.

I am not talking about Longus, whose naïve fable doubtless needed to be naïve in order not to be obscene, and now owes the greater part of its attraction to the inimitable style of an old translator; Longus was only a Greek, and a Greek of the Low Empire; but look at the veritable poets of love, Gesner,[1] Klopstock and Bernardin de Saint-Pierre, who enchains your soul in the ingenuous and almost fraternal tenderness of his Paul and Virginie, from the mat on which they confounded their infantile amities to the nuptial grave that reunited them forever in the shade of grapefruit trees; look at Chateaubriand, who has entered more boldly into that fiction of ancient love, and who has only veiled it with the atrabiliary passions of our times.

Alas, what affection will ever be worth as much as that sympathy of the sister formed on the threshold of the paternal house amid touching concerns and delectable hopes, in a perpetual exchange of anxieties and joys? And what would the wife of our choice be, once the frivolous illusions of pleasure have vanished, if she did not come to sit down, like a sister, by the dolorous bedside of the invalid and place a sisterly kiss on the icy cheeks of the dying man?

---

1 Salomon Gessner (1730-1788) was a painter and poet best known for his idylls.

When Esther, moved to pity for her people, fainted because of the excess of her trouble and confusion before the glory of Ahasuerus, he did not raise her up, by touching her with his golden scepter, in the name of mistress or wife. "I am your brother and you are my sister," he said to her, "come to me, Esther, and have no fear . . . !"

How fortunate and pure the was old age of the ancestor when he saw increasing and multiplying, in a proportion that escapes the calculations of science, the generations emerge from him, all nourished by the recent traditions that he had received from his forefathers, and doctrines that had been communicated to him by the very mouth of the Lord, under the symbolic appearance of a dream, or through the errant gleams that dance and catch fire around desert bushes, or in the shelter of the awnings of palms and reeds with which he had shaded his banqueting hall in order to celebrate the arrival of some traveling angel.

Family alliances, a matter of necessity among young peoples, were maintained for a long time in the laws coming from on high; and the only human police, which was held to have emanated directly from God, made a religious obligation of what became, by a strange perturbation of ideas, a crime before morality.

If one asks now what power long unknown to primitive societies could have snatched the Moabite from the patriarchal bed of Boaz and substituted, with an incomprehensible authority, its capricious institutions for those of religion, amour and liberty, I will respond that it names itself, like almost all the ideas for the meaning of which on searches in the elements of their name. Morality is the expression of the customs and prejudices of a country, for mores are never anything else in the exact meaning of the word, and our languages have conserved the trace of that profane usurpation of natural sentiments by social conventions, since we still talk about good and bad morals, which contains explicitly enough a confession that thought is obliged to make, shuddering, in order to acquire the truth. That is that there is nothing positive, nothing absolute and nothing essentially true in morality and in mores. Etymology has never revealed a mystery more profound and more frightening.

From that day on, the empire of caprice, fashion and custom replaced in degenerate humans the intimate and pure law that the instinct of their organization, the tradition of their forefathers and the revelations of their God had engraved within them. From that innocent world that no longer existed the virtues surged forth and were thus named, astonished by their own existence because a virtue only has real existence in relation to the admitted existence of the vice that is contrary to it. Love, as it was understood by ingenuous races, fled the tent with ignorance, and chastity, which had only been until then a discreet modesty of the soul, learned while blushing the mysteries of its veil and its girdle. The most chaste of sympathies, which enabled the brother and sister to pass from the paternal foreside into the spousal bed, was proscribed under the name of the *unchaste*, or *incest*, which is the same word, and that revolution carried away all that remained of the Golden Age. The candor and innocence of the human species was ended forever.

It is necessary not to search for love in the heroic ages. Dominated by imperious and grim religions, by an omnipotent theocracy or a tyranny armed with its prestige, by the illusions of glory and liberty, it was only a fanatical and brutal devotion stimulated by hatred and vanity; it was no longer a sentiment.

Love was even less among the great historic peoples among which it would have been so difficult to live. Have you read those insipid romances in which pale intrigues, relieved by all the efforts of a flaccid style and an almost-extinct genius develop at length in cold peripeties? There is Greek romance in all the energy of its inventions, because there is Greek love in all the energy of its tenderness and its sacrifices; do not ask any more of it. Have you seen the Greek Amour, that ideal type of the most beautiful creations of antiquity? That is Greek love in its entirety: straight and harmonious lines, of which no emotion has yet altered the suave severity; a grave and mild outline, colder than the marble in which the chisel has sought it; an eye that has never rolled the radiance of desire, impatience or anger; a mouth that has never quivered with jealousy, despair or disdain; a forehead over which the corrosive finger of care has never once passed in order to trace the location of a wrinkle; that is Greek love, that is what they meant by love. The Venus of Greek sculpture is a miracle of form; admire her, as you can, without fear of adoring her. The fire that animated Pygmalion's statue has never touched that insensible image, as one can scarcely imagine that she would have had a soul if she had chanced to come to life. She is a masterpiece of art, a divinity of the human hand, a stone, but she is not Venus.

The literature of the ancients is so poor in love that it is unnecessary to be astonished that it disappeared a long time ago from the education of women. Only Virgil found a few of its chords that vibrate in the heart, and skillful sophists would be able to draw that induction in order to refuse it, with old Hardouin,[1] to the finest parts of the *Aeneid*. Virgil united, fortunately for his glory, all the conditions that explain in a human soul the prescience of an unknown sentiment. He was born poor and lived unhappily. A physiognomy devoid of charm, a timid and anxious irritability, and a somber and solitary melancholy rendered him incapable of inspiring love;

1 The Jesuit Classical scholar Jean Hardouin (1646-1729), who alleged that many of the classic works of antiquity—he excepted Homer, Herodotus and Virgil, and a few others—had been forged by Medieval monks. He also challenged the authenticity of the New Testament.

but add genius to that and you would have in any era a man who divines a love that the vulgar do not know, its enchantments its chimeras and its poetry. The hearts that have loved the most are those that have only been loved poorly, if at all. It is not to those confident in the law that the delights of the promised land are reserved.

And then, according to all appearance, there was already in Virgil's time I know not what revelation of a future that must have manifested itself more rapidly on the shores of Lake Mantua than in the feasts of Maecenas. The form of society was about to change, and that immense change only ever happens when it is announced by some moral phenomenon in the life of a people, and especially in the organization of certain chosen individuals who weigh more than peoples in the balance of destiny. When the sun rises, it has already blanched the horizon for some time by its approach, but the summits of the highest mountains are struck by it first. One might think that it has chosen a throne before launching forth into a cradle. It is the same for new civilizations; fortunate are those that are not born in darkness, for the day the latter will endure will be nebulous and baleful.

Christianity was about to be born, and it is Christianity that has invented, so to speak, all of our sentiments. The shepherds of the cowshed arrived with their hands full of flowers, like the shepherds of the poet, and lavished them in the renewed world like the pledge of a new spring. The most precious of those benefits, so cruelly misunderstood today, was liberty, was love.

That Christian love, perhaps conceived in the silent contemplations of Pythagoras, gestated in the sublime reveries of Plato, nursed by the dreamy faith of the Essenes, and exalted by the romantic sensibility of the Therapeutae,[1] took several

---

1 The Therapeutae were a sect described in the first century by Philo of Alexandria in opposition to the Essenes, supposedly representing the contemplative life while the Essenes exemplified the active life. Nothing

centuries to emerge from the proofs of martyrdom and the exile of the catacombs. It emerged chaste and mild, but sad, pale and suffering, like the lamb that had just been sacrificed for the last feast of the people. Afterwards, in fact, love was quite finished; the imagination could not conceive anything to replace it, and that was why it was born in a tomb, the love whose last flames were to be extinguished in the eternal tomb of nations.

What distinguishes Christianity among all human religions is that instead of placing its sanctuary in the imagination it has placed it in the heart; it is that instead of coming for the rich and privileged of life, it came for the poor and the unfortunate; it is that instead of imposing a new yoke on the future, it broke the iron yoke that had weighed upon the head of past generations. Even the hallucinations of its thaumaturges and solitaries have a mildness that enchants and a splendor that dazzles. To it was reserved mysticism, the marvelous muse of the faith, which sustains the soul in sublime regions, as incomprehensible as itself, its origin and its destiny. To it was reserved asceticism, the melancholy genius of the Thebaids who consumed themselves above all terrestrial affections in contemplative effusions and perhaps imaginary tenderness, because it found nothing in living and sensible creation that was worthy of being loved as it loves. To it was reserved ecstasy, the sensuality of saints, into which is plunged, in order to love and enjoy God, thought disengaged from all corporeal bonds. At its voice, two as-yet unnamed virtues, which would take their place among the others, tolerance and charity, were added to vulgar chorus of pagan virtues. Liberty sounded before it the first fanfares of its triumph, and the people accompanied it joyfully, making the debris of their broken irons resound around them.

Love is so intimate to Christianity that an affectionate and passionate soul can easily misunderstand it, and the Middle

---

else is known about them and they might have been entirely hypothetical.

Ages often confounded it among its emblems. The giant Christophorus who revolts the shameful and grim ignorance of our iconoclasts is the Hercules of the new civilization, the Christian Prometheus bearing love in his arms.

And then, who can ever comprehend, in all the plenitude of its graces, the delectable mystery of Christian love.

"Love is a great thing, the sole wealth of life; it alone renders light what is heavy, it alone is able to support all vicissitudes with constancy and equality; for it submits to its burden without feeling the weight and it changes all bitterness into tenderness.

"It is generous and enterprising, borne to great things, insatiable for perfection.

"Love always wants to rise, and nothing down here is sufficient for it.

"Love wants to be independent and disengaged from all affection that distracts it from the person it possesses, in order that no illusion can seduce it and no pain can repel it.

"There is nothing sweeter than love, nothing stronger, nothing more elevated, nothing more extensive, nothing more gracious. Nothing more perfect and better in Heaven and on earth, because love is born of God and can only repose in God, above all created objects.

"The man who loves runs, flies and rejoices; he is free, and nothing stops him.

"He gives all for all; he possesses everything he loves, because what he loves is everything and contains everything. He does not fear giving himself entire, because everything is given to him.

"Love knows no limits; it crosses them and leaves them behind.

"No obstacle worries it, no labor frightens it; it attempts more than it can do, for it does not know the impossible. It believes that all efforts are permitted to it and that all successes are assured to it.

"Love is capable of anything; it undertakes, it pursues, it accomplishes things that discourage and defeat the heart that does not love.

"Love is always awake, and does not sleep in slumber.

"It torments without fatigue, constrains itself without hindrance, is excited and alarmed without being troubled; but like a living flame, ardent and light, it burns, rises up and passes with assurance.

"It is only those who love who can understand that language."

I have always thought like the incomparable author of *The Imitation of Christ*—the most beautiful book, Fontenelle says, that ever emerged from the human hand, since the Bible did not—but do not seek that divine language in the masterpieces of Greek and Rome; do not ask it of those geniuses of antiquity whose example is still the example of your rules and the light of your schools; do not expect it from the naïve and pompous inspirations of Homer or the touching melancholies of the other Homer who sang of the amours of Dido, nor the voluptuous confidences of fortunate Propertius, nor the regrets of exiled Ovid. It rises from the cell of a poor Christian hermit mortified by fasting, privation and pain, who has not left us his name,[1] and whose writings the savant perfectibility of the sovereign people delivered to the waves and the fire the other day in the capital of the world with the Epictetus of the Gospel and the Demosthenes of the Church.

The form of Christian love was not as immutable as its principle. In accordance with its nature, it followed the various modifications of Christian society, but without deteriorating, at least until the days of decadence in which we are living, the imposing character of which reveals its origin . . .

---

1 The author of *The Imitation of Christ* was generally believed in 1831, as now, to have been Thomas à Kempis, but Nodier never makes that attribution, respecting the author's *incognito*.

I shall not follow it through its temporary phases, the influence of which only affects the aspect and the surface of sentiments. It is the frame of a great tableau, the execution of which would have been frightened my weakness at any time, and the page that remains for me to cover in the tablets of my life is scarcely large enough to receive a sketch. It is the subject of a vast and sublime history, and my failing pen warns me, in escaping from my fingers, that not enough time remains to me even to finish a summary. It requires in any case, the young impressions of young souls. It is not when the mirror that reflects thought is darkened by so many disillusionments that it can reflect purely and brightly, as in the years of strength and hope. Cheerful scenes of happiness require cheerful colors, and the painters of my generation only have tears and blood on their palette.

You, who for whom beauty has always had inspirations, for whom love has always had a gaze and a language, say that beauty and love unite enchantments in the chronicles of the Middle Ages, in the suave songs of troubadours and in romantic fables of paladins; and if you do not possess the secret of resuscitating the past, if you do not know the words that raise the dead erect in their coffins, in the mildness of their innocence and the freshness of their courage, with bouquets of betrothal and the armor of knights, ask Victor Hugo and ask Vigny for one of those palingeneses, which are only child's play for their magic wand.

Here, already, is the decoration that unfurls with its almost cyclopean towers, its lanceolate ogives, its casements veiled by ivy, its light and broad balconies, which the patient graver of the sculptors has crowned with an awning of foliage that seems to quiver, or enveloped with a girdle of lace that seems to float. Here is the profound gallery with sonorous paving stones, and that pensive young woman who paces it incessantly, stopping at every stride is the chatelaine who has been waiting for two years for a squire coming from Palestine, for the return of whom she no longer dares to hope, for she is weeping. That soldier, however, can only bring an uncertain message, a consolation perhaps betrayed by a hundred battles, a rosary blessed in the holy places, or a bloody scarf, fortunate if it is not some fatal sheath in which a heart that has ceased to beat for her is gradually desiccating. Is it Godefroy, Tancred or Courcy? I do not know, I no longer know anything of those mysteries; but what I do know positively is that the amours of Achilles and Aeneas were stupid amours.

Or read Petrarch, and forgive him the fastidious richness of his mind;

Or read the episode of Francesca di Rimini in Dante's *Inferno*;

Or read that of Isabella and Zerbino in Ariosto's *Orlando*;

Or read two or three of the rhapsodic elegies of Marot;[1]

Or read Shakespeare's *Romeo and Juliet* in its entirety.

And go no further into modern times. The formal Apollo of the classics had raked thoroughly the ashes of the library of Alexandria; he had hidden in the monasteries, he had come to take the bonnet at the Sorbonne and to sustain theses at the university; he had come to sit down in the Académie, laden with pedantic furs and artificial laurels, under the purple of Richelieu, between La Mesnardière and Chapelain.[2]

It does not take up much room in the history of amour, the literary history of classical times. One could believe that there never existed a man more antipathetic to love than Malherbe,[3] who finally arrived and could have dispensed with

---

1 The Renaissaance poet Clément Marot (1496-1544)

2 Hippolyte-Jules Pilet de La Mesnardière (1610-1663) and Jean Chapelain (1595-1674) were both among the original members of the Académie française, although their literary worth was generally reckoned to be a trifle dubious.

3 The poet and courtier François Malherbe (1555-1628), notoriously, only saw his wife twice in twenty years, but he did have a son (allegedly).

arriving without inconvenience. It is even worse with Jean-Baptiste Rousseau,[1] whose name could have howled that of amour, but who never bothered; and I leave you to decide whether that is a lyre on which love never vibrated. In order to arrive at the final term of that negative progression, there is fortunately Voltaire to discover. Take away a few shreds of love and tolerance from him, the profane spoils of the Christianty of which he made his fine days, and you will see that he had only, in order to veil his sad philosophy, the hideous rags of an atheist with entrails of iron.

Apart from a small number of admirable scenes by Molière, a small number of admirable effusions by La Fontaine, a few leaps of *Phèdre* and *Ariane* and a few tears of *Andromaque*, fine impulses of *Le Cid* and one sublime hemistich in *Sertorius*,[2] the classics have no more understood love than liberty. All that they knew of love you could enclose in ten pages. There are ten times more in the *Confessions* of Saint Augustine and the works of Saint Thérèse.

Is not a crushing revelation for a people a literature in which all the fables of drama and romance repose on love, and in which poetic love is no longer understood by its natural interpreters? Is not a phenomenon in the social order the existence of a people in which the last sparks of moral sentiment, stifled in its sanctuary, no longer consume anything but the hearts of children, disavowed, embittered and crumpled by customs and by laws? What would you do with it if it were virile, and with what aliments would you nourish the generous passions that your imbecile decrepitude has betrayed?

---

1 Jean-Baptiste Rousseau (1671-1741) was more famous for his cynical epigrams than his poetry; many obscene and libellous verses were attributed to him, of which he probably only penned a few. Prosecuted for defamation of character in 1712, he failed to contest the charge and spent the rest of his life in exile.
2 Jean Racine's *Phèdre* (1677) and Thomas Corneille's *Ariane* (1672) are often coupled by critics. Racine also wrote *Andromaque* (1667) and Corneille *Le Cid* (1636) and *Sertorius* (1662).

That is very little, however; and an offended cynicism has come to scourge what remains of love, like a repulsive insect that has spoiled the debris of a rose with its impure drool. A metaphysics more precious than it is subtle has been introduced into well-born people in the commerce of the heart. Sensibility has become as pedantic as the philosophy of the encyclopedists, and sensuality as dirty and as brutal as the lingams of the Parc-aux-Cerfs.[1] The question is then reduced to knowing which is worth more for the happiness of life: a sophisticated adultery in the style of the fay Moustache[2] or an orgy in a place of ill repute, perfumed by the artificial flowers of the Opéra and the gilded brothel of La Popelinière.[3] But love is not mingled with it; it had no longer been there for a long time.

Where had it taken refuge? That is no great mystery: where elevated human thoughts always take refuge when society abandons them. It returned to the people, because it is in the people that all the elements of civilization are conserved, developed and renewed, as it is in the soil that all creative seeds are hidden in order to be reborn, the flourishing resurrection of which renews the aspect of nature in spring. It is there that it resided, anxious, turbulent, passionate and tragic, bloodying the altars of Lyon with the double suicide of a milliner and a master of arms, and the theaters of London with the double

---

1 The Parc-aux-Cerfs was a country house where Louis XV accommodated his mistresses, probably only one at a time, although the legend that he kept an entire harem there was much bandied about. Nodier's text refers to "spinthrées," an esoteric word of which few people but him would have known the meaning, but I thought it reasonable to substitute the more commonplace "lingam."

2 La fée Moustache [the fay Moustache] is featured in one of the classics of libertine literature, Pierre de Marivaux's multi-volume account of *La Vie de Marianne* (1731-1745).

3 The tax-farmer and patron of the arts Alexandre Le Riche de La Popelinière (1693-1762) was notorious for his princely lifestyle, and his lavish suppers were attended by singers and dancers from the Opéra, but the description of his house at Passy as a *lupanar* [brothel] is a libel.

murder of Hackman;[1] it was there, as young and vivacious as in the Middle Ages, when the last age awoke, already ripe for death, to the noise of a revolution.

The question is sometimes asked of where that revolution came from. It came from where the agony of everything that has ever lived came from: from the necessity of dying, common to all created beings, and from which the vain knowledge of sophists has not preserved thus far either the individual or the species. If you look with a little attention you will find all the conditions of that last crisis of life, the anguish of dissolution and the need for change, the convulsions of pain and the gleams of apotheosis. It is quite simply that God has written on the forehead of species, as on that of the individual: "Thou art born of dust and to dust thou shalt return."

The peoples who surround us, while peoples remain somewhere, have arrived, some sooner and others better than us, at the same result, perhaps because they went less rapidly. There are some who have cast a profound glance into the abyss and measured it for a long time before obeying the invincible necessity that pushes us all thereinto. What remain to us in France of solemn ideas, in this chaos that we call society out of habit or by derision, we owe to Germany, the assured refuge of all that remains of soul in our expiring civilization, and whose generous impulse, twice in the first fifteen years of our present century, provided an admirable lesson for oppressed nations. Klopstock, Schiller and Goethe are the geniuses emerged from that mold known in our literature, of which

---

1 James Hackman (1752-1779) shot Martha Ray, the concubine of Lord Sandwich, with whom he was besotted, outside a theater in Covent Garden, and was hanged in consequence—the execution presumably constituting, in Nodier's view, a second murder. The case was sensational, not least because Hackman had just been ordained as a priest. The reference to a double suicide in Lyon might be taken from an incident in 1770 reported by Voltaire in an essay "De Caton et du suicide," but there is no reference therein to the professions of the two lovers, who had been denied permission to marry by the young woman's parents.

Abbadonna,[1] Charles Moor[2] and Werther have multiplied the type throughout the world, while cold madrigals, lewd parades and musky elegies were made in Paris. The time had truly come.

The last song of genius is a song of despair. It is the clamor that is heard one day in the middle of the sea and which announced to the frightened world that God was dead.

Love could only bring to that catastrophe a tribute of melancholy and grief, and the sinister aspect under which it appeared then in the societies that were not yet completely incapable of understanding it was such that it is not astonishing that the vulgar have not recognized it, for it was not given to Moses, Hesiod or Tasso to divine it. All its illusions have given way to regrets, all it ecstasies to frenzy. It no longer brandishes in its hands anything but murderous arrows; nothing any longer rises in the heart but thoughts of annihilation, because it is animating the last generations of the earth, and those generations, condemned before birth, have nothing more to engender but nothingness.

All that remains of it is a language; that is poetry, which ought to accompany the funeral procession of humankind with one last song, as it enchanted the celebrations of its cradle with a hymn of tenderness and joy. And that tearful voice has been saddened for more than half a century by the death-throes of a world that is ready to dissolve. It drags itself in long lamentations, with Young, to the tomb of Narcissus; it moans on the marble of the cemetery with Hervey;[3] it murmurs the

1 The seraph Abbadonna is one of the rebels featured in Klopstock's *Der Messias* (1748-73), who regrets his error; he attracted particular attention from Madame de Staël, who gave French Romanticisme its name and celebrated its German models.

2 Charles, or Karl Moor is a character in Schiller's *Die Räuber* (1781) who is unjustly persecuted by his father and brother, goes to the bad but remains irredeemably melancholy, and ends up killing his lover and surrendering to the law.

3 Edward Young (1683-1765), author of *Night Thoughts* (1742-45) and James Hervey (1714-1758), author of *Meditations and Contemplations*

lugubrious refrains of the Apocalypse with Jean-Paul;[1] it howls with indignation in the frantic imprecations of Faust; it is intoxicated by sardonic wrath in the verses of Byron; it exhales a bitter and profound cry on the steps of André Chénier's scaffold;[2] it bursts into sobs on the edges of American lakes with René; it still weeps one more time and then fades away and dies on the angelic lyre of Lamartine.

And you want to know where that comes from? And you cannot imagine why the highest expression of human genius has become as convulsive as a death-rattle and as plaintive as a sigh that no sigh will ever follow! And you say: "It's because they're romantic and mad, for the earth is young and merry." And yet, if you put your hand on the place where the heart of the social body is beating, you will feel that it is no longer beating.

When the angel of the last day comes to sit down pensively in the sublime tragedy of *Adam* on the mat of the patriarch, the father of men says to him: "Why, you seem to be consumed by sorrow today, you whom I saw radiant with such a pure sensuality when I showed Eve's gaze marvel after marvel in the garden of the Lord."

"That's because today," the angel replies to him, "before the sun disappears behind the mountain, you must de."

The response that I am making to you is what poetry is making today to the entire race of Adam.

"What does it matter to us?" you might reply to me. "Have we not deftly reconstructed civilization on entirely new bases? And if the conflagration you fear is imminent, do we not have the elements to remake what time has destroyed? Repose, surly dreamer, from the cares that are consuming you; and if you

(1748) were both classified in the "Graveyard school" of English Poetry that preceded the growth of the Gothic element of English Romanticism.
1 The German Romantic poet Jean Paul [Richter] (1763-1825)
2 The proto-Romantic poet André Chenier (1762-1794) was guillotined three days before the Reign of Terror ended.

remain obstinately infatuated with primitive forms of Biblical composition, at least write about the genesis of philosophy and perfectibility; that is a subject worthy of occupying human meditation!

"To begin with, we have not had the advantage of making everything from nothing, which leaves the spirit of creation with such a vast latitude; but we have succeeded in making nothing out of everything, which certainly supposes another power, for it is very doubtful that your God has reserved it for himself.

"Then, for the pivot on which you have made the political sphere revolve, always faithful to an immobile axis, which you have called the social spirit, we have substituted another, which is called the spirit of association, and which is much better for us, you will agree, once every segment of the sphere that our axis traverses contains its nucleus. If it breaks one day into little pieces, the social spirit will doubtless perish, but the spirit of association will necessarily survive, for the great consolation of the future; and we will owe the law, without contradiction, to legislators of a new species, which we can also flatter ourselves with having created in our image.[1]

---

1 Author's note attached to the version of the essay reprinted in *Rêveries* (1832): "My thought will never attack species or individuals. The conscience of men of good faith is inviolable. This was written two months before there was question for the first time of association properly speaking, of which there is no longer any question today. I had in view the theory of association in general, because I regard it as essentially antipathetic to the conditions of a unified society, compact and unbreakable; which would not prevent me, I admit, from participating in a national association against the excesses of the power on the day when it allows itself to be dominated by the ascendancy of a faction to the extent of reopening the Empires oubliettes or rebuilding the guillotine of the Terror. Outside of those extreme cases, an intelligent and active entity that has his own will in an intelligent and active being that is no longer master of its own, is what was once called and obsession, and will end in death." The reference within the quote is presumably to the formation in 1831 of an Association Nationale to ensure the independence of France and the expulsion of the elder branch of the Bourbons: an organization that soon become redundant.

"Christianity was good, but it was timid; it was content to free slaves, to proclaim the rights of the people and to consecrate moral equality to all, subordinating the duties of each to the social fiction under the empire of which it was born.

"We have gone much further. What Christianity has done, we have defined.

"We have liberty, which is the right to do what one wants when one is the master, and which imposes the duty to suppress everything that one cannot prevent.

"We have equality, which consists of going first when one is the stronger or when one believes that one is, which is absolutely the same thing in politics.

"We have the sovereignty of the people, which is a very ancient and very natural dogma, very convenient for destroying, very inconvenient for renewing, and which all social authority must know how to break when it no longer has any need to manipulate it. That does not concern prudent, peaceful, tolerant and conscientious authorities, which are subject to its impulsion without soliciting it. It concerns us.

"We have the representative system, which is, as you know, the expression of the interests of a few thousand rich people, more or less freely chosen by a few hundred thousand well-to-do people, to the exclusion of a few million honest poor people, about whom we hardly care, although, to tell the truth, they compose a certain fraction of the sovereign people we mentioned just now. But centuries have their exigencies, and without going further, you will be told on the floor of the Bourse that money is the vehicle or ours. Your own legislator gave the poor the kingdom of Heaven. It is permitted to us to give the opulent the kingdom of the earth. Those are luminous ideas, legislative revelations of which Lycurgus and Jesus Christ were never informed.

"You have mentioned genius. We also mention it a great deal, with an impartiality so disinterested that it can only be compared with yours, but we have something better; we have industry, which is the art of producing as much as possible with very little, and see, in order to convince yourself of it, what revolutions make of us!

"Of religion we have no lack. We have one ready-made, which is less mystical than Theophilanthropy but much more reasonable; a material religion, you understand, a positive religion, a religion of interests admirably suited to our epoch, and which only lacks one bagatelle—a God, perhaps.

"As for love, that's something else. We agree that it has a high price today, and that the graces and virtues of a young woman count for little among us when they cannot be completed in a good cash dowry, a pretty guarantee of eligibility, but who the devil advises the proletariat to have amiable and sage daughters and petty landowners to be infatuated with the children of the poor, as in the days of King Pelagius?[1] We have said at the tribune, without being contradicted: Whoever is not rich is not worthy to be. It's so easy to become rich!

"Fortunately, moral love, which is good to amuse the sentimental idleness of a people backward in civilization, is only the most insignificant of *hors-d'oeuvres* among positive peoples. All those fantasies of the heart, appropriate to the ages of speculation when people had time to feel, pass for follies in ages of calculation, when one only has time to count. That is because we have the best to offer you in that genre, which is the law of divorce, which is legal adultery, and, if necessary, the community of women, which is a social adultery much more convenient than anything imagined before us. Perhaps that is love . . . ?"

Well, no, Messieurs, that is no more love than your liberty is liberty. But don't think that in collecting, under the

---

1 Pelagius is the Latinized name of Pelayo el Connquistador (c685-737), the first king of Asturias. Alexandre Guiraud's *La Tragedie de Pelage* had been staged at the Théâtre-Français in 1820., following up an 1814 opera by Gaspare Spontini.

impression of your works, the accurate definition of the last resorts of our political organization, and reducing them to their value under the forms of an involuntary irony repugnant to my intelligence, which is new under my pen, that I have conceived the design of casting the slightest disfavor on your intentions. They are pure, sincere and natural because they are the essential expression of your education and your experience, which are the essential expression of your epoch. You can no more judge and act otherwise than you could force the sun to turn back toward the signs that it traveled in its youth or the sea to return to the limits against which it has broken for so many centuries.

What you say is the truth, because all that we know of truth is the lies appropriate to the times from which they come, and the last times have come. The person among us who talks in an unusual language and who marches in deserted paths is me, who has never lived in the world that you inhabit and has never been subjected to its influences, and who no longer knows any society but that which can be divined in solitude. It is therefore evident that the relative error is mine, and that is not astonishing, for I have not grown a day older without making amends for an error. I am therefore reduced to making use of the sole liberty that your institutions concede to me, that of writing and publishing my thoughts, and in that I am only obeying the rigorous conditions of a mission of misfortune.

The danger of that is not very great, only the weight of my words. Reassure yourselves also regarding their authority, for I have received neither the revelation that expired in the books of Numa not that which expired in the pulpit of the apostles; and regarding their consequences, for there are not five hundred men on the surface of the globe who participate in my dolor.

What consternates us in the utmost depths of the soul, we who have emerged from such a strong and passionate generation, is seeing our inheritors living on our theories, and that they have left our memories, our sentiments our sympathies and our enthusiasms in the waste-bin. There was a naivety in our political faith, a tenderness in our frenzies, a future and even a past in our present. We did not revolve around an idea that might only be a word, at the behest of a sectarian who might only be an impostor, with the mechanical impassivity of an automaton or the grim submission of a fanatic. We went forth to the uncertain conquest of universal happiness in inexhaustible hopes.

We did not all have golden mouths to proffer eloquent words, but we did not have hearts of bronze. We debated with the abandon of devotion, with the impetuosity of age, questions that were matters of life or death for us, but we would have refrained carefully from touching them if they had interested the fate of the people in the responsibility of our passions.

It is necessary to agree that what distinguished that epoch was not the absence of the exalted emotions and stormy follies of youth. Even less was it the aptitude to grasp the material realities of life, the aplomb of a dry and positive philosophy, the imperious assurance of knowledge; it was an inexhaustible effusion of tenderness for the human race, an instinct of hatred and horror for the wicked. We would have shuddered at the contact of the muddy and bloody foam of large populations where, in our time, only crime would have gone in search of auxiliaries. The untimely solidarity of a scoundrel in the most generous conspiracy would have condemned us forever to the cloister and to despair.

Children, our turbulent expansion was that of an ingenuous fervor for the truth, in which we believed for a long time, but was promptly embittered by the disappointments of life, by which one is quickly disillusioned; it was the sharp fever of love betrayed, of patriotism abused, of disenchantment with impossible social felicity, instead of which we had found behind the veils of politics, lifted by experience, only the grimace of a triumphant sniggering hypocrisy.

We had your errors, and others besides, but we did not convert them into a system, because we obeyed spontaneous inspiration and not instructions. Nor were we struggling, in the days of which I am speaking, against the attempts of a well-intentioned power that was striving to conciliate liberty with order. The enemy of us all was the false liberty that hid by turns under its mask the vanity of a rabble-rouser or the ambition of a soldier, and you know whether we were mistaken. We too had to suffer from the injustice of men, the ingratitude of parties, the natural anxieties of those in power and the officious cruelty of their agents. You only have one inappreciable advantage over us that institutions have conquered: our prisons had no echoes; they were deaf, like tyrants.

I have said nothing about the opinions that divided us then. What do the opinions matter of a man who has been, involuntarily, the witness of a complete history, who has seen factions and their projects at close range, events and their results—who has lived?

I am not imploring you to go backwards toward concluded centuries. The last vibration of their funeral knell is expiring in the wailing of the tocsin that is summoning so many peoples to the possession of a brief and tumultuous independence, a future patrimony of despotism, like herds returning to the cowshed who want to be butchered. Nor am I imploring you to save religious sentiment, which is perhaps no more, or liberty, which never was

Save love, if you can. It is a god of your age.

OTHER BOOKS BY CHARLES NODIER IN THIS SERIES

Outlaws and Sorrows
Jean Sbogar and Other Stories
The Story of the King of Bohemia and His Seven Castles
The Memoirs of Maxime Odin
Perfectibility and Resurrection

SOME OTHER SNUGGLY BOOKS

G. ALBERT AURIER *Elsewhere and Other Stories*
CHARLES BARBARA *My Lunatic Asylum*
S. HEZOLNRY BERTHOUD *Misanthropic Tales*
LÉON BLOY *The Tarantulas' Parlor and Other Unkind Tales*
ÉLÉMIR BOURGES *The Twilight of the Gods*
CYRIEL BUYSSE *The Aunts*
FÉLICIEN CHAMPSAUR *The Latin Orgy*
BRENDAN CONNELL *Spells*
DELPHI FABRICE *The Red Spider*
BENJAMIN GASTINEAU *The Reign of Satan*
EDMOND AND JULES DE GONCOURT *Manette Salomon*
REMY DE GOURMONT *From a Faraway Land*
GUIDO GOZZANO *Alcina and Other Stories*
GUSTAVE GUICHES *The Modesty of Sodom*
EDWARD HERON-ALLEN *The Complete Shorter Fiction*
J.-K. HUYSMANS *Knapsacks*
COLIN INSOLE *Valerie and Other Stories*
MAURICE LEVEL *The Shadow*
JEAN LORRAIN *Errant Vice*
GEORGES DE LYS *An Idyll in Sodom*
ARTHUR MACHEN *Ornaments in Jade*
CATULLE MENDÈS *Mephistophela*
ÉPHRAÏM MIKHAËL *Halyartes and Other Poems in Prose*
LUIS DE MIRANDA *Who Killed the Poet?*
OCTAVE MIRBEAU *The Death of Balzac*
CHARLES MORICE *Babels, Balloons and Innocent Eyes*
GABRIEL MOUREY *Monada*
DAMIAN MURPHY *Daughters of Apostasy*
KRISTINE ONG MUSLIM *Butterfly Dream*
OSSIT *Ilse*
RACHILDE *The Princess of Darkness*
MONTAGUE SUMMERS *Six Ghost Stories*
LÉO TRÉZENIK *The Confession of a Madman*
AUGUSTE VILLIERS DE L'ISLE-ADAM *Isis*

www.ingramcontent.com/pod-product-compliance
Lightning Source LLC
Chambersburg PA
CBHW050512110726
47899CB00005B/1431